FRAGILE

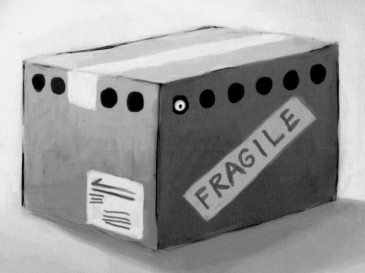

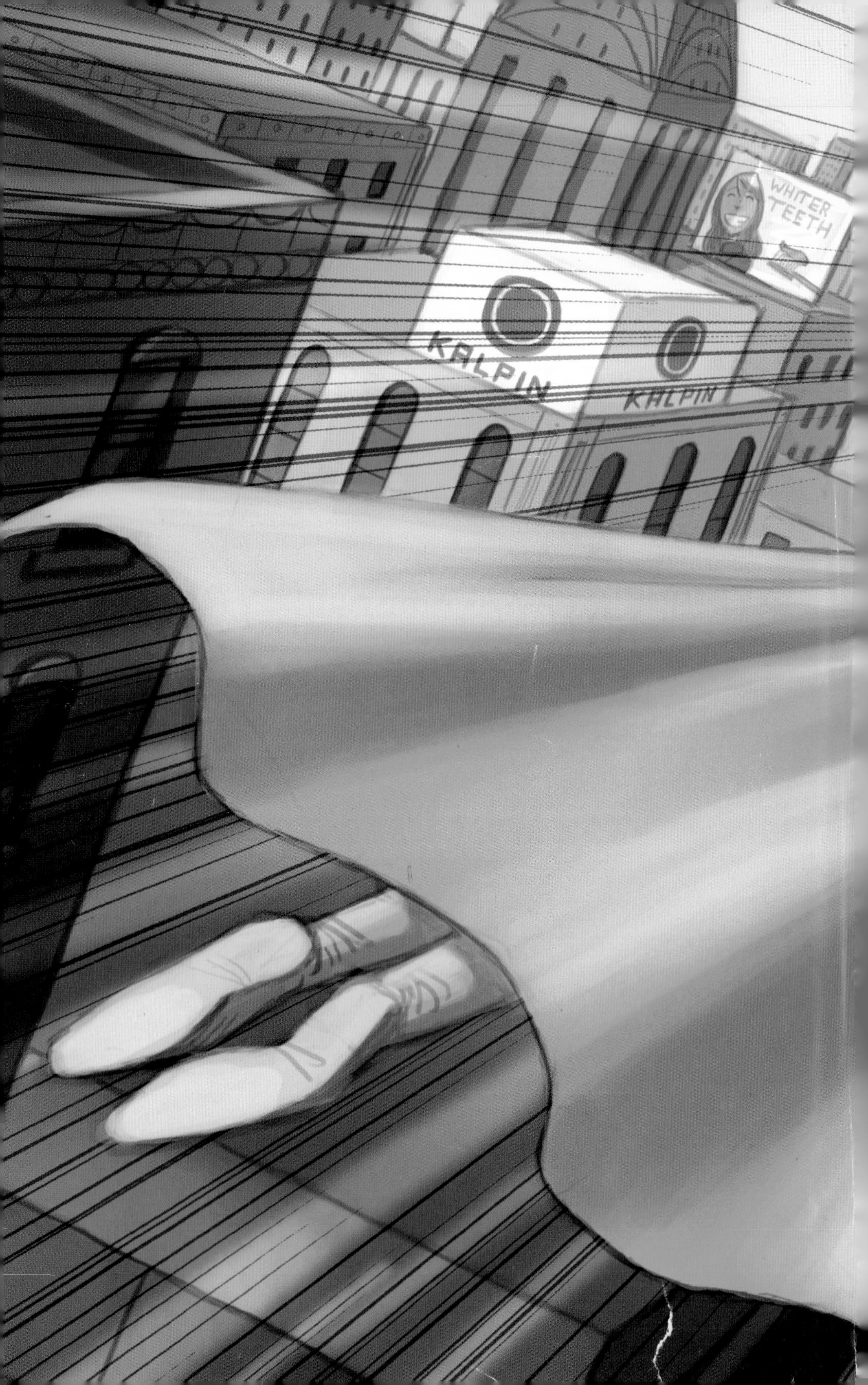
WHITER TEETH
KALPIN
KALPIN

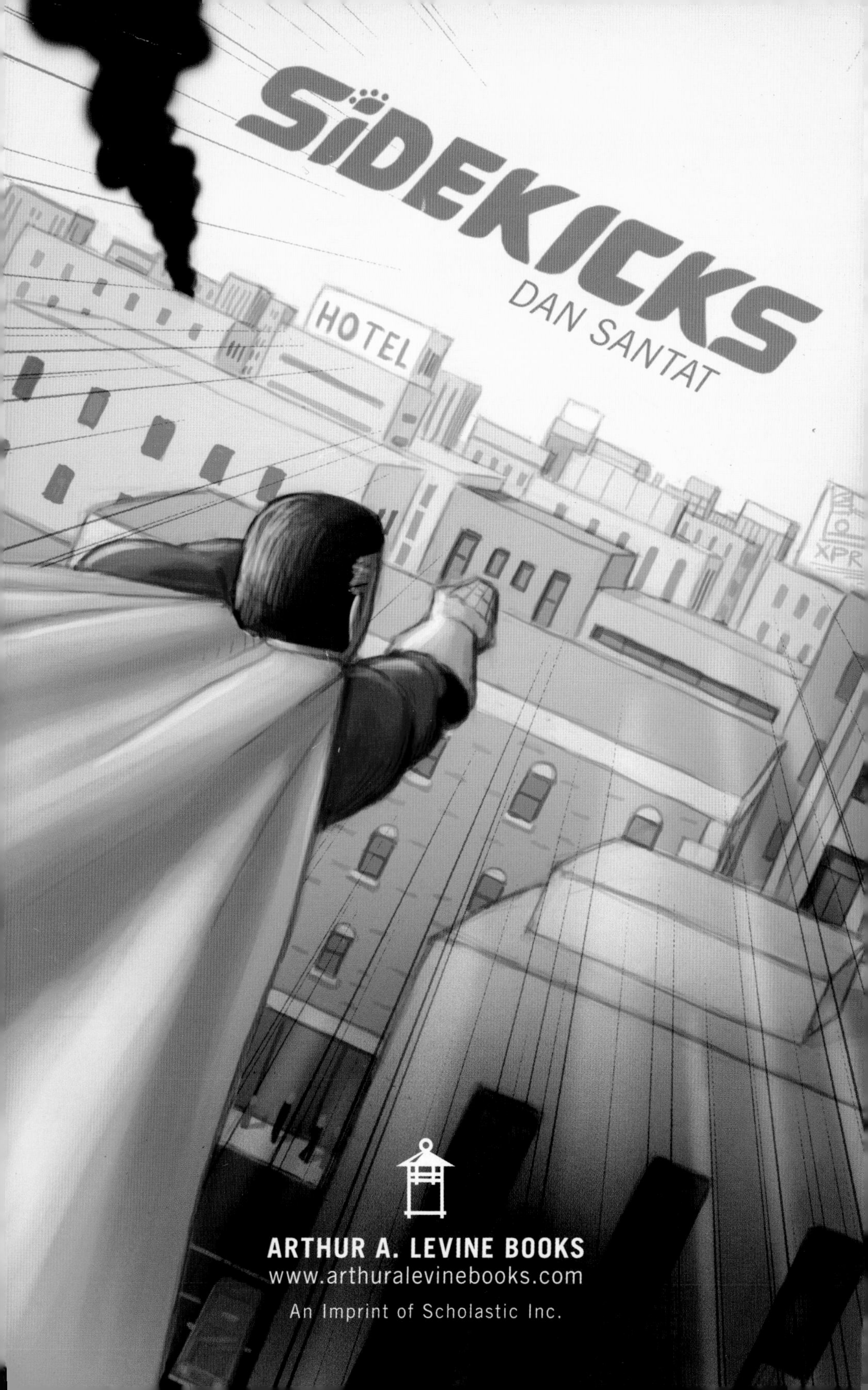
HOTEL
XPR

SIDEKICKS

DAN SANTAT

ARTHUR A. LEVINE BOOKS
www.arthuralevinebooks.com
An Imprint of Scholastic Inc.

LIBRARY OF CONGRESS CATALOGING-IN-PUBLICATION DATA

SANTAT, DAN.
SIDEKICKS / WRITTEN AND ILLUSTRATED BY DAN SANTAT. -- 1ST ED.
P. CM.
ISBN 978-0-439-29811-7 (HARDCOVER)
ISBN 978-0-439-29819-3 (PAPERBACK)
1. GRAPHIC NOVELS. (1. GRAPHIC NOVELS. 2. SUPERHEROES--FICTION. 3. PETS--FICTION.)
I. TITLE.
PZ7.7.S17SI 2011
741.5'973--DC22

                                    2010034704

24 23 22 21 20   20 21 22

BOOK DESIGN BY DAN SANTAT AND PHIL FALCO
LETTERING BY JOHN GREEN

FIRST EDITION, JULY 2011

PRINTED IN CHINA   62

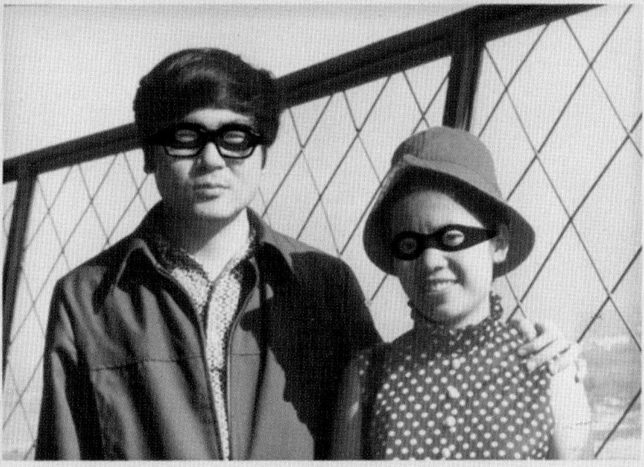

FOR MY PARENTS.

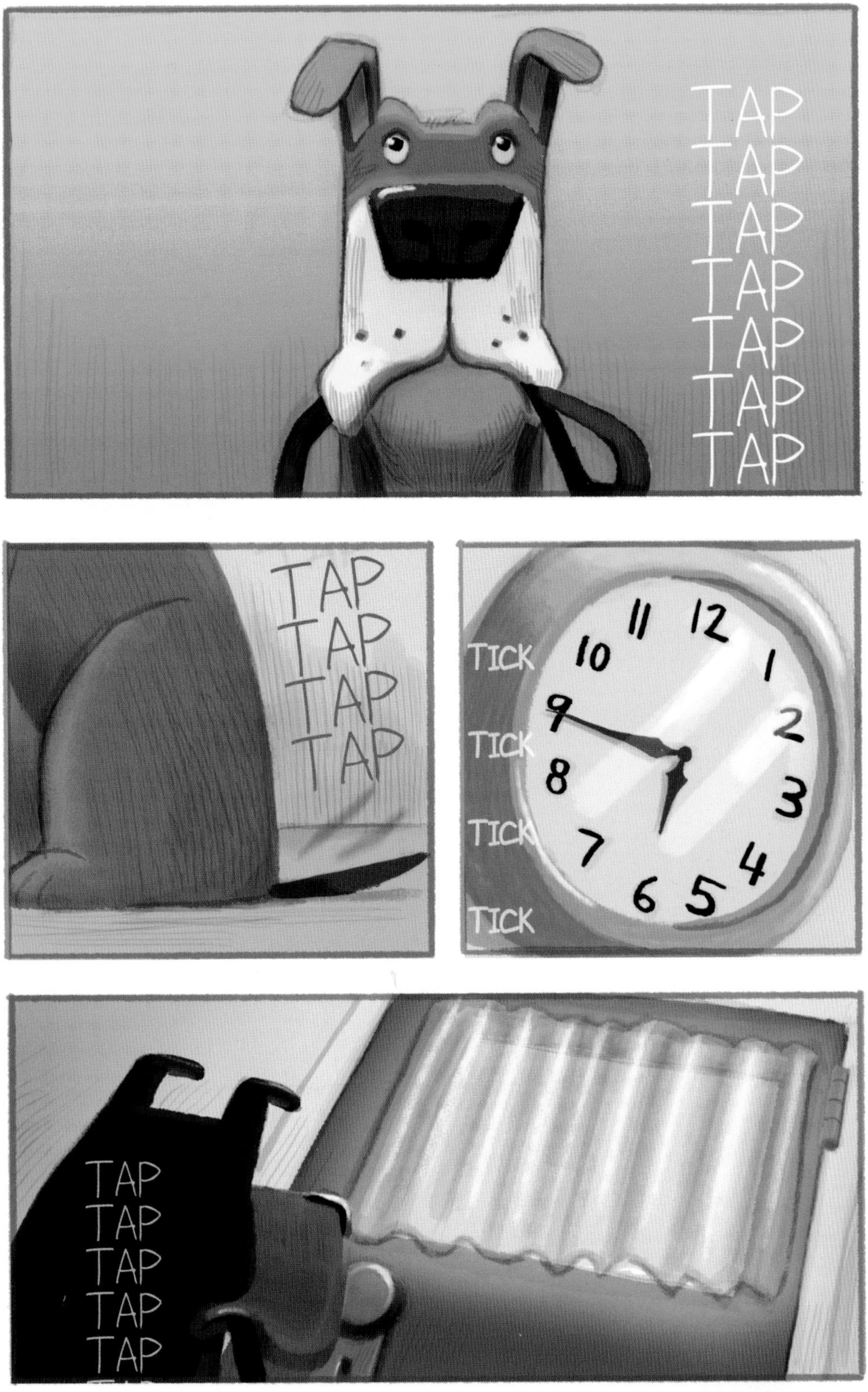
TAP
TAP
TAP
TAP
TAP
TAP
TAP
TAP
TAP
TAP
TAP
TICK
TICK
TICK
TICK
TAP
TAP
TAP
TAP
TAP

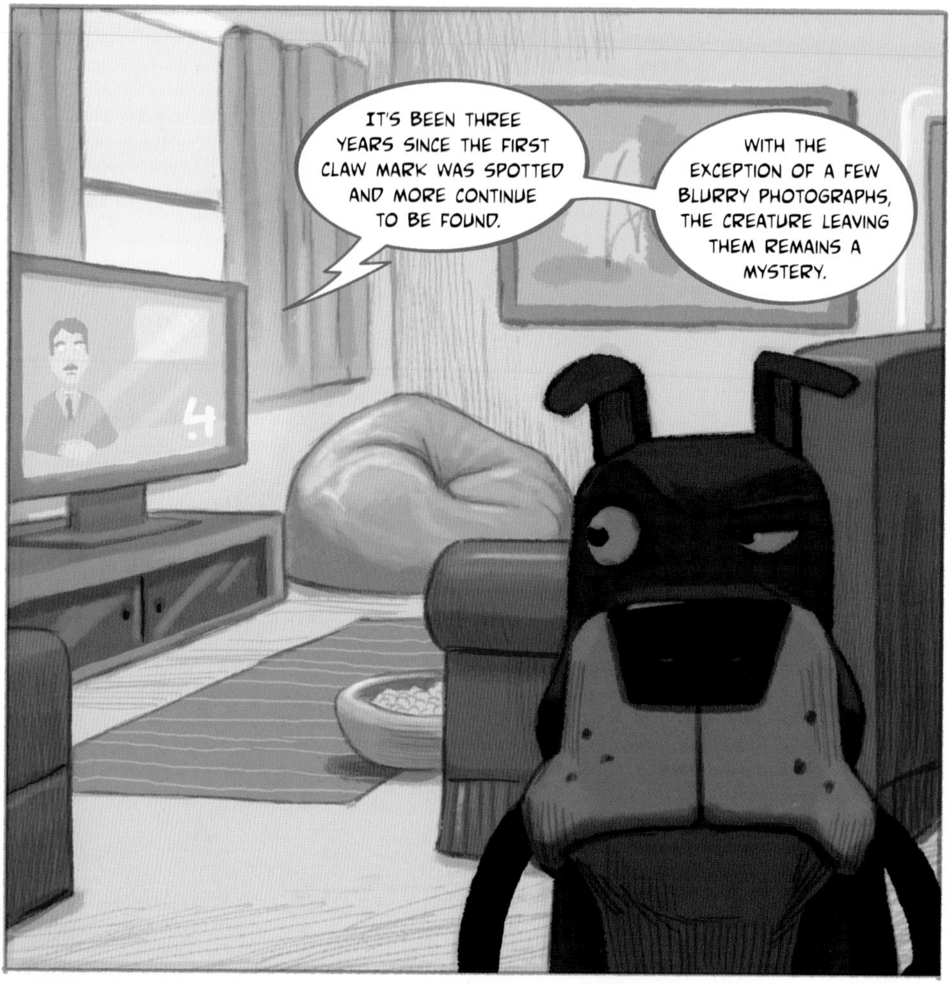
IT'S BEEN THREE YEARS SINCE THE FIRST CLAW MARK WAS SPOTTED AND MORE CONTINUE TO BE FOUND.
WITH THE EXCEPTION OF A FEW BLURRY PHOTOGRAPHS, THE CREATURE LEAVING THEM REMAINS A MYSTERY.
4

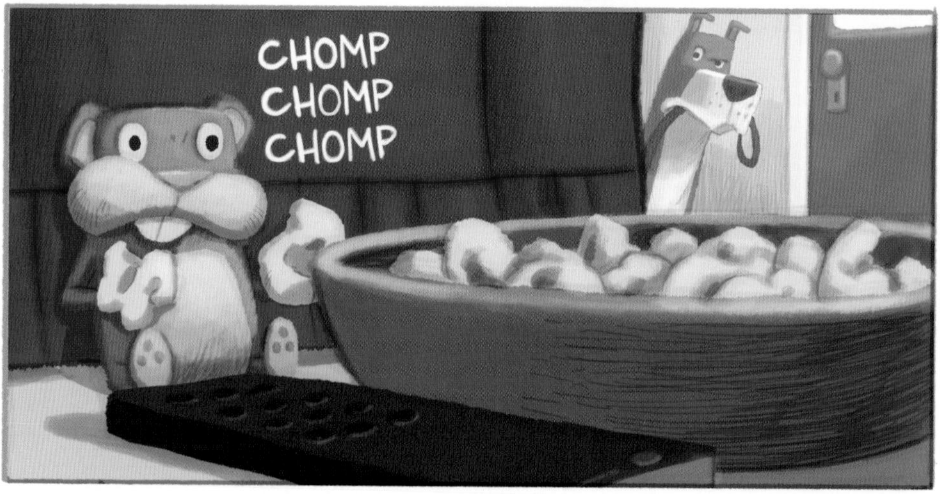
CHOMP
CHOMP
CHOMP

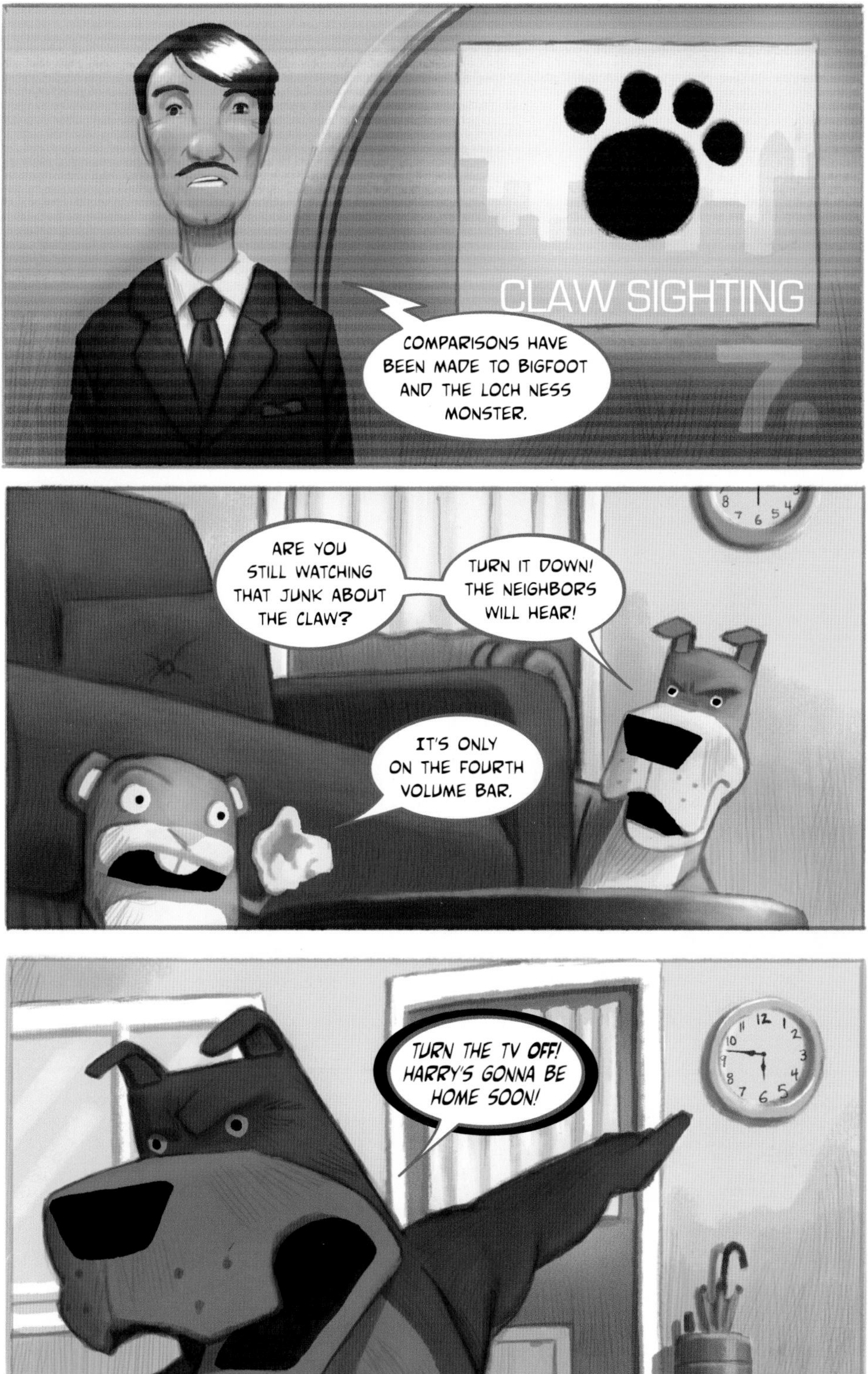
CLAW SIGHTING
COMPARISONS HAVE BEEN MADE TO BIGFOOT AND THE LOCH NESS MONSTER.
ARE YOU STILL WATCHING THAT JUNK ABOUT THE CLAW?
TURN IT DOWN! THE NEIGHBORS WILL HEAR!
IT'S ONLY ON THE FOURTH VOLUME BAR.
TURN THE TV OFF! HARRY'S GONNA BE HOME SOON!

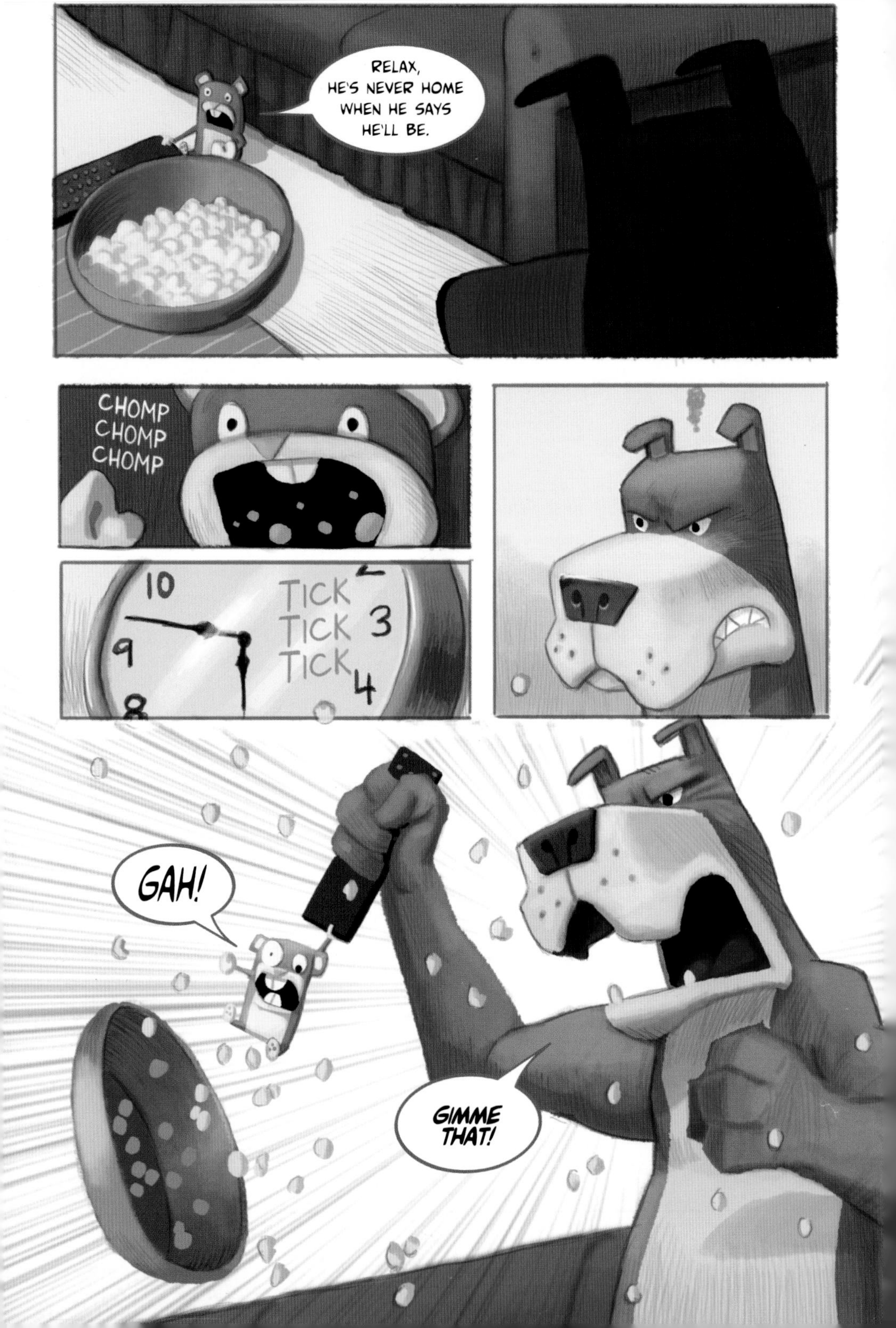
RELAX, HE'S NEVER HOME WHEN HE SAYS HE'LL BE.
CHOMP CHOMP CHOMP
TICK TICK TICK
GAH!
GIMME THAT!

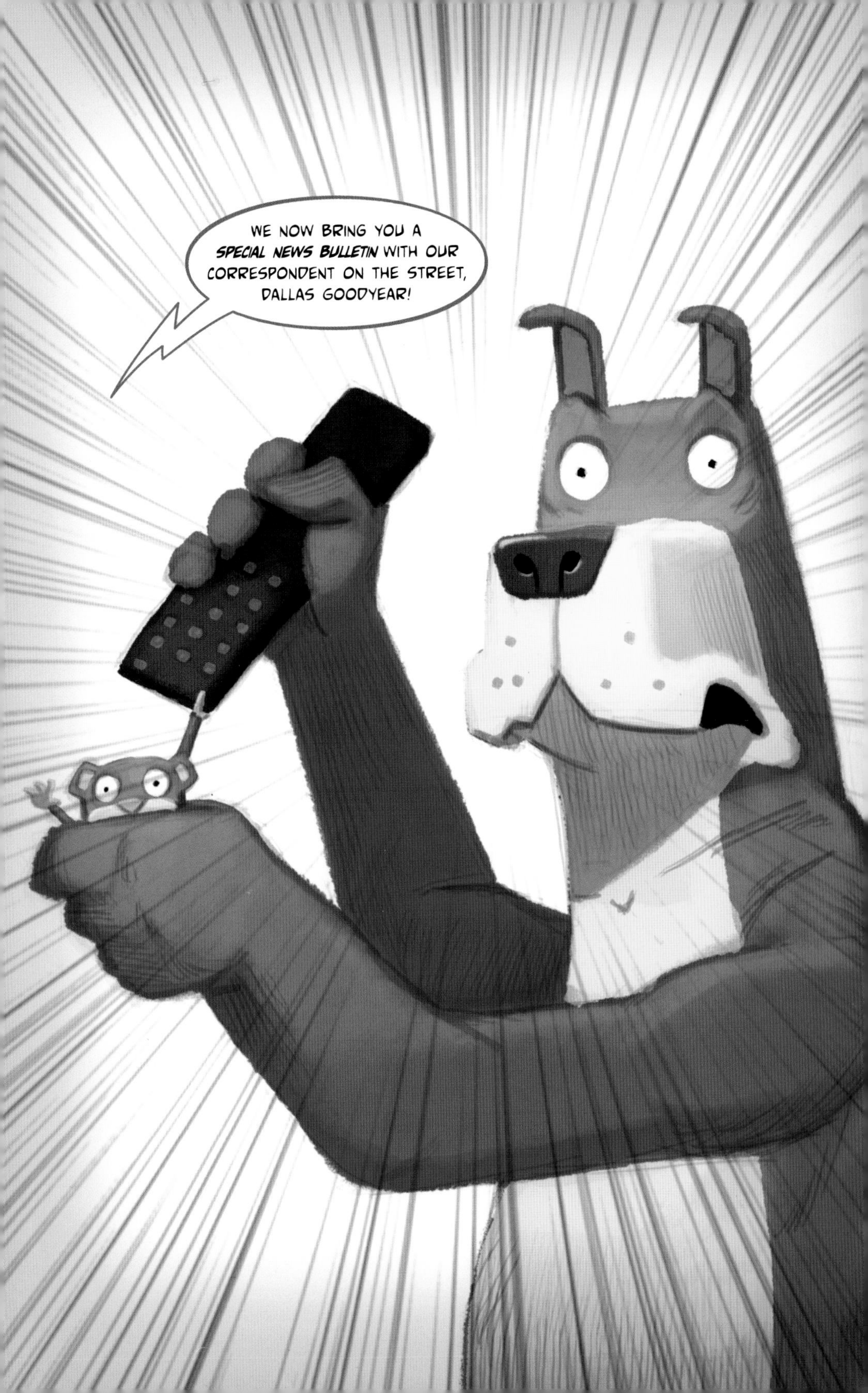
WE NOW BRING YOU A SPECIAL NEWS BULLETIN WITH OUR CORRESPONDENT ON THE STREET, DALLAS GOODYEAR!

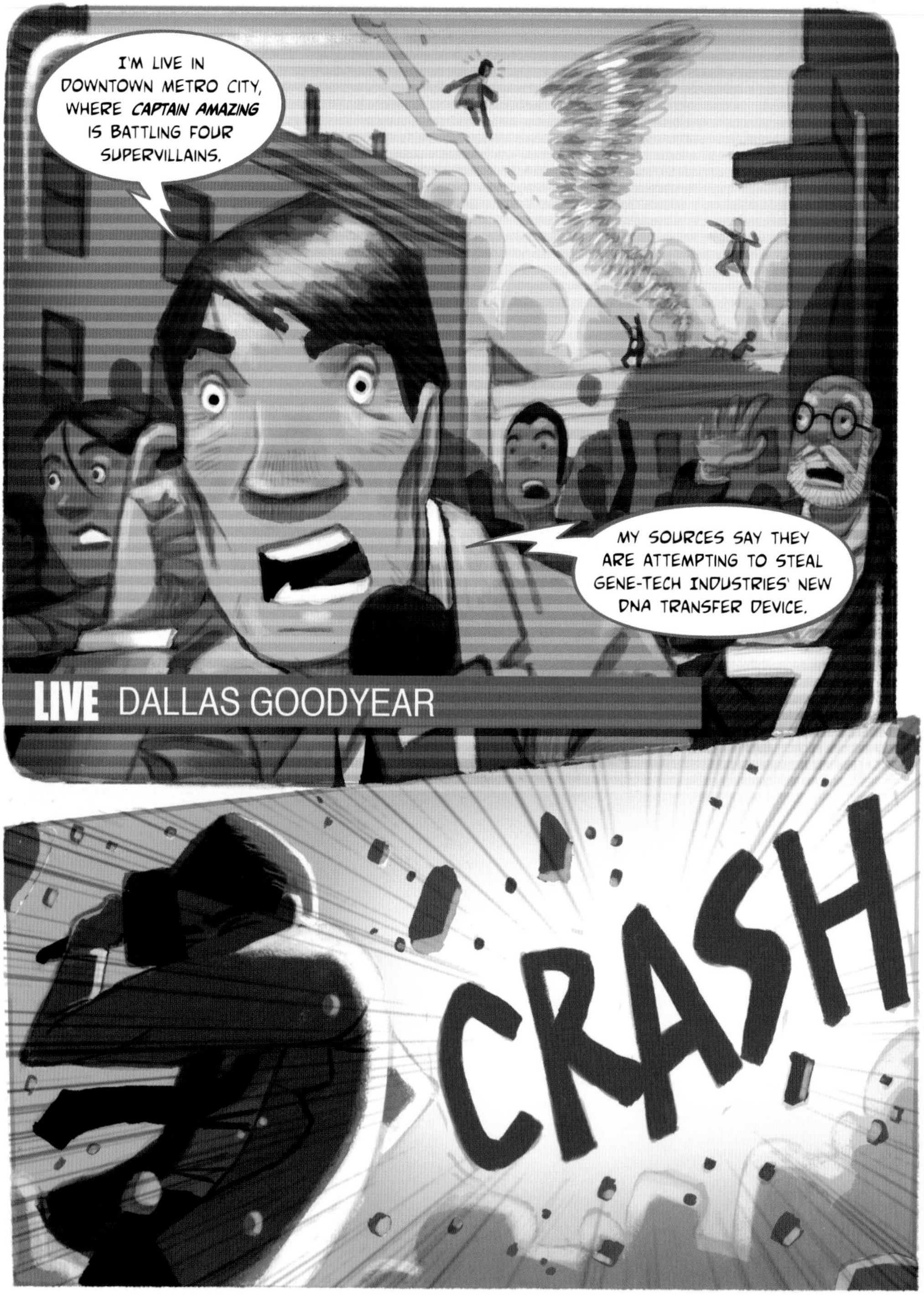
I'M LIVE IN DOWNTOWN METRO CITY, WHERE *CAPTAIN AMAZING* IS BATTLING FOUR SUPERVILLAINS.
MY SOURCES SAY THEY ARE ATTEMPTING TO STEAL GENE-TECH INDUSTRIES' NEW DNA TRANSFER DEVICE.
LIVE DALLAS GOODYEAR
7
CRASH

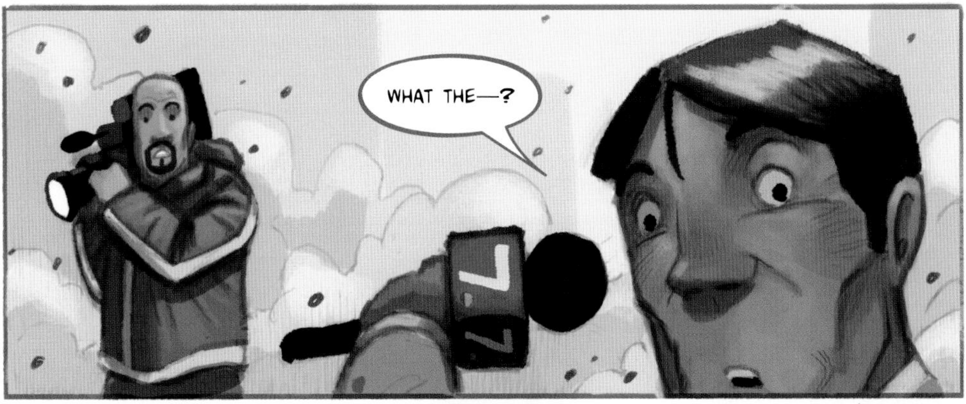
WHAT THE—?
7

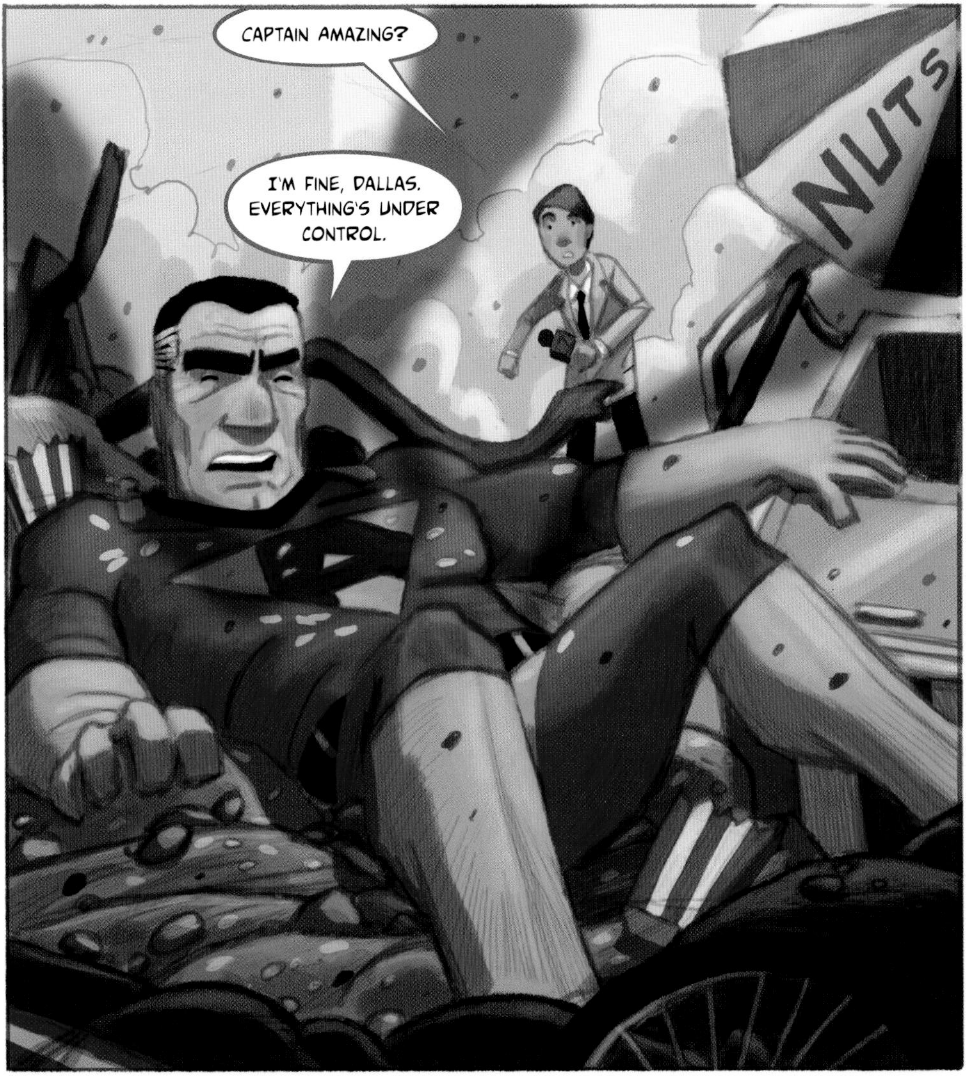
CAPTAIN AMAZING?
I'M FINE, DALLAS. EVERYTHING'S UNDER CONTROL.
NUTS

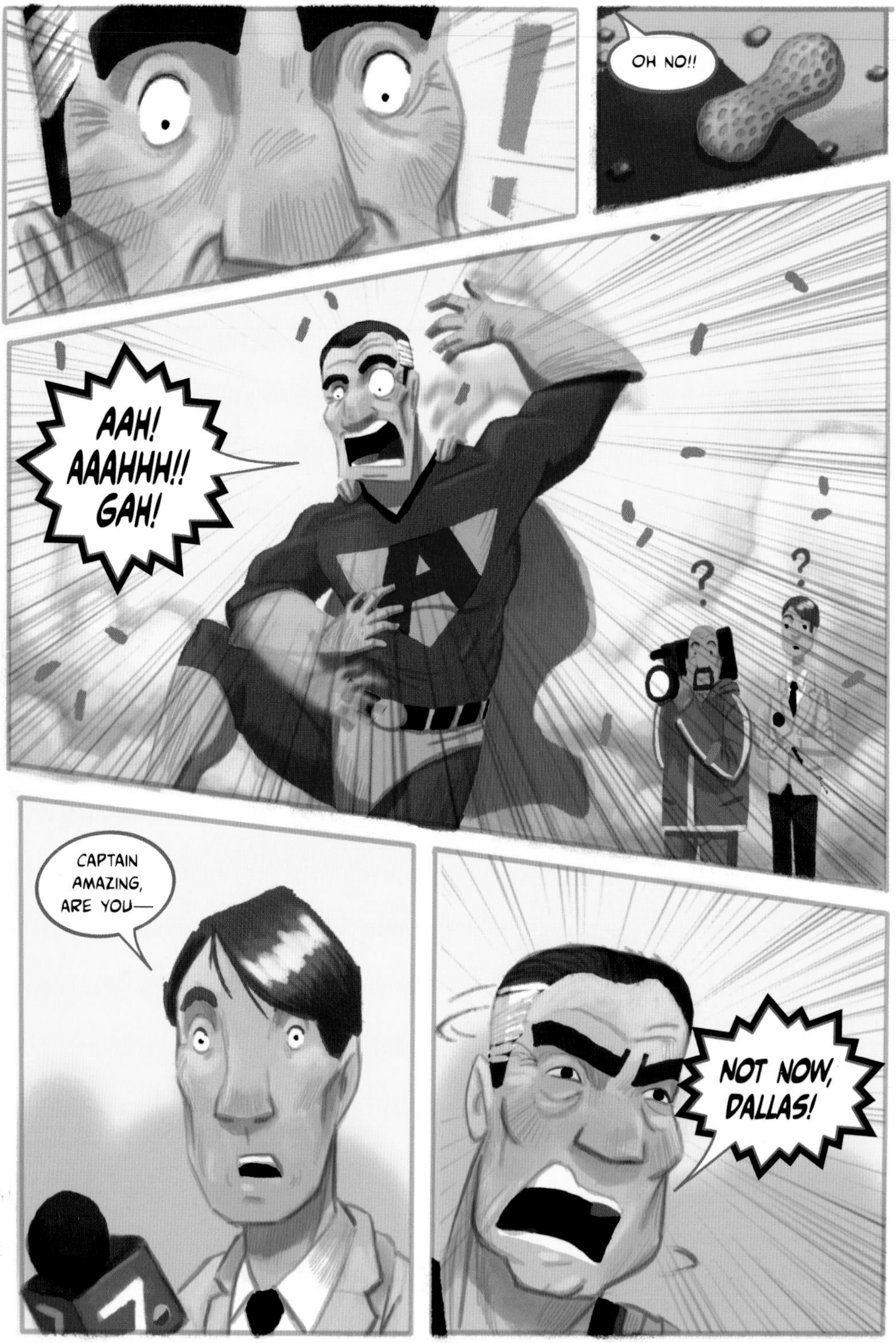
OH NO!!
AAH! AAAHHH!! GAH!
CAPTAIN AMAZING, ARE YOU—
NOT NOW, DALLAS!

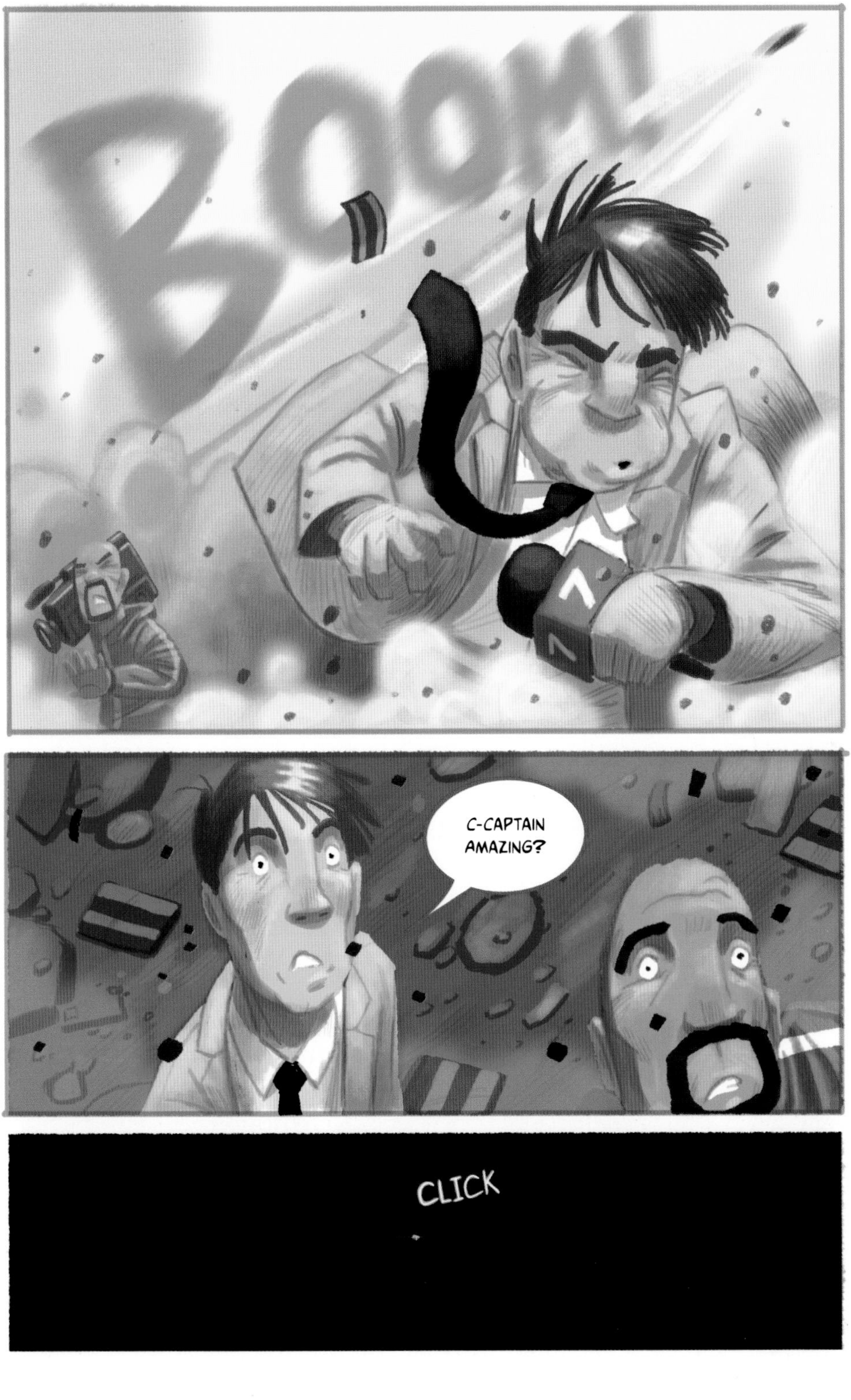
BOOM!
C-CAPTAIN AMAZING?
CLICK

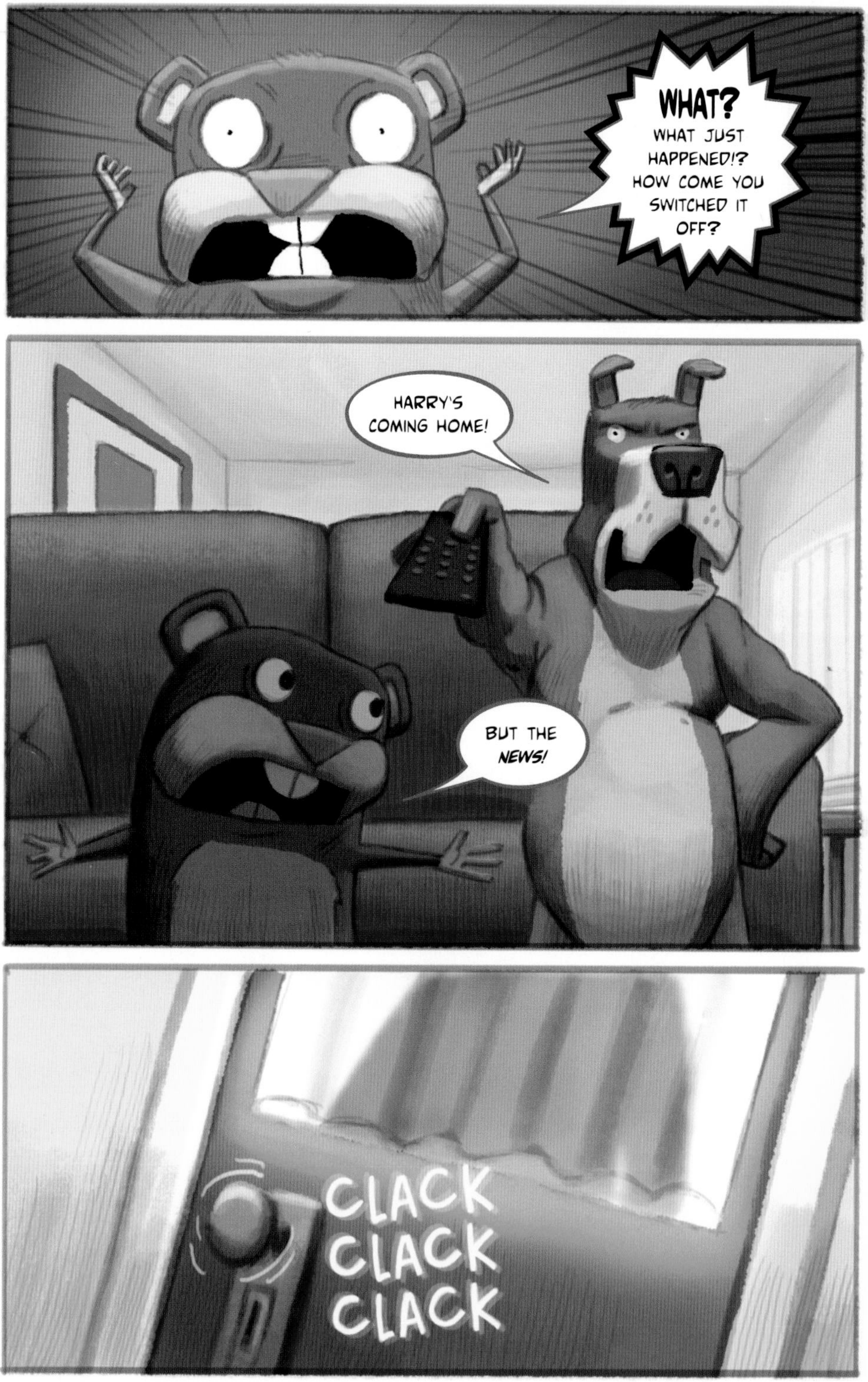
WHAT? WHAT JUST HAPPENED!? HOW COME YOU SWITCHED IT OFF?
HARRY'S COMING HOME!
BUT THE *NEWS!*
CLACK CLACK CLACK

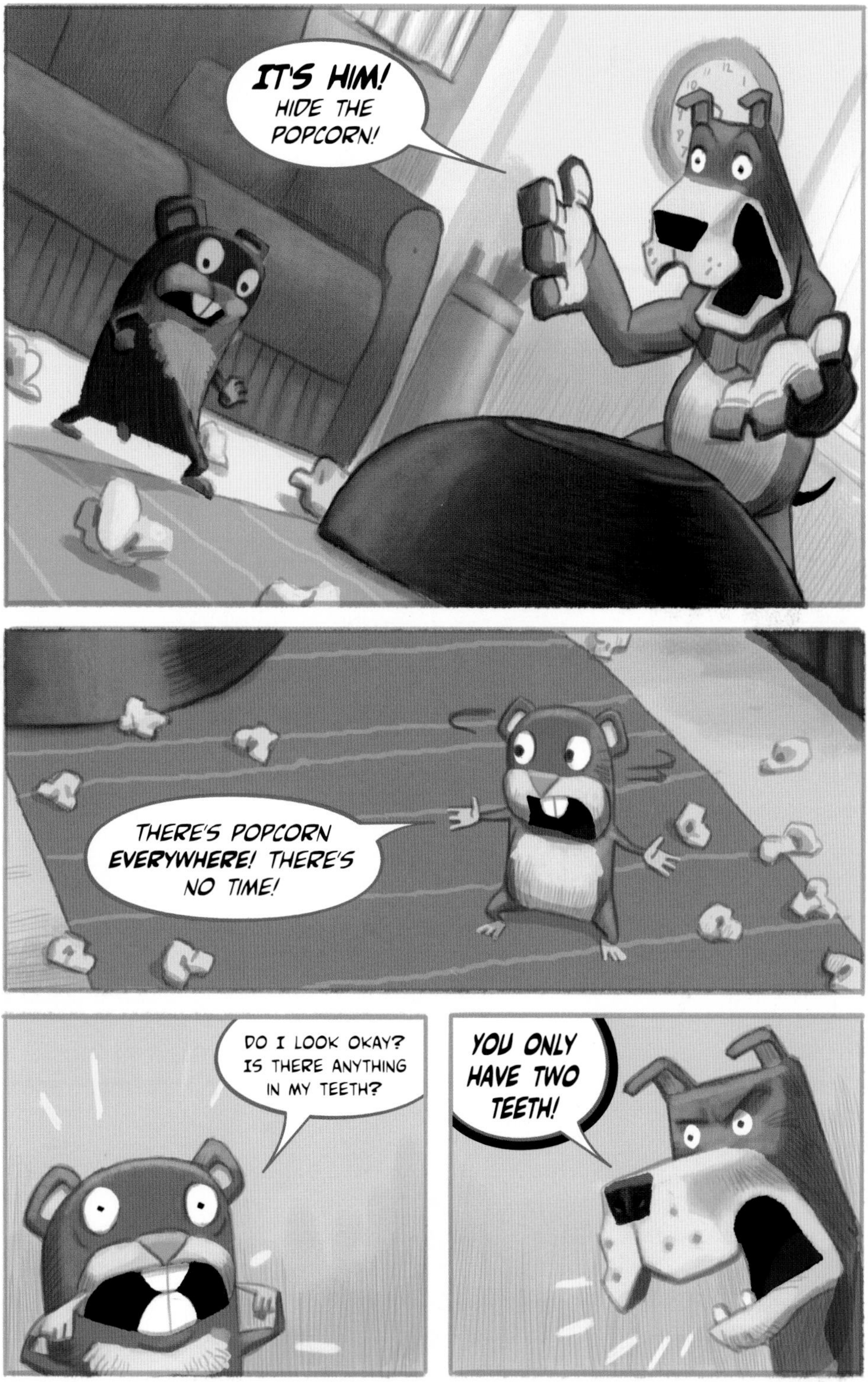
IT'S HIM! HIDE THE POPCORN!
THERE'S POPCORN EVERYWHERE! THERE'S NO TIME!
DO I LOOK OKAY? IS THERE ANYTHING IN MY TEETH?
YOU ONLY HAVE TWO TEETH!

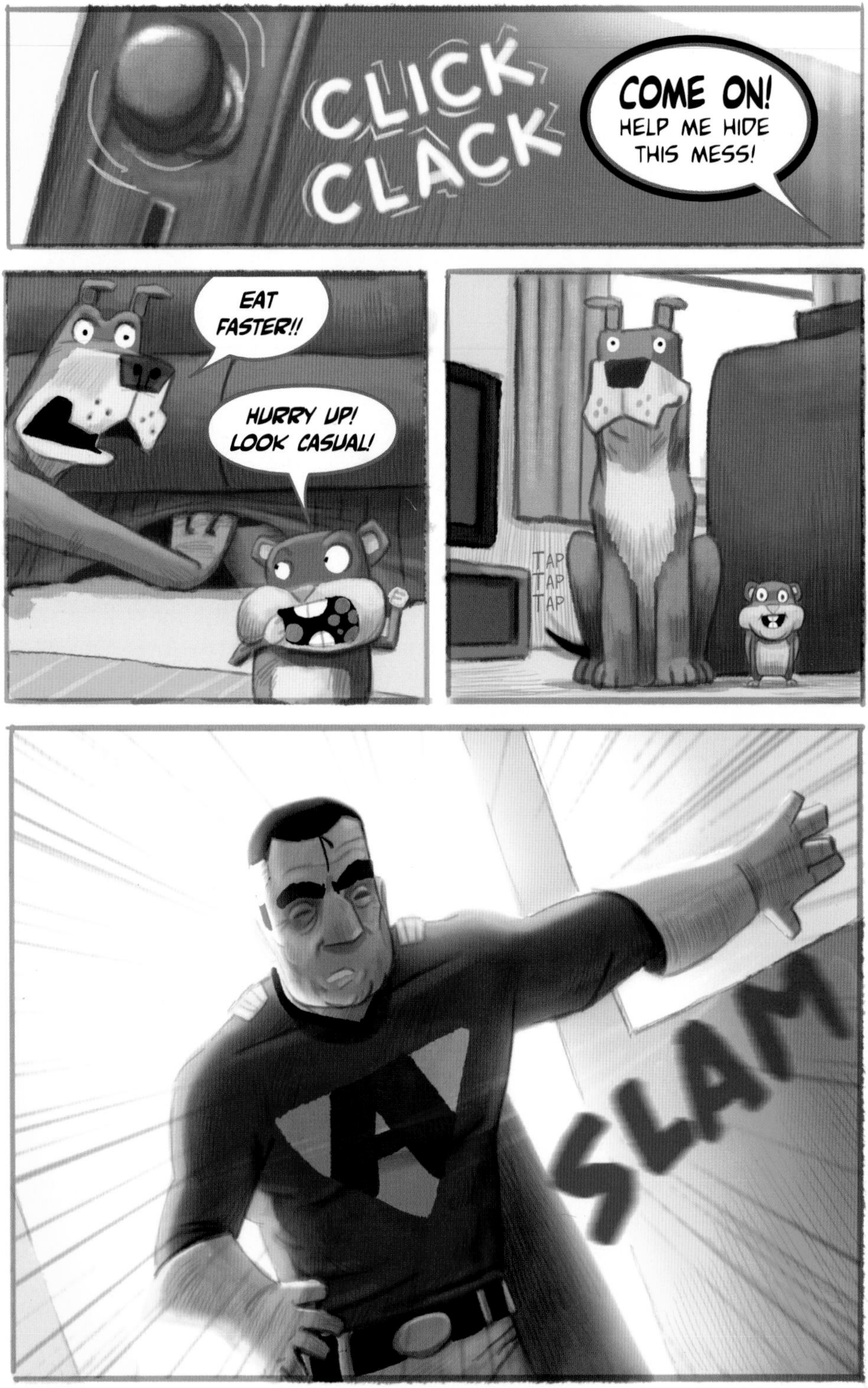
CLICK
CLACK
COME ON! HELP ME HIDE THIS MESS!
EAT FASTER!!
HURRY UP! LOOK CASUAL!
TAP
TAP
TAP
SLAM

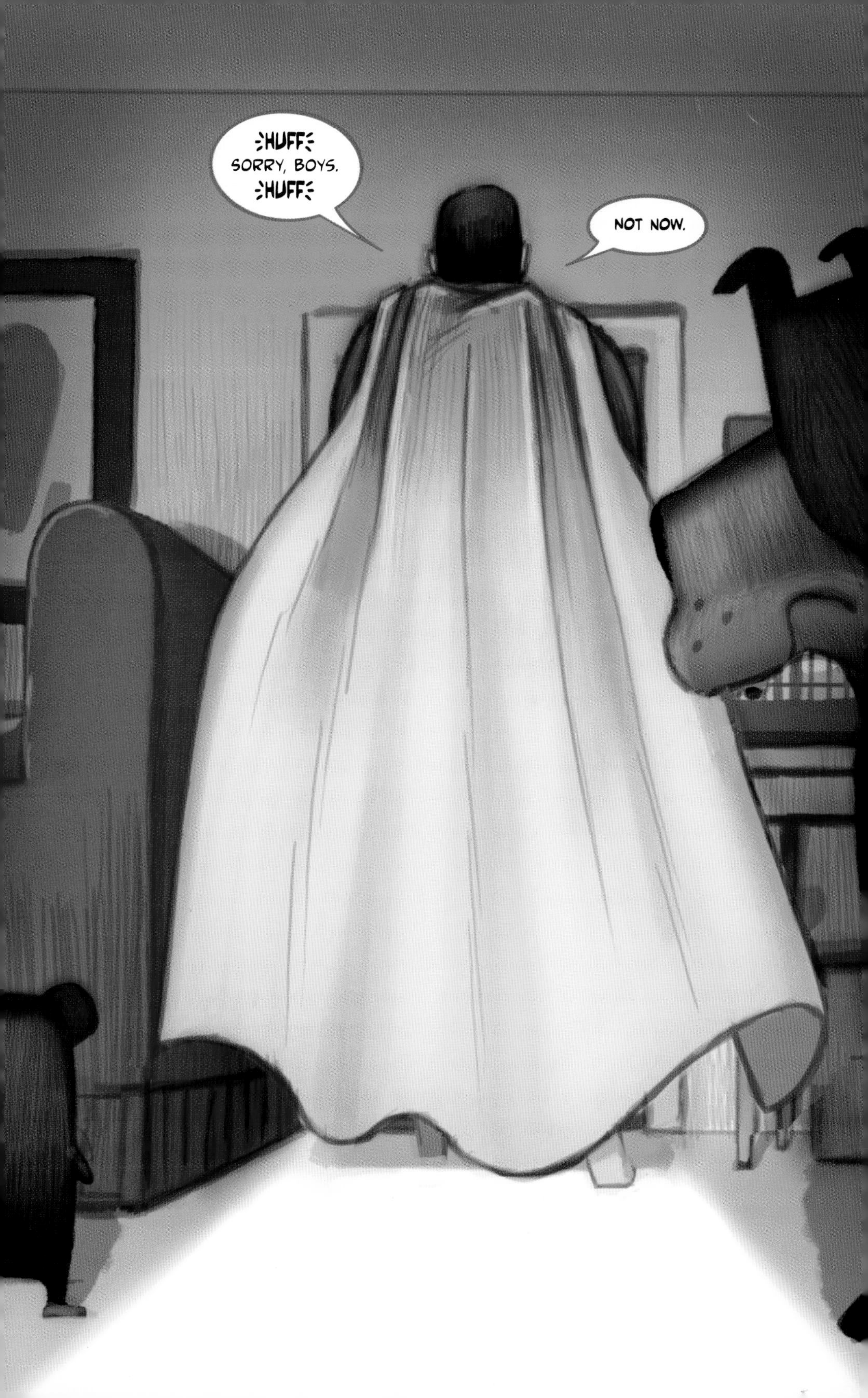
HUFF
SORRY, BOYS.
HUFF
NOT NOW.

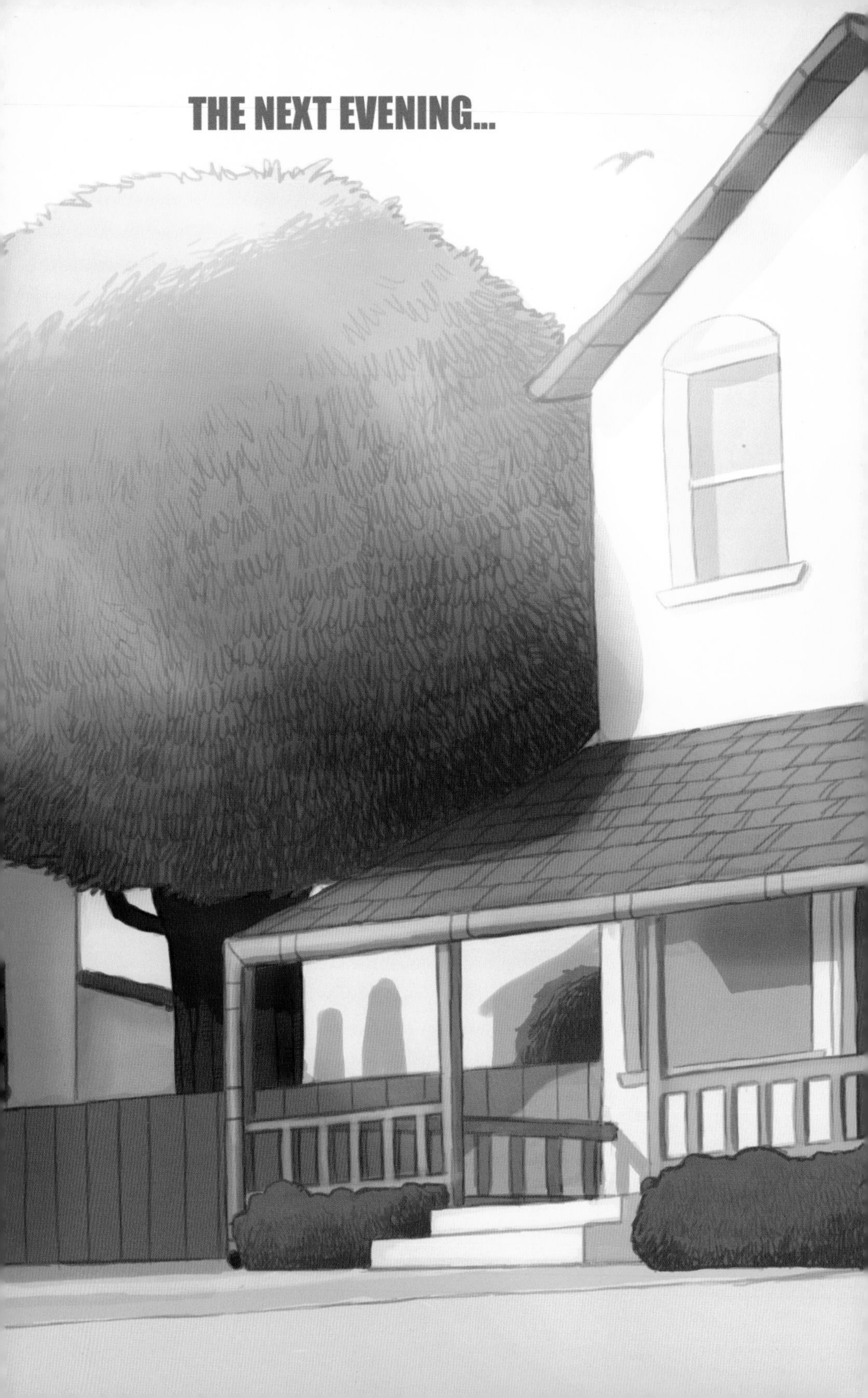
THE NEXT EVENING...

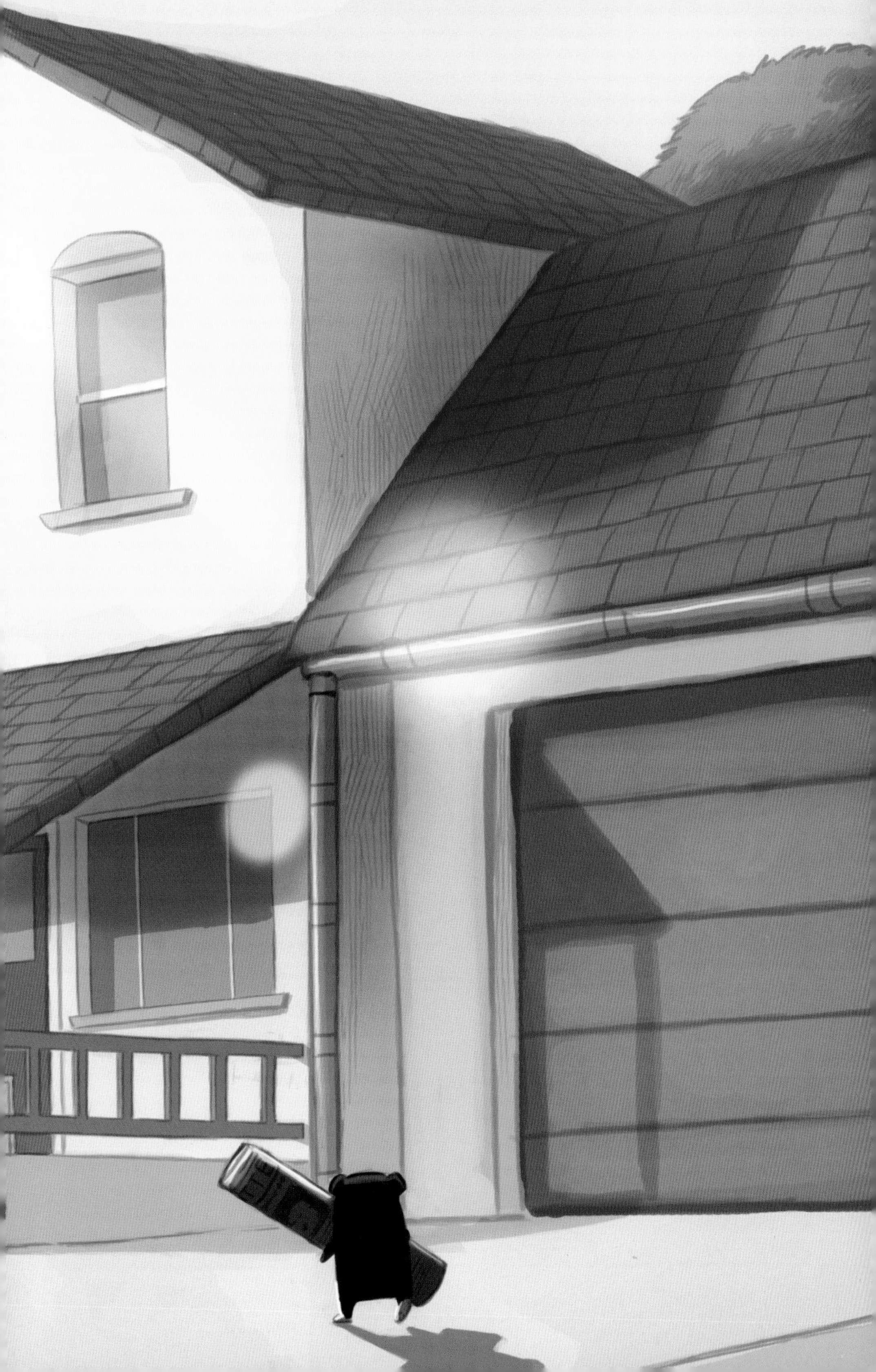

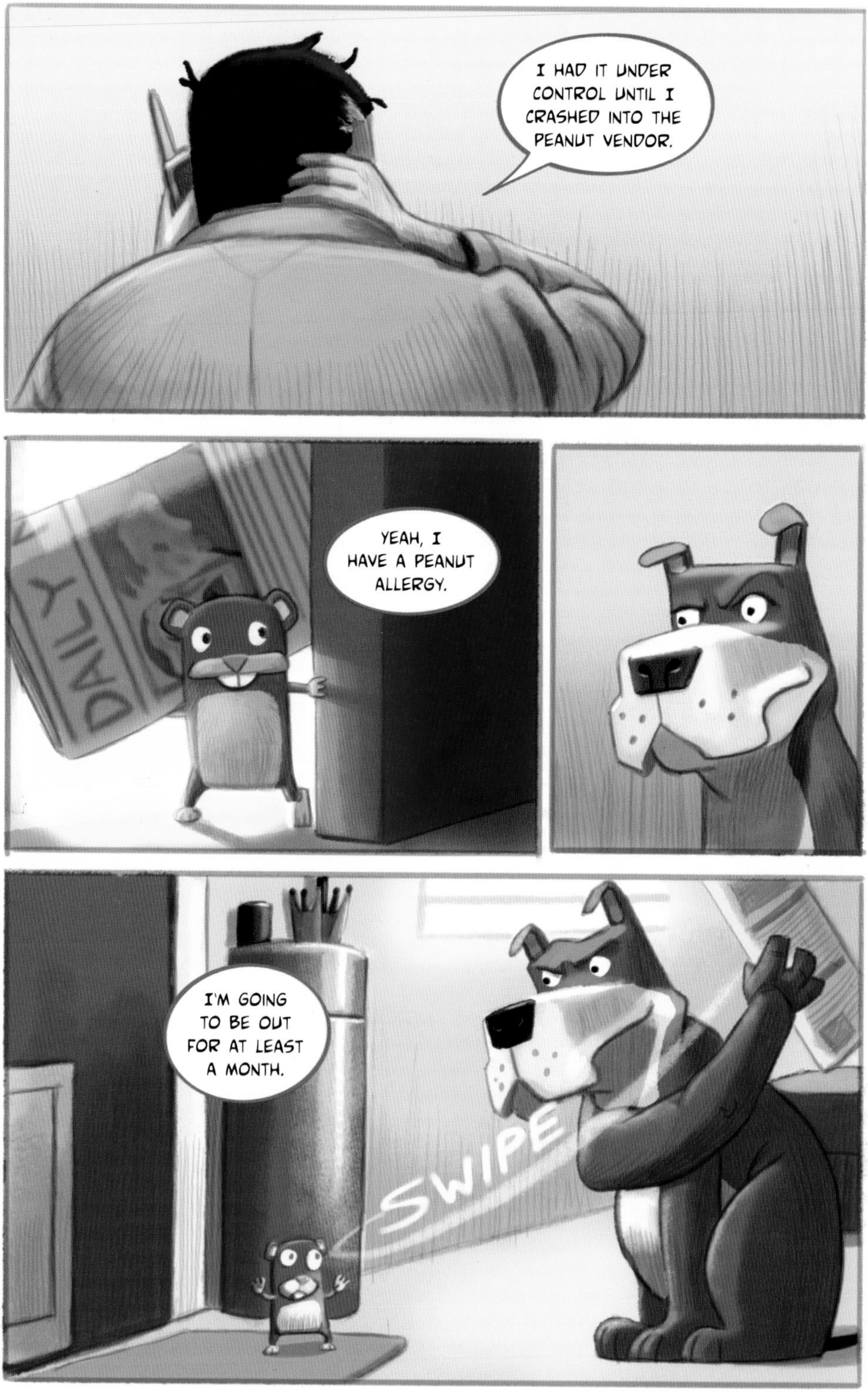
I HAD IT UNDER CONTROL UNTIL I CRASHED INTO THE PEANUT VENDOR.
DAILY
YEAH, I HAVE A PEANUT ALLERGY.
I'M GOING TO BE OUT FOR AT LEAST A MONTH.
SWIPE

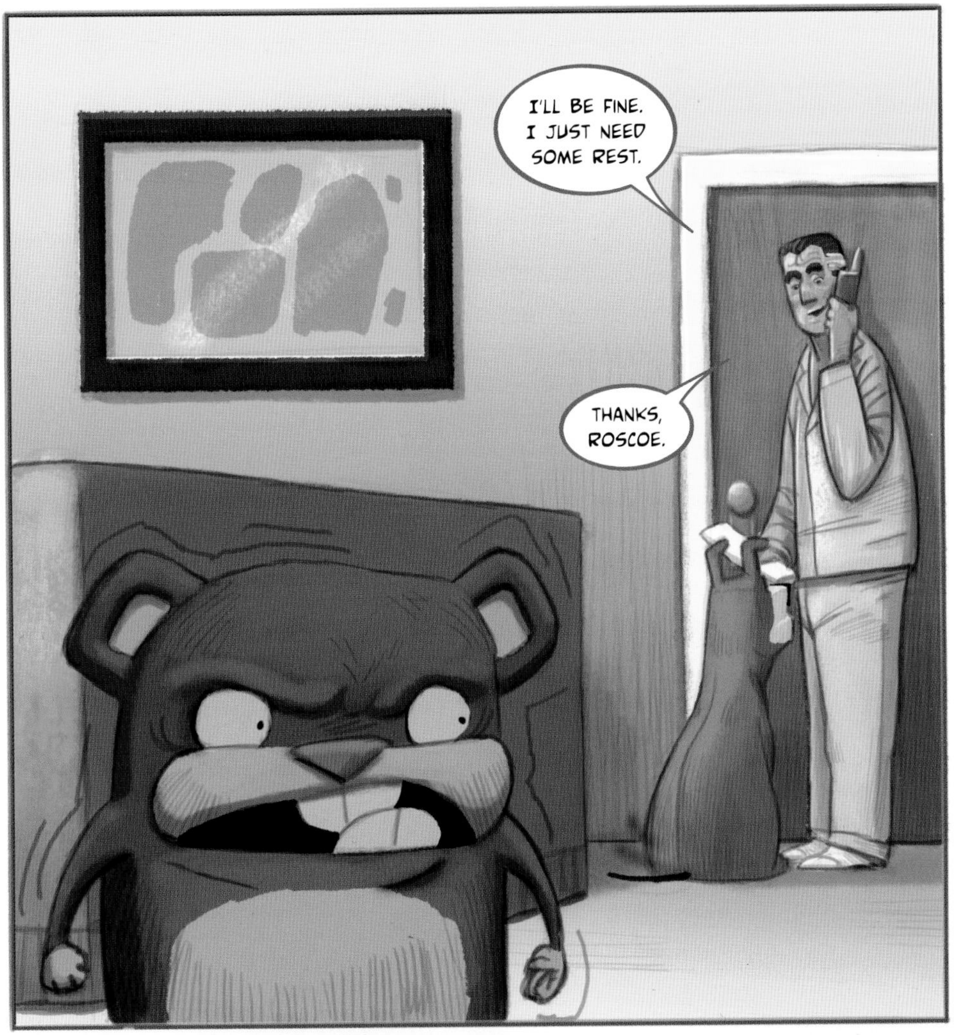
I'LL BE FINE. I JUST NEED SOME REST.
THANKS, ROSCOE.

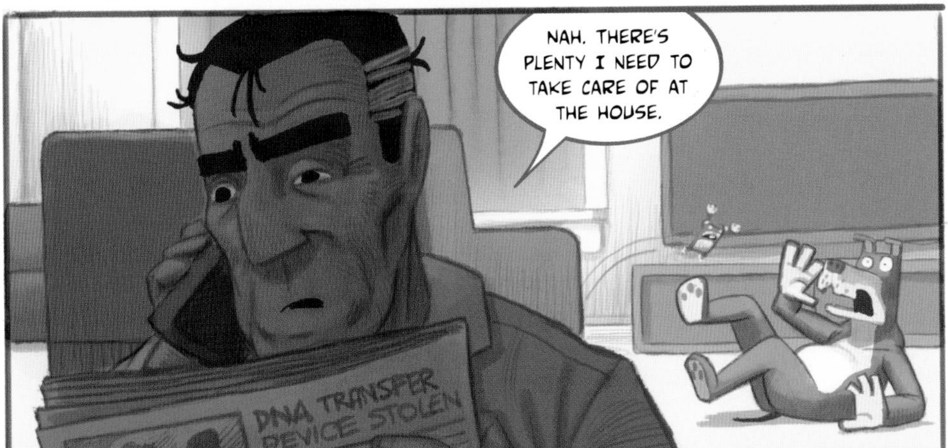
NAH. THERE'S PLENTY I NEED TO TAKE CARE OF AT THE HOUSE.
DNA TRANSFER DEVICE STOLEN

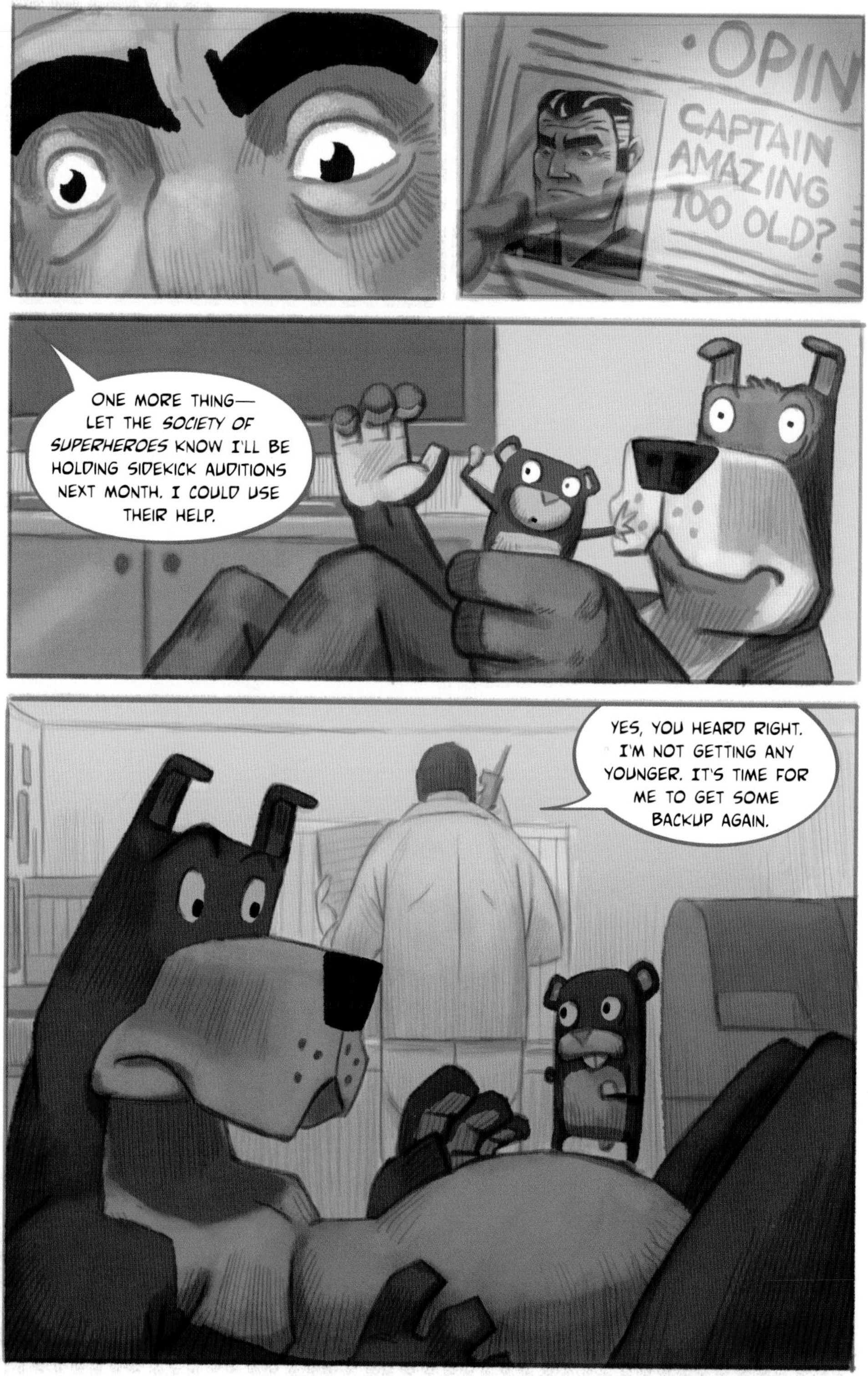
OPIN
CAPTAIN AMAZING TOO OLD?
ONE MORE THING— LET THE *SOCIETY OF SUPERHEROES* KNOW I'LL BE HOLDING SIDEKICK AUDITIONS NEXT MONTH. I COULD USE THEIR HELP.
YES, YOU HEARD RIGHT. I'M NOT GETTING ANY YOUNGER. IT'S TIME FOR ME TO GET SOME BACKUP AGAIN.

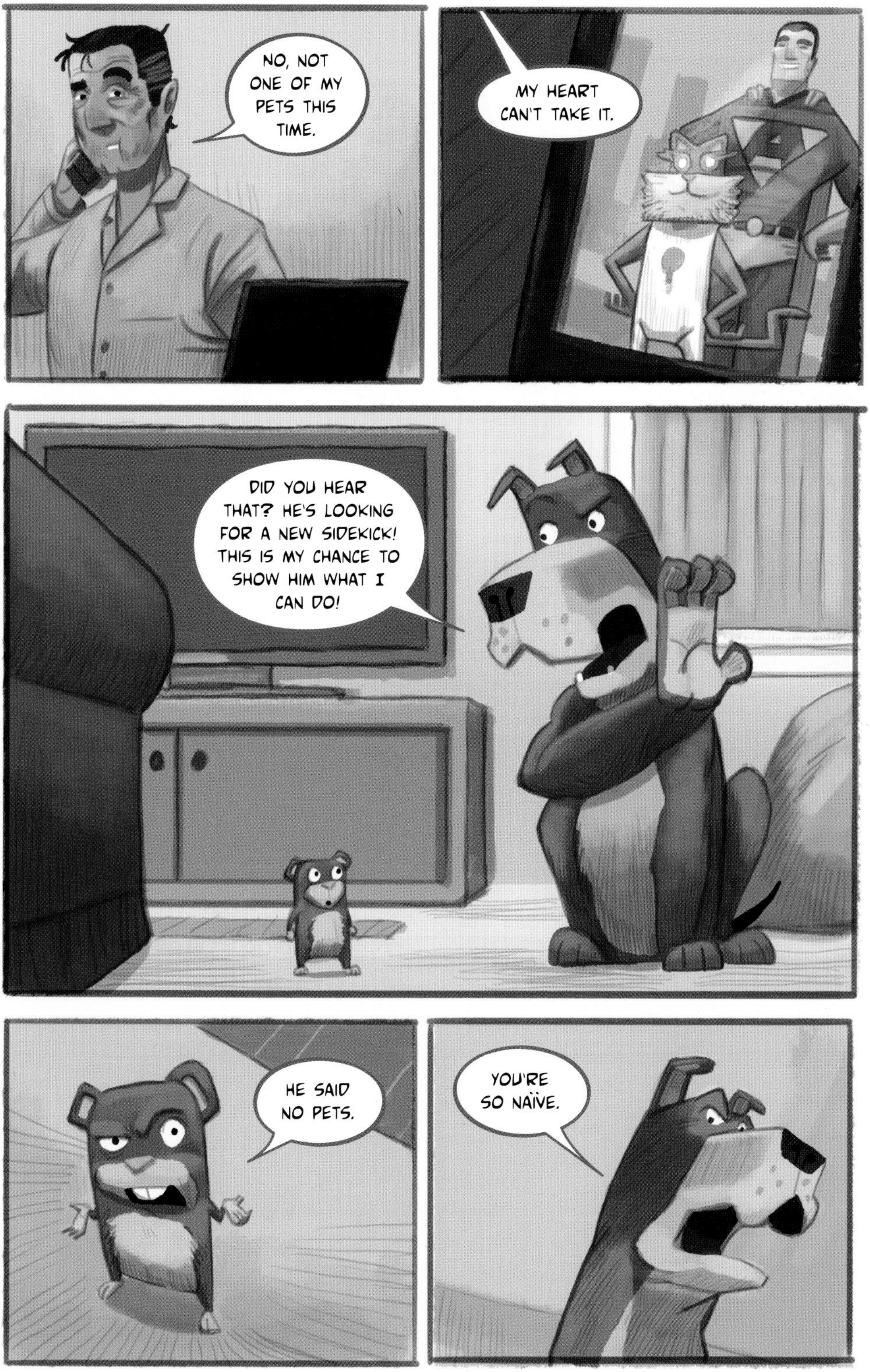
NO, NOT ONE OF MY PETS THIS TIME.
MY HEART CAN'T TAKE IT.
DID YOU HEAR THAT? HE'S LOOKING FOR A NEW SIDEKICK! THIS IS MY CHANCE TO SHOW HIM WHAT I CAN DO!
HE SAID NO PETS.
YOU'RE SO NAÏVE.

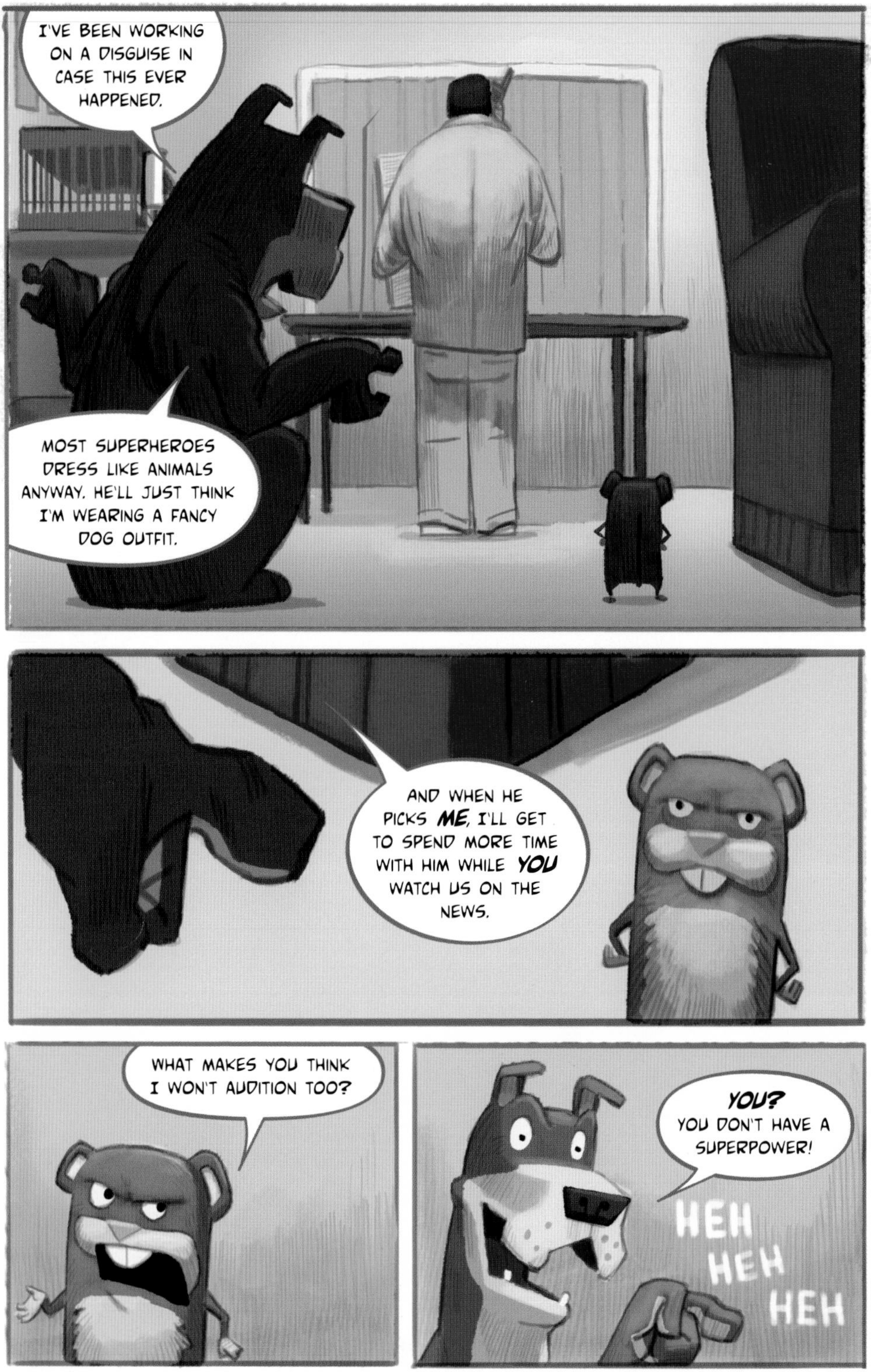
I'VE BEEN WORKING ON A DISGUISE IN CASE THIS EVER HAPPENED.
MOST SUPERHEROES DRESS LIKE ANIMALS ANYWAY. HE'LL JUST THINK I'M WEARING A FANCY DOG OUTFIT.
AND WHEN HE PICKS ME, I'LL GET TO SPEND MORE TIME WITH HIM WHILE YOU WATCH US ON THE NEWS.
WHAT MAKES YOU THINK I WON'T AUDITION TOO?
YOU? YOU DON'T HAVE A SUPERPOWER!
HEH HEH HEH

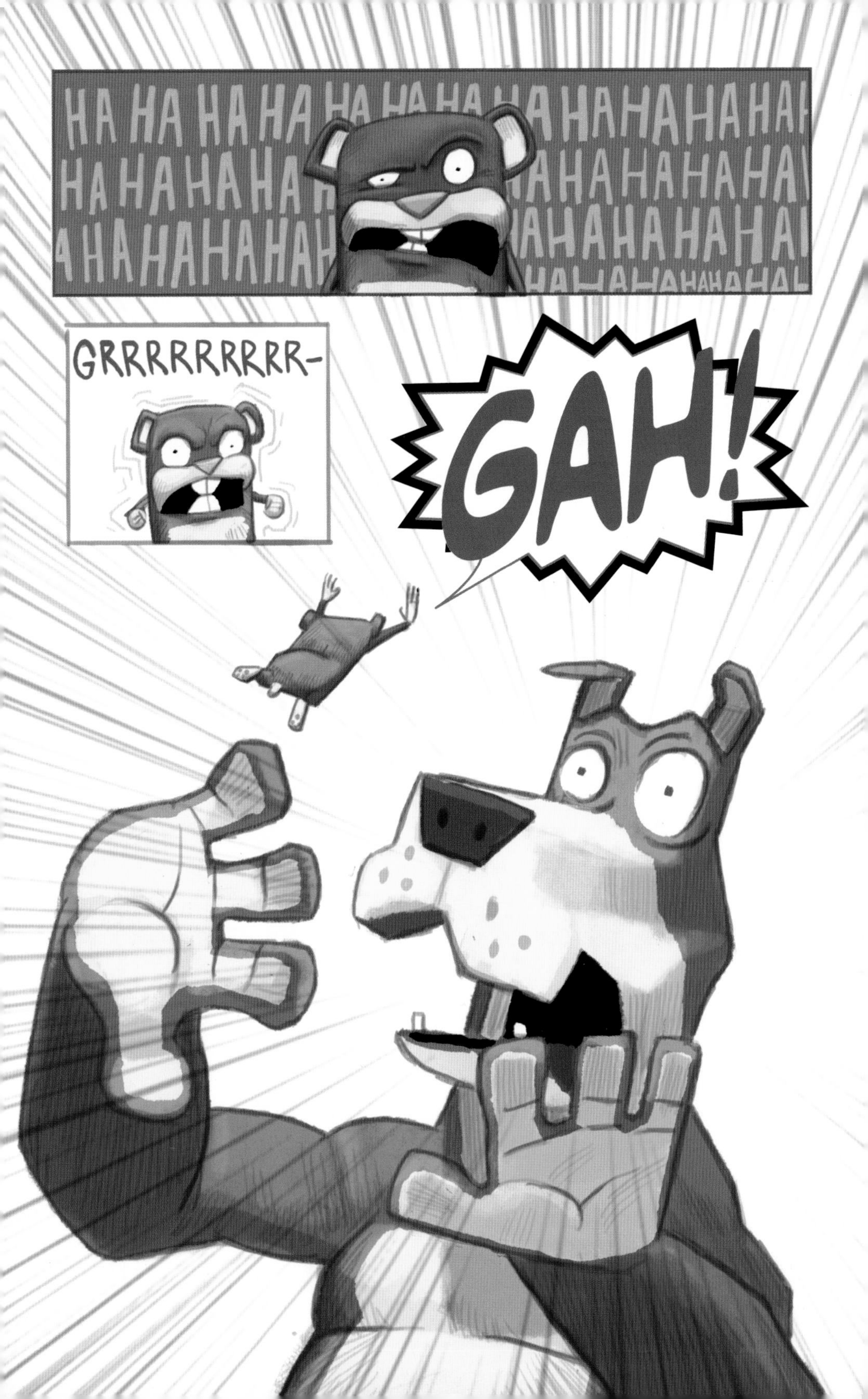
HA HA HA HA HA HA HA HA HAHAHAHAHA
HA HAHAHAHA HAHAHAHAHA
HAHAHAHAHAH HAHAHA HA HA
HAHAHAHAHAHA
GRRRRRRRRR-
GAH!

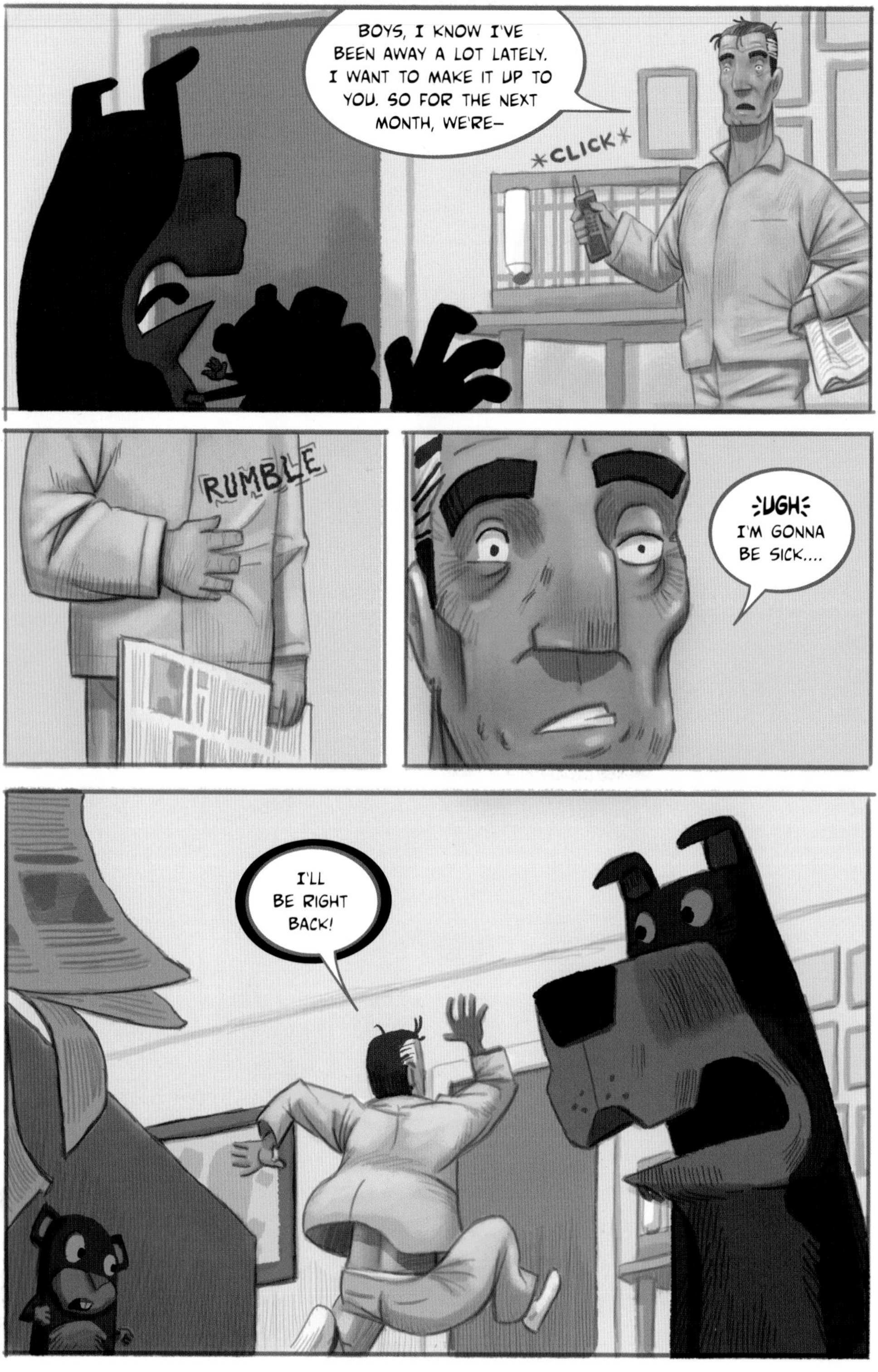
BOYS, I KNOW I'VE BEEN AWAY A LOT LATELY. I WANT TO MAKE IT UP TO YOU. SO FOR THE NEXT MONTH, WE'RE–
CLICK
RUMBLE
UGH
I'M GONNA BE SICK....
I'LL BE RIGHT BACK!

DING DONG
DELIVERY FOR HARRISON BLAKE!
SWIPE!
FRAGILE

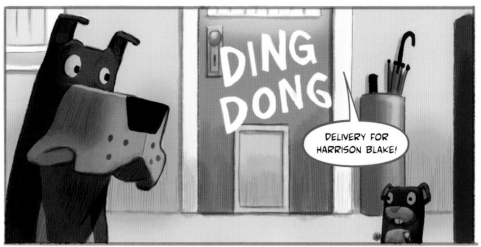

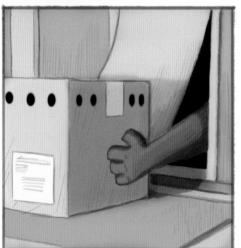

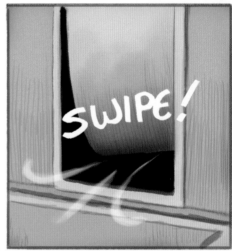

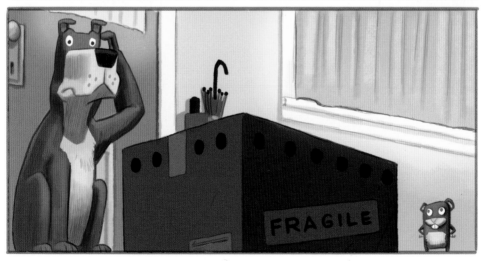

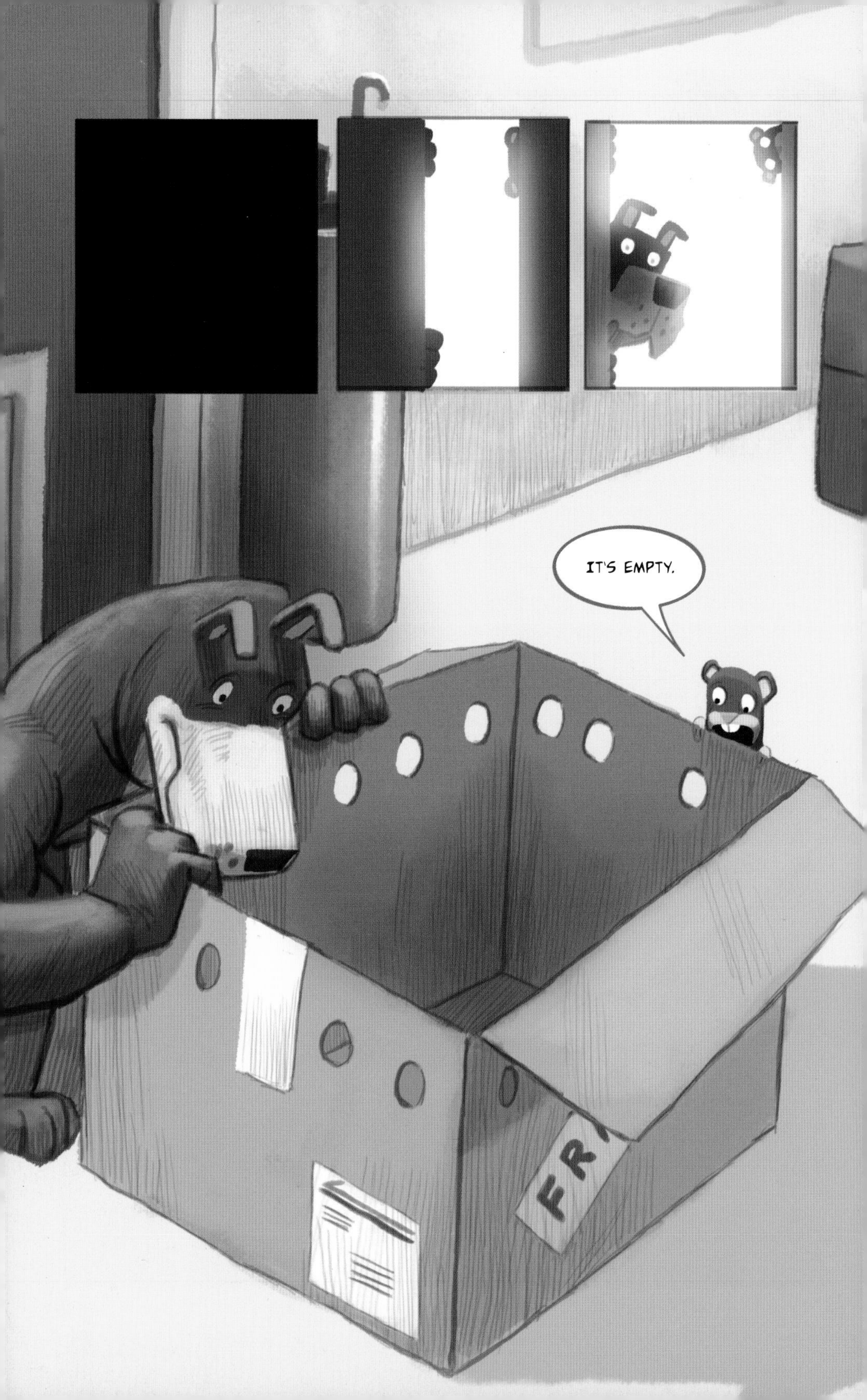
IT'S EMPTY.

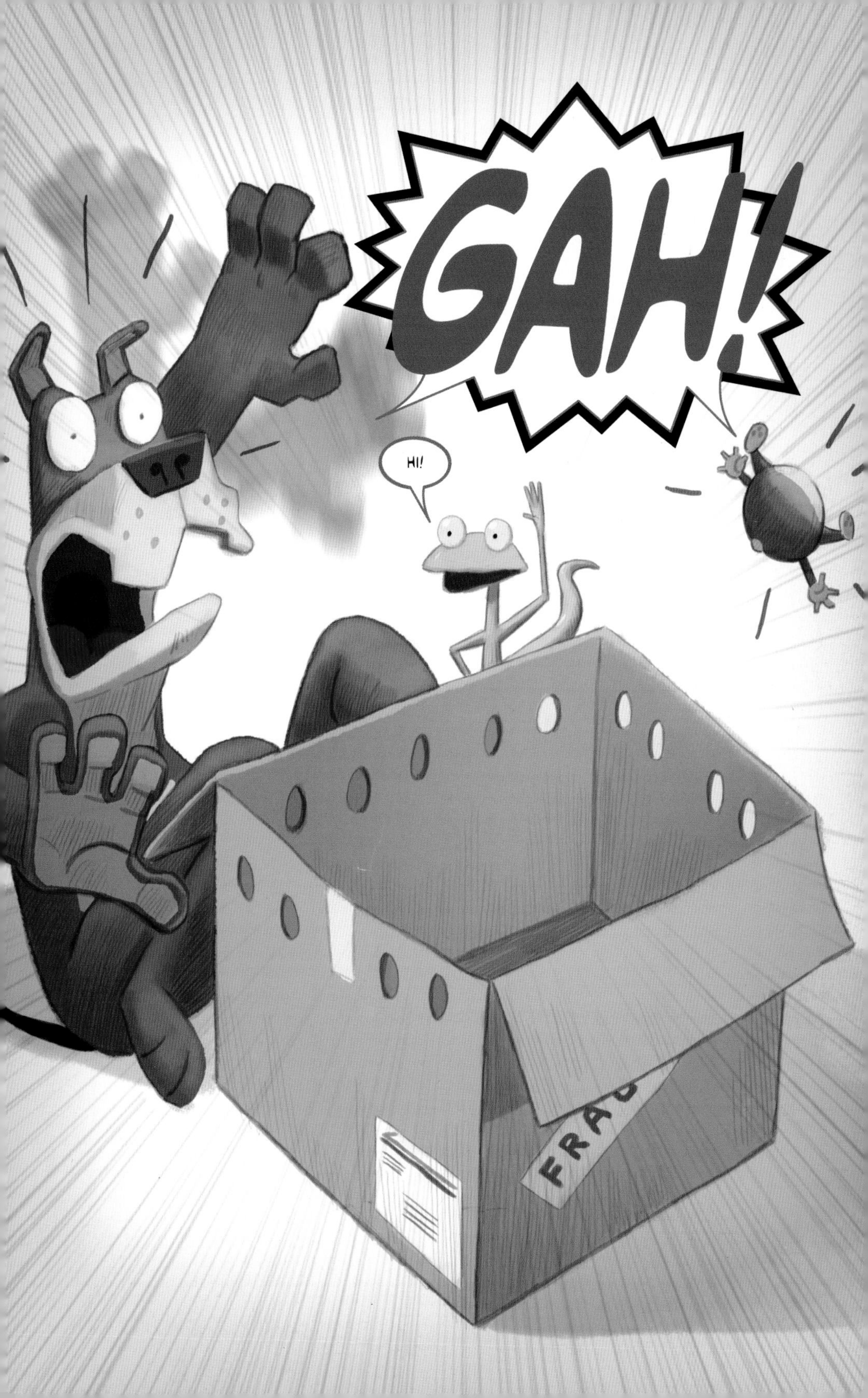
GAH!
HI!
FRA

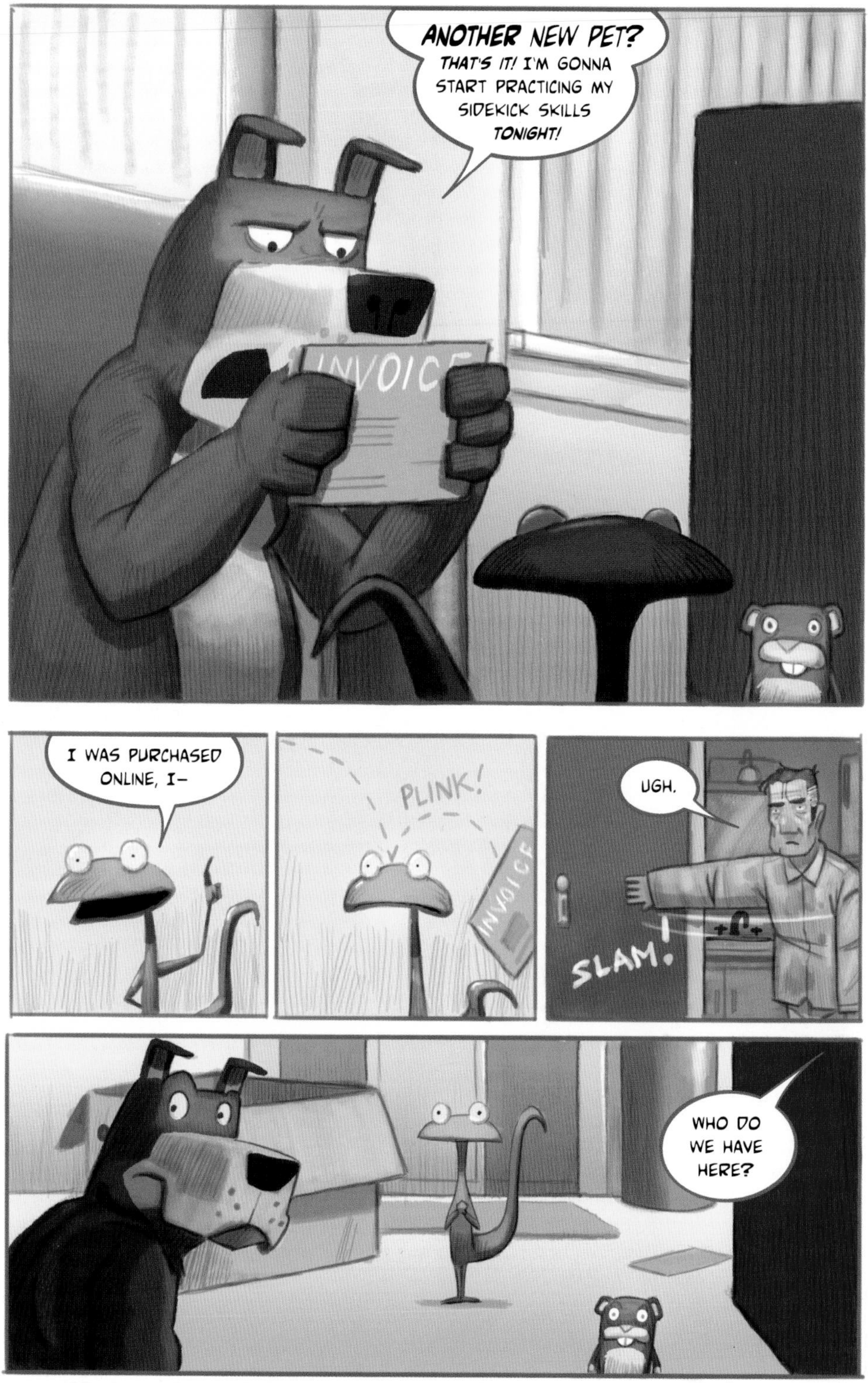
ANOTHER NEW PET? THAT'S IT! I'M GONNA START PRACTICING MY SIDEKICK SKILLS TONIGHT!
INVOICE
I WAS PURCHASED ONLINE, I–
PLINK!
INVOICE
UGH.
SLAM!
WHO DO WE HAVE HERE?

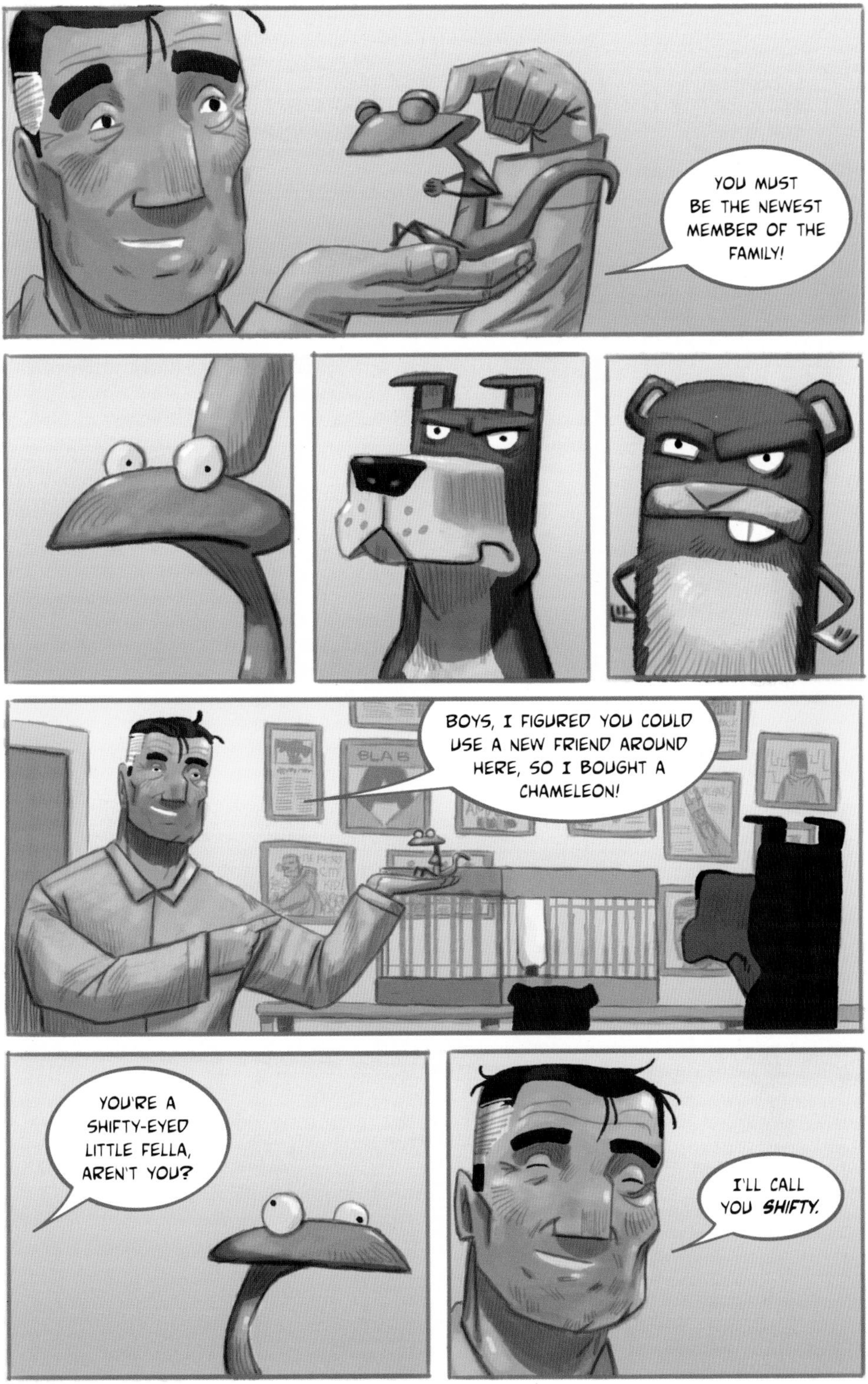
YOU MUST BE THE NEWEST MEMBER OF THE FAMILY!
BOYS, I FIGURED YOU COULD USE A NEW FRIEND AROUND HERE, SO I BOUGHT A CHAMELEON!
YOU'RE A SHIFTY-EYED LITTLE FELLA, AREN'T YOU?
I'LL CALL YOU ***SHIFTY.***

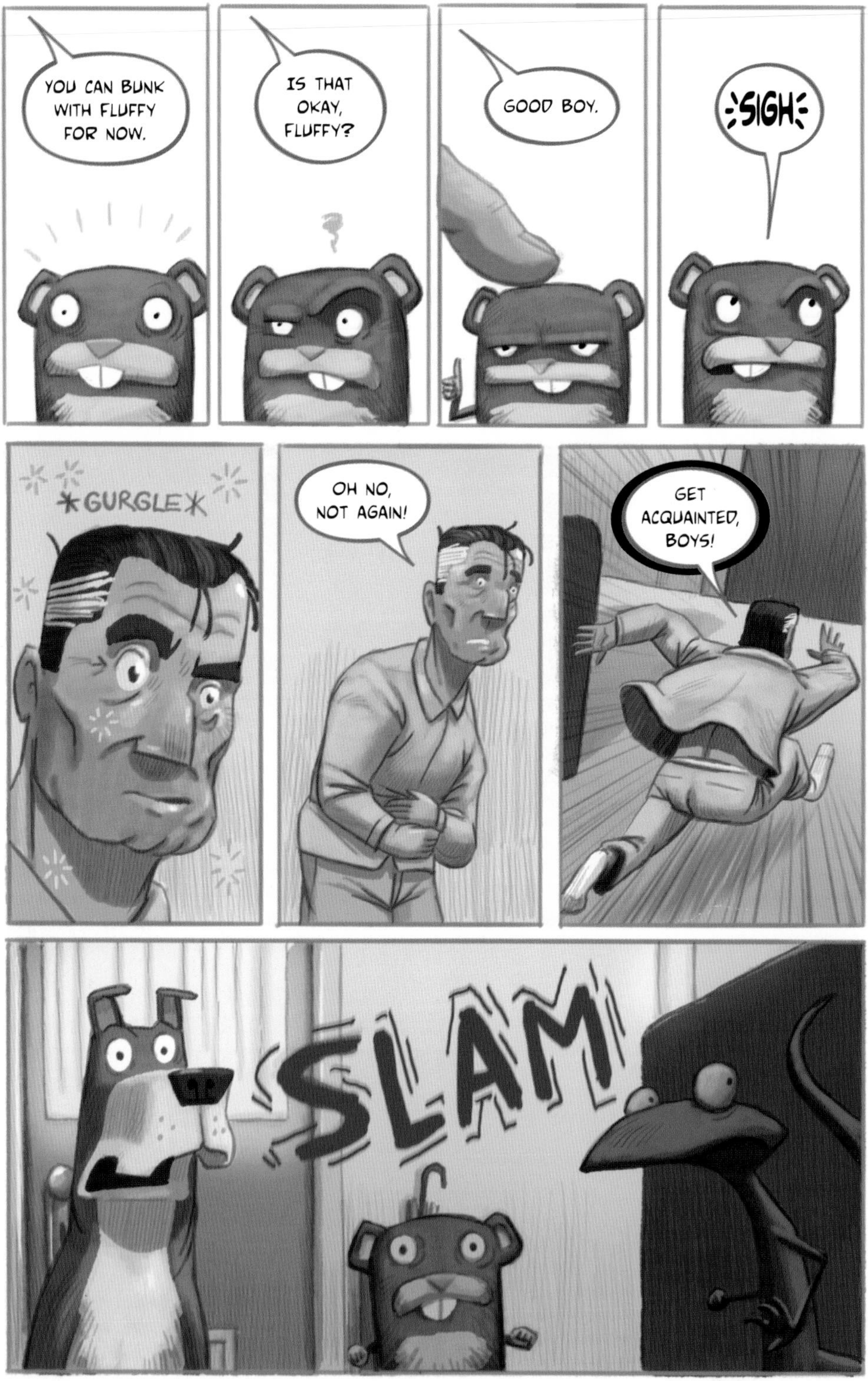
YOU CAN BUNK WITH FLUFFY FOR NOW.
IS THAT OKAY, FLUFFY?
GOOD BOY.
SIGH
GURGLE
OH NO, NOT AGAIN!
GET ACQUAINTED, BOYS!
SLAM

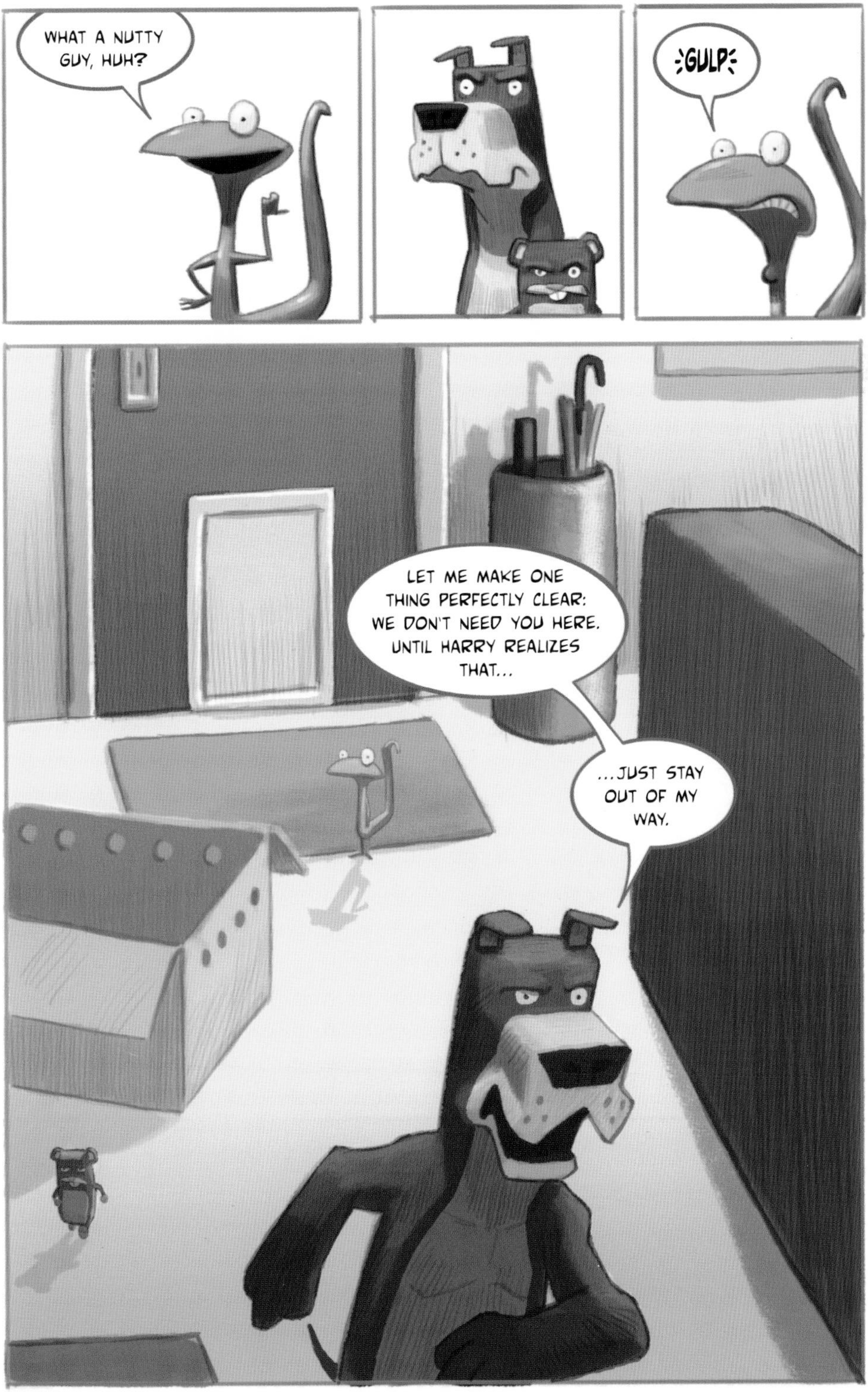
WHAT A NUTTY GUY, HUH?
GULP
LET ME MAKE ONE THING PERFECTLY CLEAR: WE DON'T NEED YOU HERE. UNTIL HARRY REALIZES THAT...
...JUST STAY OUT OF MY WAY.

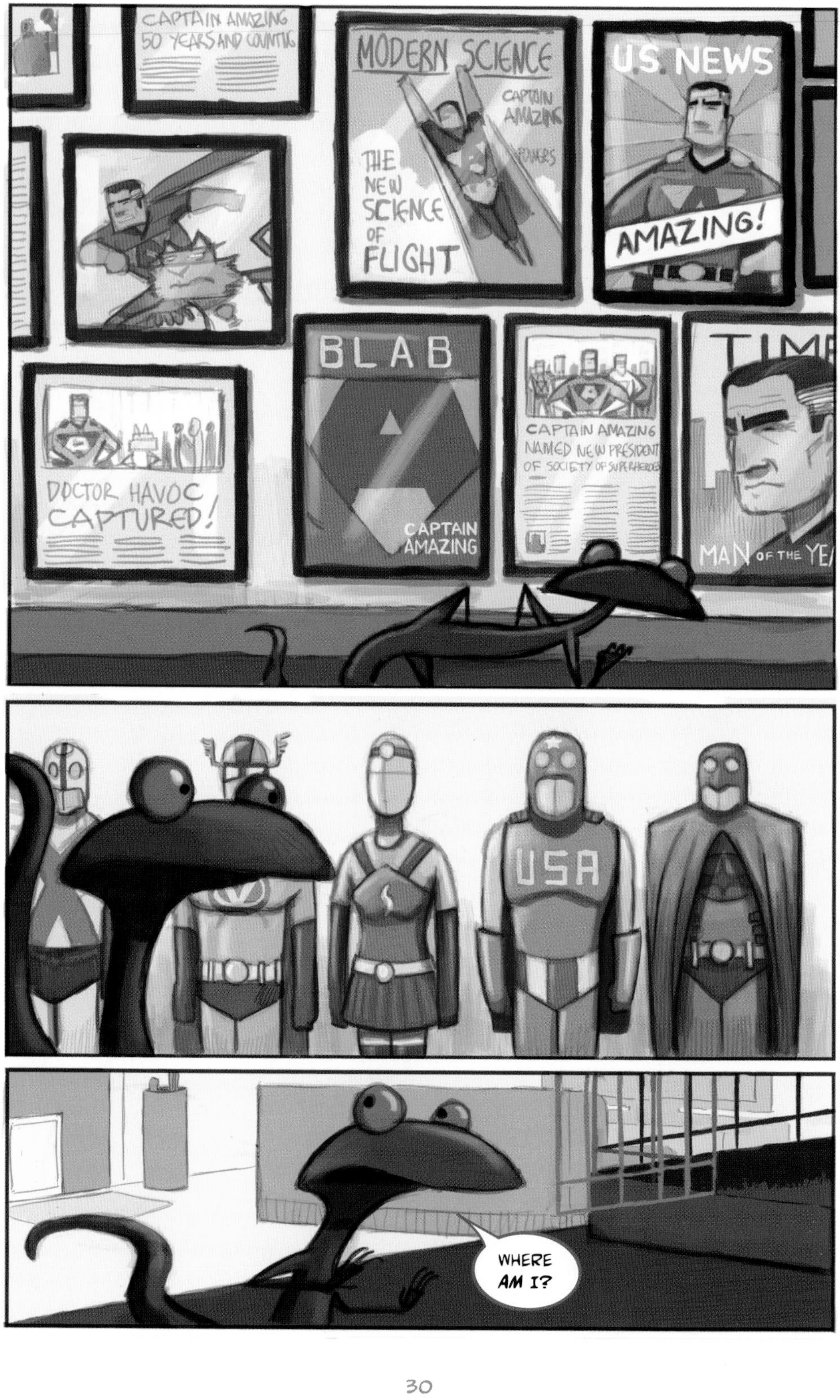
CAPTAIN AMAZING 50 YEARS AND COUNTING
MODERN SCIENCE
CAPTAIN AMAZING
THE NEW SCIENCE OF FLIGHT
U.S. NEWS
AMAZING!
BLAB
CAPTAIN AMAZING
CAPTAIN AMAZING NAMED NEW PRESIDENT OF SOCIETY OF SUPERHEROES
DOCTOR HAVOC CAPTURED!
USA
WHERE AM I?

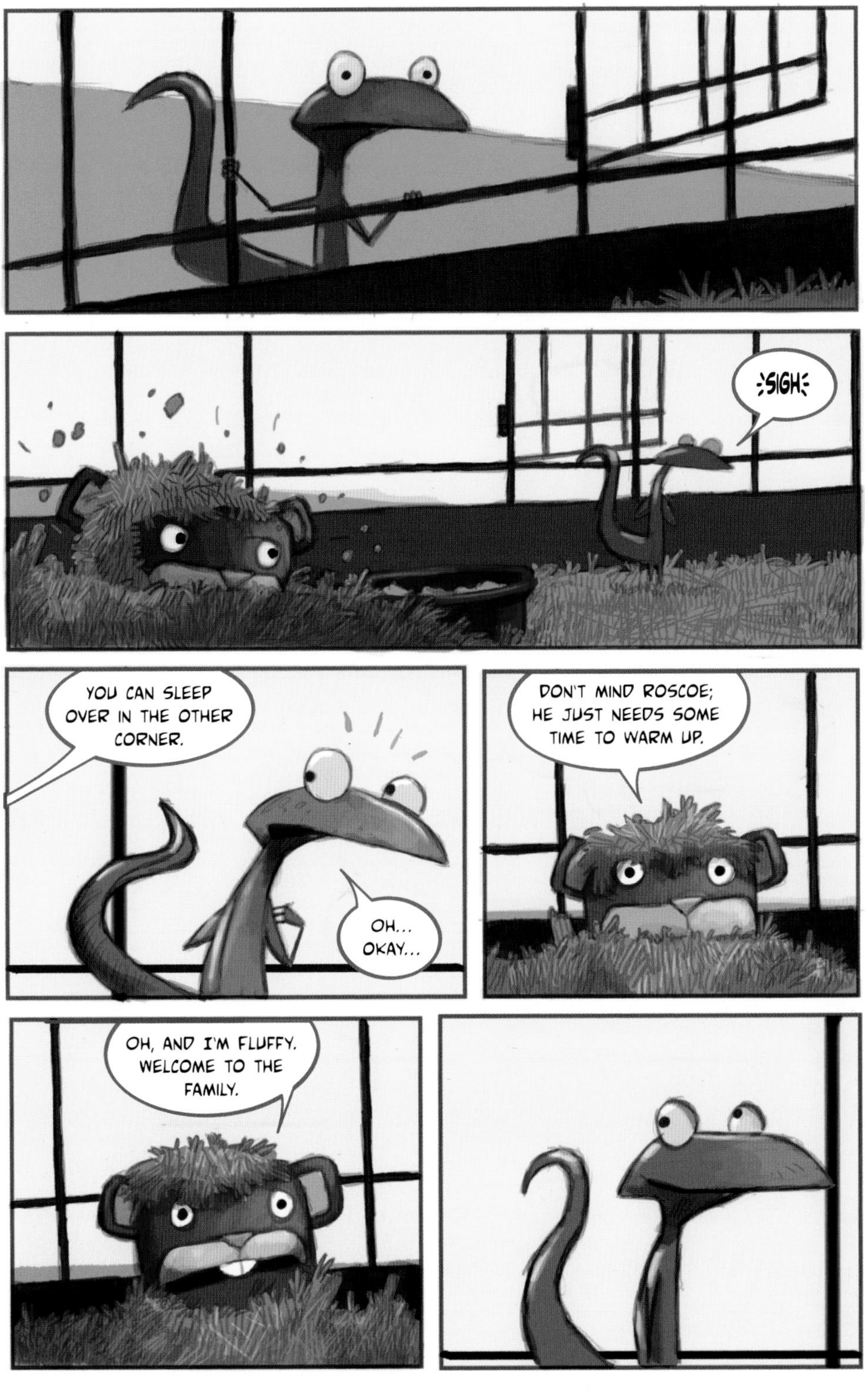
SIGH
YOU CAN SLEEP OVER IN THE OTHER CORNER.
OH... OKAY...
DON'T MIND ROSCOE; HE JUST NEEDS SOME TIME TO WARM UP.
OH, AND I'M FLUFFY. WELCOME TO THE FAMILY.

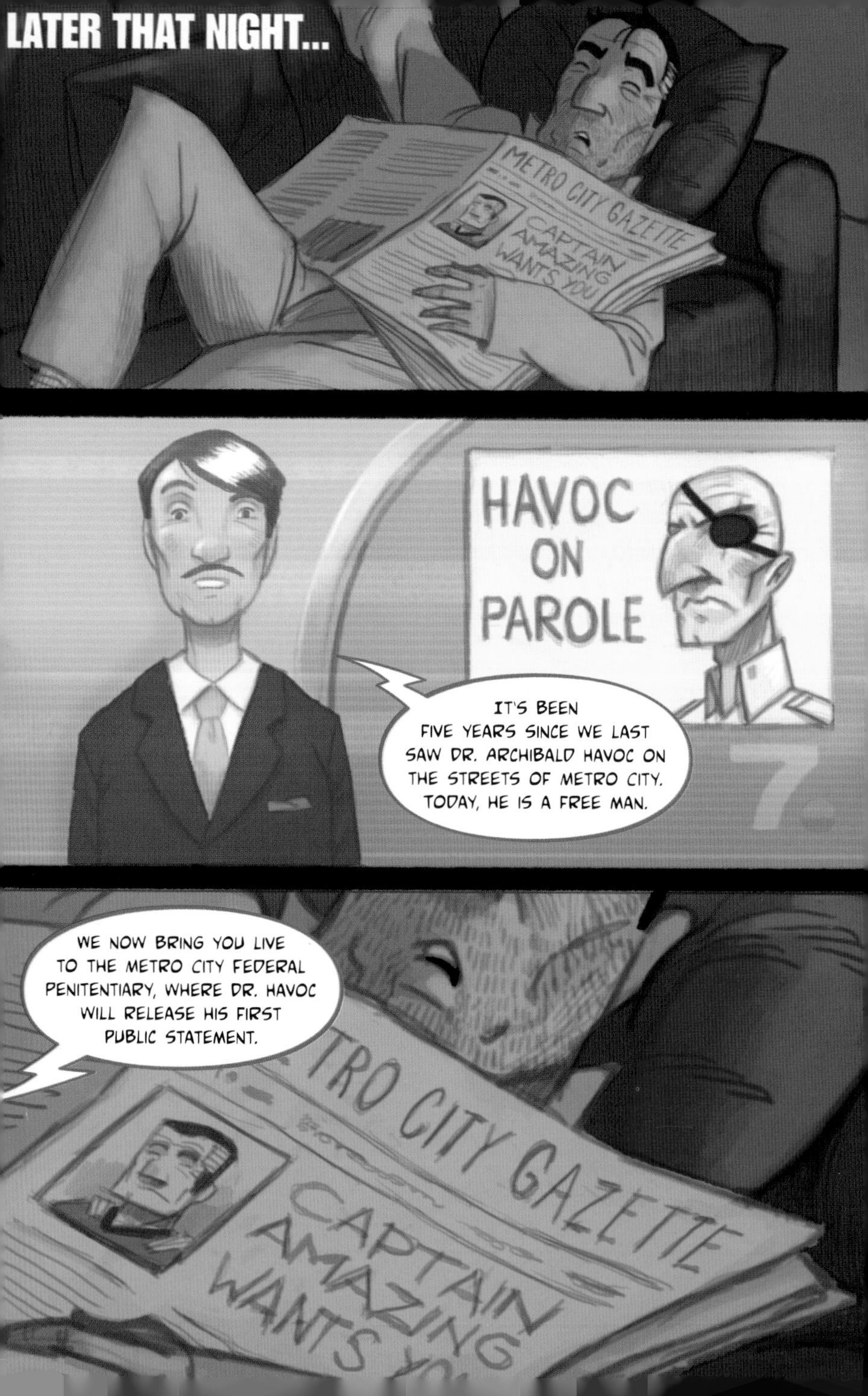
LATER THAT NIGHT...
METRO CITY GAZETTE
CAPTAIN AMAZING WANTS YOU
HAVOC ON PAROLE
IT'S BEEN FIVE YEARS SINCE WE LAST SAW DR. ARCHIBALD HAVOC ON THE STREETS OF METRO CITY. TODAY, HE IS A FREE MAN.
7.
WE NOW BRING YOU LIVE TO THE METRO CITY FEDERAL PENITENTIARY, WHERE DR. HAVOC WILL RELEASE HIS FIRST PUBLIC STATEMENT.
CAPTAIN AMAZING

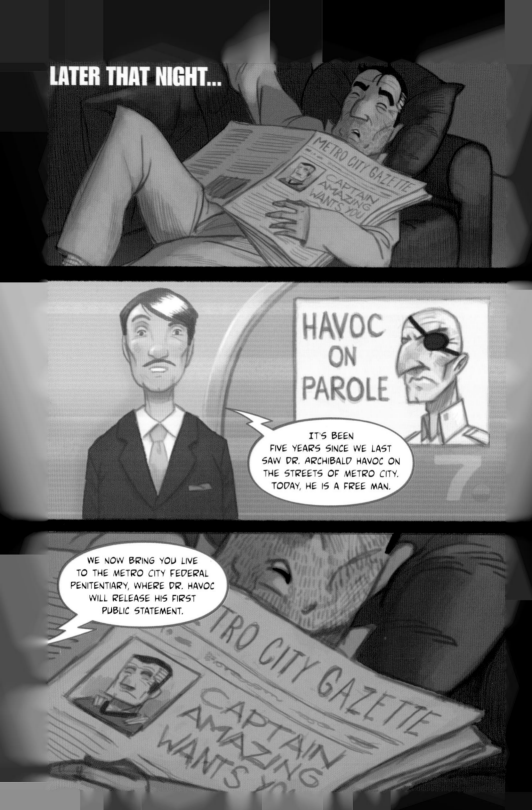

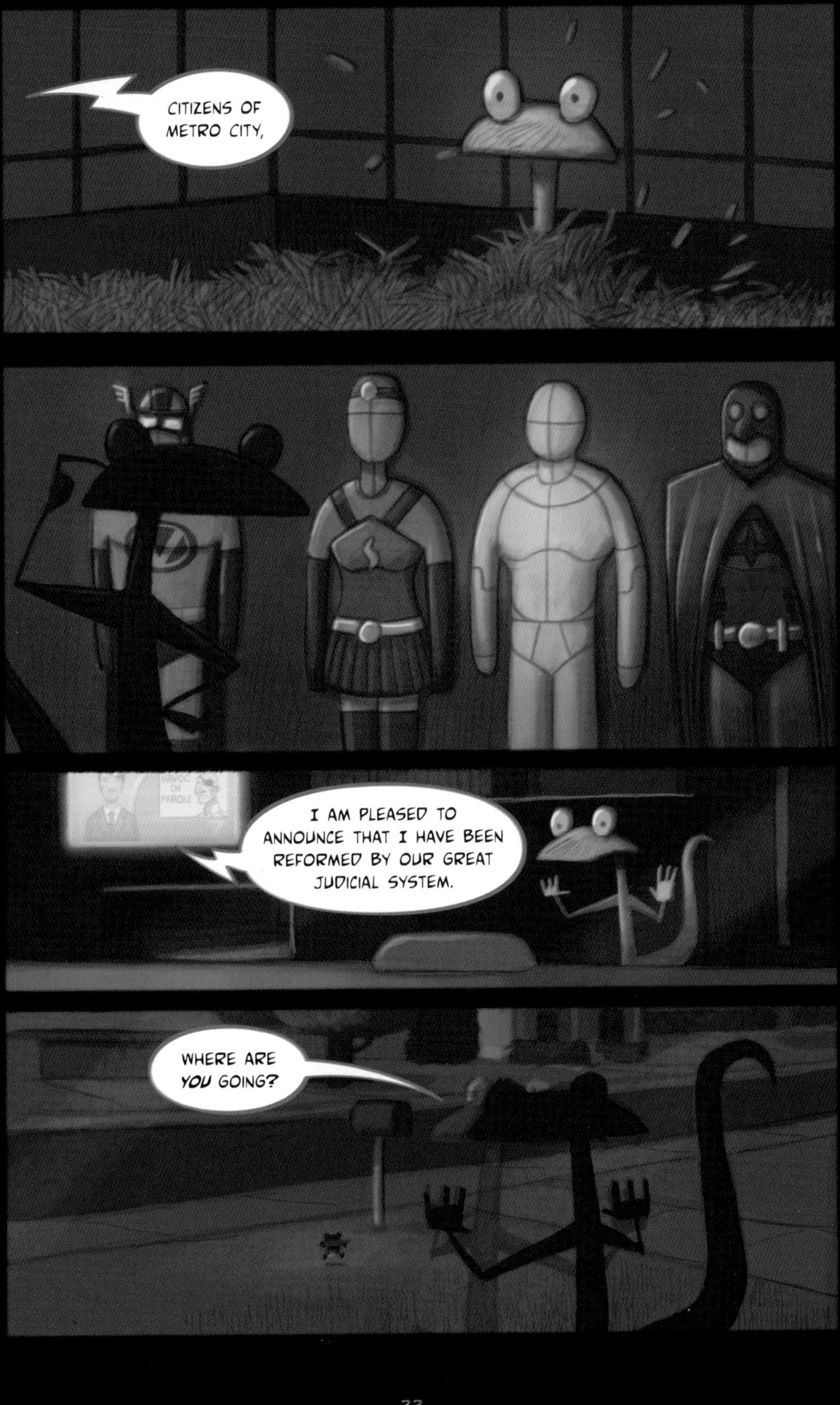
CITIZENS OF METRO CITY,
HAVOC ON PAROLE
I AM PLEASED TO ANNOUNCE THAT I HAVE BEEN REFORMED BY OUR GREAT JUDICIAL SYSTEM.
WHERE ARE YOU GOING?

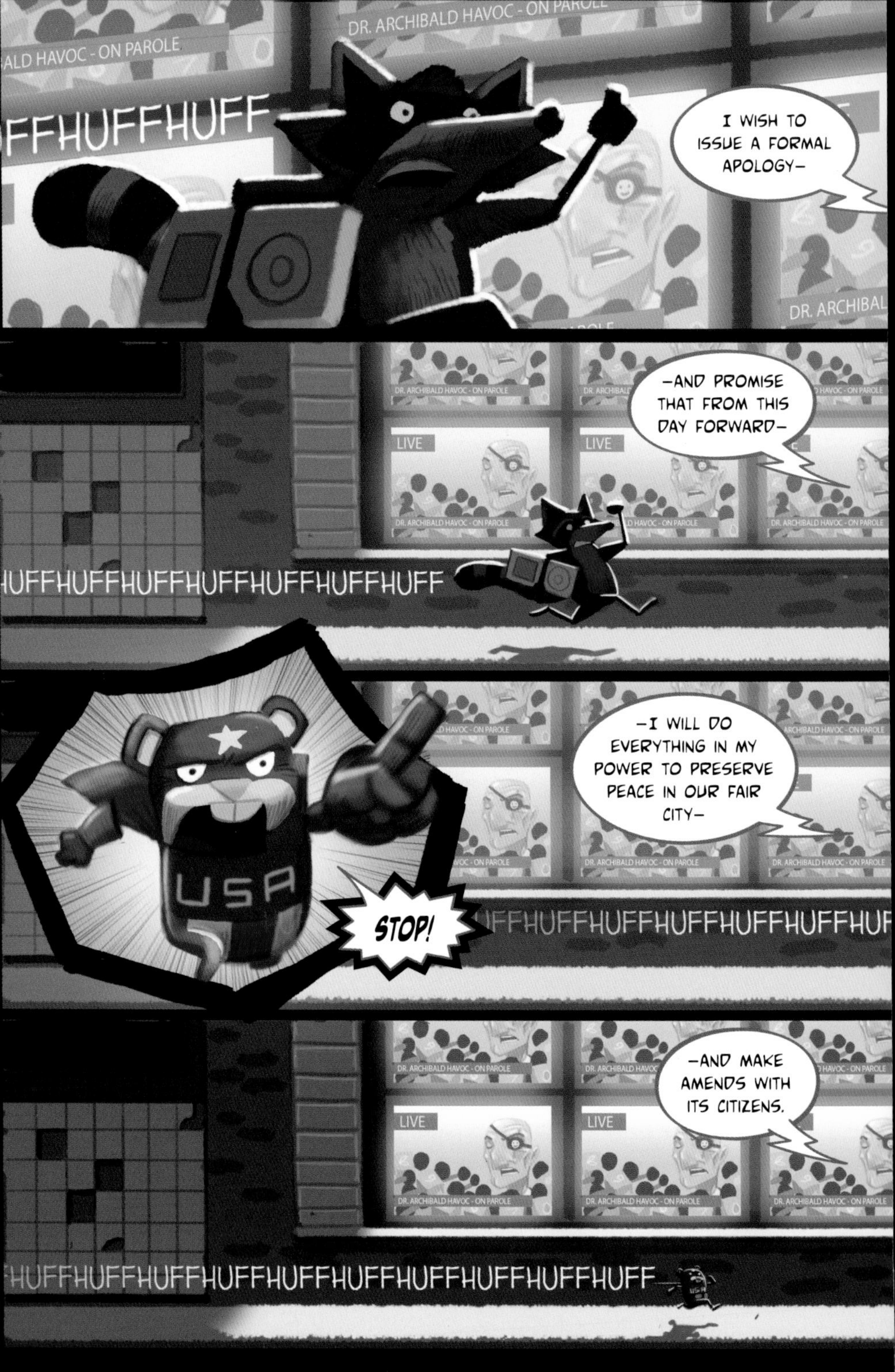
DR. ARCHIBALD HAVOC - ON PAROLE
FFHUFFHUFF
I WISH TO ISSUE A FORMAL APOLOGY—
—AND PROMISE THAT FROM THIS DAY FORWARD—
LIVE
HUFFHUFFHUFFHUFFHUFFHUFFHUFF
—I WILL DO EVERYTHING IN MY POWER TO PRESERVE PEACE IN OUR FAIR CITY—
USA
STOP!
FFHUFFHUFFHUFFHUFFHUFFHUF
—AND MAKE AMENDS WITH ITS CITIZENS.
HUFFHUFFHUFFHUFFHUFFHUFFHUFFHUFFHUFF

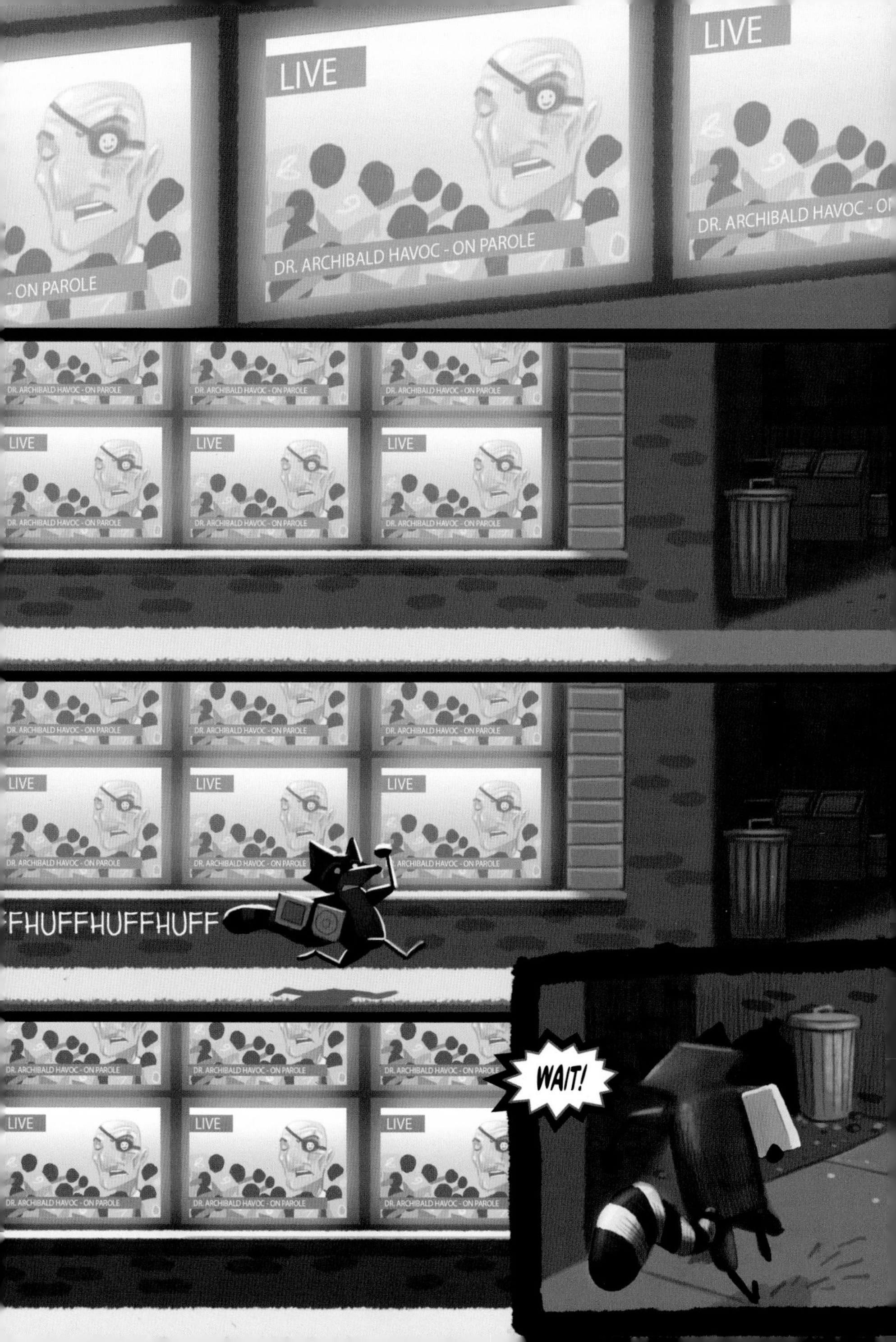
LIVE
DR. ARCHIBALD HAVOC - ON PAROLE
LIVE
DR. ARCHIBALD HAVOC - ON PAROLE
LIVE
DR. ARCHIBALD HAVOC - ON PAROLE
FHUFFHUFFHUFF
WAIT!

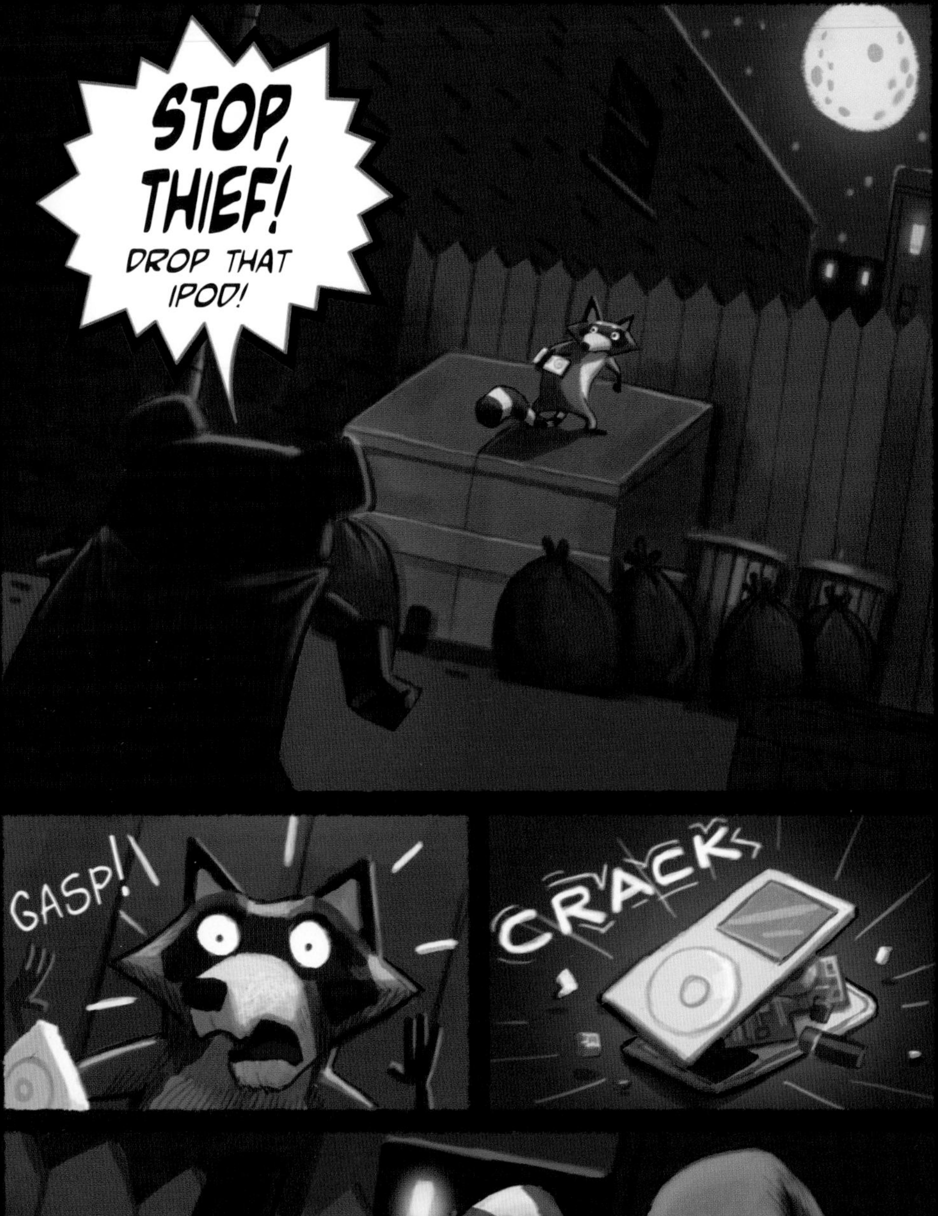
STOP, THIEF! DROP THAT IPOD!
GASP!
CRACK
WHOA, WAIT!
HEY, GET BACK HERE!
SCRAPE
SCRAPE
SCRAPE
SCRAPE
SCRAPE

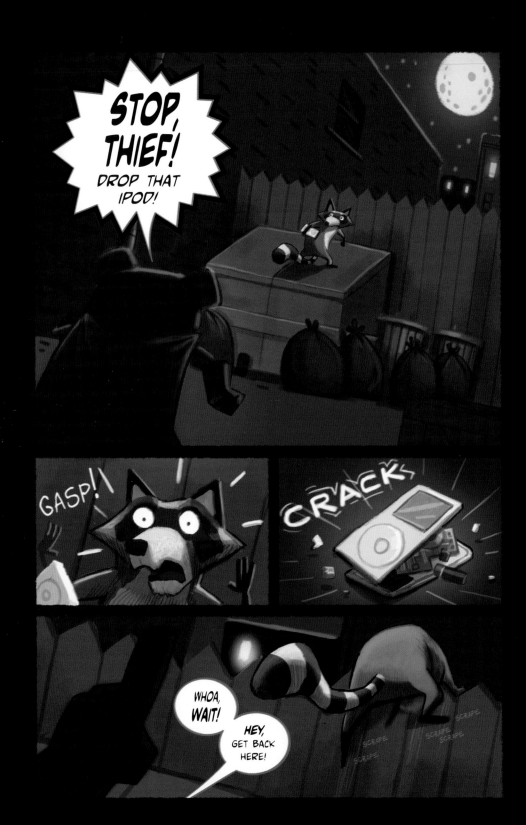

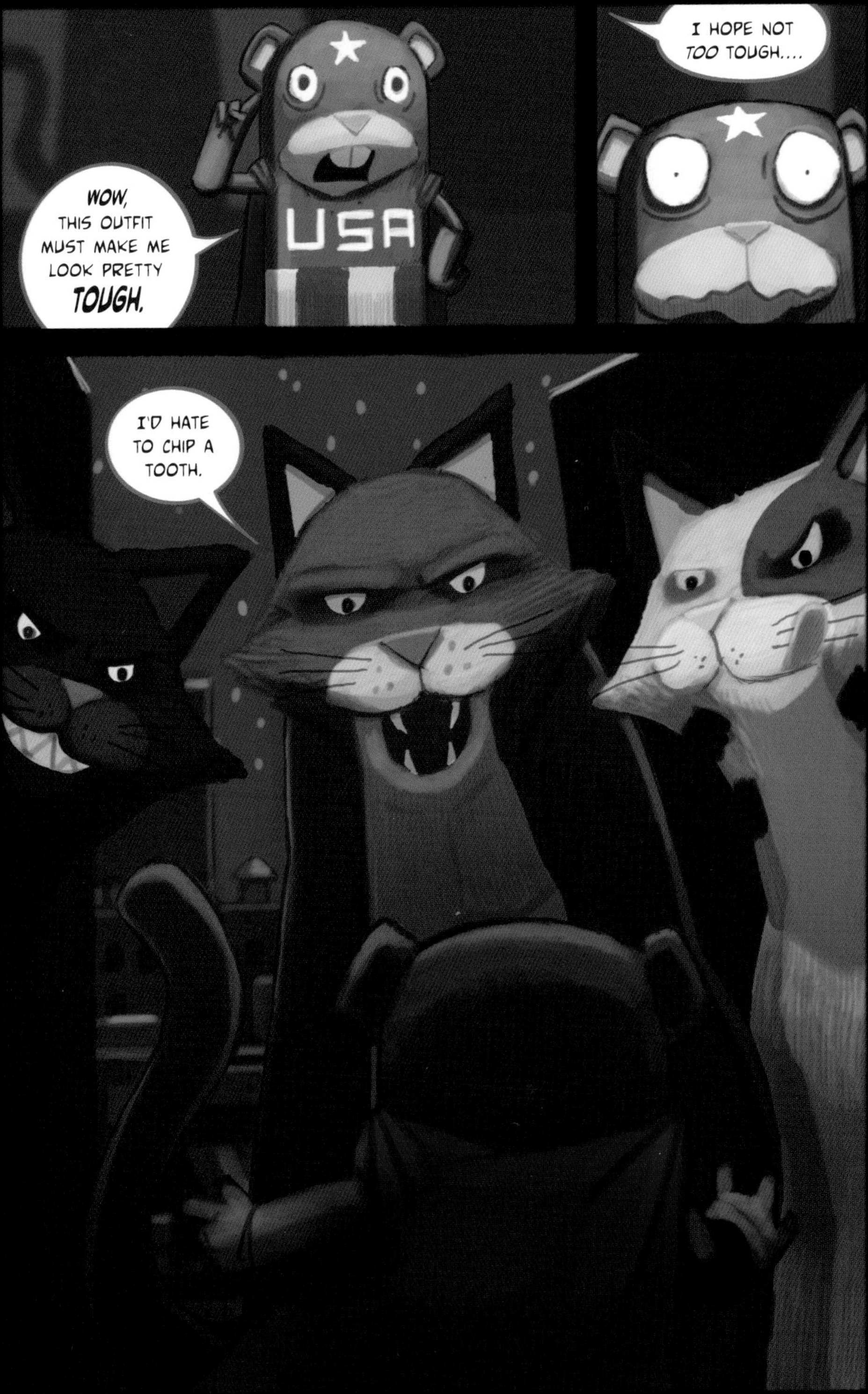
WOW, THIS OUTFIT MUST MAKE ME LOOK PRETTY TOUGH.
I HOPE NOT TOO TOUGH....
I'D HATE TO CHIP A TOOTH.

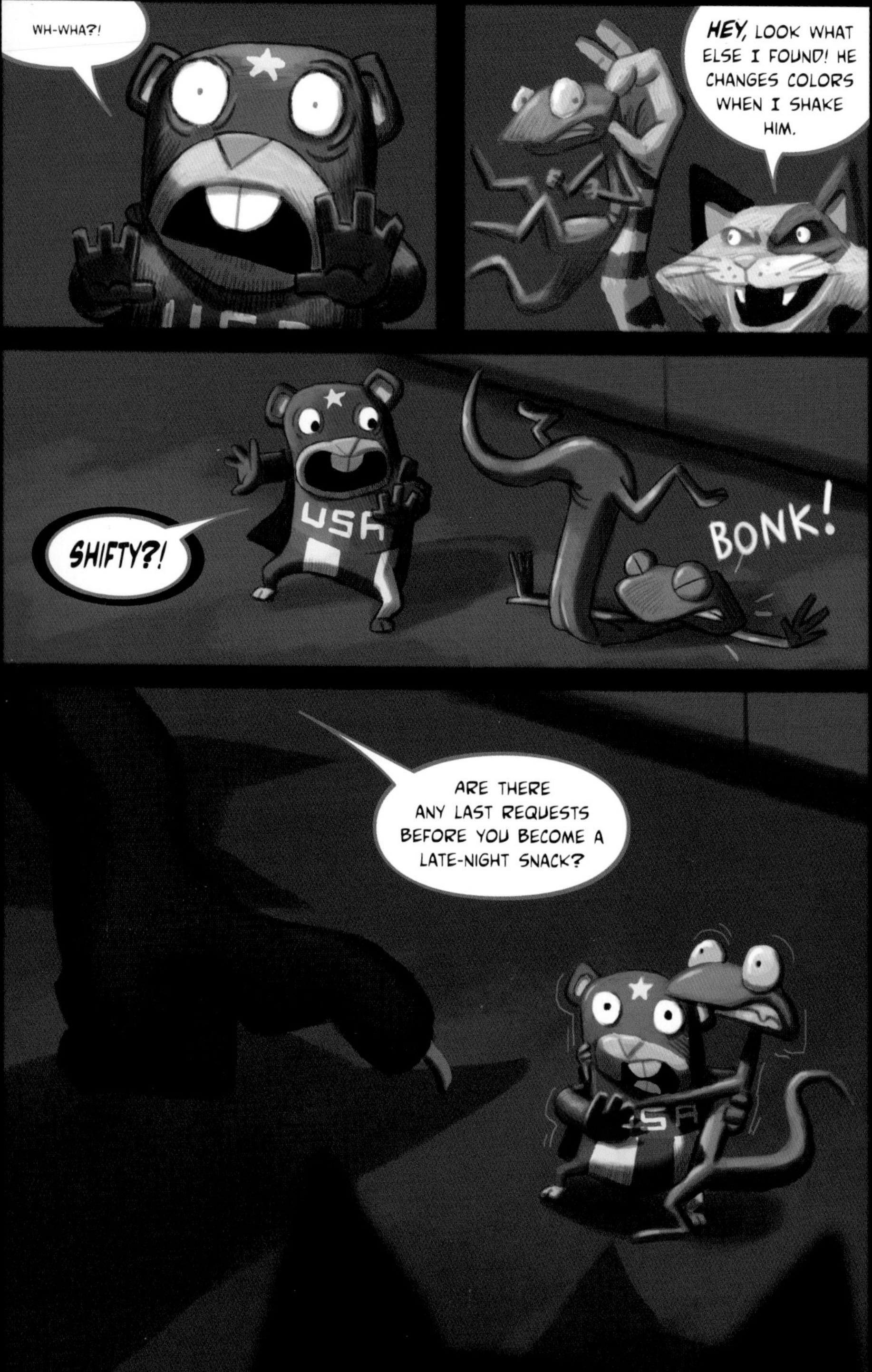
WH-WHA?!
HEY, LOOK WHAT ELSE I FOUND! HE CHANGES COLORS WHEN I SHAKE HIM.
SHIFTY?!
BONK!
USA
ARE THERE ANY LAST REQUESTS BEFORE YOU BECOME A LATE-NIGHT SNACK?

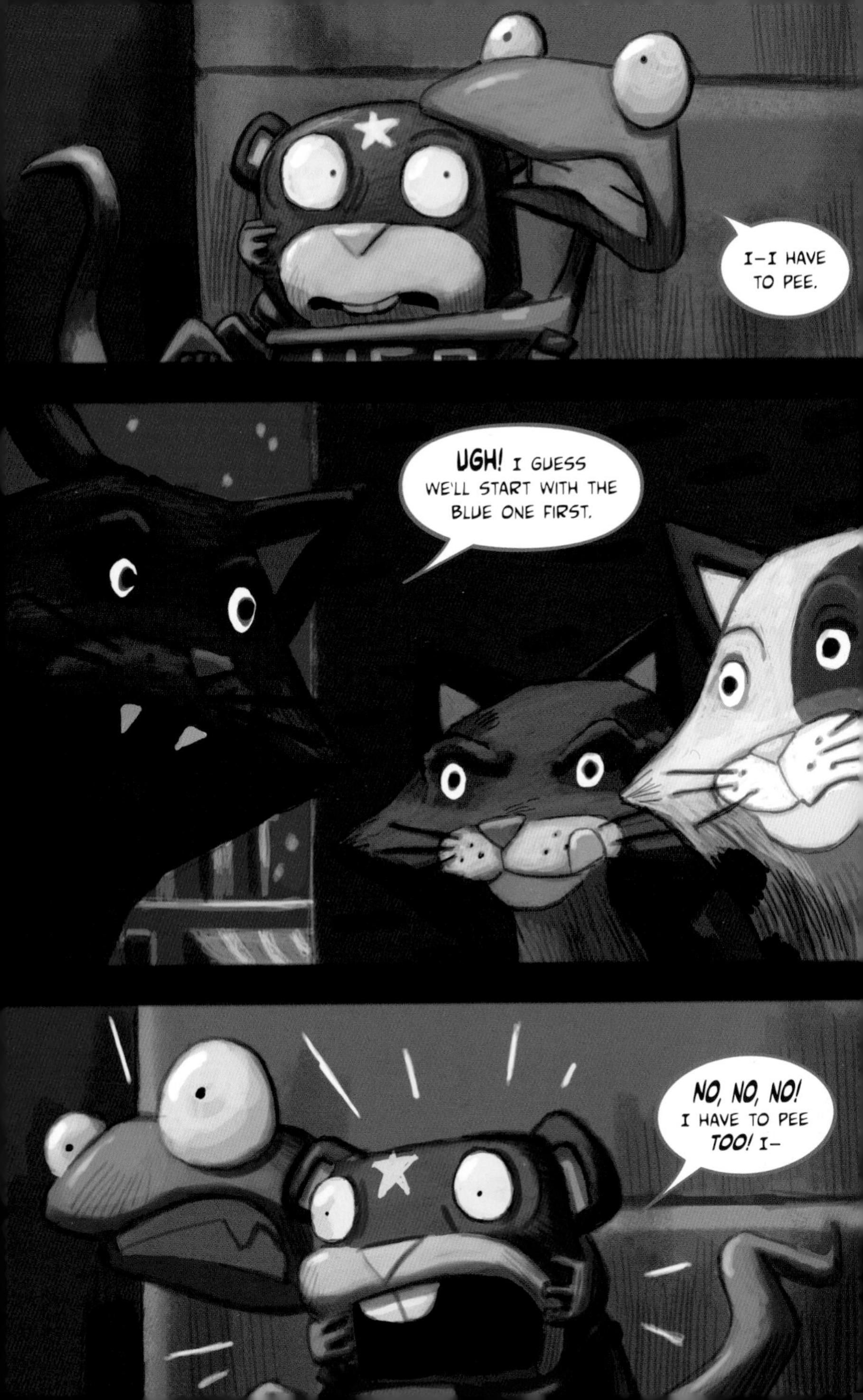
I–I HAVE TO PEE.
UGH! I GUESS WE'LL START WITH THE BLUE ONE FIRST.
NO, NO, NO! I HAVE TO PEE TOO! I–

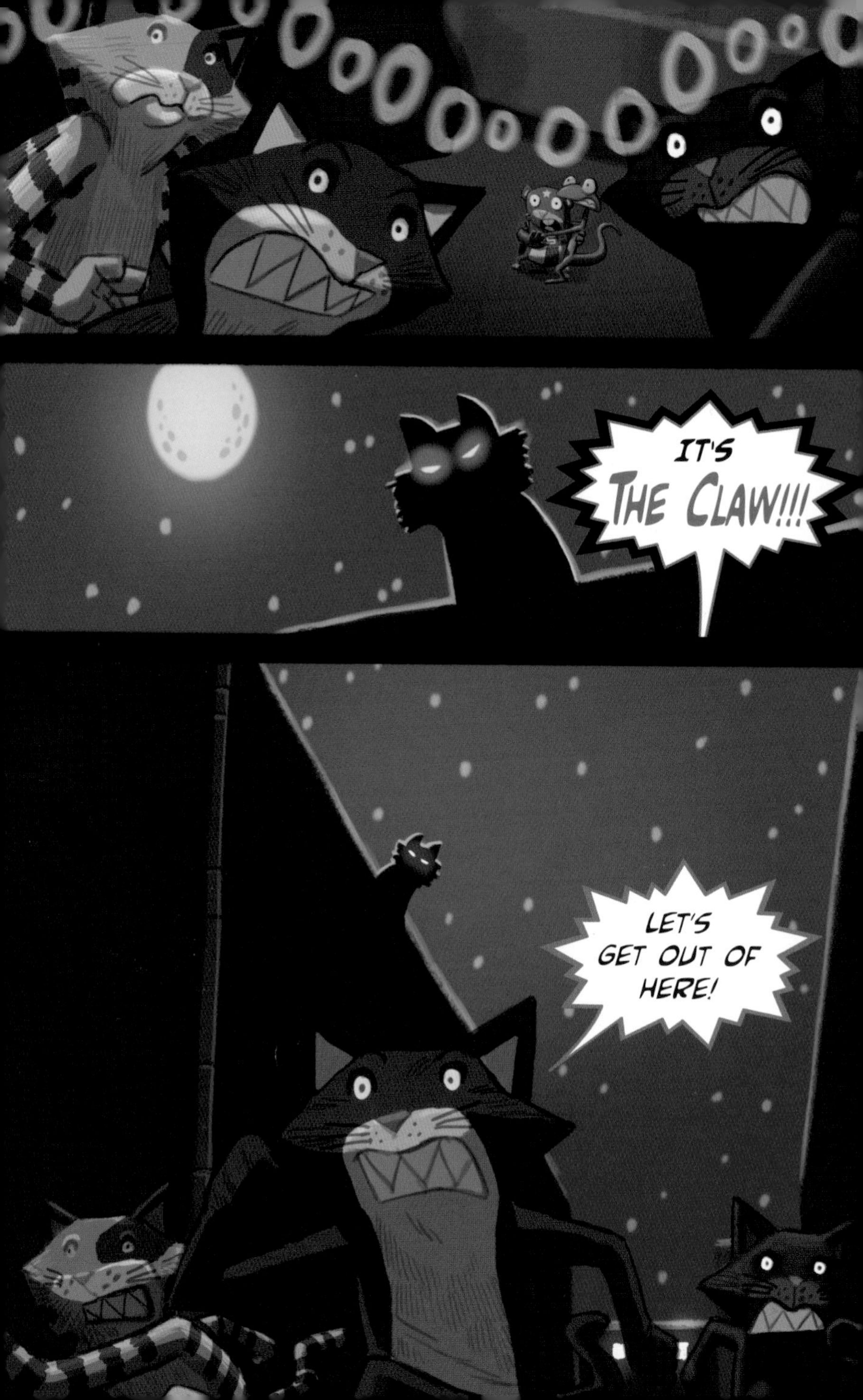
IT'S THE CLAW!!!
LET'S GET OUT OF HERE!

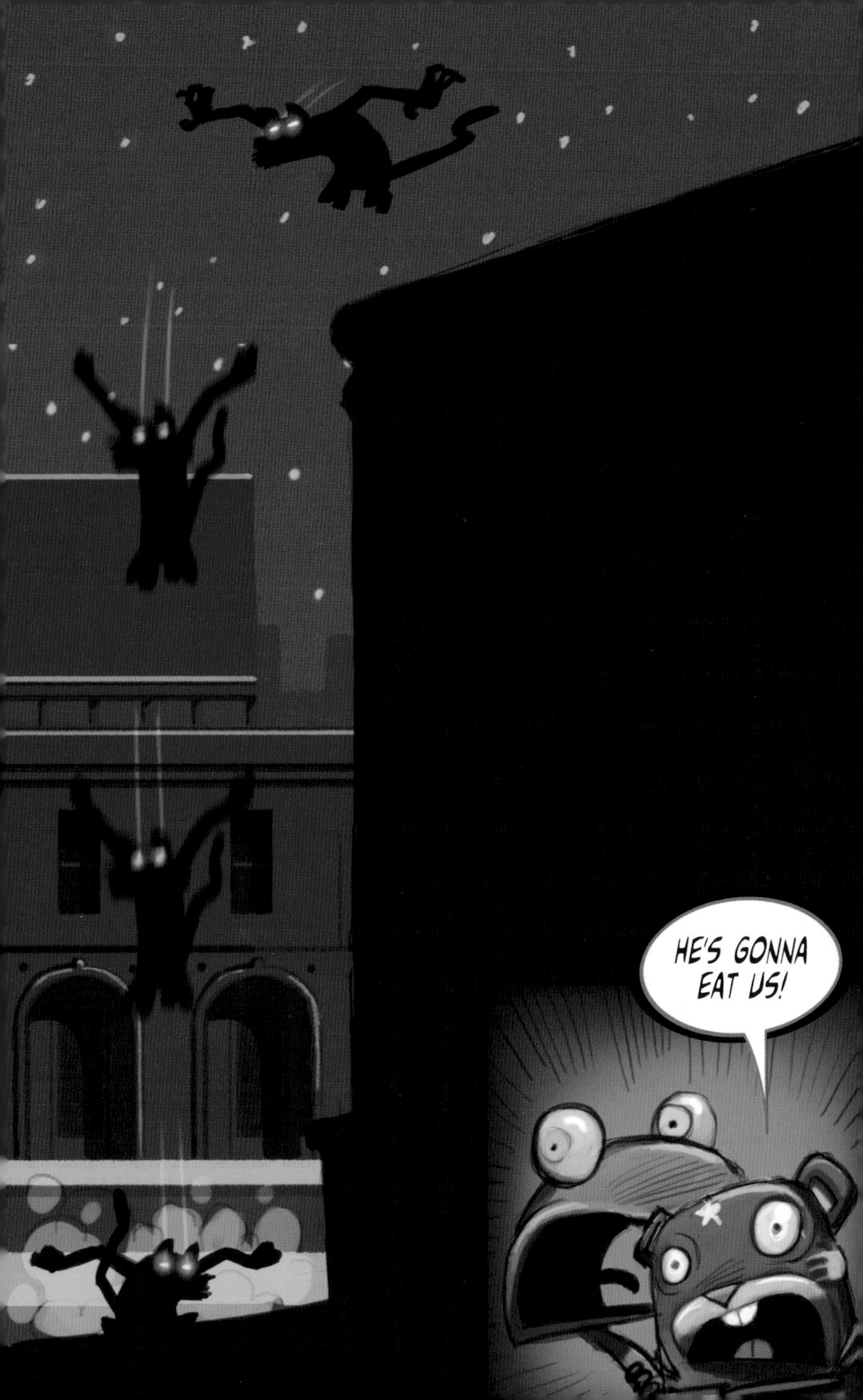
HE'S GONNA EAT US!

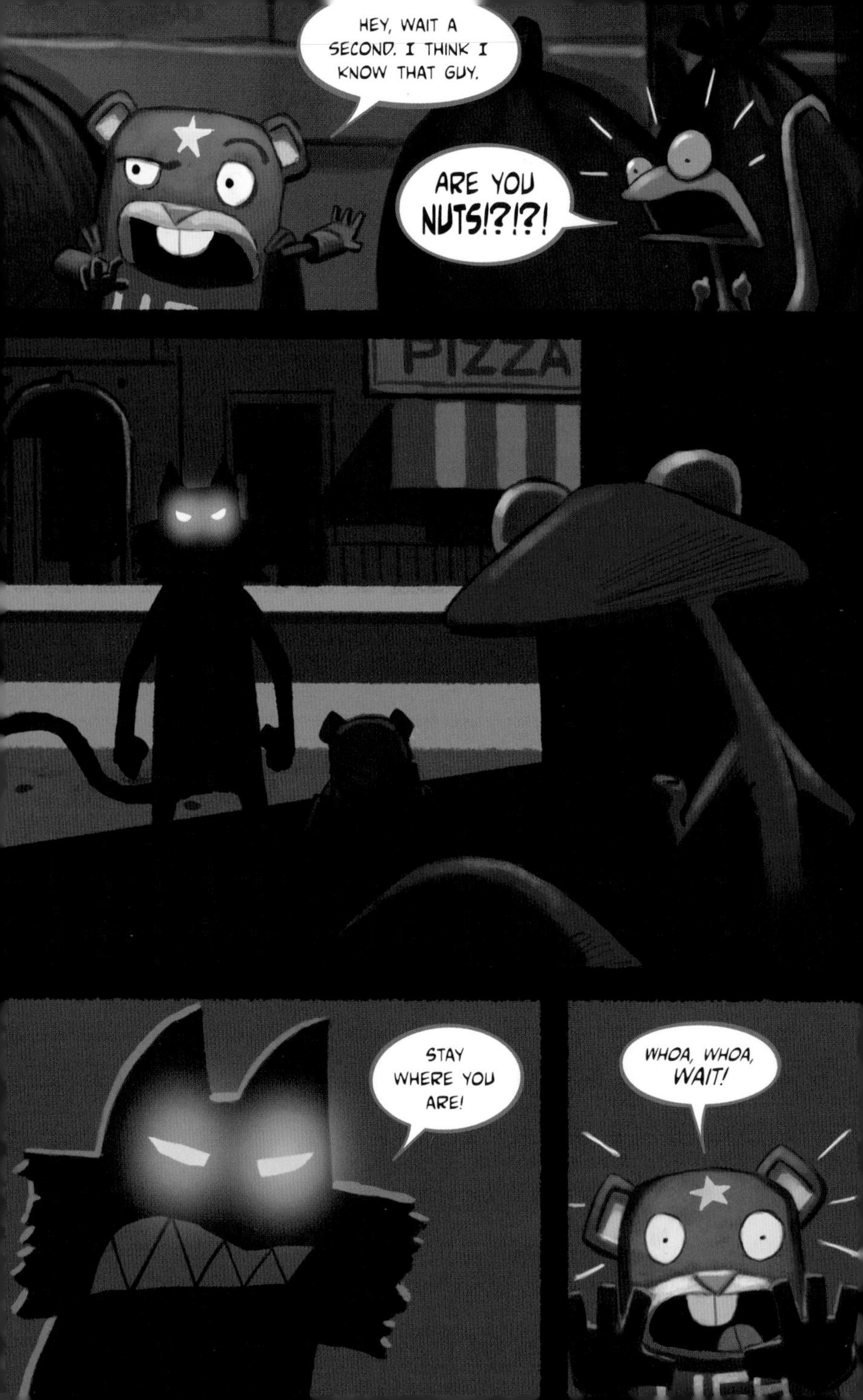
HEY, WAIT A SECOND. I THINK I KNOW THAT GUY.
ARE YOU NUTS!?!?!
PIZZA
STAY WHERE YOU ARE!
WHOA, WHOA, WAIT!

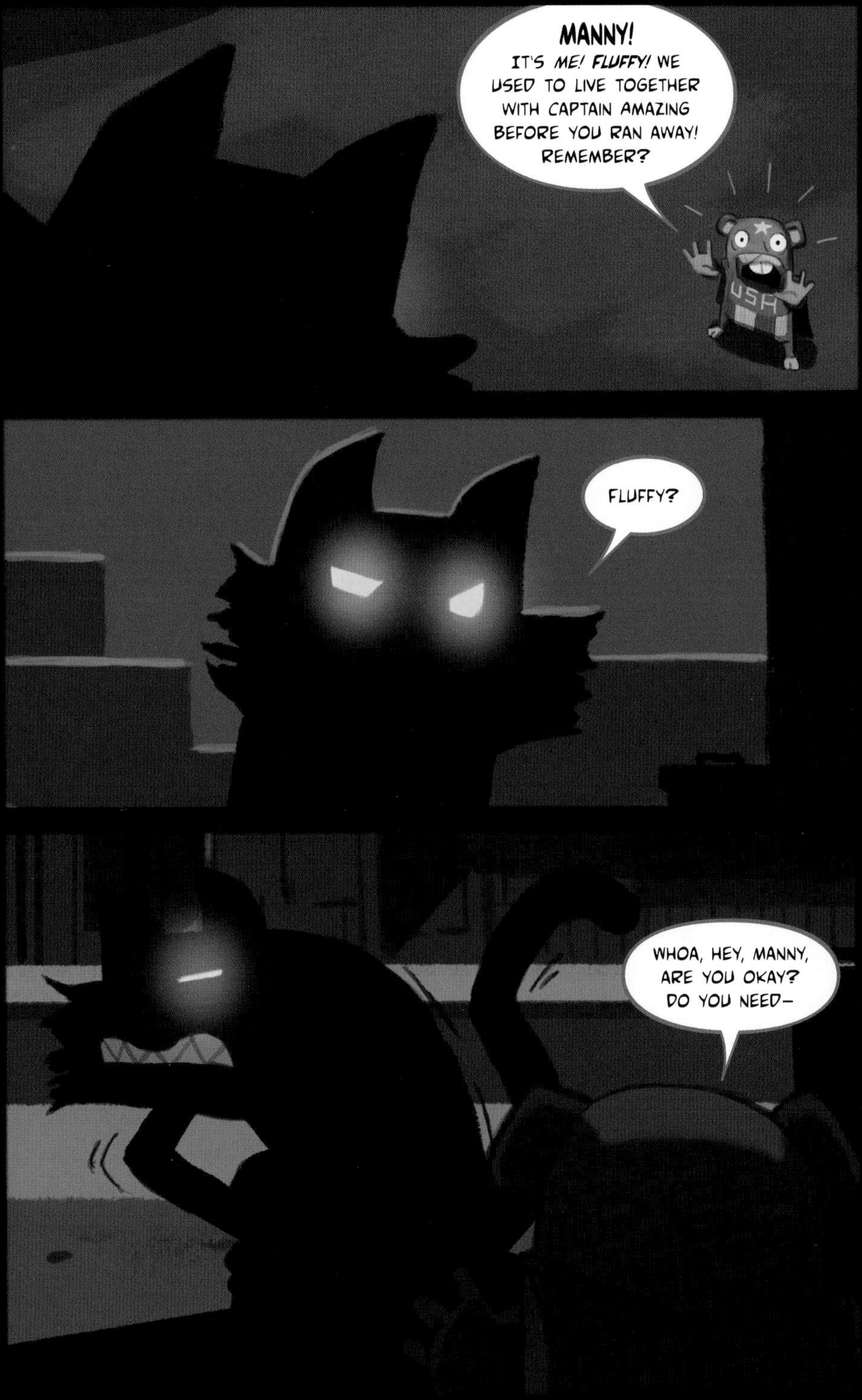
MANNY!
IT'S *ME!* ***FLUFFY!*** WE USED TO LIVE TOGETHER WITH CAPTAIN AMAZING BEFORE YOU RAN AWAY! REMEMBER?
USA
FLUFFY?
WHOA, HEY, MANNY, ARE YOU OKAY? DO YOU NEED—

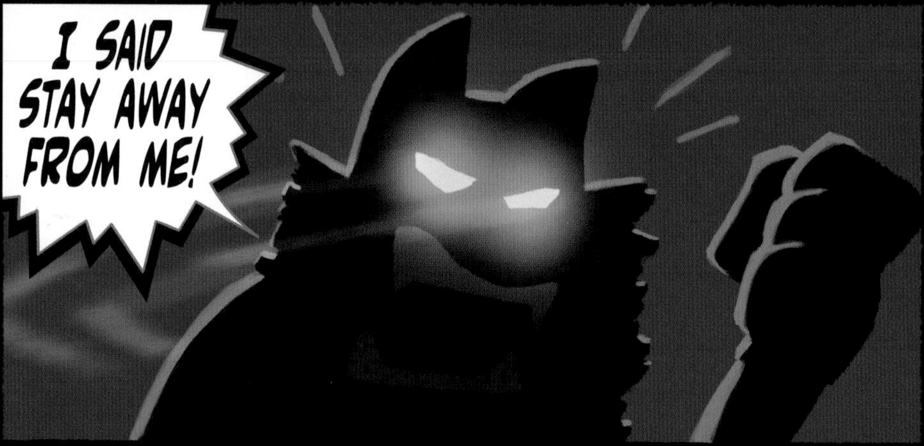
I SAID STAY AWAY FROM ME!

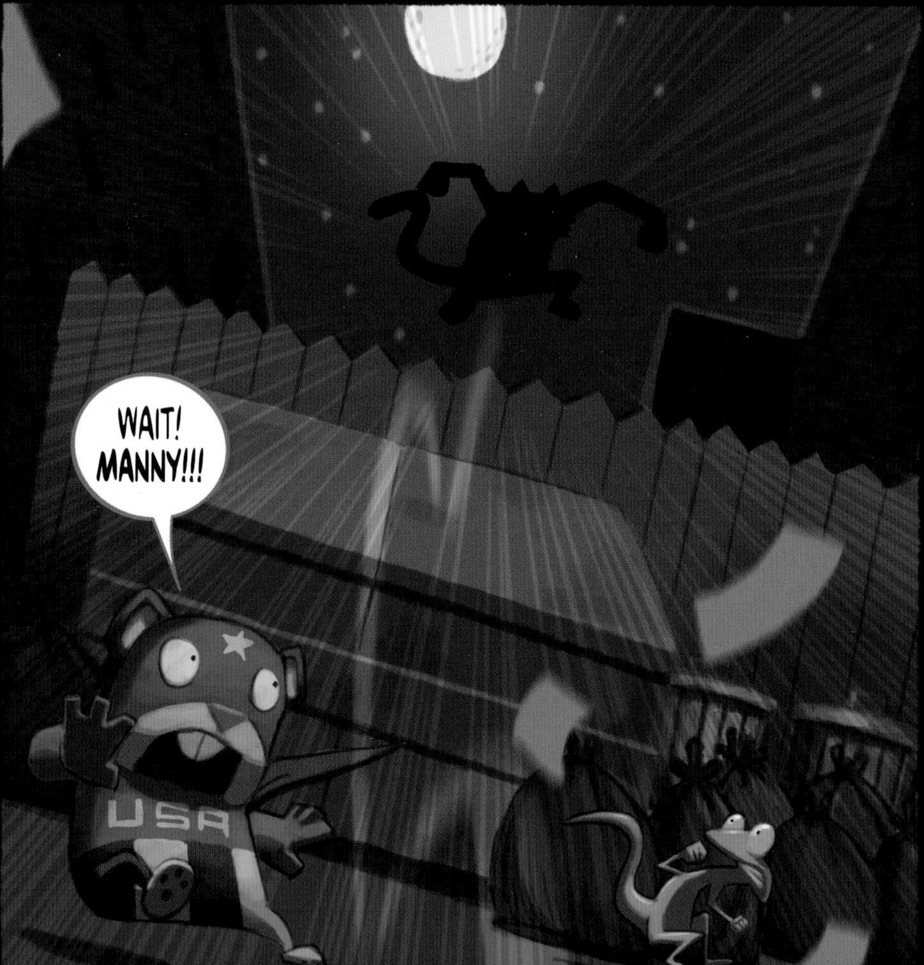
WAIT! MANNY!!!

THAT. WAS.

AWESOME!!

I DIDN'T KNOW YOU KNEW *THE CLAW!* I—

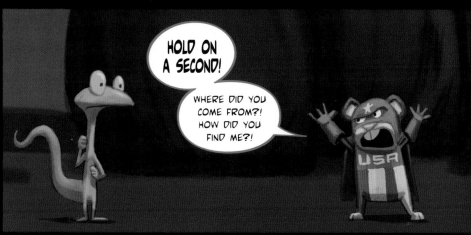

HOLD ON A SECOND!

WHERE DID YOU COME FROM?! HOW DID YOU FIND ME?!

I SAW YOU LEAVE. I THOUGHT MAYBE YOU COULD USE A SIDEKICK, YOU KNOW? SOMEONE TO HELP YOU OUT.

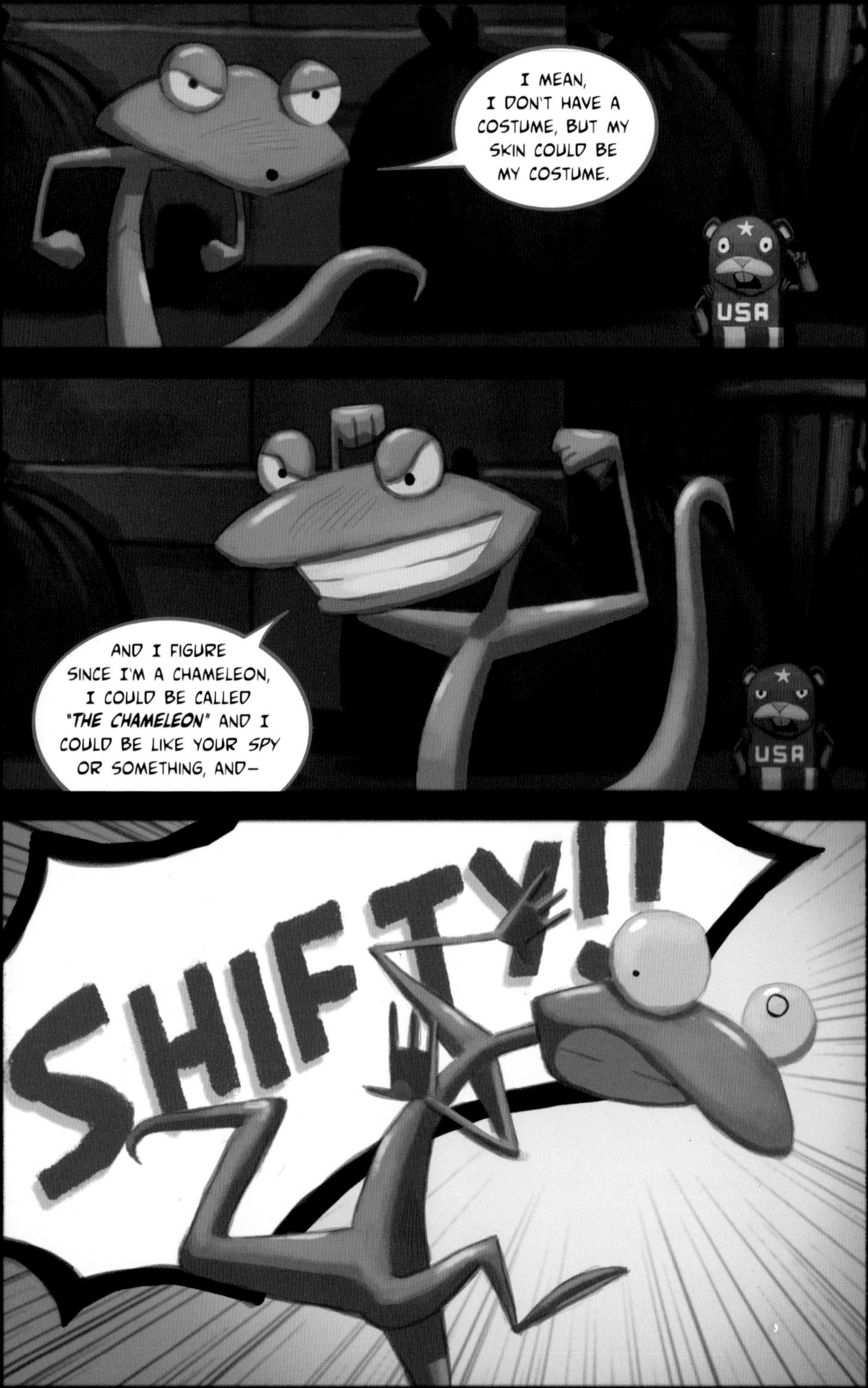
I MEAN, I DON'T HAVE A COSTUME, BUT MY SKIN COULD BE MY COSTUME.
USA
AND I FIGURE SINCE I'M A CHAMELEON, I COULD BE CALLED "*THE CHAMELEON*" AND I COULD BE LIKE YOUR *SPY* OR SOMETHING, AND—
USA
SHIFTY!!

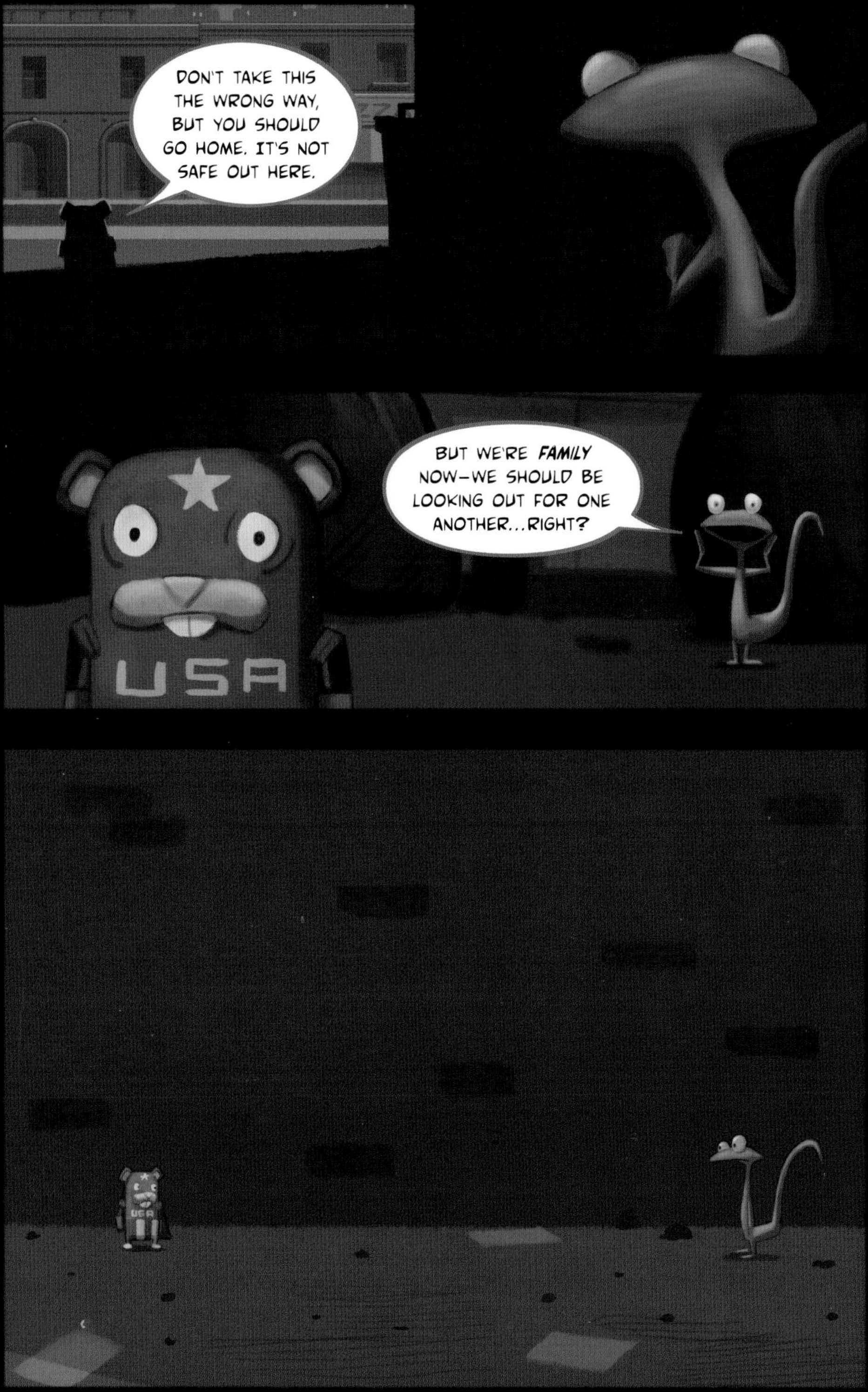
DON'T TAKE THIS THE WRONG WAY, BUT YOU SHOULD GO HOME. IT'S NOT SAFE OUT HERE.
BUT WE'RE *FAMILY* NOW—WE SHOULD BE LOOKING OUT FOR ONE ANOTHER...RIGHT?
USA

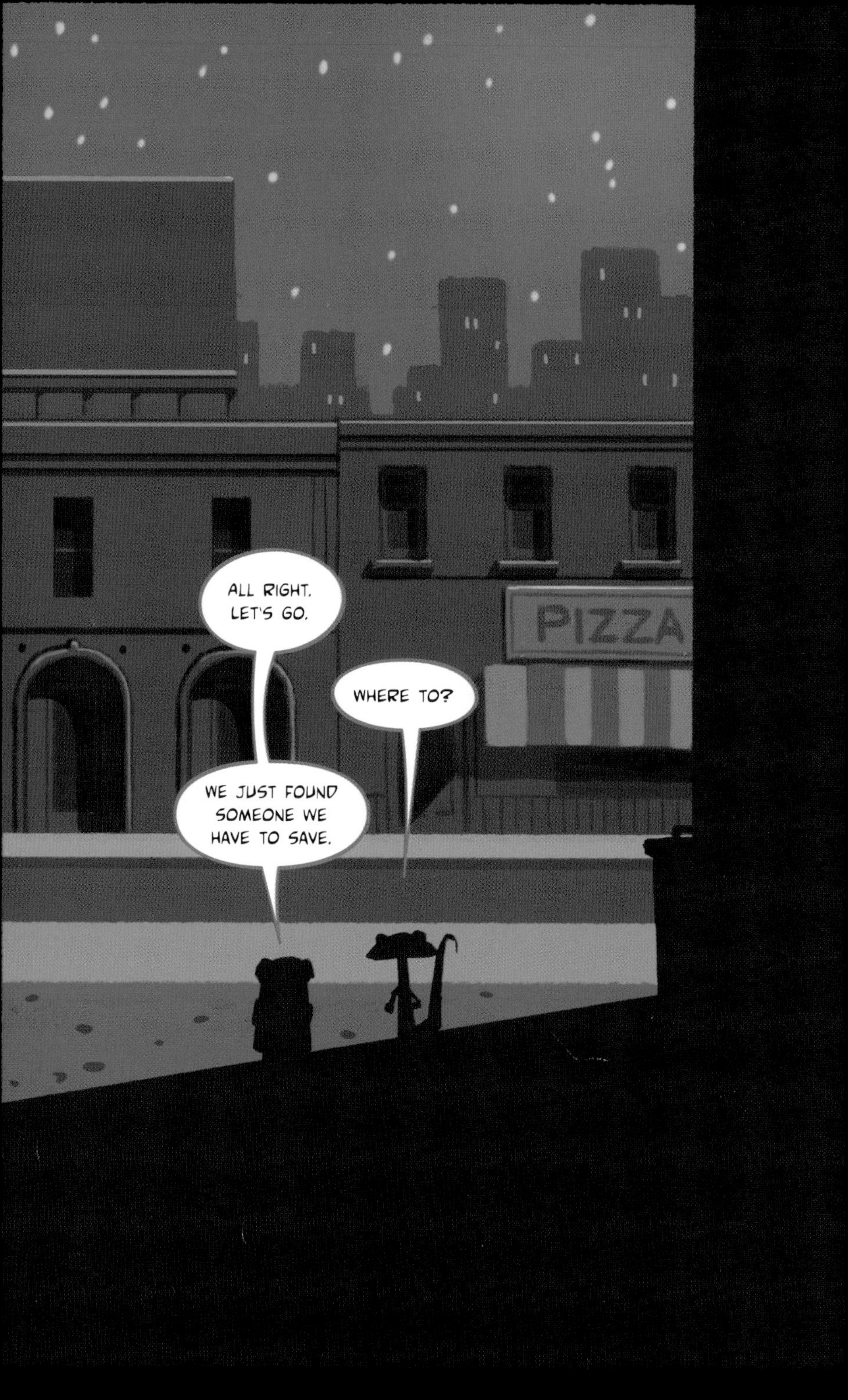
ALL RIGHT. LET'S GO.
WHERE TO?
WE JUST FOUND SOMEONE WE HAVE TO SAVE.
PIZZA

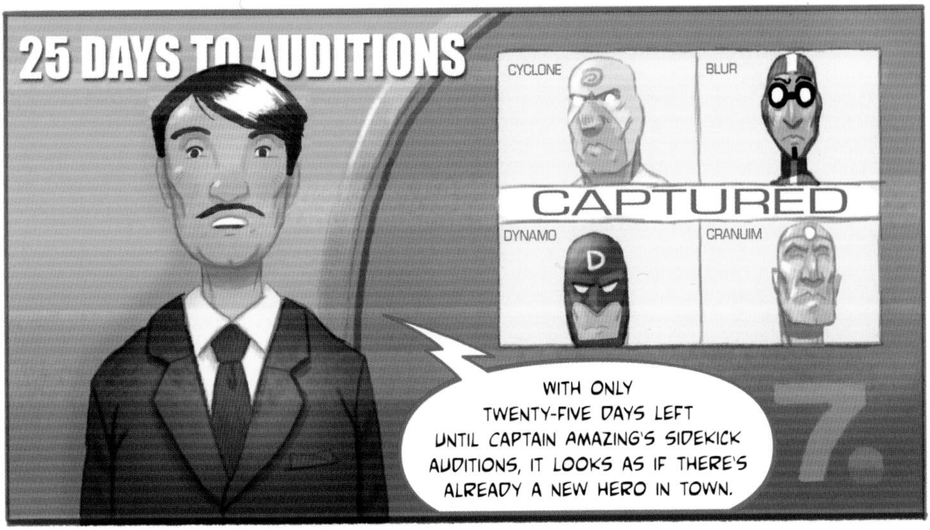
25 DAYS TO AUDITIONS
CYCLONE
BLUR
CAPTURED
DYNAMO
CRANUIM
WITH ONLY TWENTY-FIVE DAYS LEFT UNTIL CAPTAIN AMAZING'S SIDEKICK AUDITIONS, IT LOOKS AS IF THERE'S ALREADY A NEW HERO IN TOWN.
7.

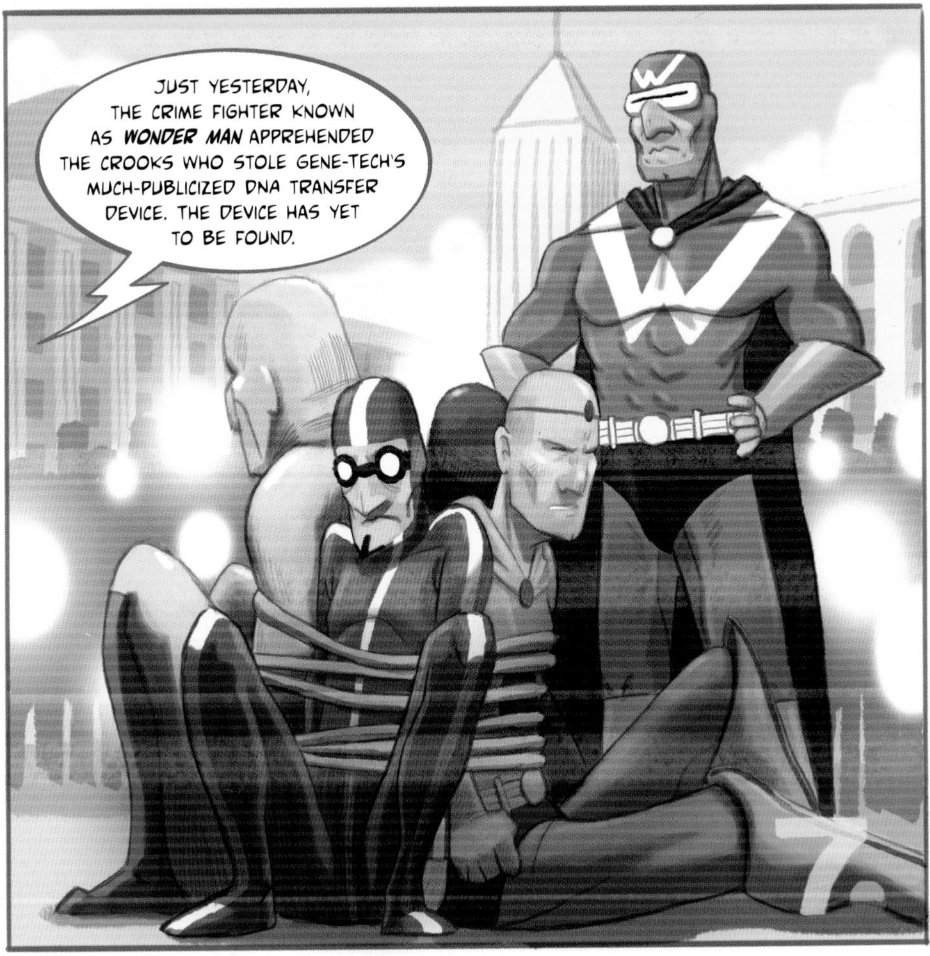
JUST YESTERDAY, THE CRIME FIGHTER KNOWN AS **WONDER MAN** APPREHENDED THE CROOKS WHO STOLE GENE-TECH'S MUCH-PUBLICIZED DNA TRANSFER DEVICE. THE DEVICE HAS YET TO BE FOUND.
7.

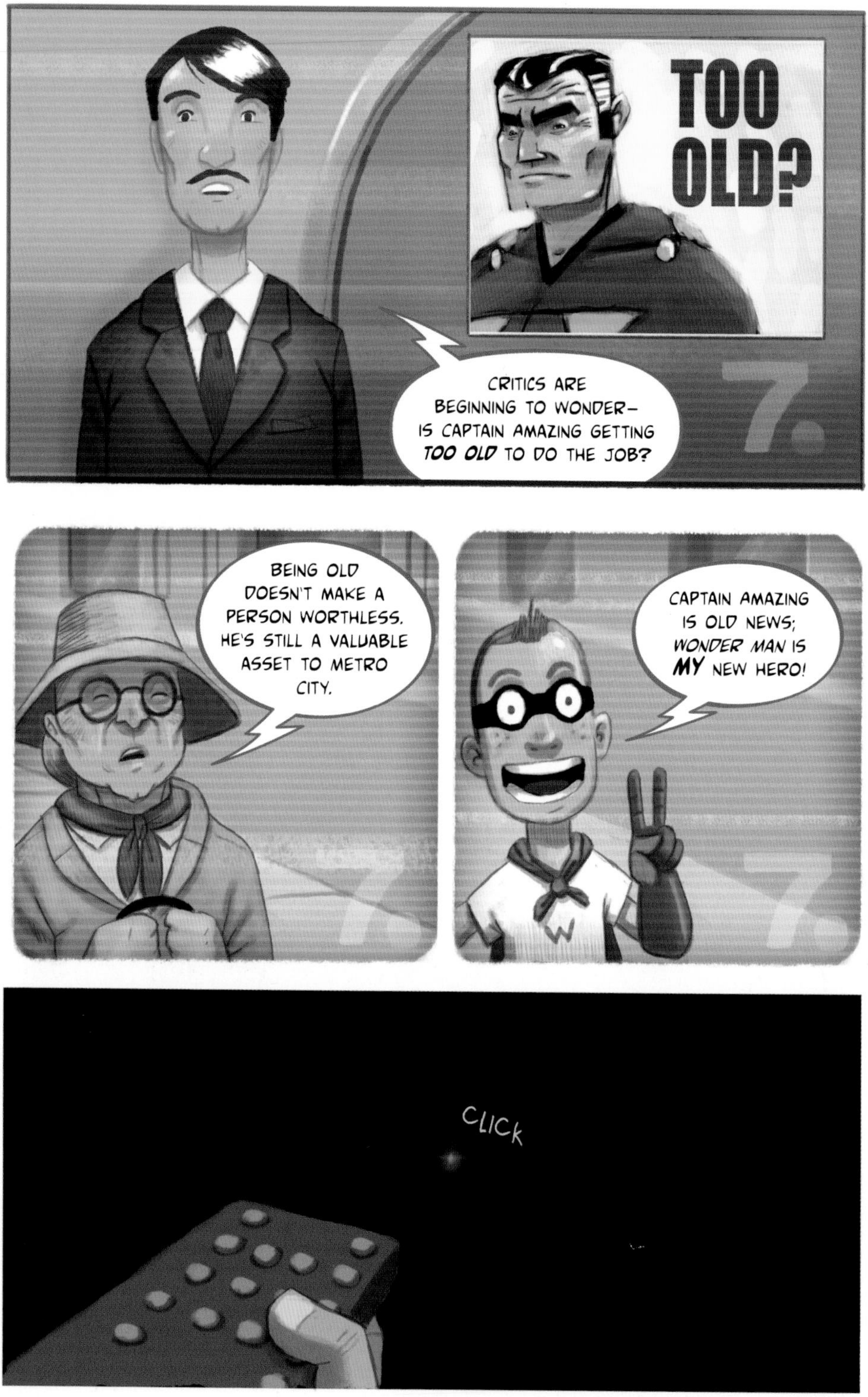
TOO OLD?
CRITICS ARE BEGINNING TO WONDER– IS CAPTAIN AMAZING GETTING TOO OLD TO DO THE JOB?
BEING OLD DOESN'T MAKE A PERSON WORTHLESS. HE'S STILL A VALUABLE ASSET TO METRO CITY.
CAPTAIN AMAZING IS OLD NEWS; WONDER MAN IS MY NEW HERO!
CLICK

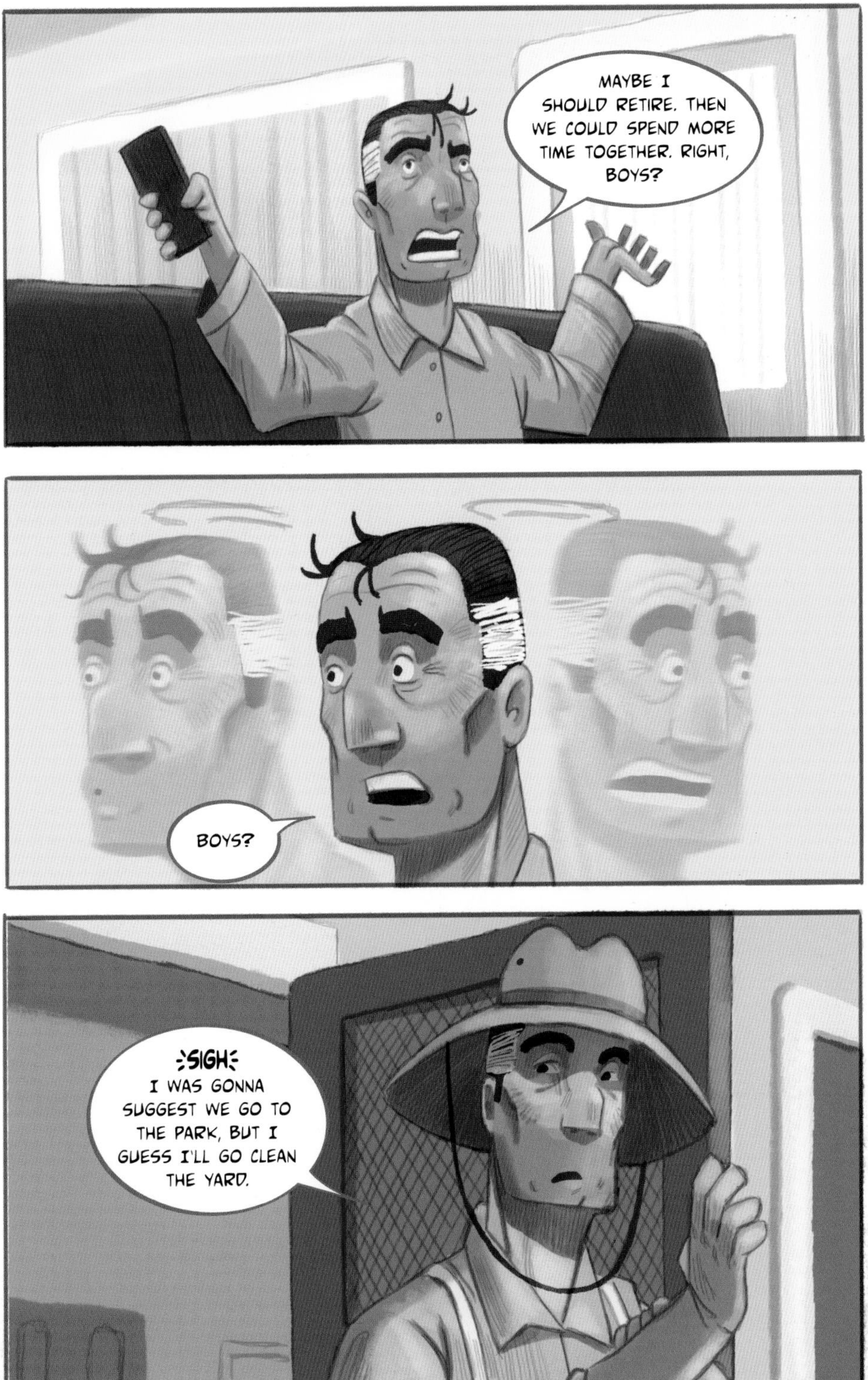
MAYBE I SHOULD RETIRE. THEN WE COULD SPEND MORE TIME TOGETHER. RIGHT, BOYS?
BOYS?
SIGH
I WAS GONNA SUGGEST WE GO TO THE PARK, BUT I GUESS I'LL GO CLEAN THE YARD.

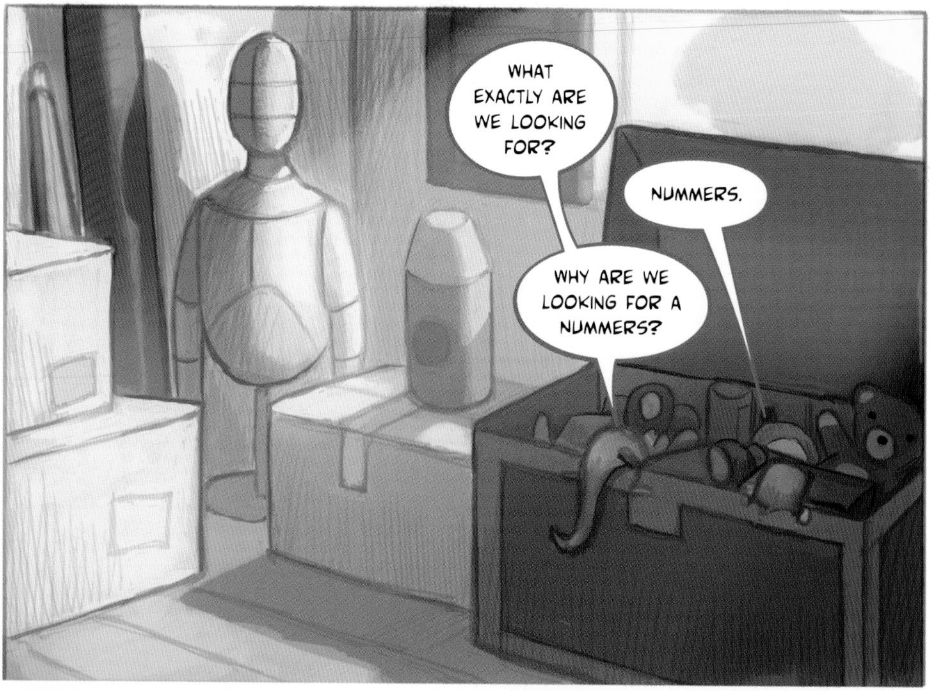
WHAT EXACTLY ARE WE LOOKING FOR?
NUMMERS.
WHY ARE WE LOOKING FOR A NUMMERS?

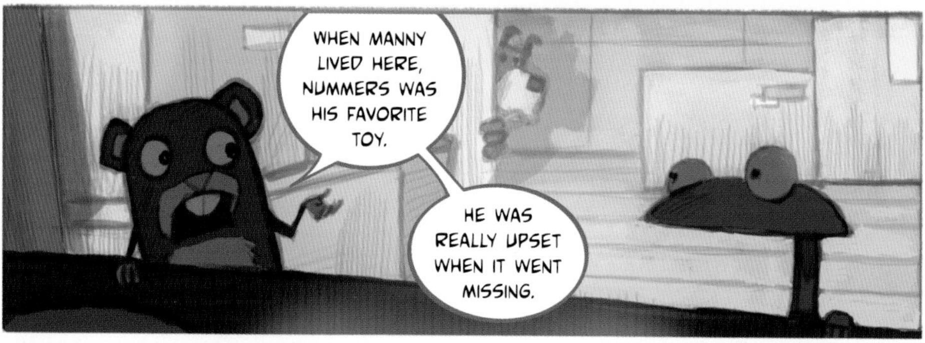
WHEN MANNY LIVED HERE, NUMMERS WAS HIS FAVORITE TOY.
HE WAS REALLY UPSET WHEN IT WENT MISSING.

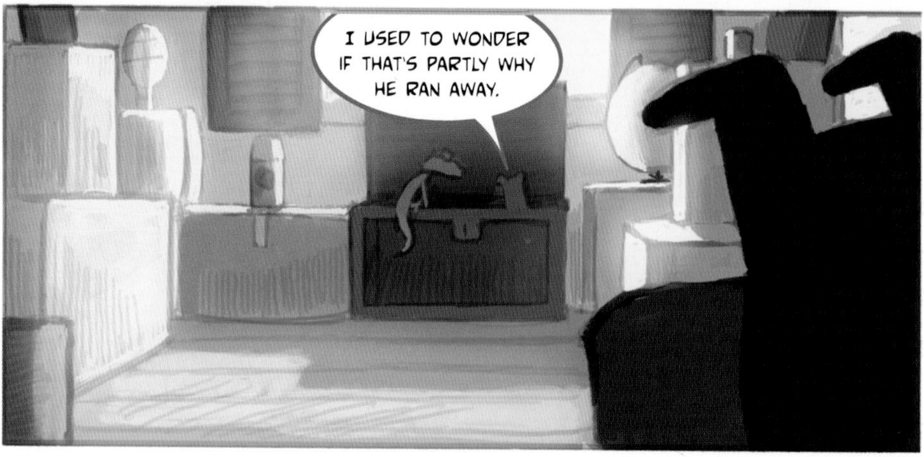
I USED TO WONDER IF THAT'S PARTLY WHY HE RAN AWAY.

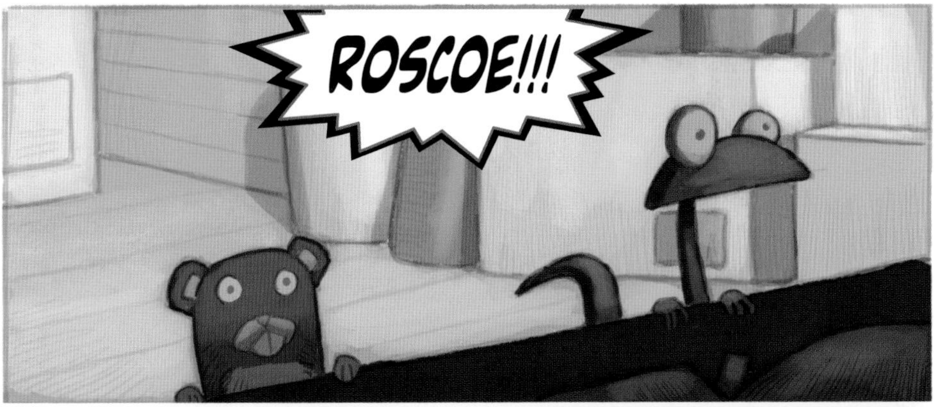
ROSCOE!!!

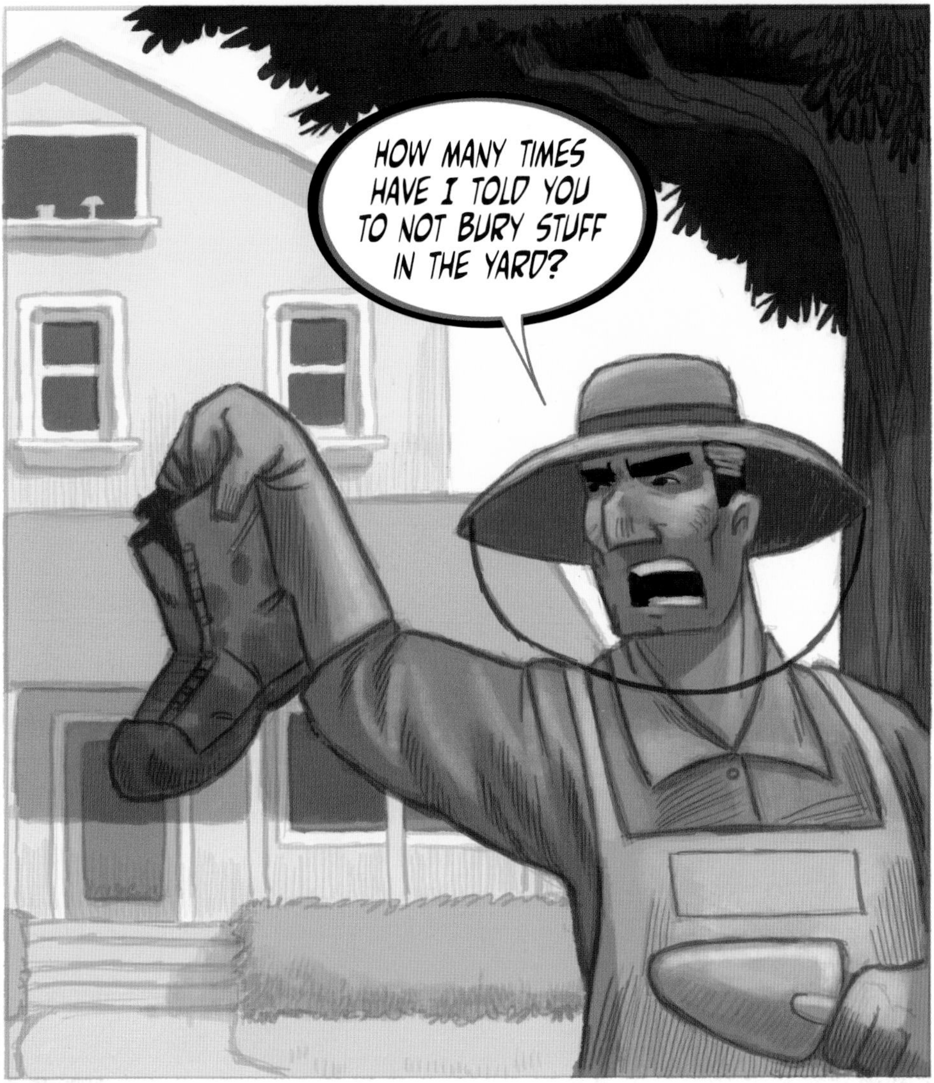
HOW MANY TIMES HAVE I TOLD YOU TO NOT BURY STUFF IN THE YARD?

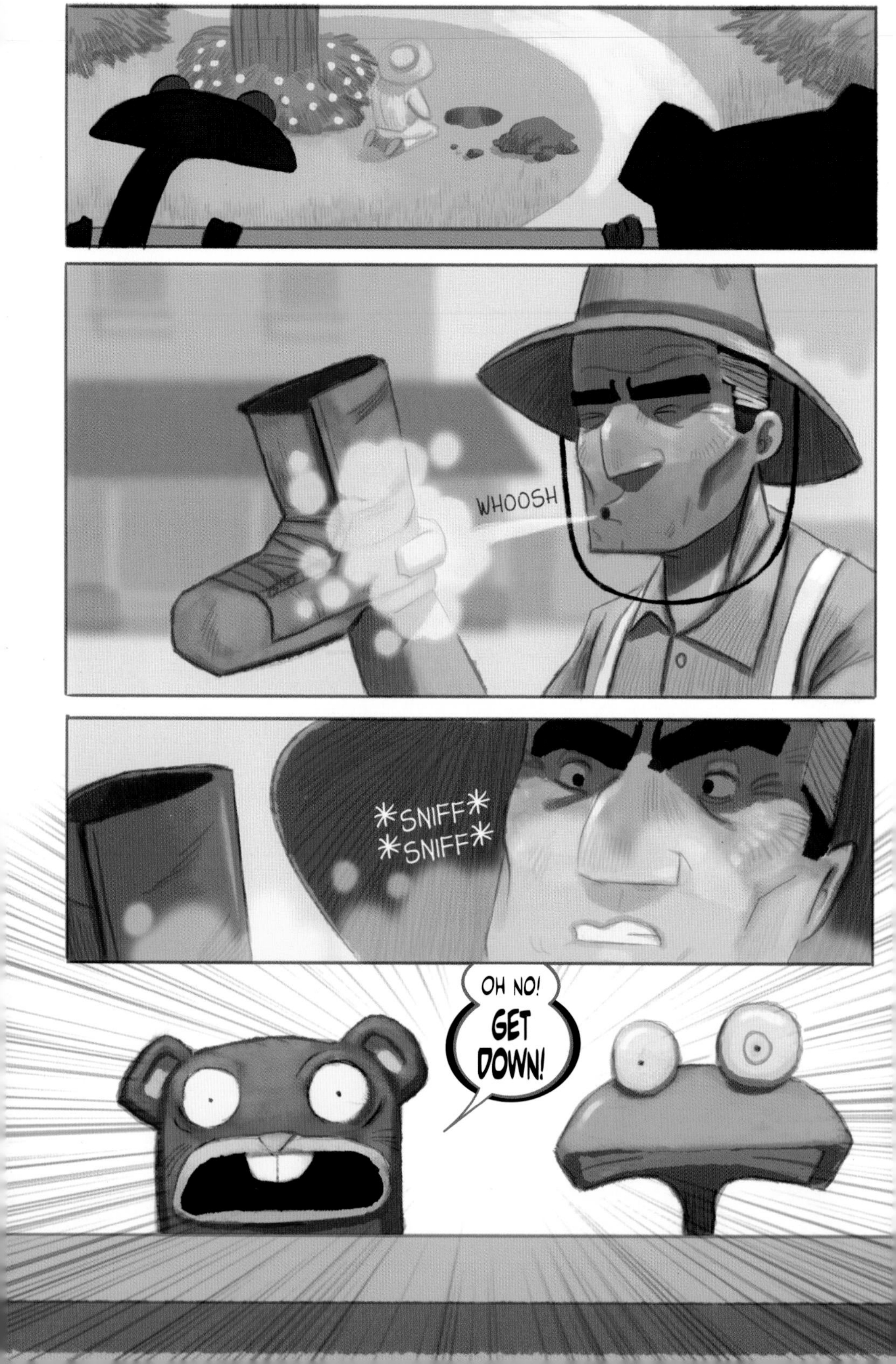
WHOOSH
SNIFF
SNIFF
OH NO! GET DOWN!

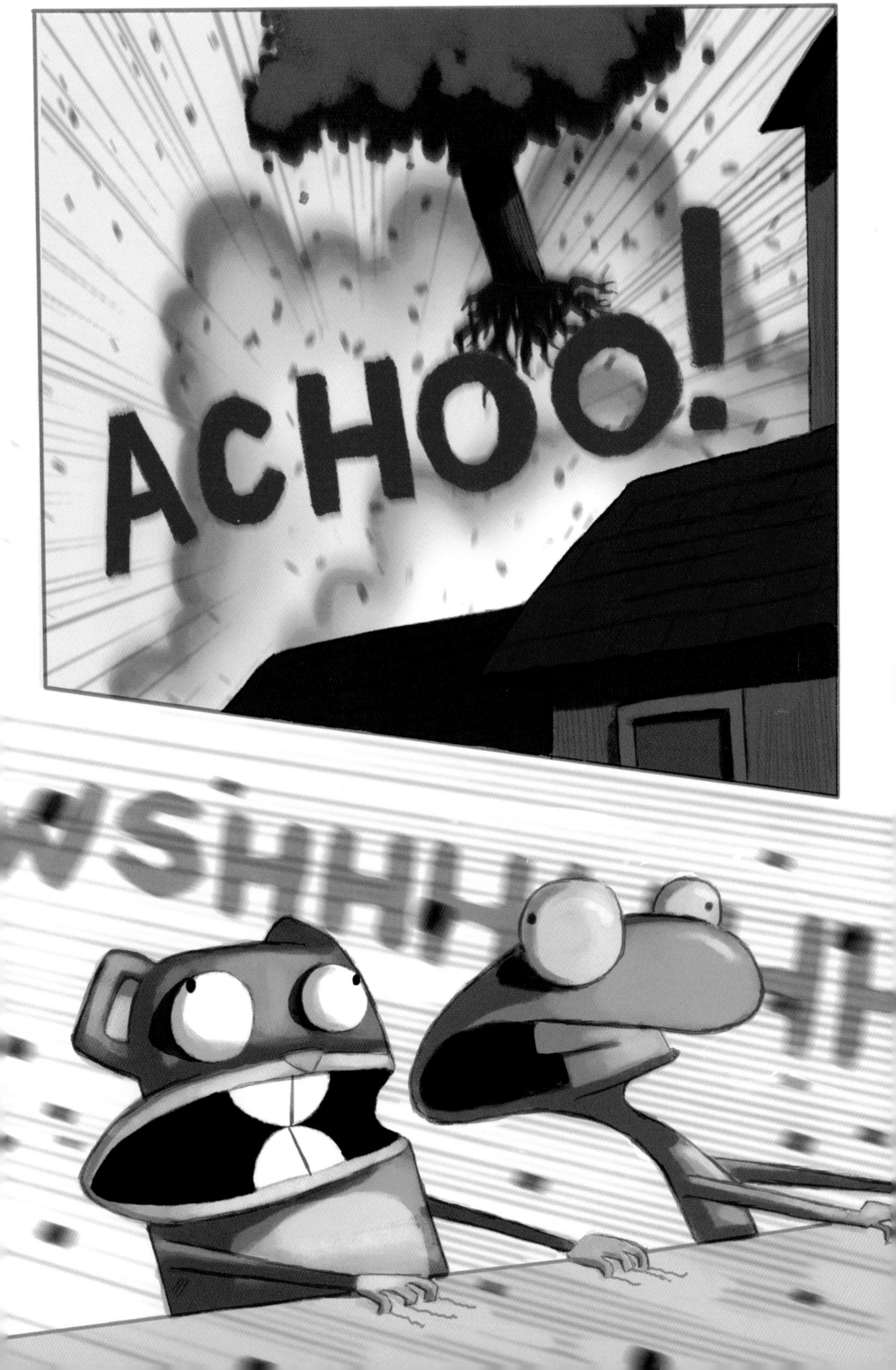
ACHOO!

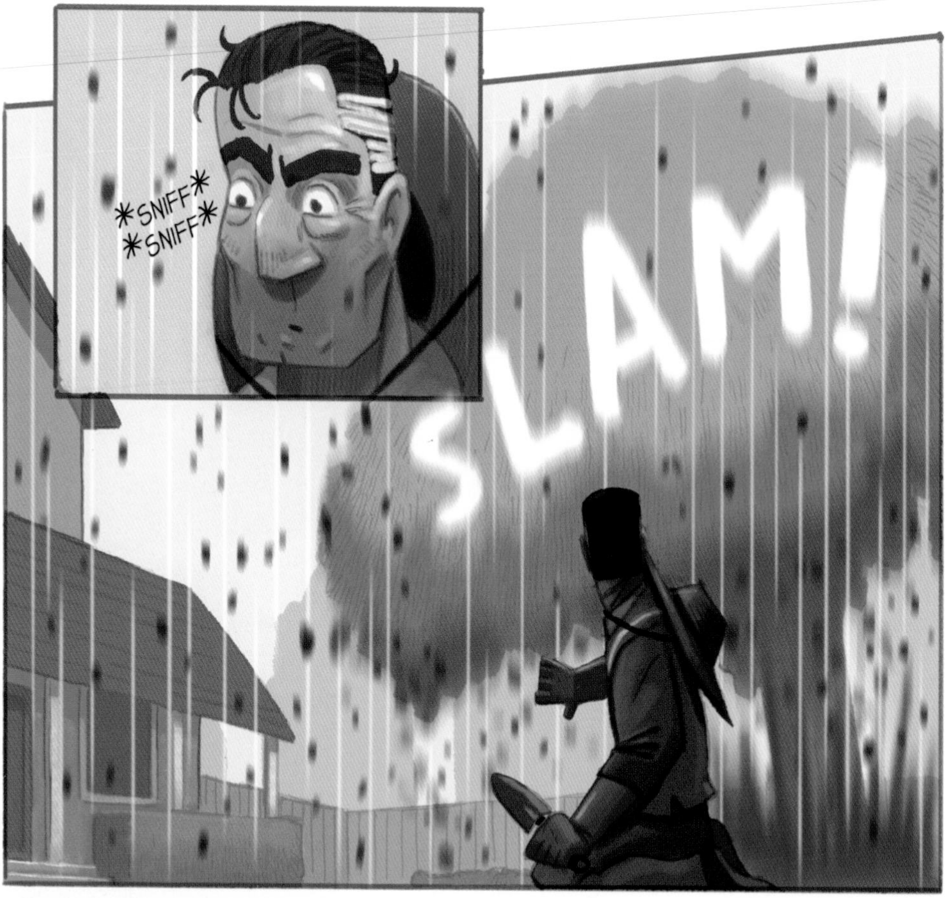
SNIFF
SNIFF
SLAM!

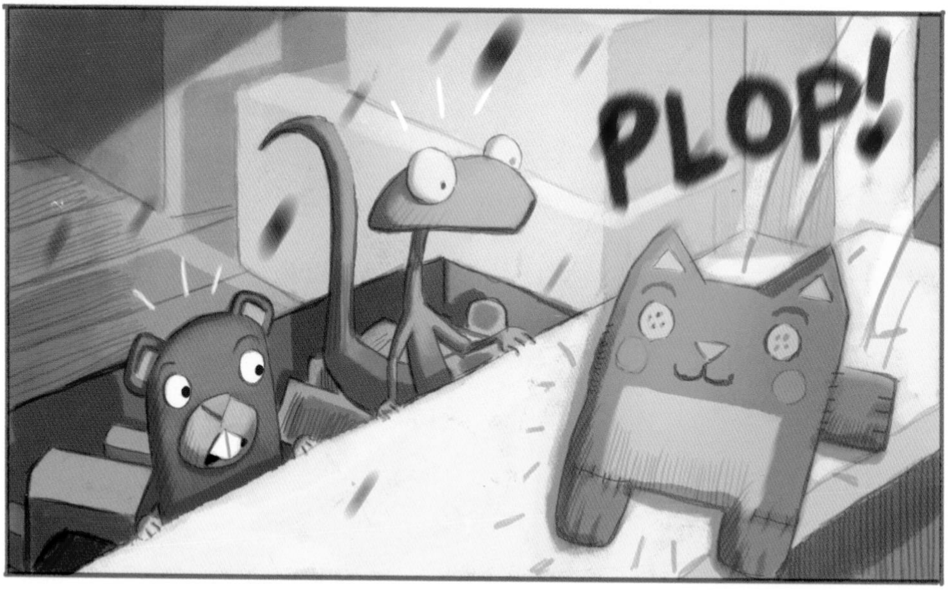
PLOP!

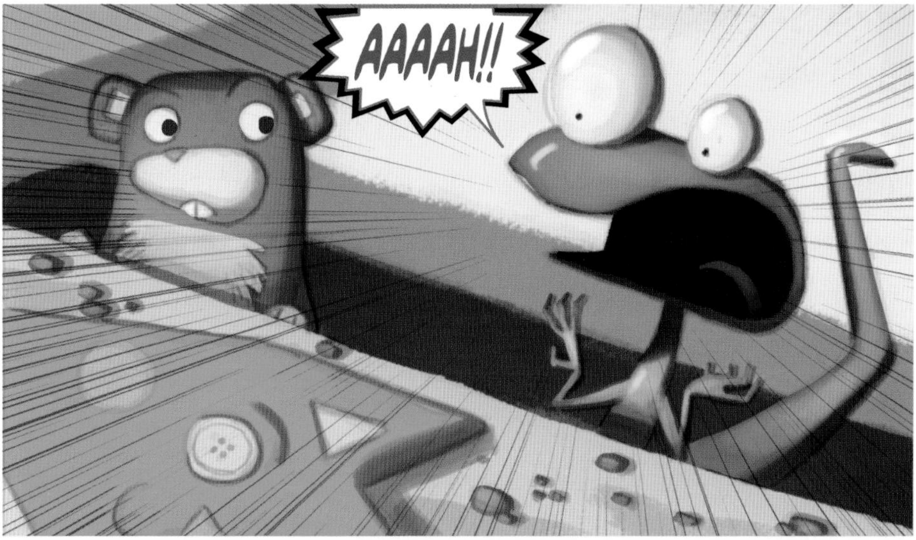
AAAAH!!

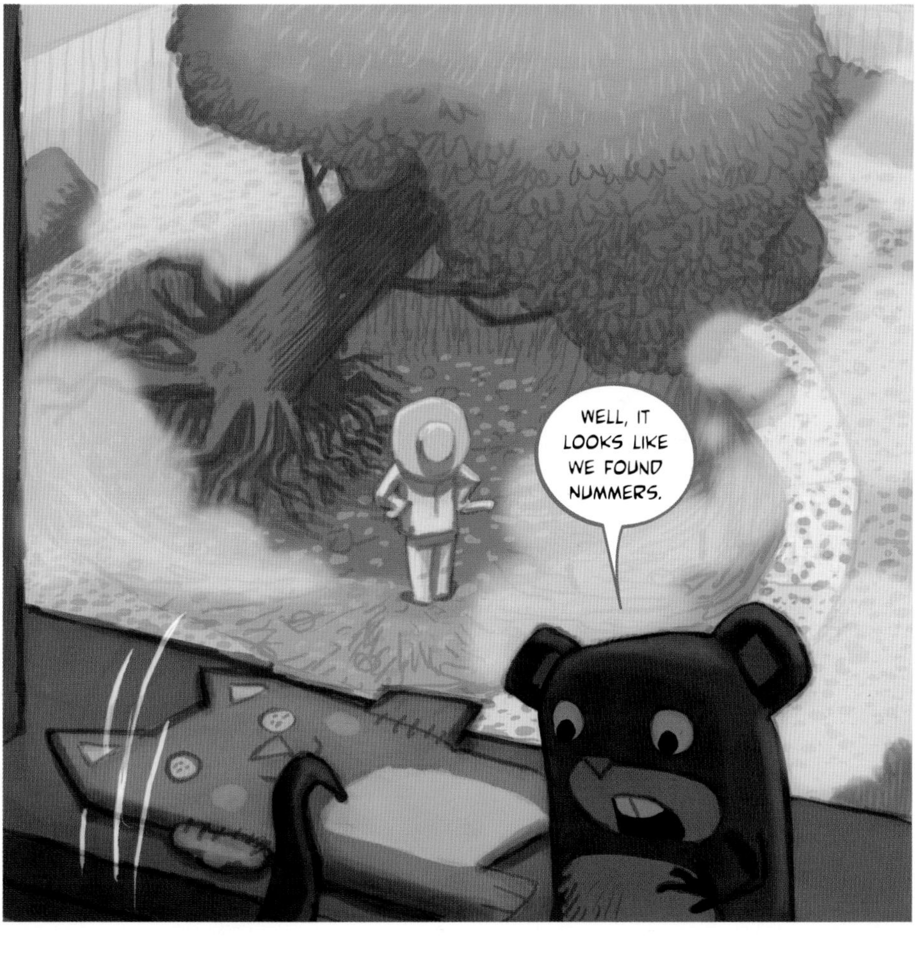
WELL, IT LOOKS LIKE WE FOUND NUMMERS.

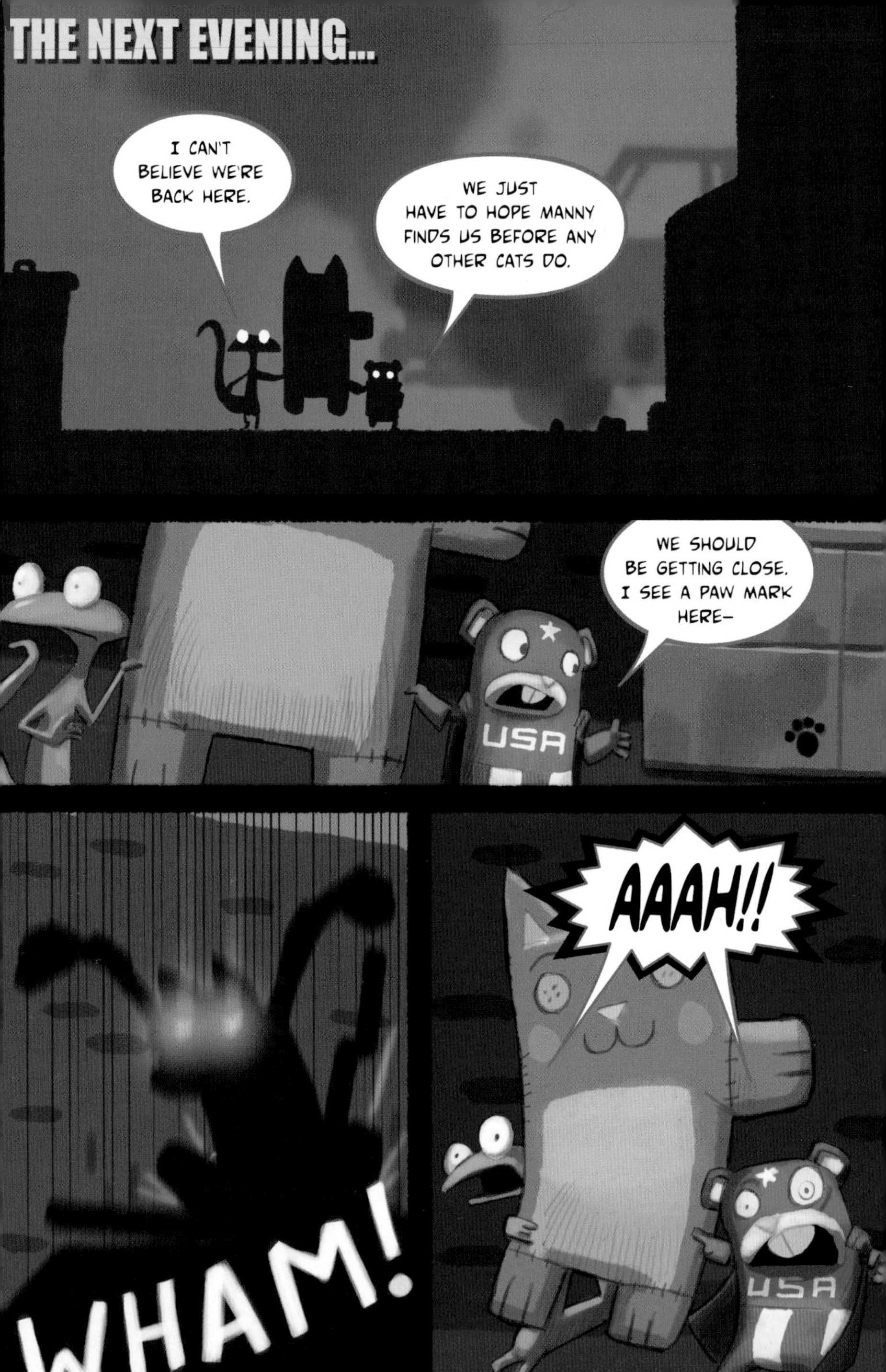
THE NEXT EVENING...
I CAN'T BELIEVE WE'RE BACK HERE.
WE JUST HAVE TO HOPE MANNY FINDS US BEFORE ANY OTHER CATS DO.
WE SHOULD BE GETTING CLOSE. I SEE A PAW MARK HERE—
USA
WHAM!
AAAH!!
USA

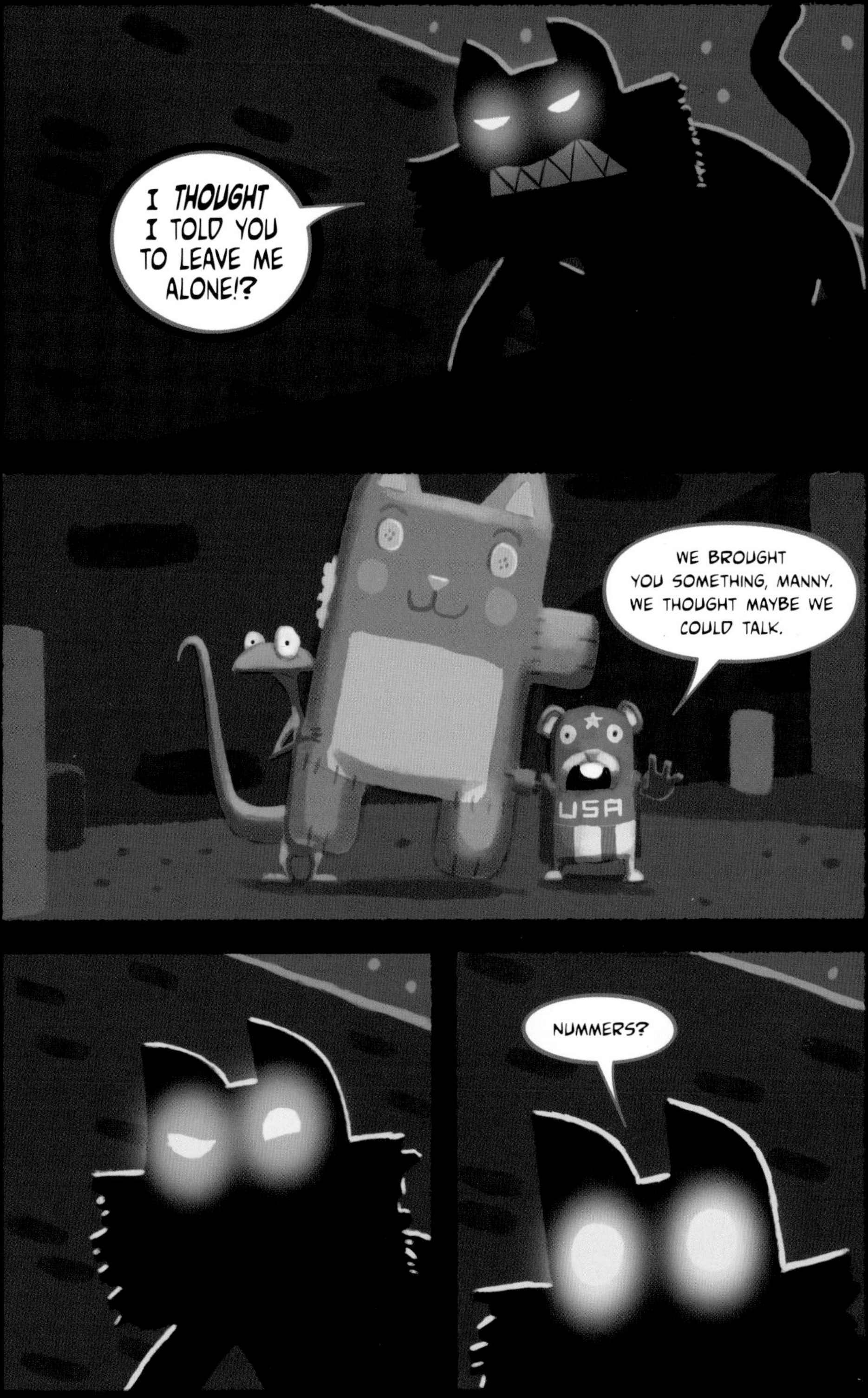
I THOUGHT I TOLD YOU TO LEAVE ME ALONE!?
WE BROUGHT YOU SOMETHING, MANNY. WE THOUGHT MAYBE WE COULD TALK.
NUMMERS?

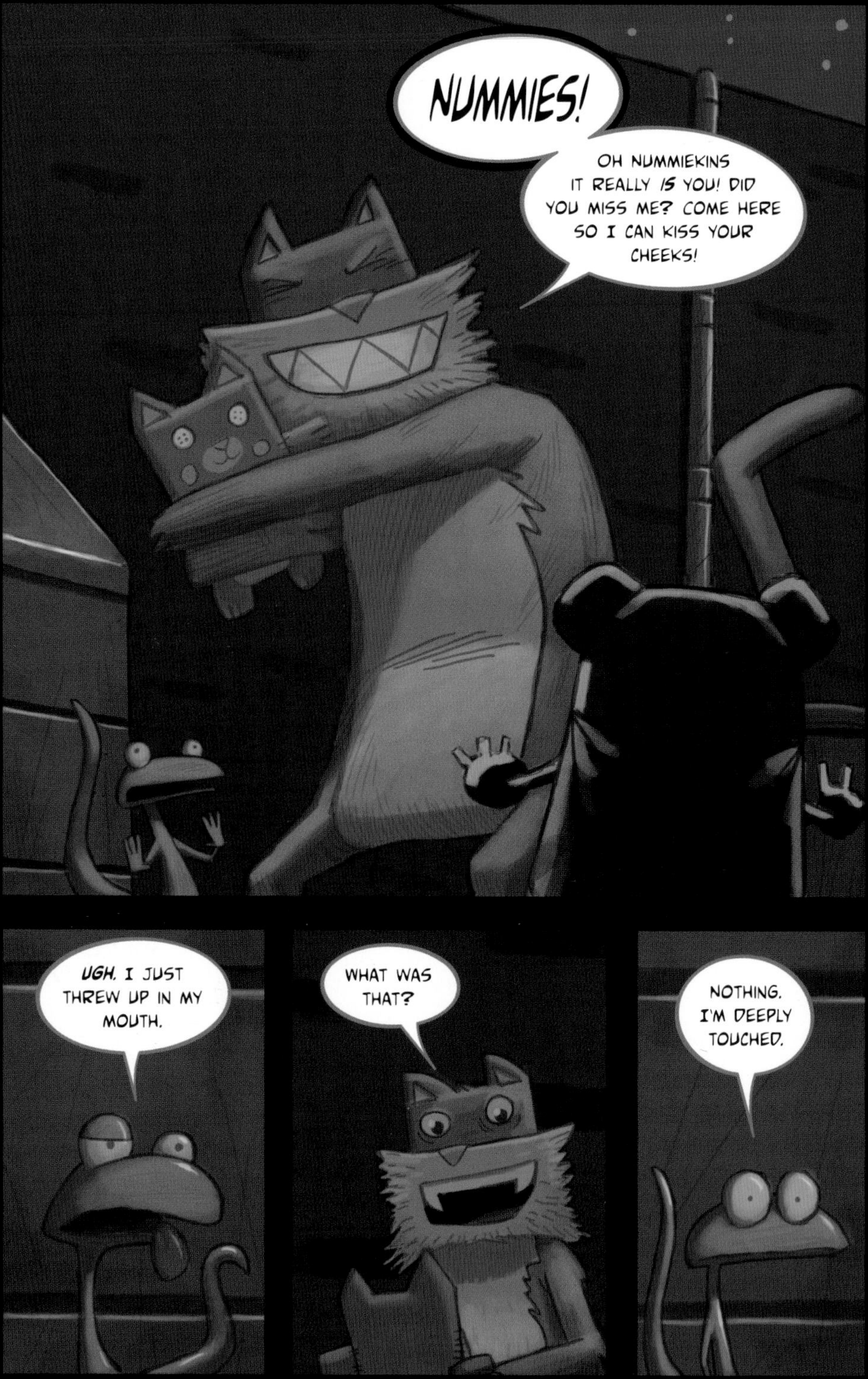
NUMMIES!
OH NUMMIEKINS IT REALLY IS YOU! DID YOU MISS ME? COME HERE SO I CAN KISS YOUR CHEEKS!
UGH. I JUST THREW UP IN MY MOUTH.
WHAT WAS THAT?
NOTHING. I'M DEEPLY TOUCHED.

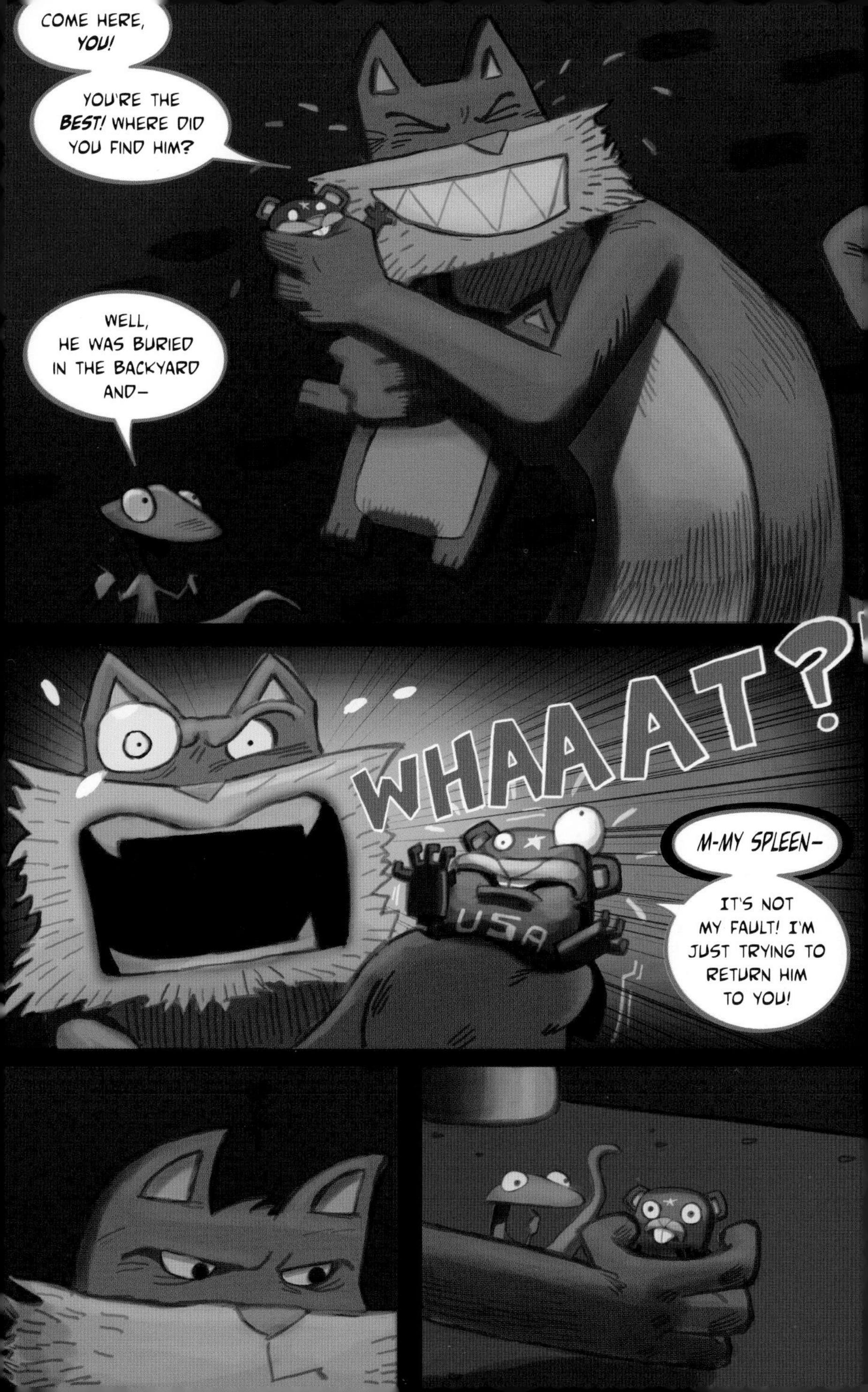
COME HERE, YOU!
YOU'RE THE BEST! WHERE DID YOU FIND HIM?
WELL, HE WAS BURIED IN THE BACKYARD AND—
WHAAAT?!
M-MY SPLEEN—
IT'S NOT MY FAULT! I'M JUST TRYING TO RETURN HIM TO YOU!
USA

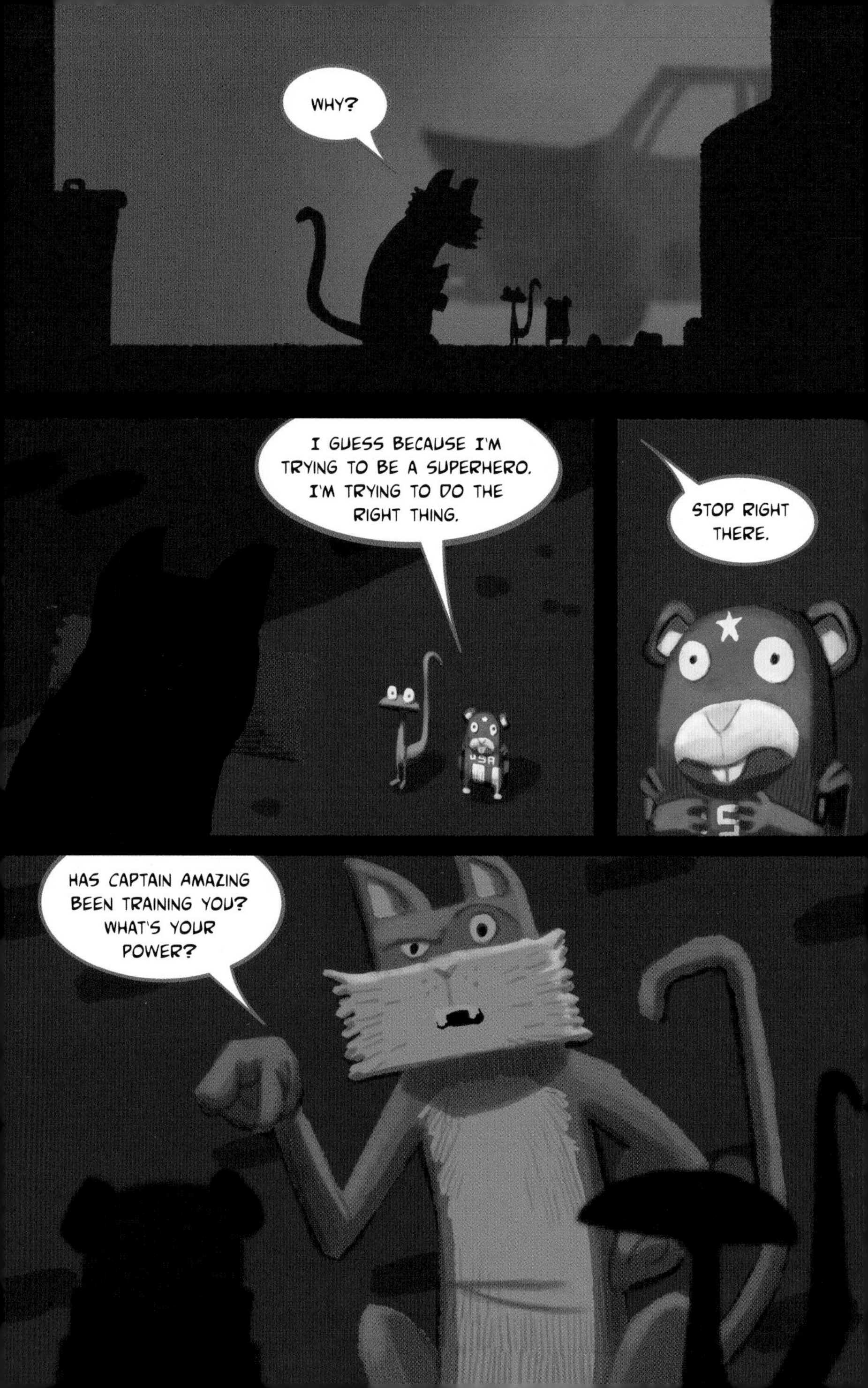
WHY?
I GUESS BECAUSE I'M TRYING TO BE A SUPERHERO. I'M TRYING TO DO THE RIGHT THING.
STOP RIGHT THERE.
HAS CAPTAIN AMAZING BEEN TRAINING YOU? WHAT'S YOUR POWER?

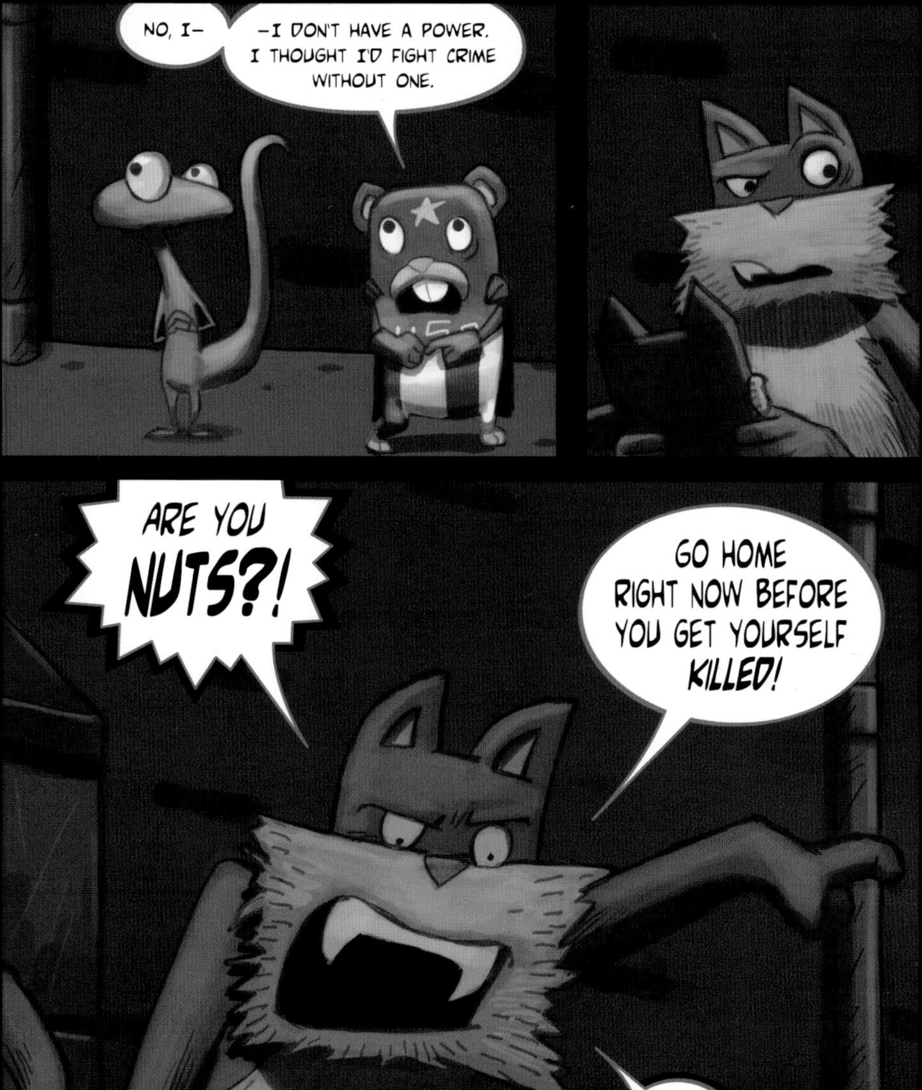
NO, I–
–I DON'T HAVE A POWER. I THOUGHT I'D FIGHT CRIME WITHOUT ONE.
ARE YOU NUTS?!
GO HOME RIGHT NOW BEFORE YOU GET YOURSELF KILLED!
BUT I–
GO!

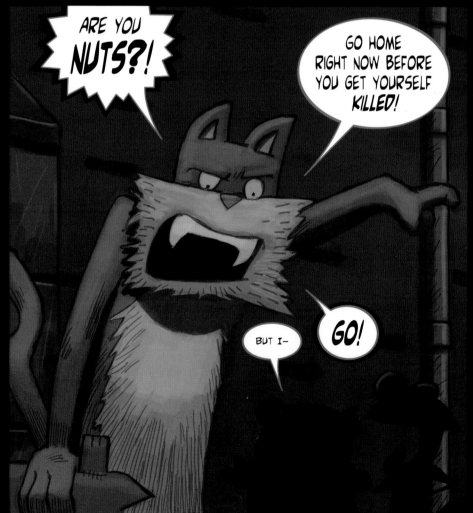

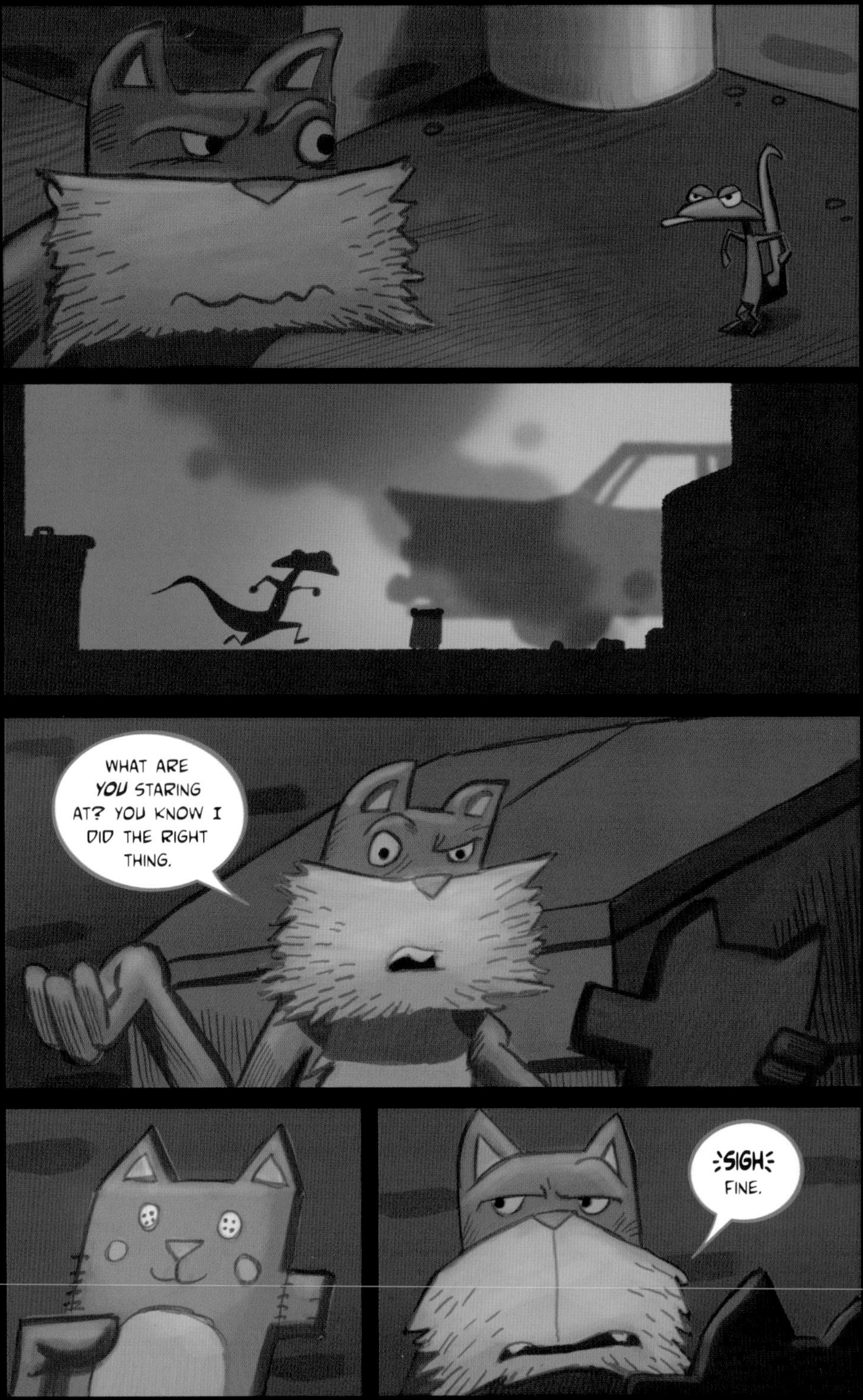
WHAT ARE YOU STARING AT? YOU KNOW I DID THE RIGHT THING.
:SIGH: FINE.

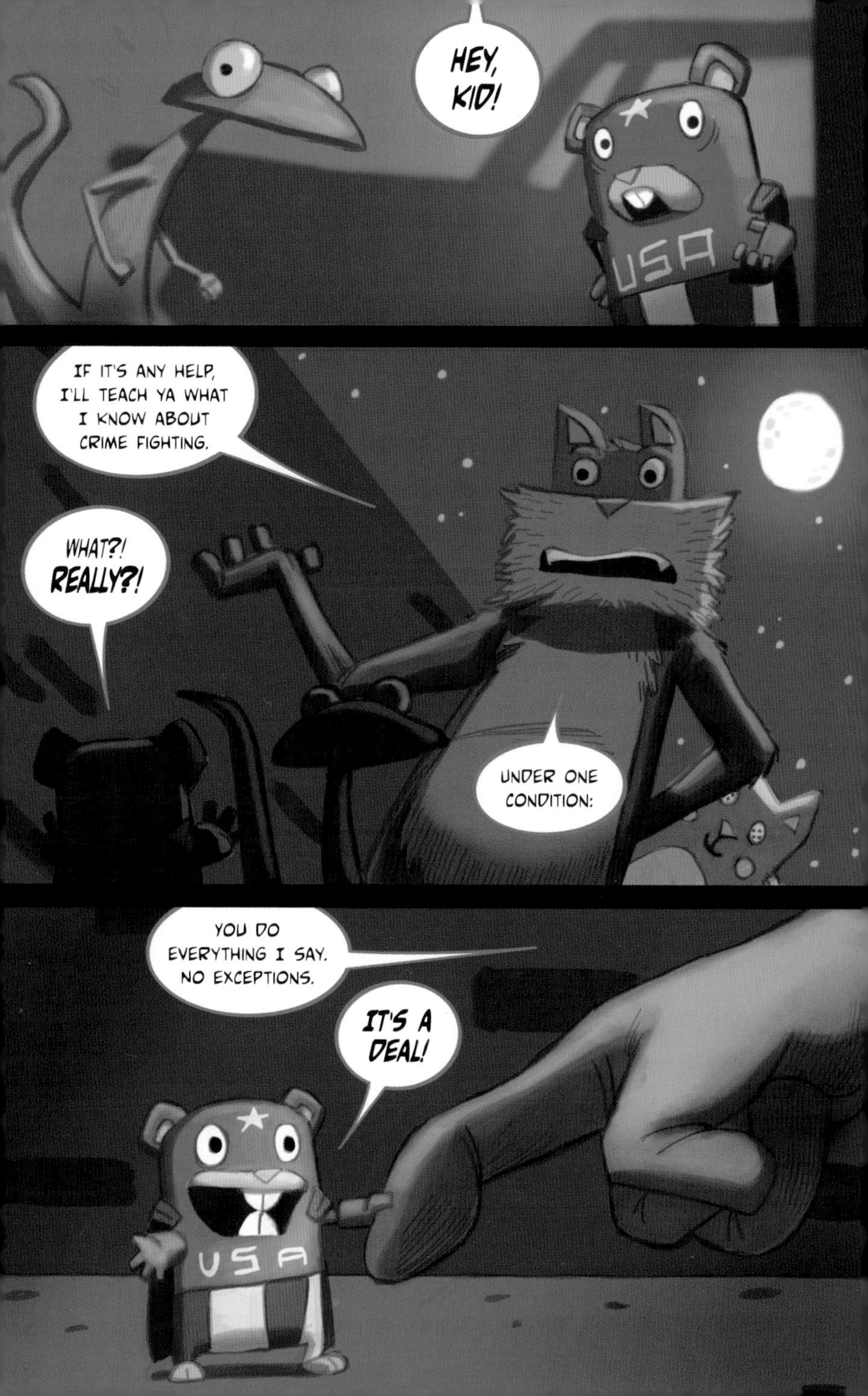
HEY, KID!
IF IT'S ANY HELP, I'LL TEACH YA WHAT I KNOW ABOUT CRIME FIGHTING.
WHAT?! REALLY?!
UNDER ONE CONDITION:
YOU DO EVERYTHING I SAY. NO EXCEPTIONS.
IT'S A DEAL!

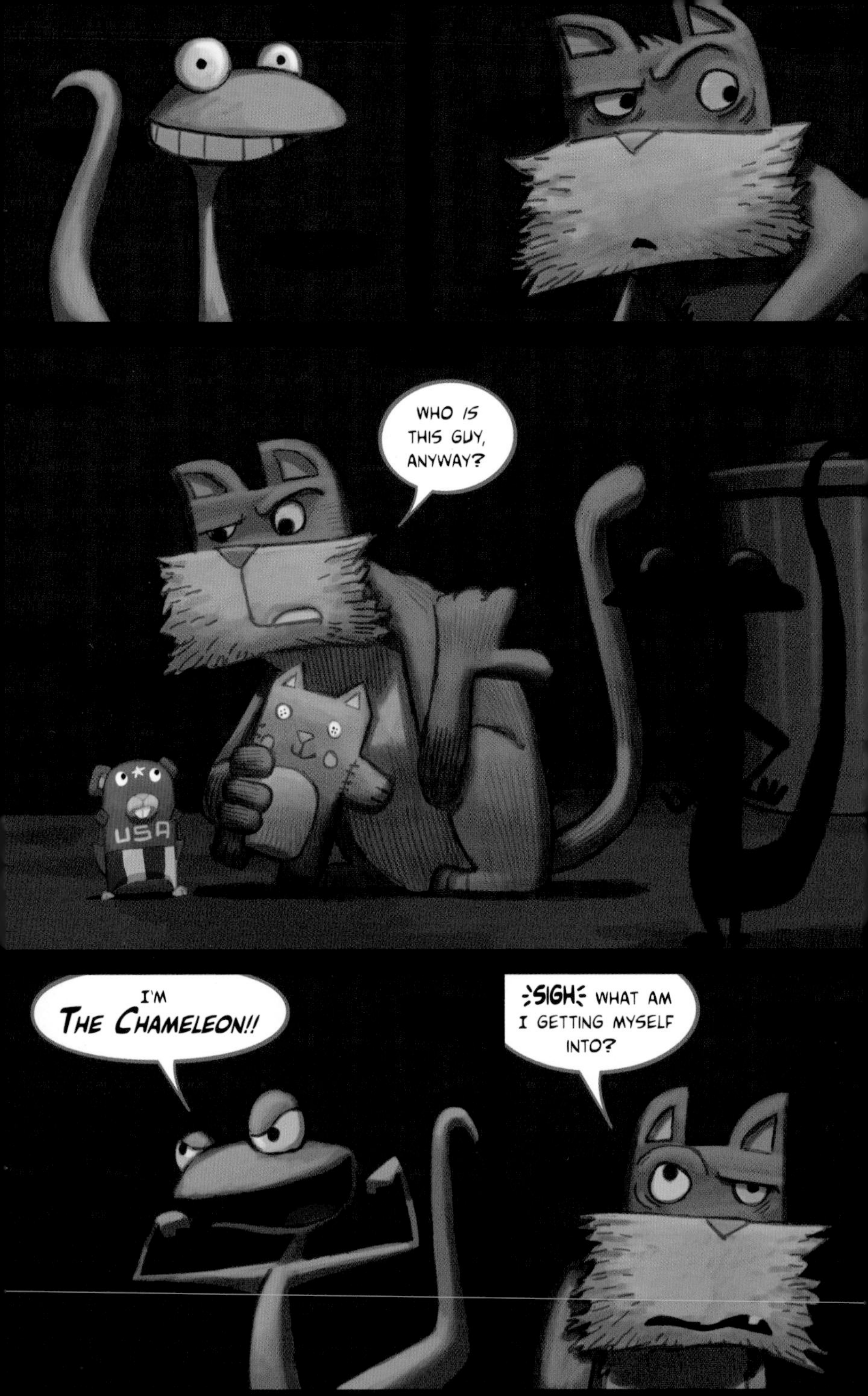
WHO IS THIS GUY, ANYWAY?
I'M THE CHAMELEON!!
SIGH WHAT AM I GETTING MYSELF INTO?

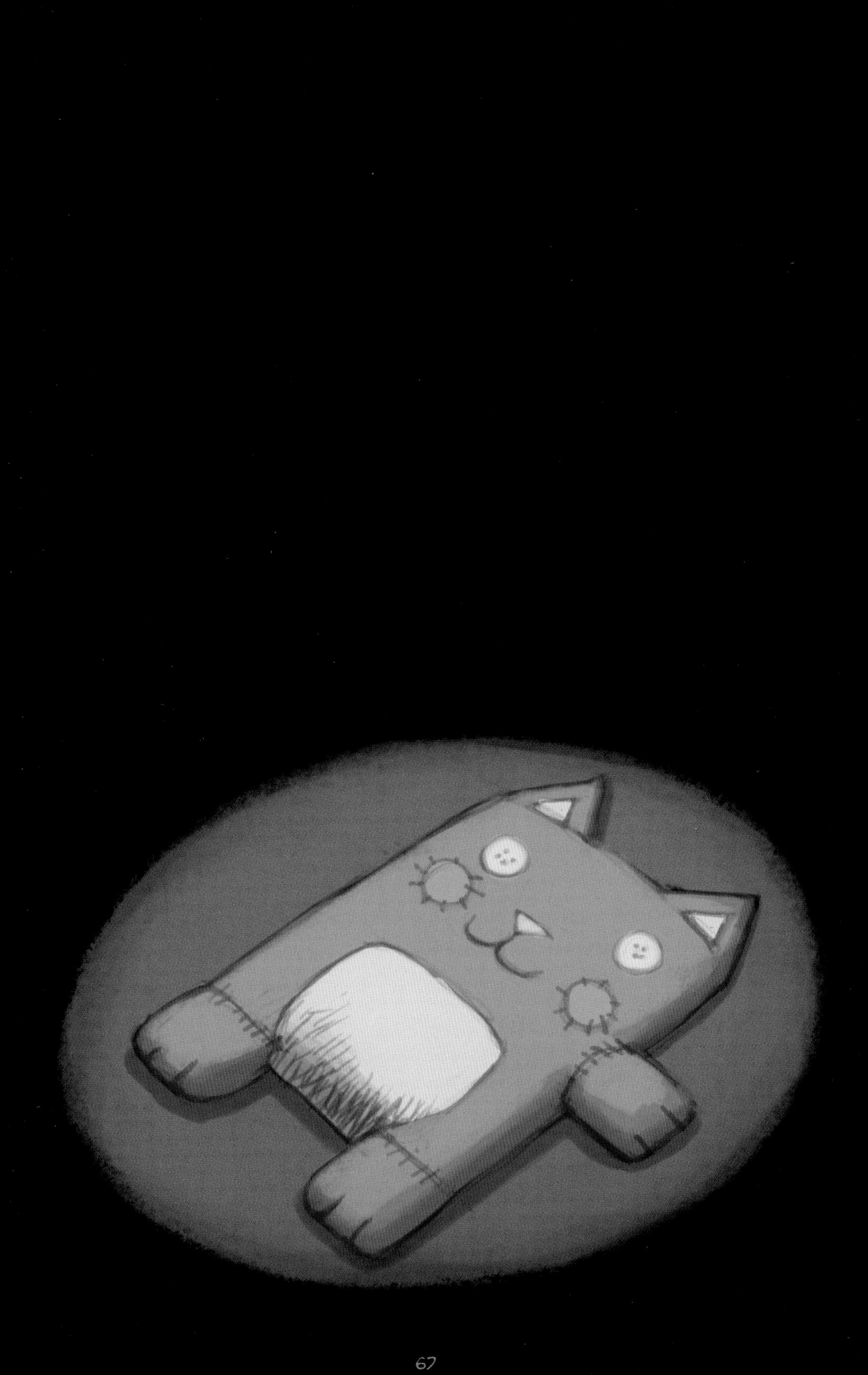

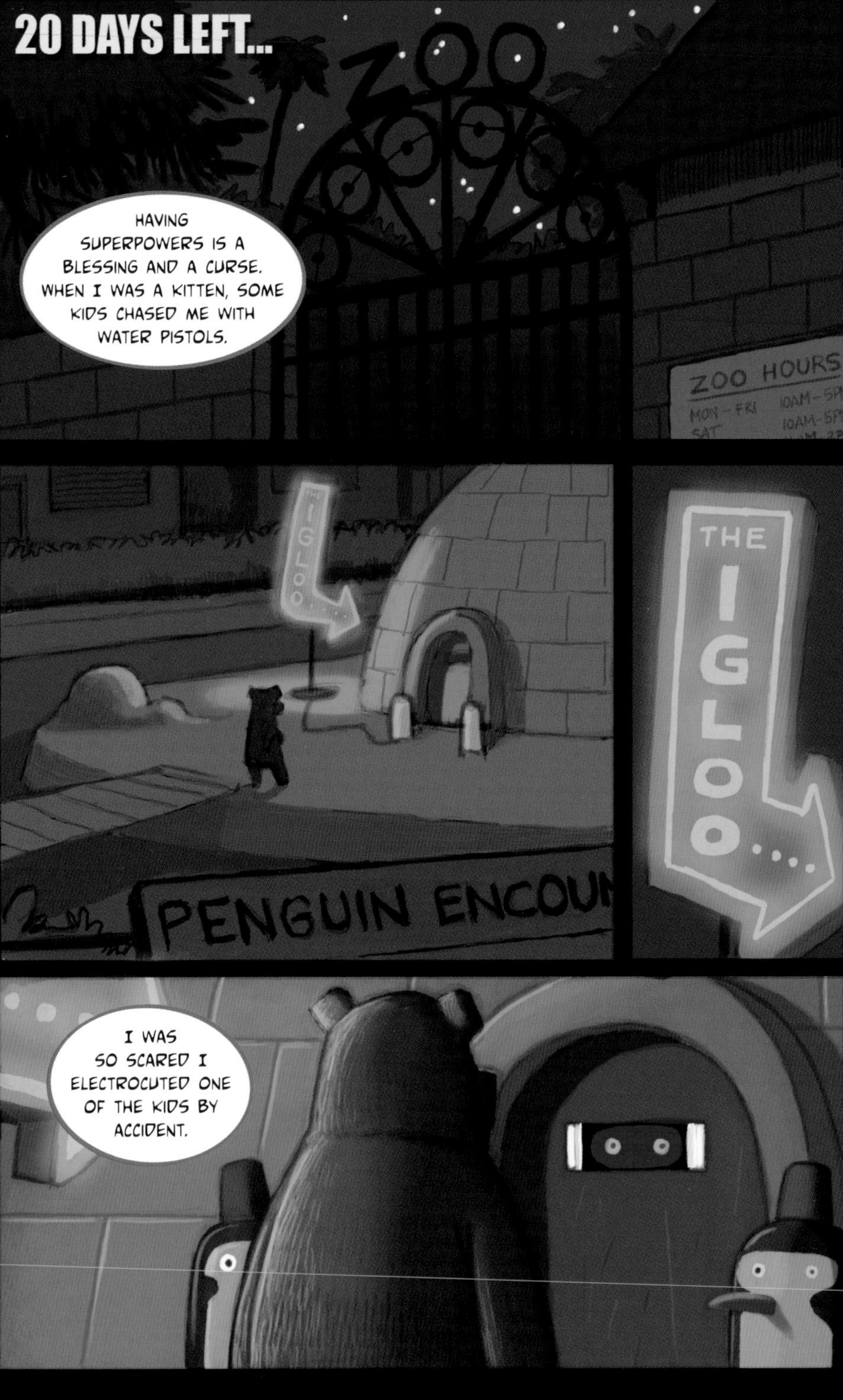
20 DAYS LEFT...
ZOO
HAVING SUPERPOWERS IS A BLESSING AND A CURSE. WHEN I WAS A KITTEN, SOME KIDS CHASED ME WITH WATER PISTOLS.
ZOO HOURS
MON - FRI 10AM-5P
SAT 10AM-5P
IGLOO
PENGUIN ENCOU
THE IGLOO....
I WAS SO SCARED I ELECTROCUTED ONE OF THE KIDS BY ACCIDENT.

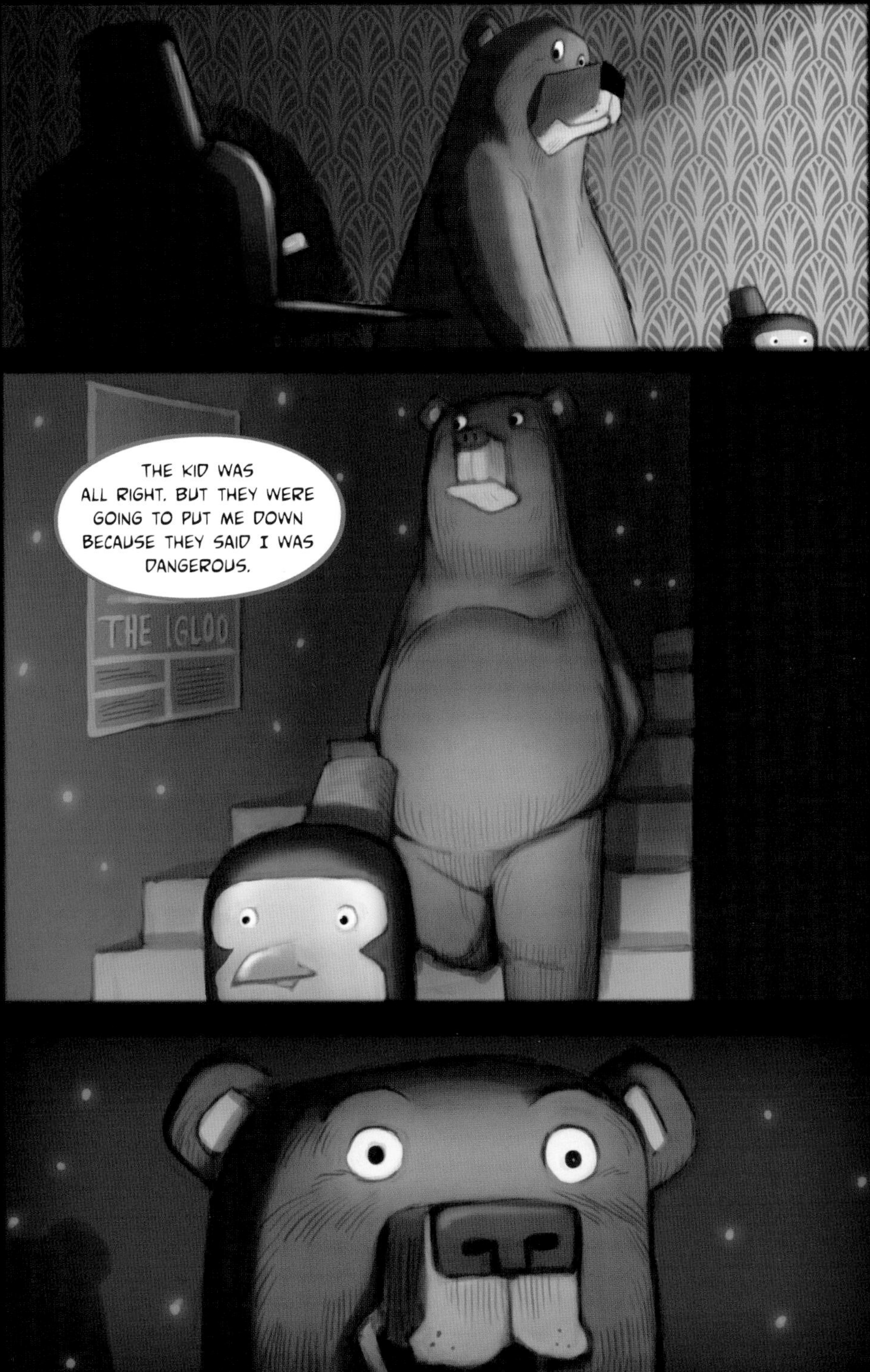
THE KID WAS ALL RIGHT. BUT THEY WERE GOING TO PUT ME DOWN BECAUSE THEY SAID I WAS DANGEROUS.
THE IGLOO

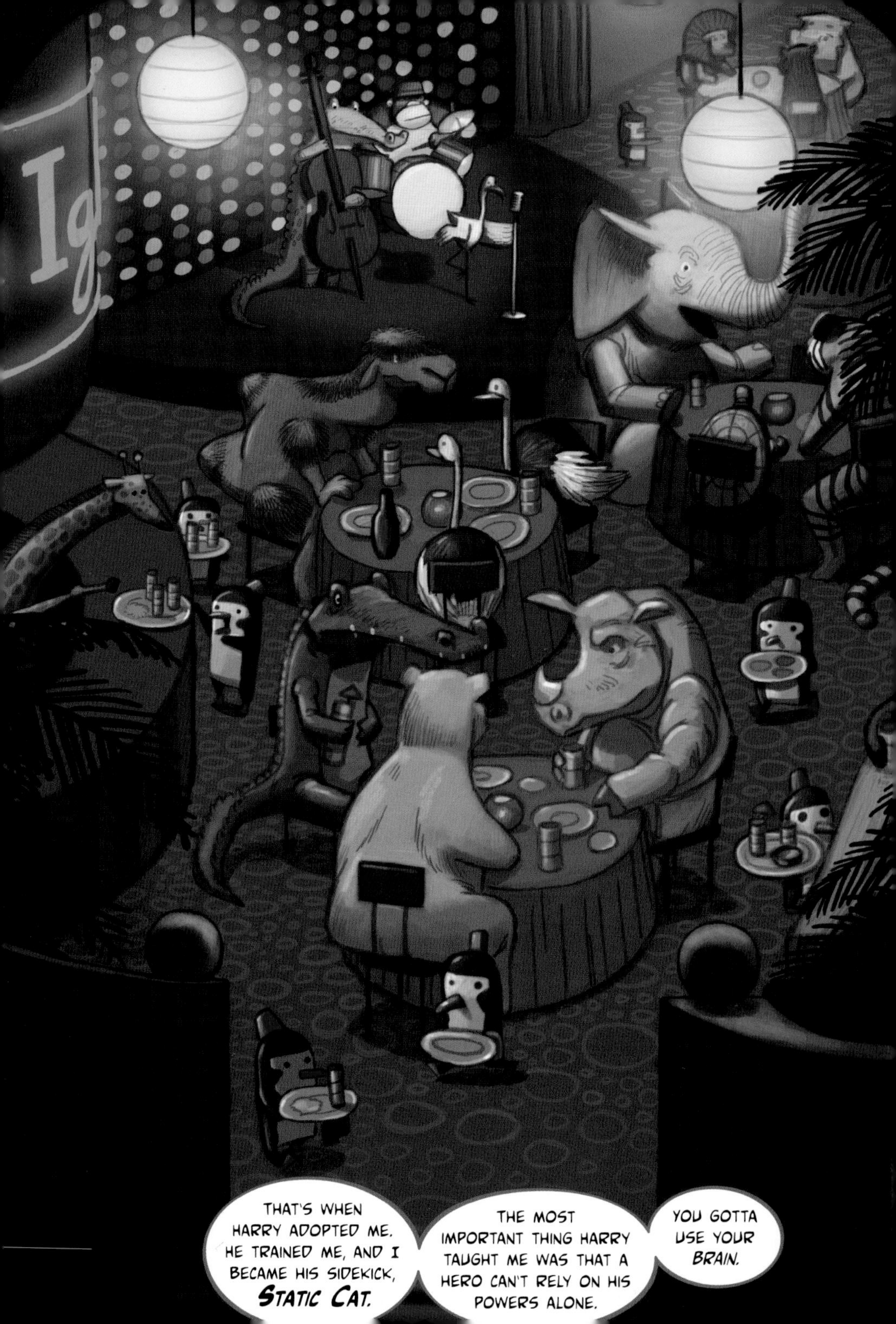
THAT'S WHEN HARRY ADOPTED ME. HE TRAINED ME, AND I BECAME HIS SIDEKICK, STATIC CAT.
THE MOST IMPORTANT THING HARRY TAUGHT ME WAS THAT A HERO CAN'T RELY ON HIS POWERS ALONE.
YOU GOTTA USE YOUR BRAIN.

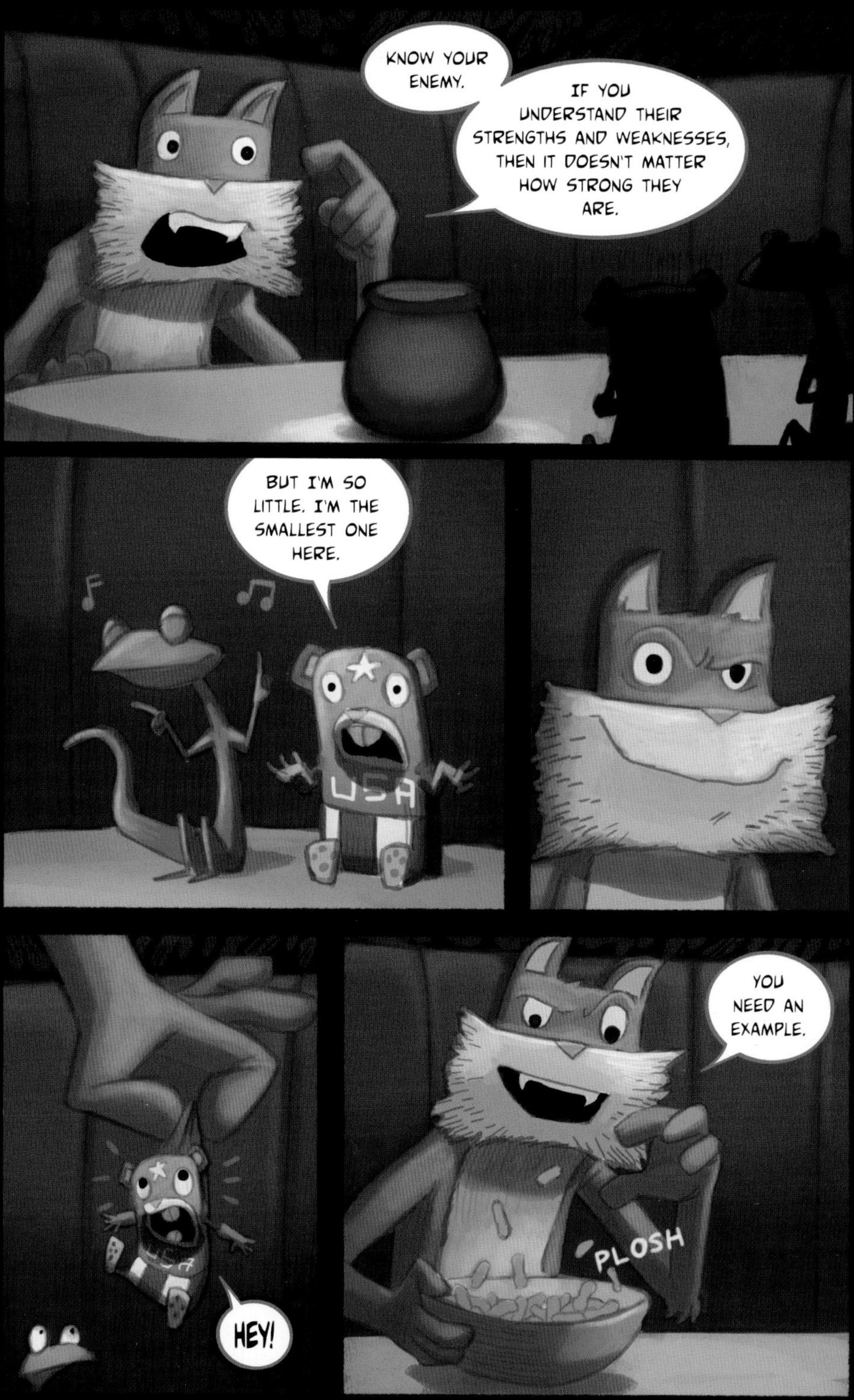
KNOW YOUR ENEMY.
IF YOU UNDERSTAND THEIR STRENGTHS AND WEAKNESSES, THEN IT DOESN'T MATTER HOW STRONG THEY ARE.
BUT I'M SO LITTLE. I'M THE SMALLEST ONE HERE.
USA
HEY!
YOU NEED AN EXAMPLE.
PLOSH

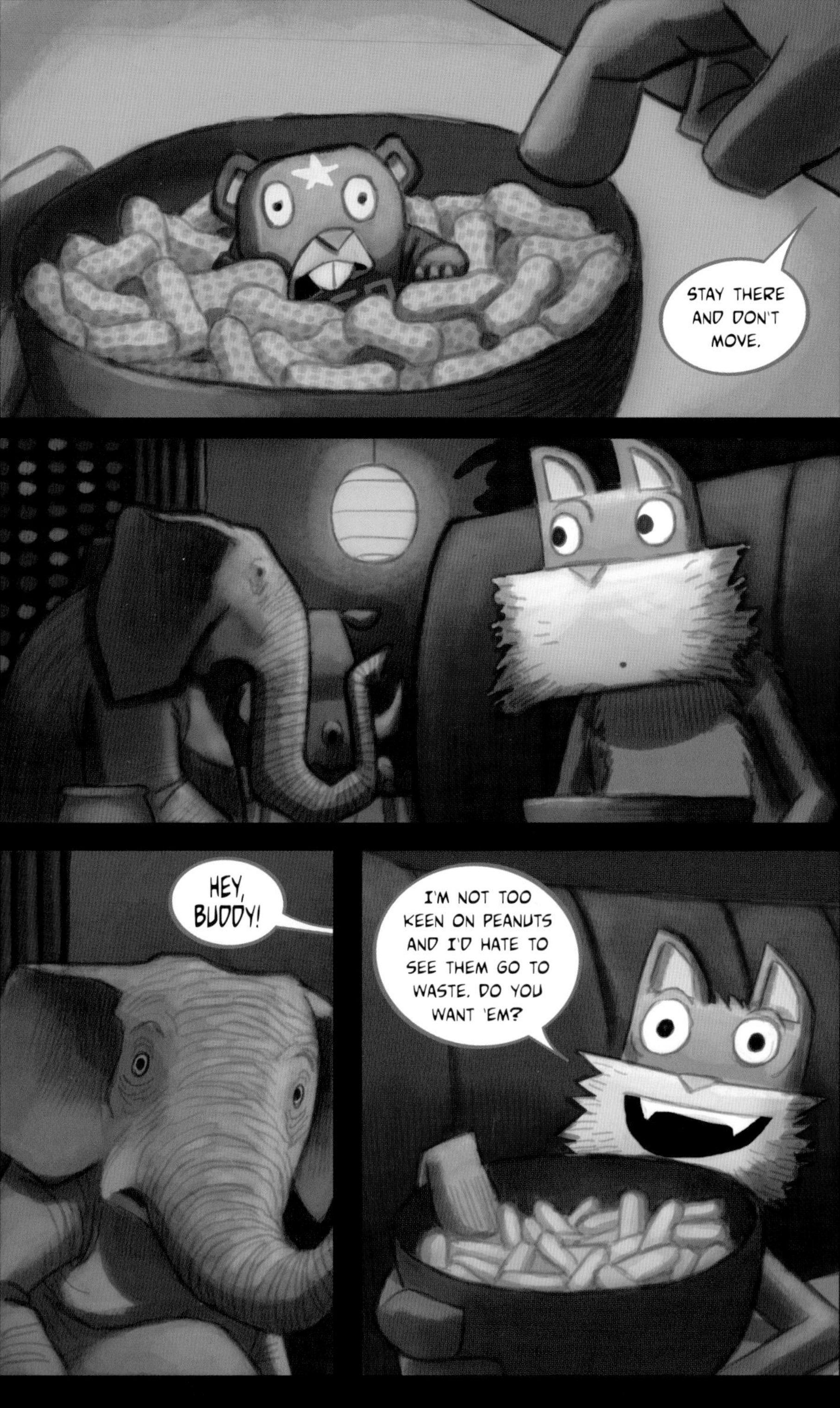
STAY THERE AND DON'T MOVE.
HEY, BUDDY!
I'M NOT TOO KEEN ON PEANUTS AND I'D HATE TO SEE THEM GO TO WASTE. DO YOU WANT 'EM?

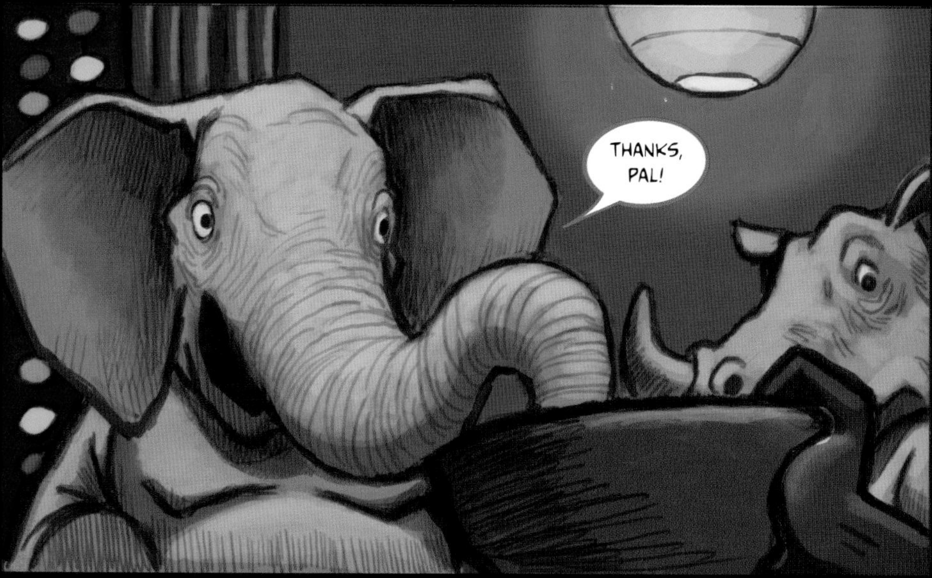
THANKS, PAL!

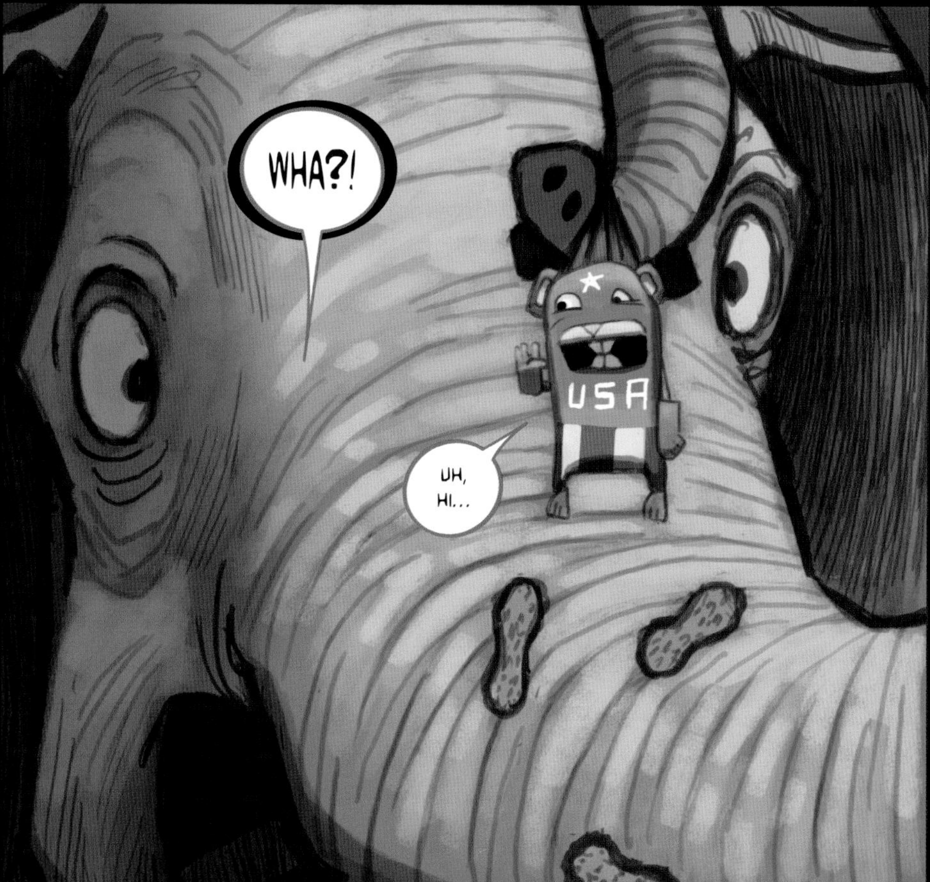
WHA?!
UH, HI...

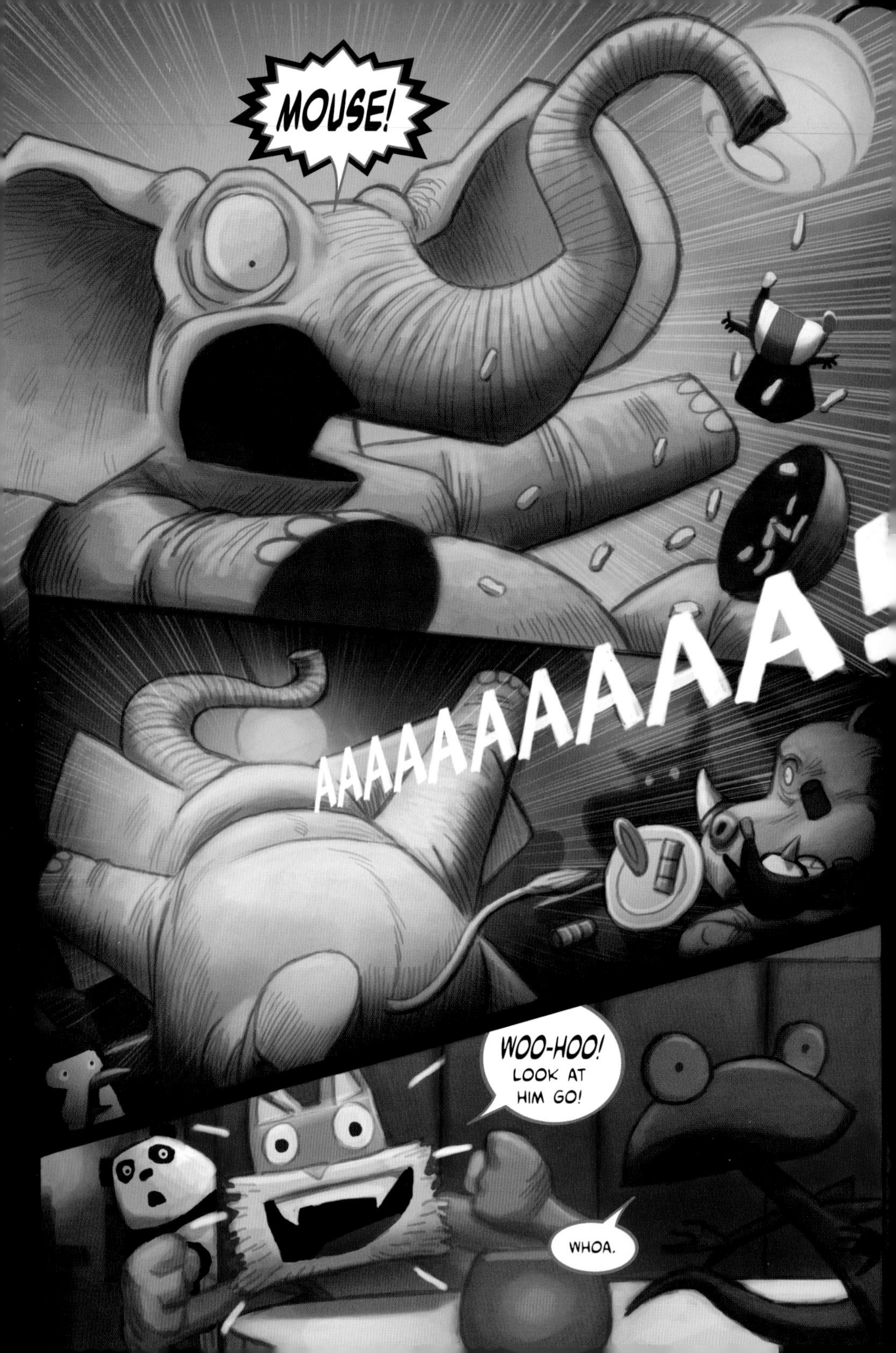

MOUSE!
AAAAAAAAAAAA!
WOO-HOO! LOOK AT HIM GO!
WHOA.

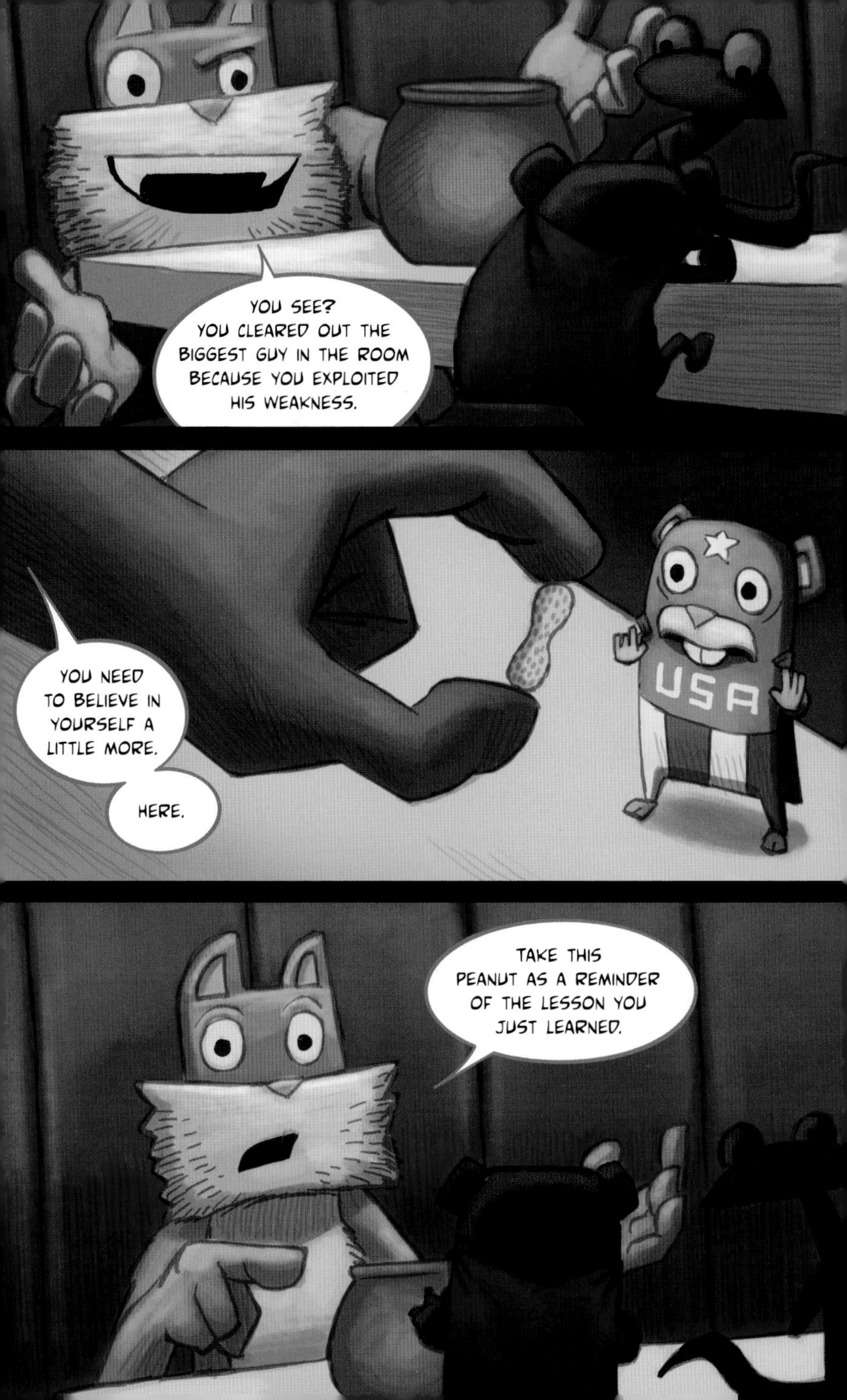
YOU SEE? YOU CLEARED OUT THE BIGGEST GUY IN THE ROOM BECAUSE YOU EXPLOITED HIS WEAKNESS.
YOU NEED TO BELIEVE IN YOURSELF A LITTLE MORE.
HERE.
USA
TAKE THIS PEANUT AS A REMINDER OF THE LESSON YOU JUST LEARNED.

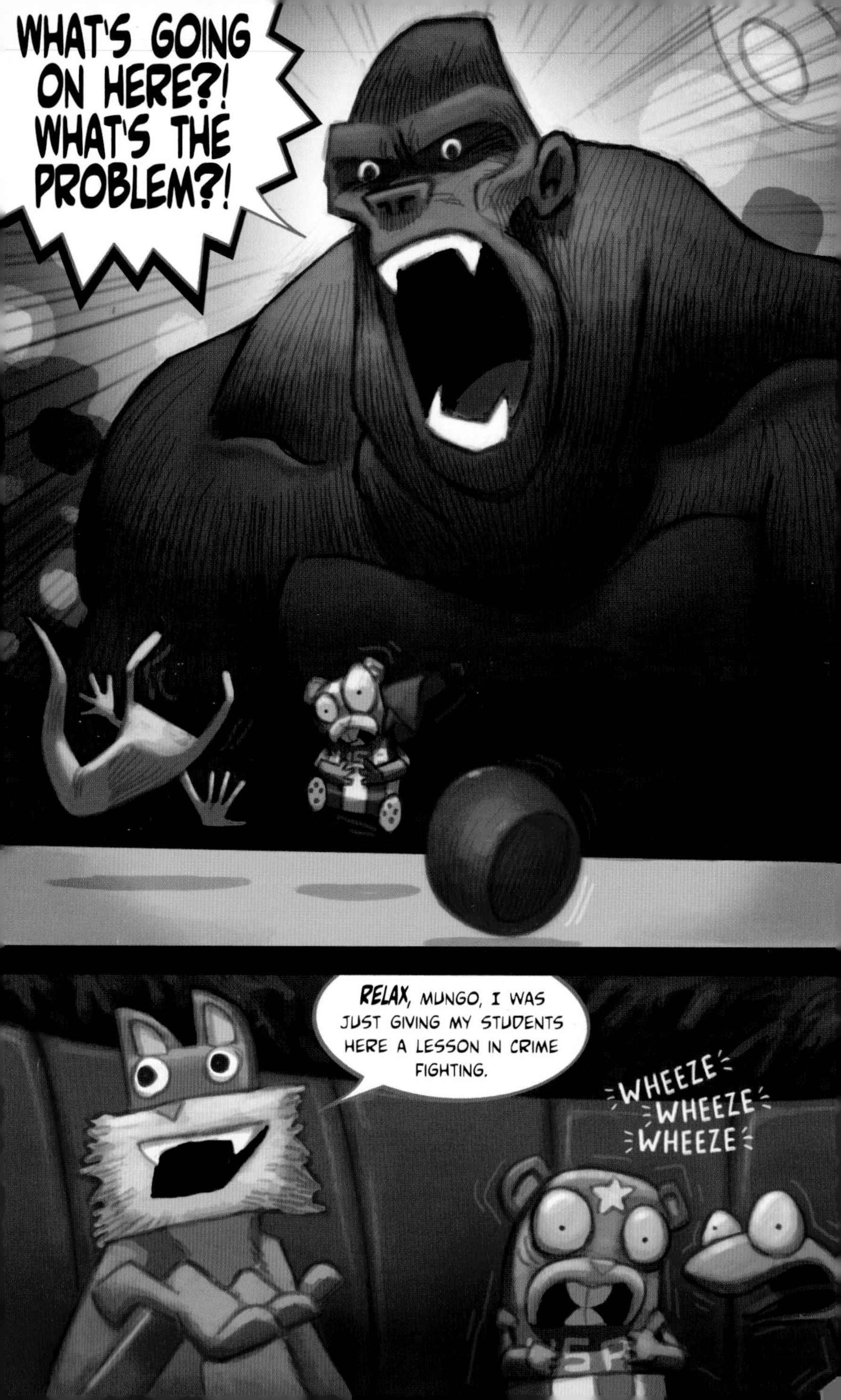
WHAT'S GOING ON HERE?! WHAT'S THE PROBLEM?!
RELAX, MUNGO, I WAS JUST GIVING MY STUDENTS HERE A LESSON IN CRIME FIGHTING.
WHEEZE
WHEEZE
WHEEZE

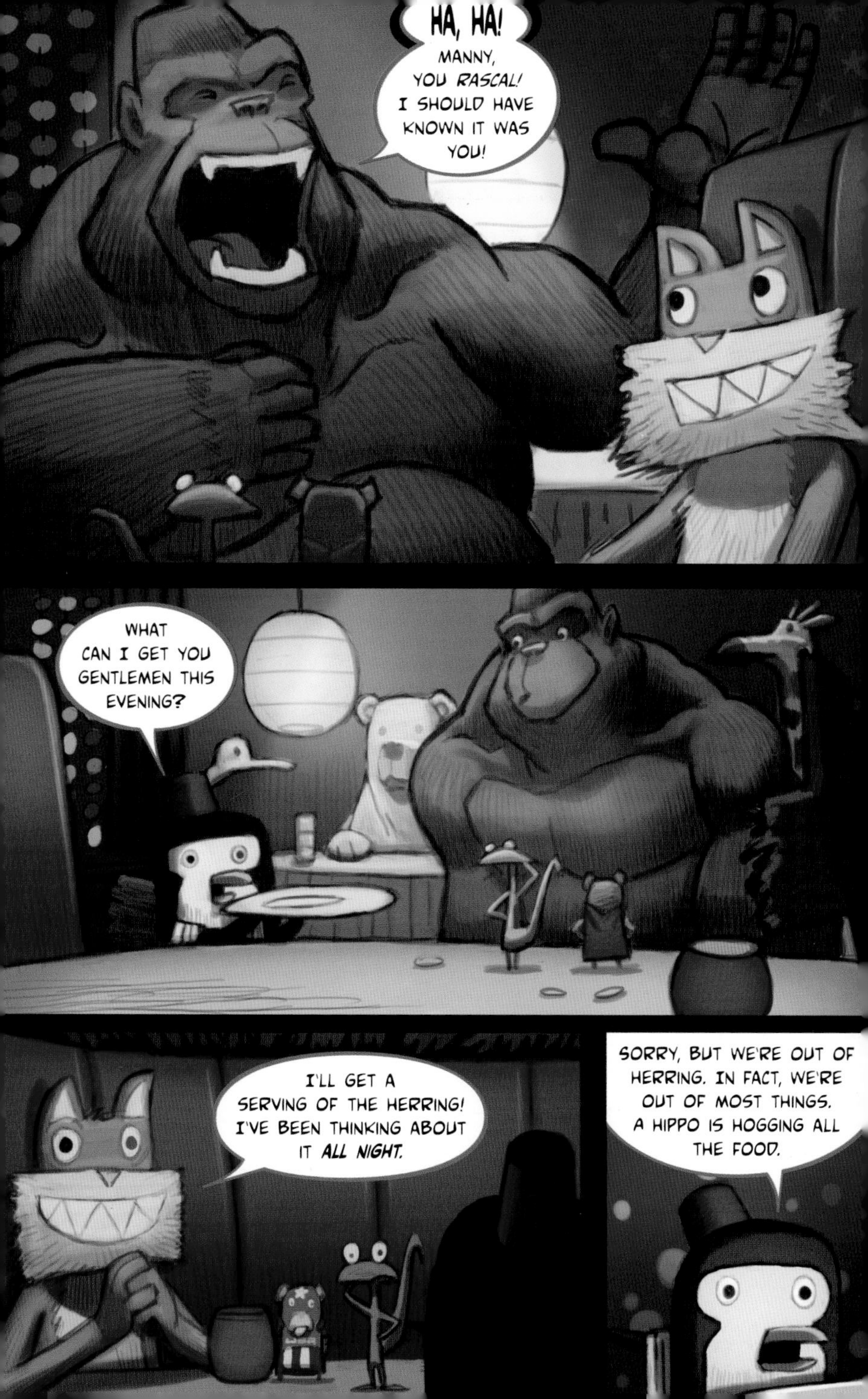
HA, HA!
MANNY, YOU RASCAL! I SHOULD HAVE KNOWN IT WAS YOU!
WHAT CAN I GET YOU GENTLEMEN THIS EVENING?
I'LL GET A SERVING OF THE HERRING! I'VE BEEN THINKING ABOUT IT ALL NIGHT.
SORRY, BUT WE'RE OUT OF HERRING. IN FACT, WE'RE OUT OF MOST THINGS. A HIPPO IS HOGGING ALL THE FOOD.

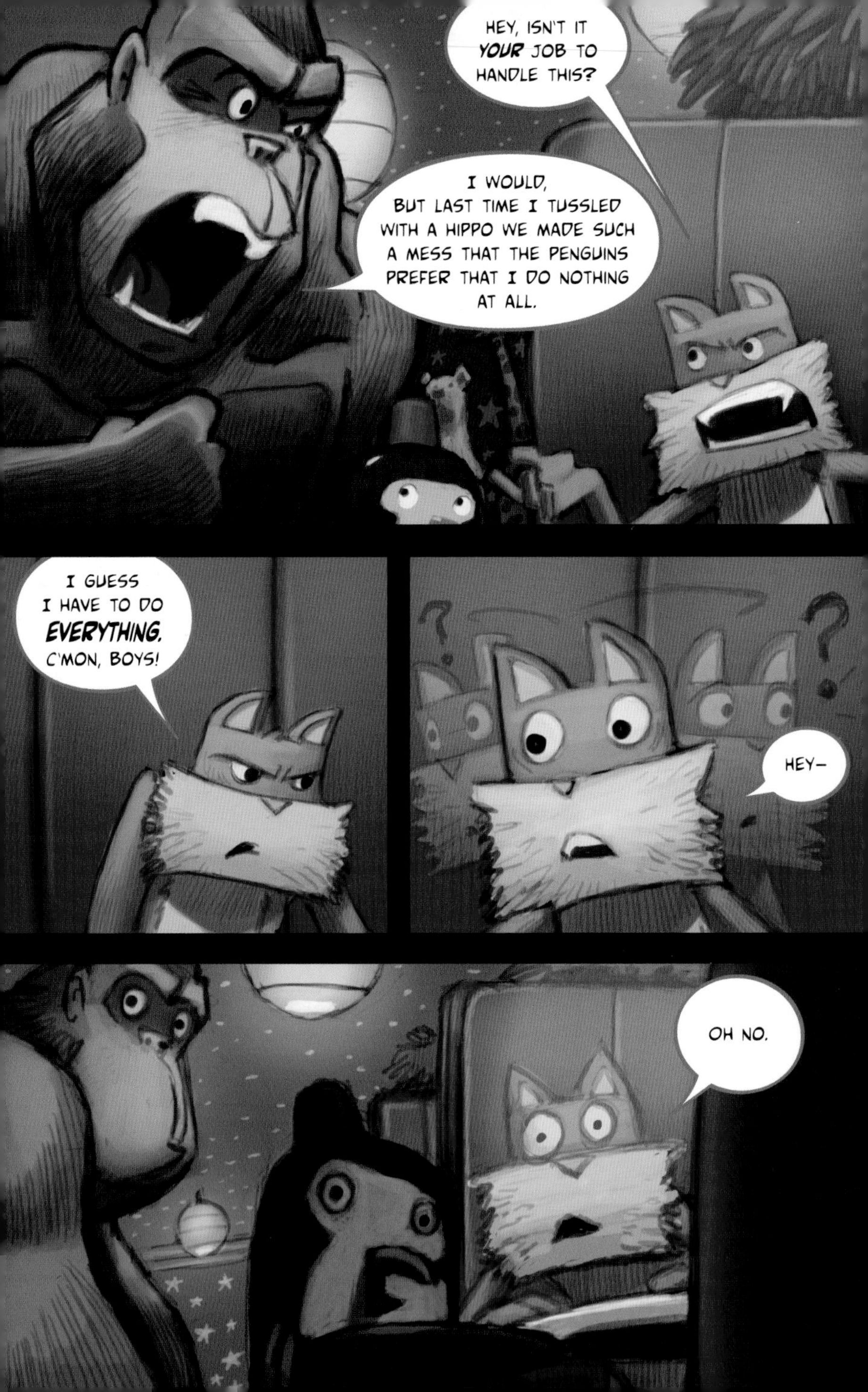
HEY, ISN'T IT YOUR JOB TO HANDLE THIS?
I WOULD, BUT LAST TIME I TUSSLED WITH A HIPPO WE MADE SUCH A MESS THAT THE PENGUINS PREFER THAT I DO NOTHING AT ALL.
I GUESS I HAVE TO DO EVERYTHING. C'MON, BOYS!
HEY–
OH NO.

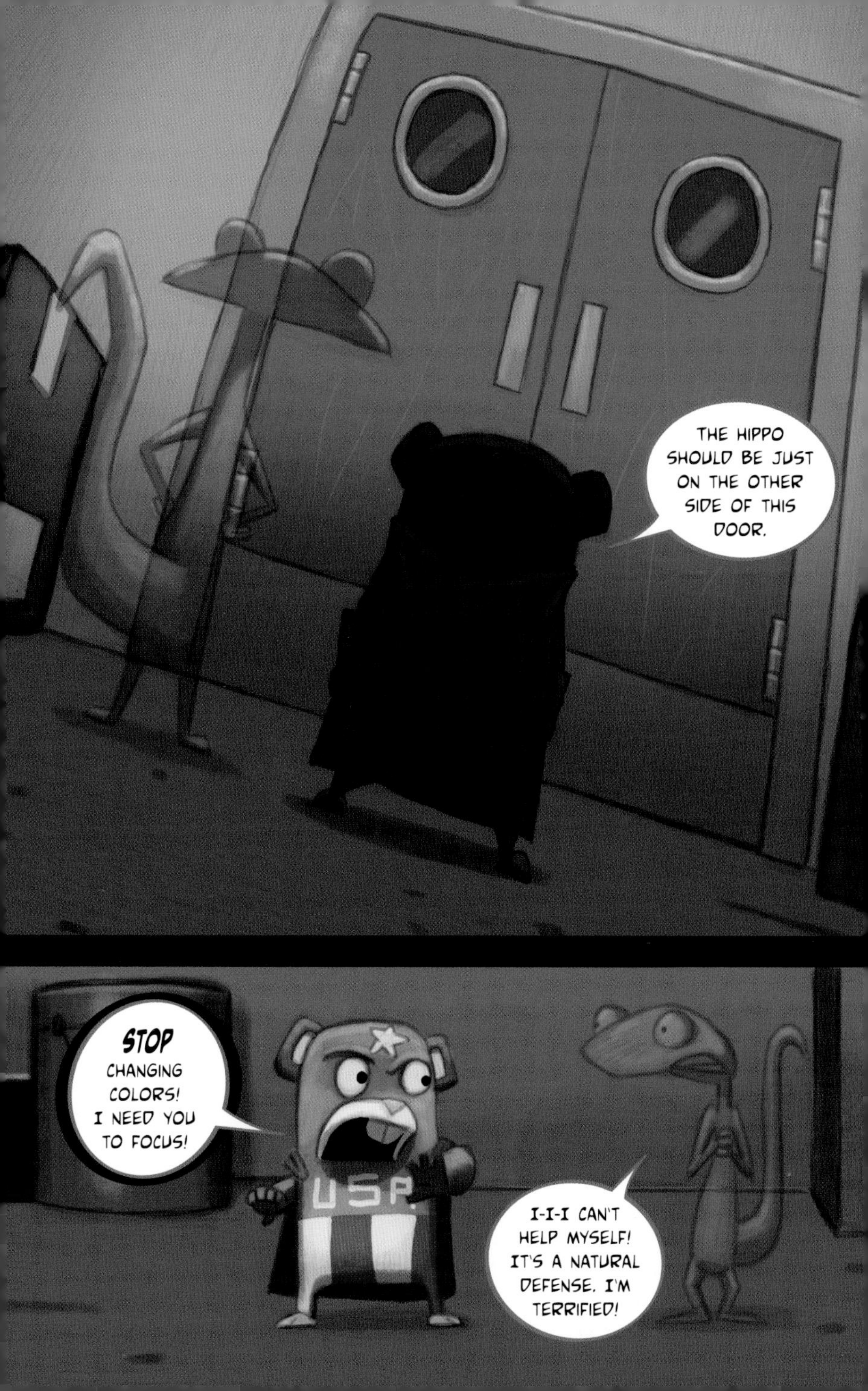
THE HIPPO SHOULD BE JUST ON THE OTHER SIDE OF THIS DOOR.
STOP CHANGING COLORS! I NEED YOU TO FOCUS!
U.S.P.
I-I-I CAN'T HELP MYSELF! IT'S A NATURAL DEFENSE. I'M TERRIFIED!

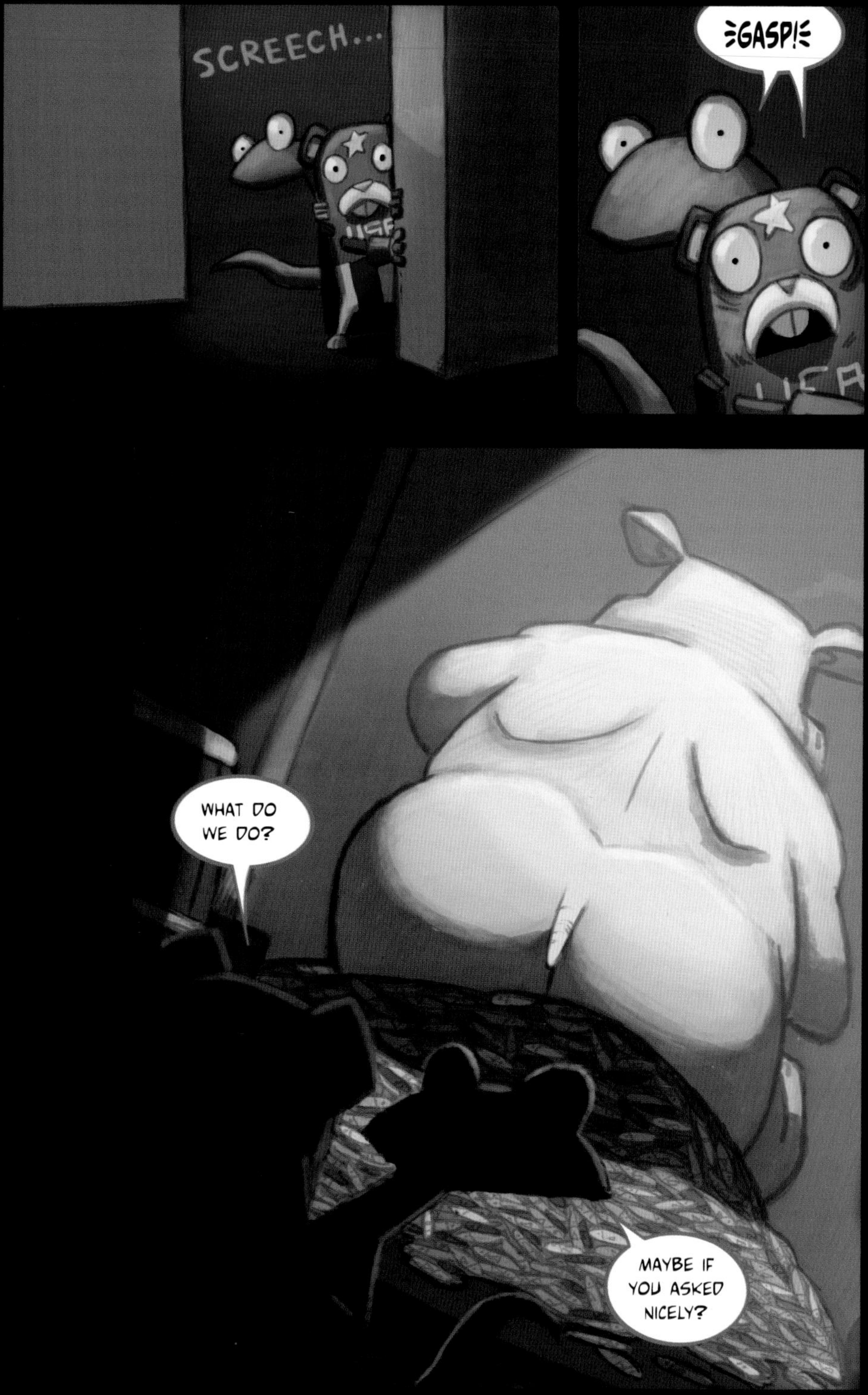
SCREECH...
GASP!
WHAT DO WE DO?
MAYBE IF YOU ASKED NICELY?

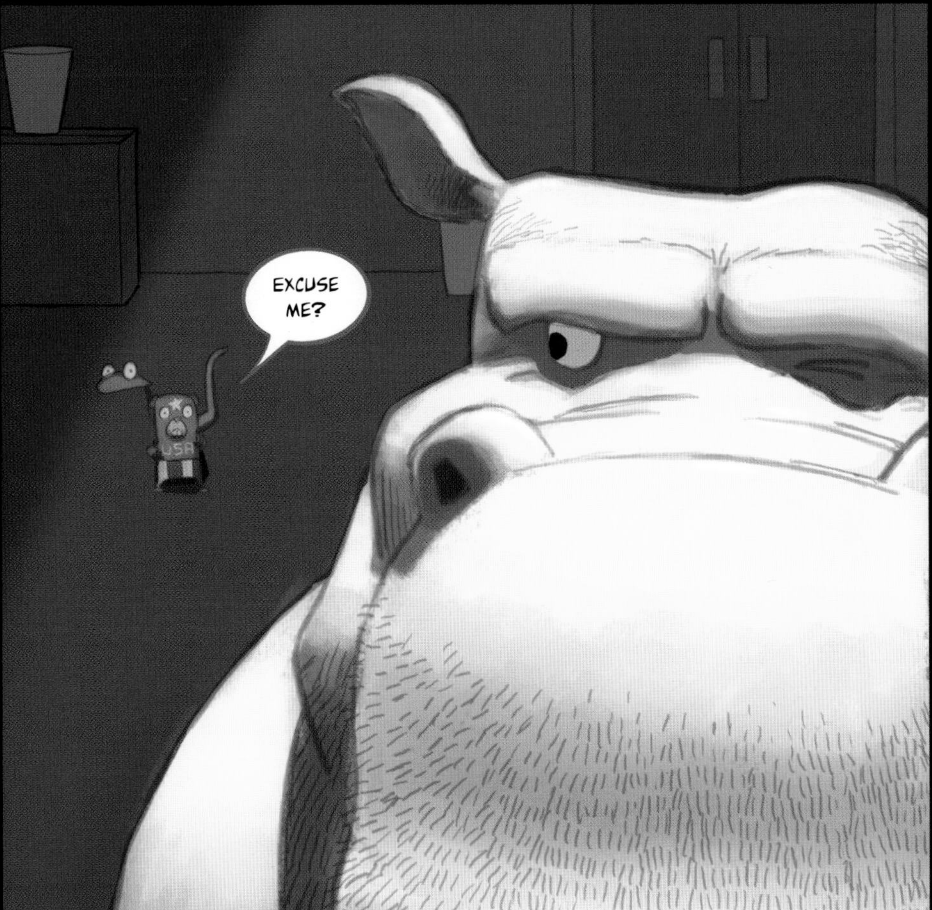
EXCUSE ME?

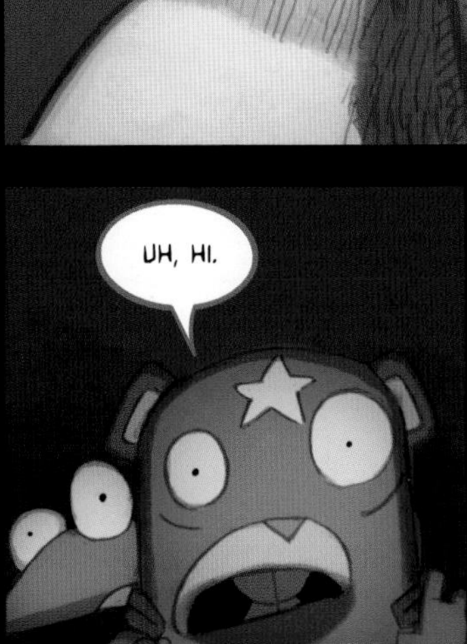
UH, HI.

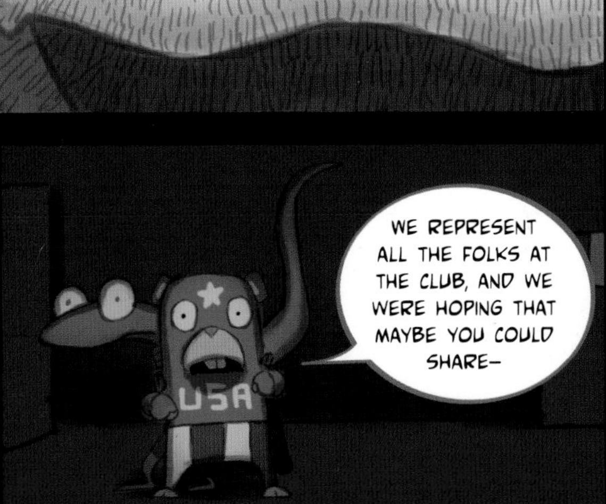
WE REPRESENT ALL THE FOLKS AT THE CLUB, AND WE WERE HOPING THAT MAYBE YOU COULD SHARE–

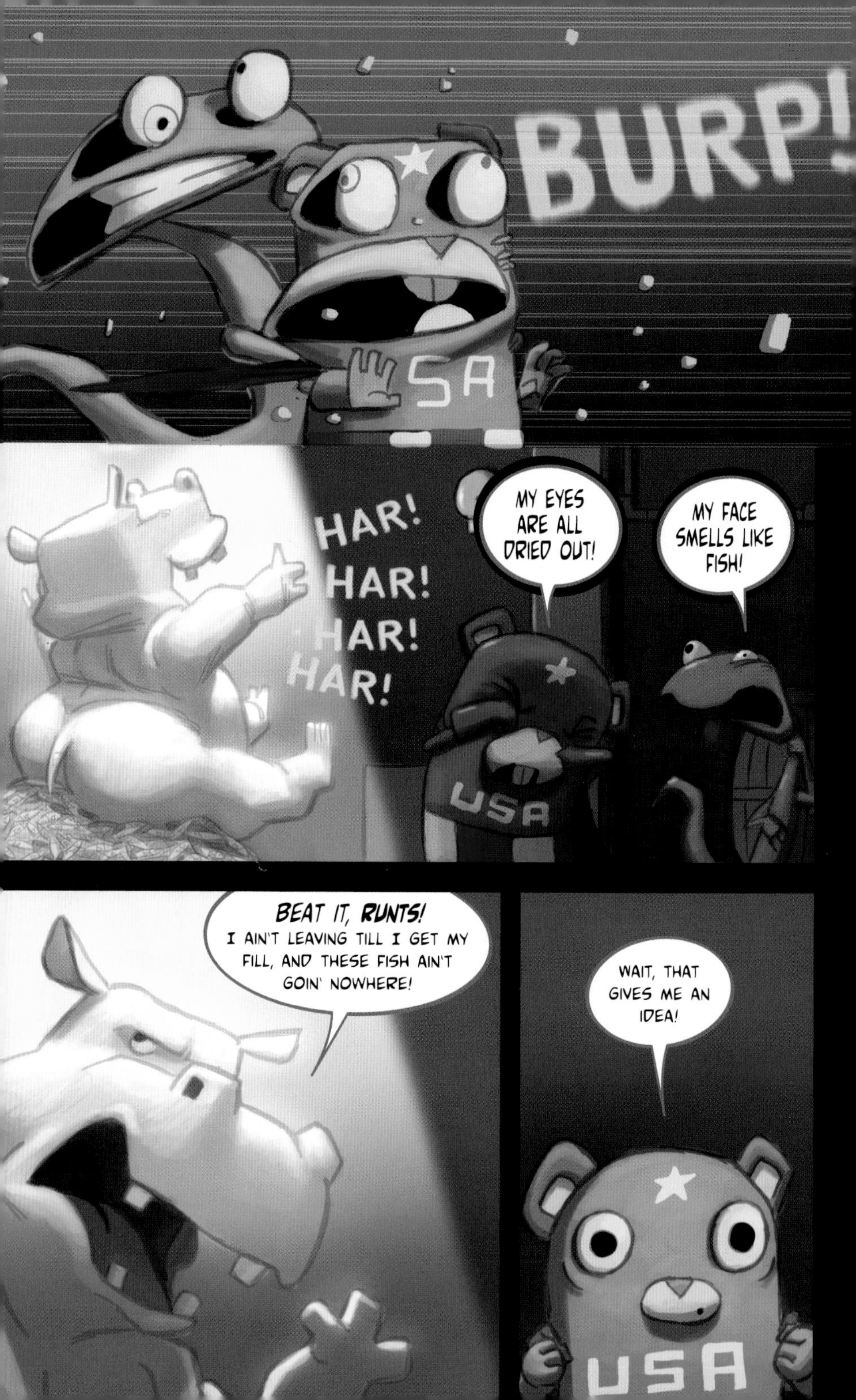
BURP!
HAR!
HAR!
HAR!
HAR!
MY EYES ARE ALL DRIED OUT!
MY FACE SMELLS LIKE FISH!
BEAT IT, RUNTS! I AIN'T LEAVING TILL I GET MY FILL, AND THESE FISH AIN'T GOIN' NOWHERE!
WAIT, THAT GIVES ME AN IDEA!

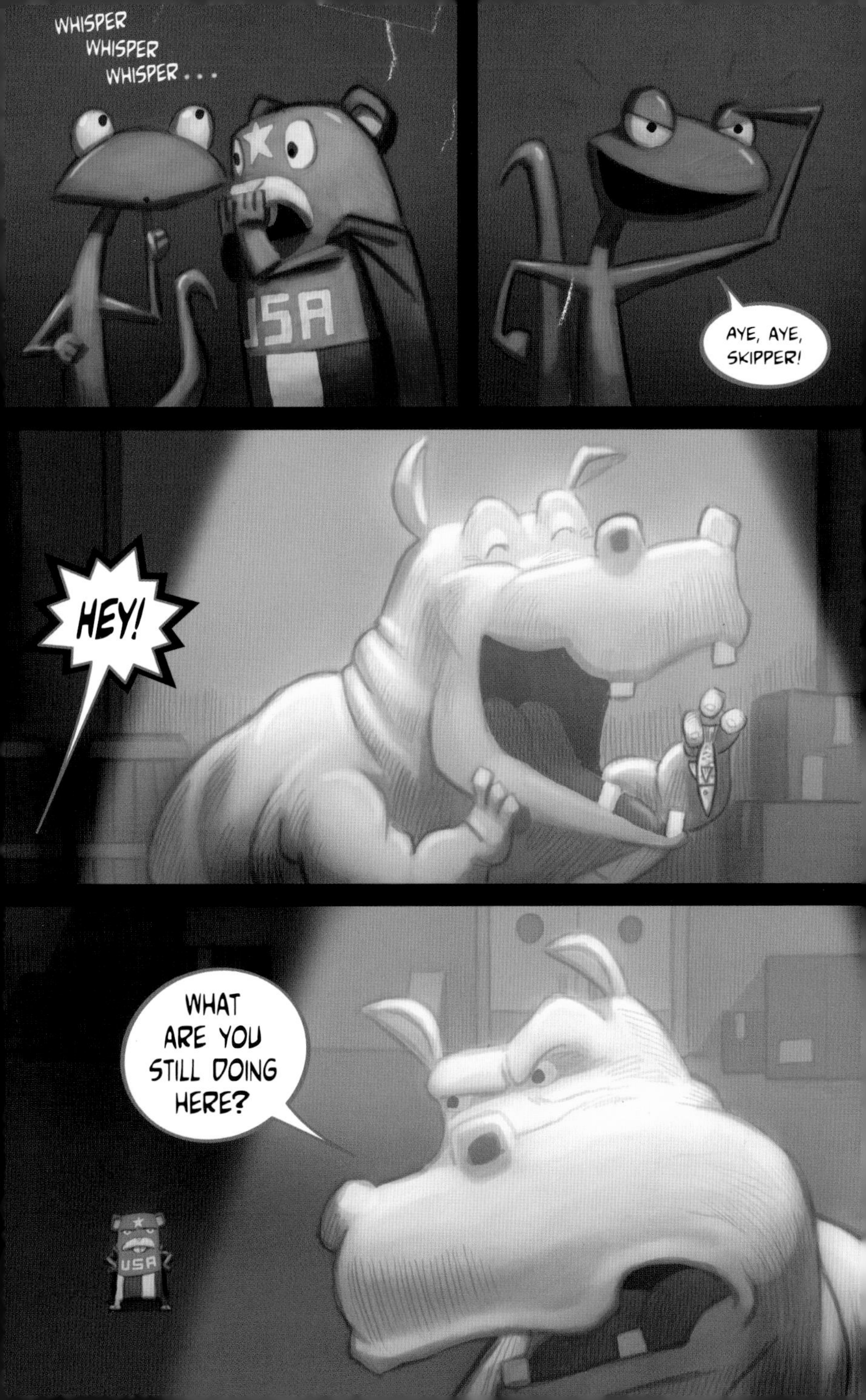
WHISPER
WHISPER
WHISPER . . .
USA
AYE, AYE, SKIPPER!
HEY!
WHAT ARE YOU STILL DOING HERE?
USA

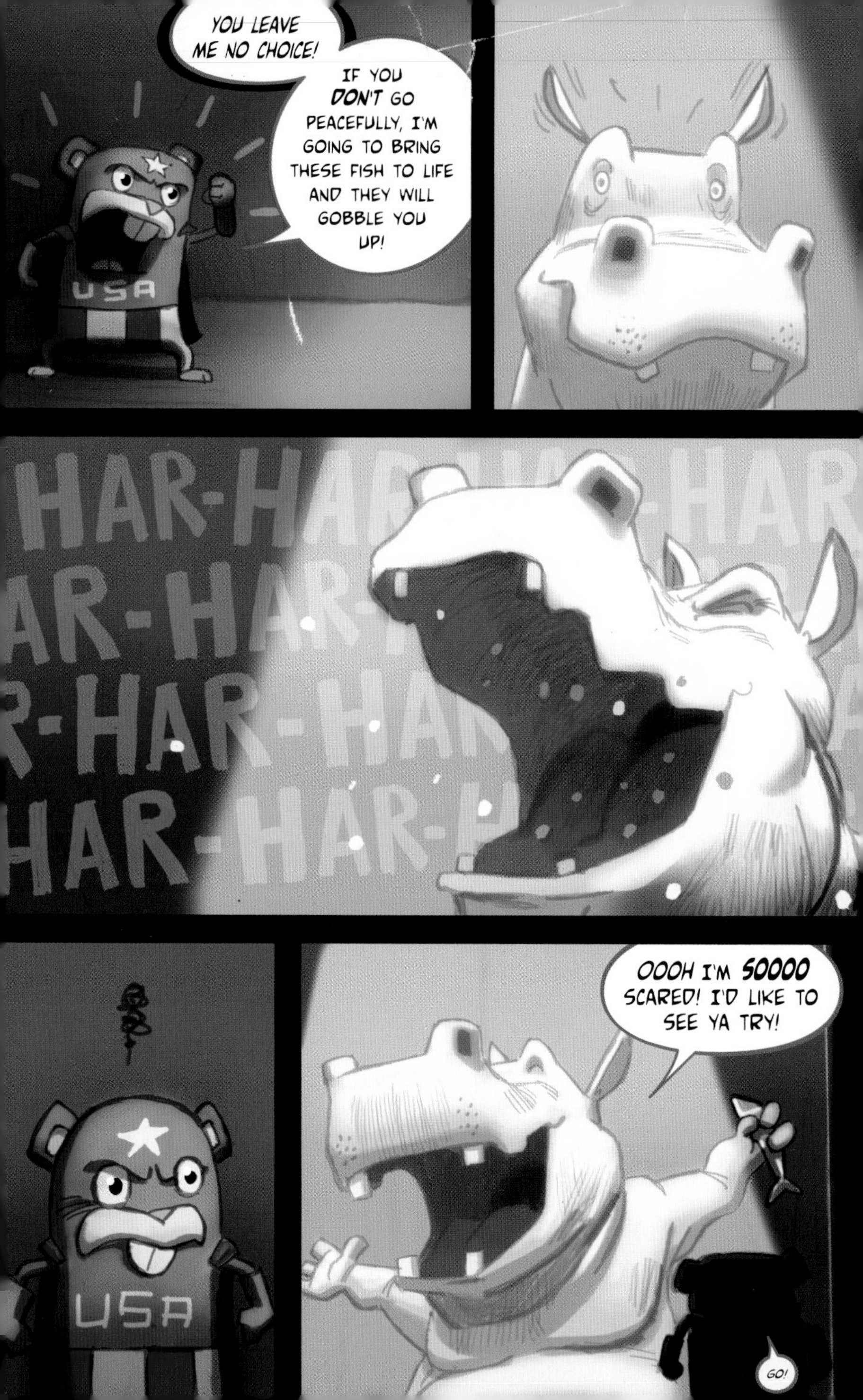
YOU LEAVE ME NO CHOICE!
IF YOU DON'T GO PEACEFULLY, I'M GOING TO BRING THESE FISH TO LIFE AND THEY WILL GOBBLE YOU UP!
HAR-HAR-HAR-HAR
AR-HAR-HAR-
R-HAR-HAR-HAR
HAR-HAR-
OOOH I'M SOOOO SCARED! I'D LIKE TO SEE YA TRY!
GO!

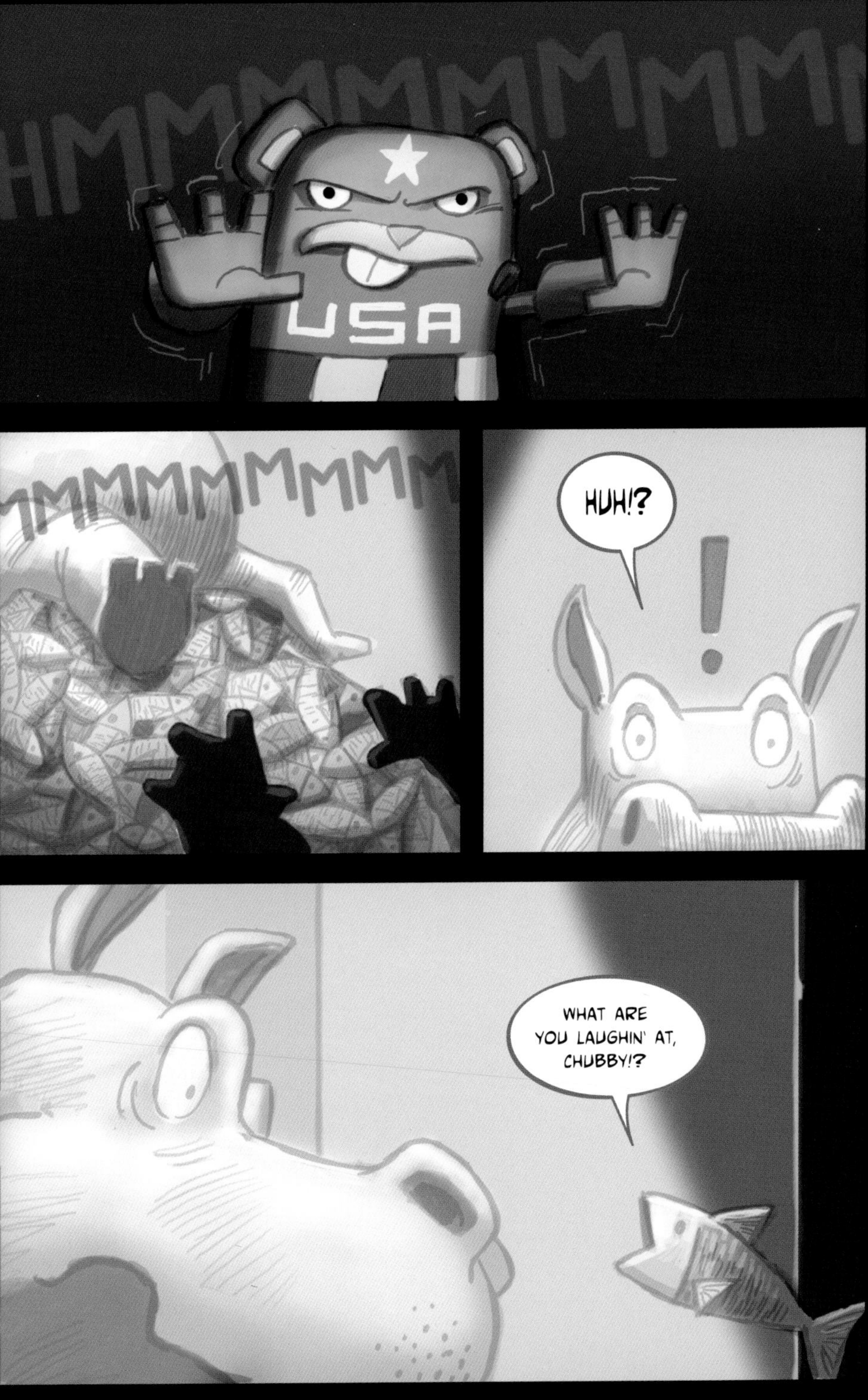
HMMMMMMMMMM
MMMMMMMMM
HUH!?
!
WHAT ARE YOU LAUGHIN' AT, CHUBBY!?

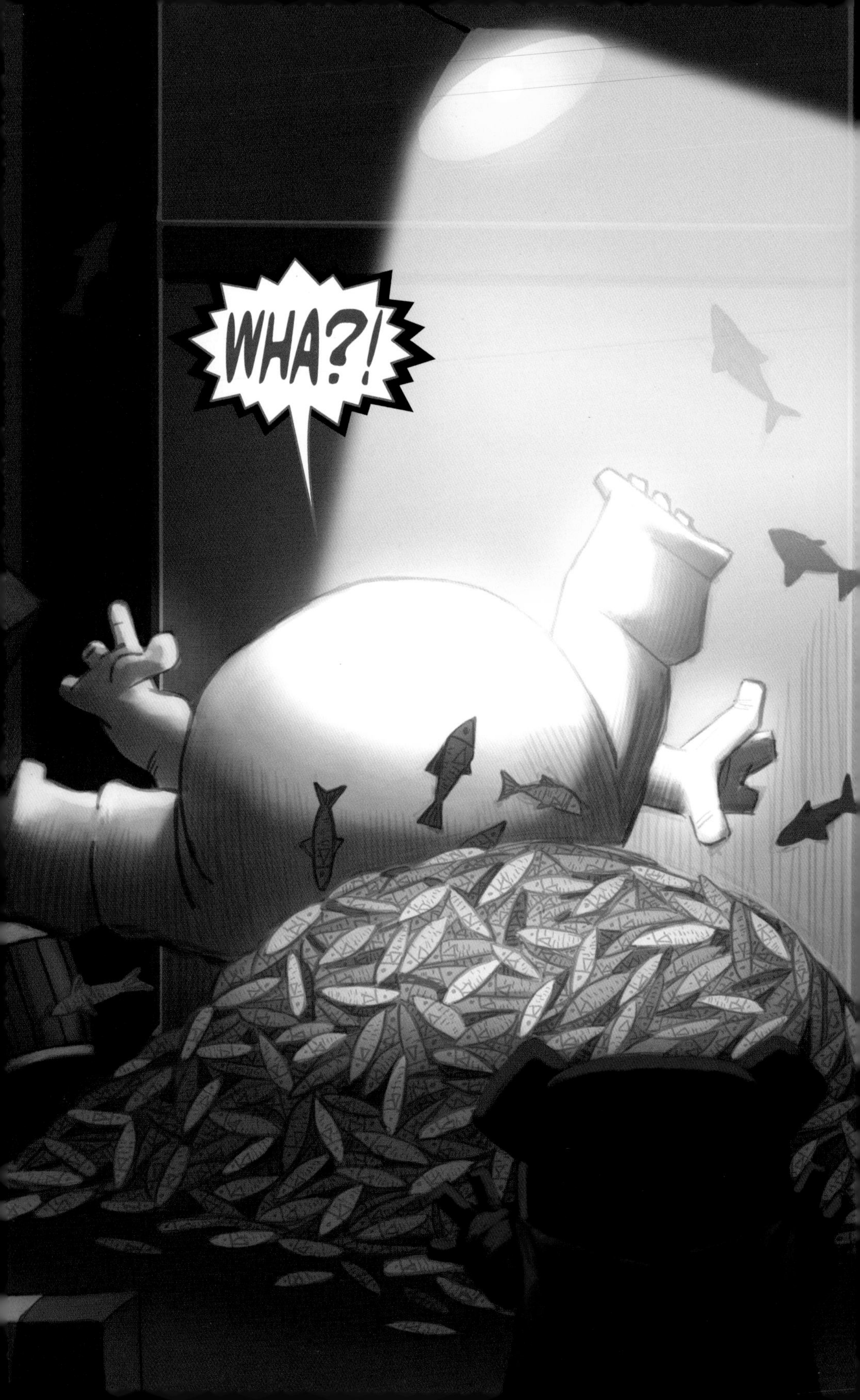
WHA?!

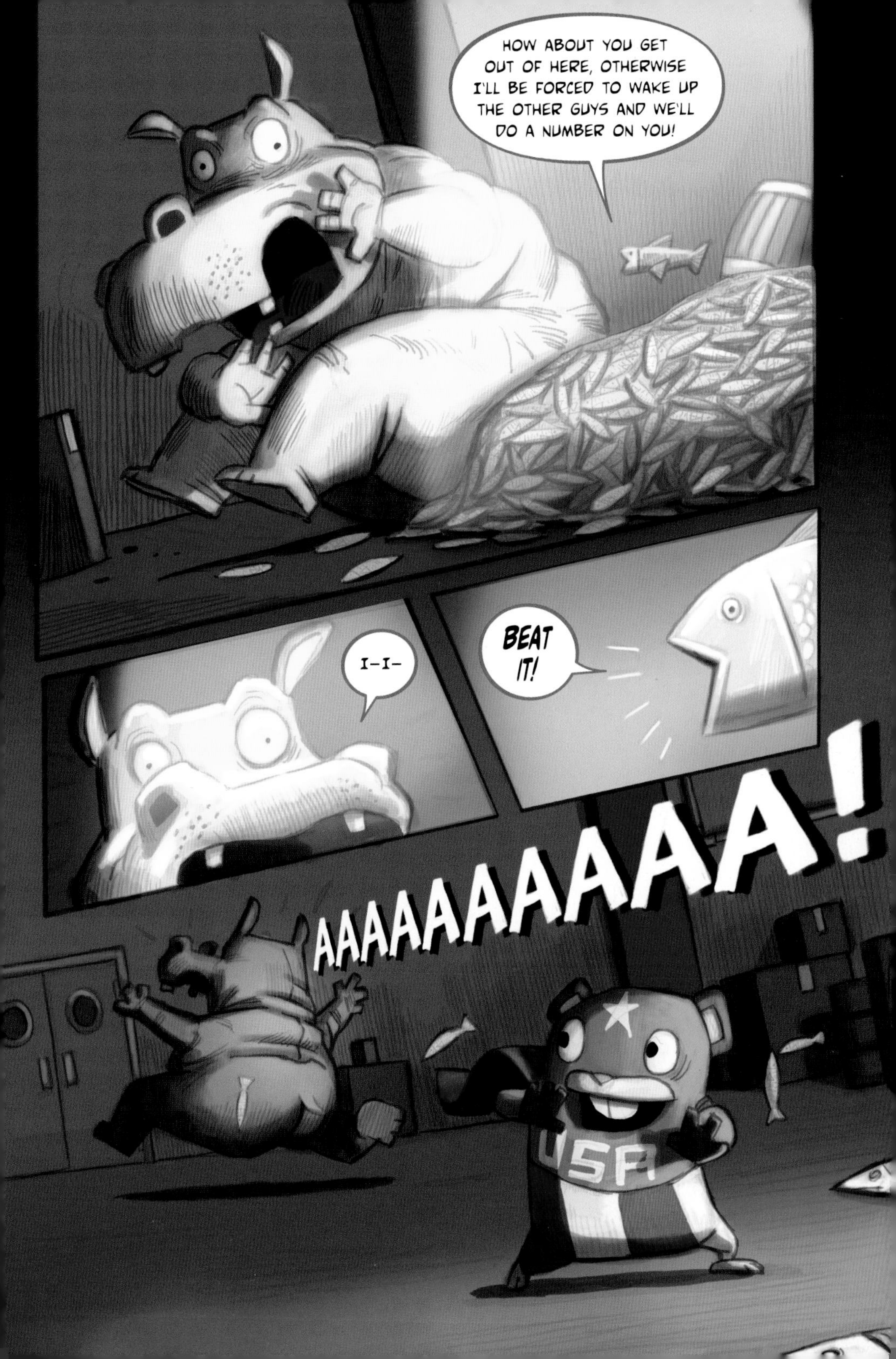
HOW ABOUT YOU GET OUT OF HERE, OTHERWISE I'LL BE FORCED TO WAKE UP THE OTHER GUYS AND WE'LL DO A NUMBER ON YOU!
I—I—
BEAT IT!
AAAAAAAAAAA!
USA

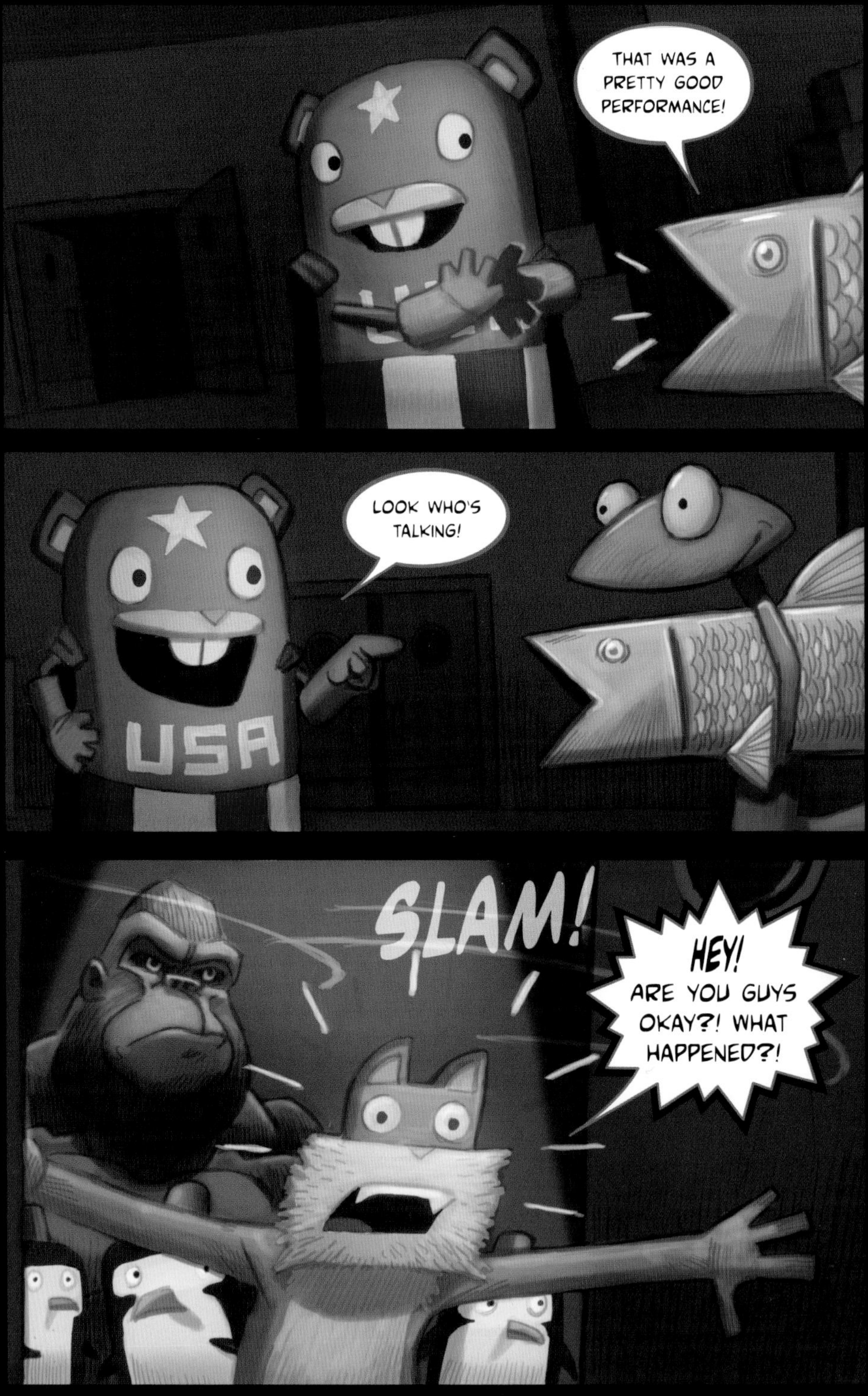
THAT WAS A PRETTY GOOD PERFORMANCE!
USA
LOOK WHO'S TALKING!
SLAM!
HEY! ARE YOU GUYS OKAY?! WHAT HAPPENED?!

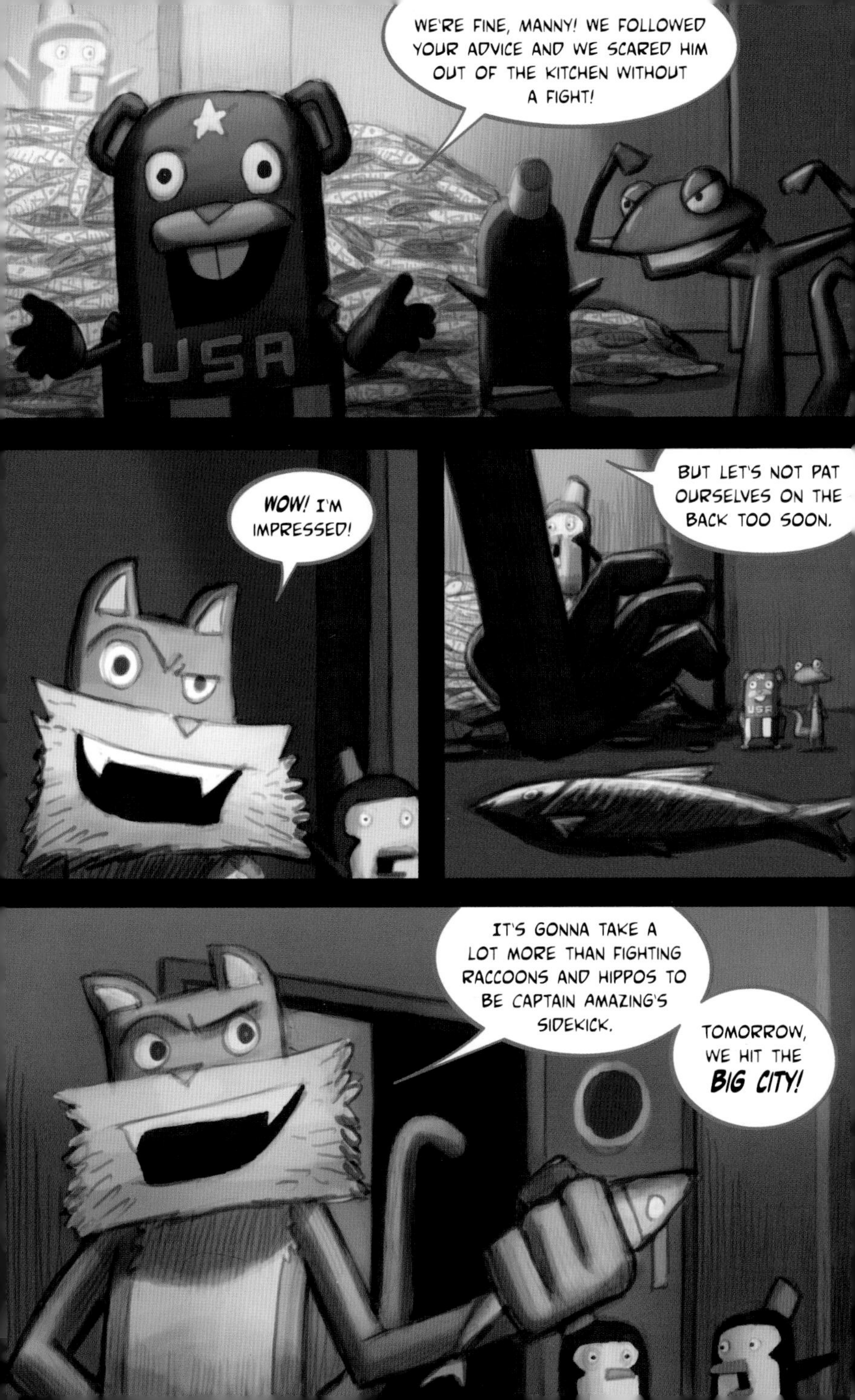
WE'RE FINE, MANNY! WE FOLLOWED YOUR ADVICE AND WE SCARED HIM OUT OF THE KITCHEN WITHOUT A FIGHT!
USA
WOW! I'M IMPRESSED!
BUT LET'S NOT PAT OURSELVES ON THE BACK TOO SOON.
IT'S GONNA TAKE A LOT MORE THAN FIGHTING RACCOONS AND HIPPOS TO BE CAPTAIN AMAZING'S SIDEKICK.
TOMORROW, WE HIT THE BIG CITY!

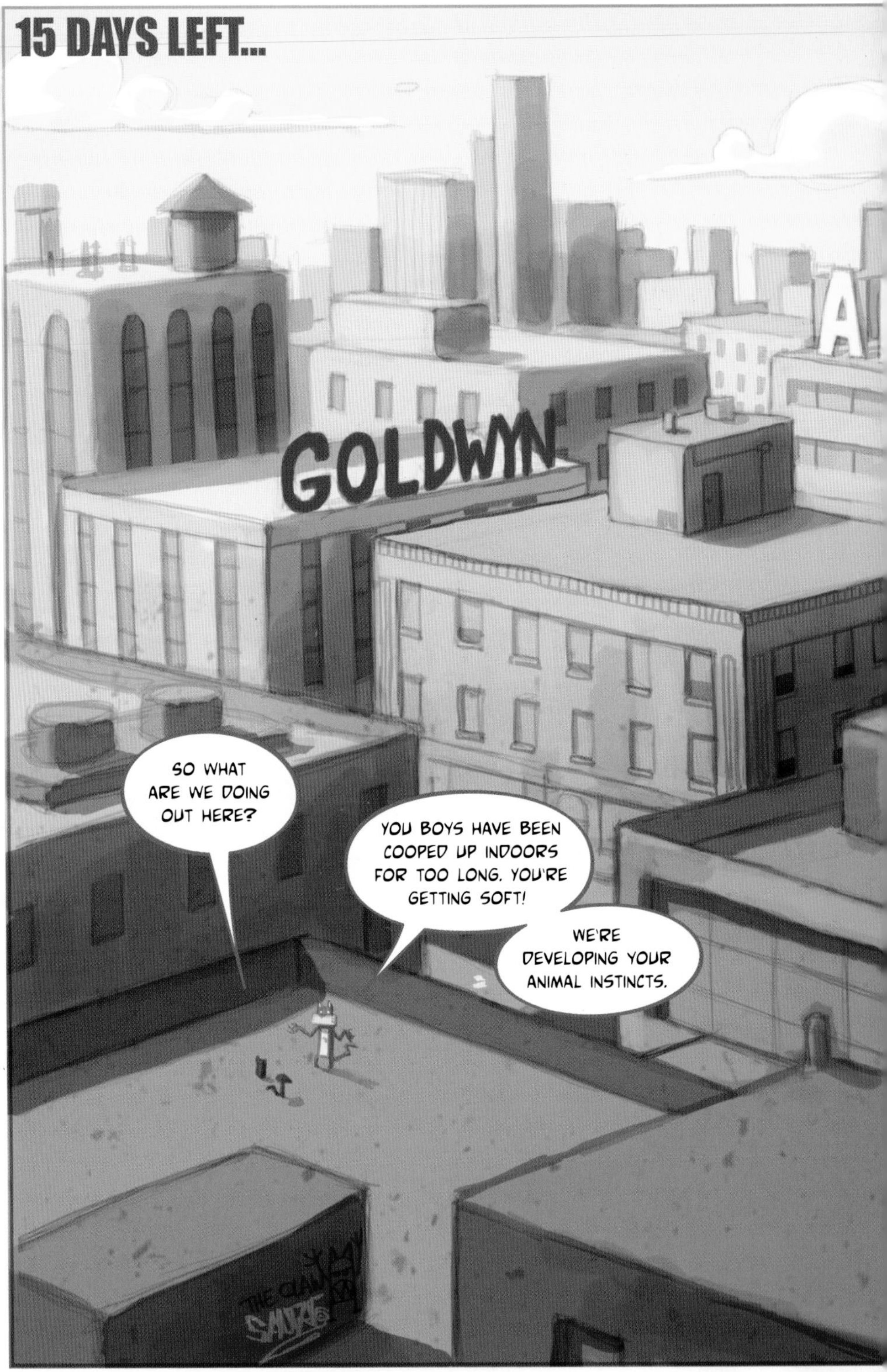
15 DAYS LEFT...
GOLDWYN
SO WHAT ARE WE DOING OUT HERE?
YOU BOYS HAVE BEEN COOPED UP INDOORS FOR TOO LONG. YOU'RE GETTING SOFT!
WE'RE DEVELOPING YOUR ANIMAL INSTINCTS.

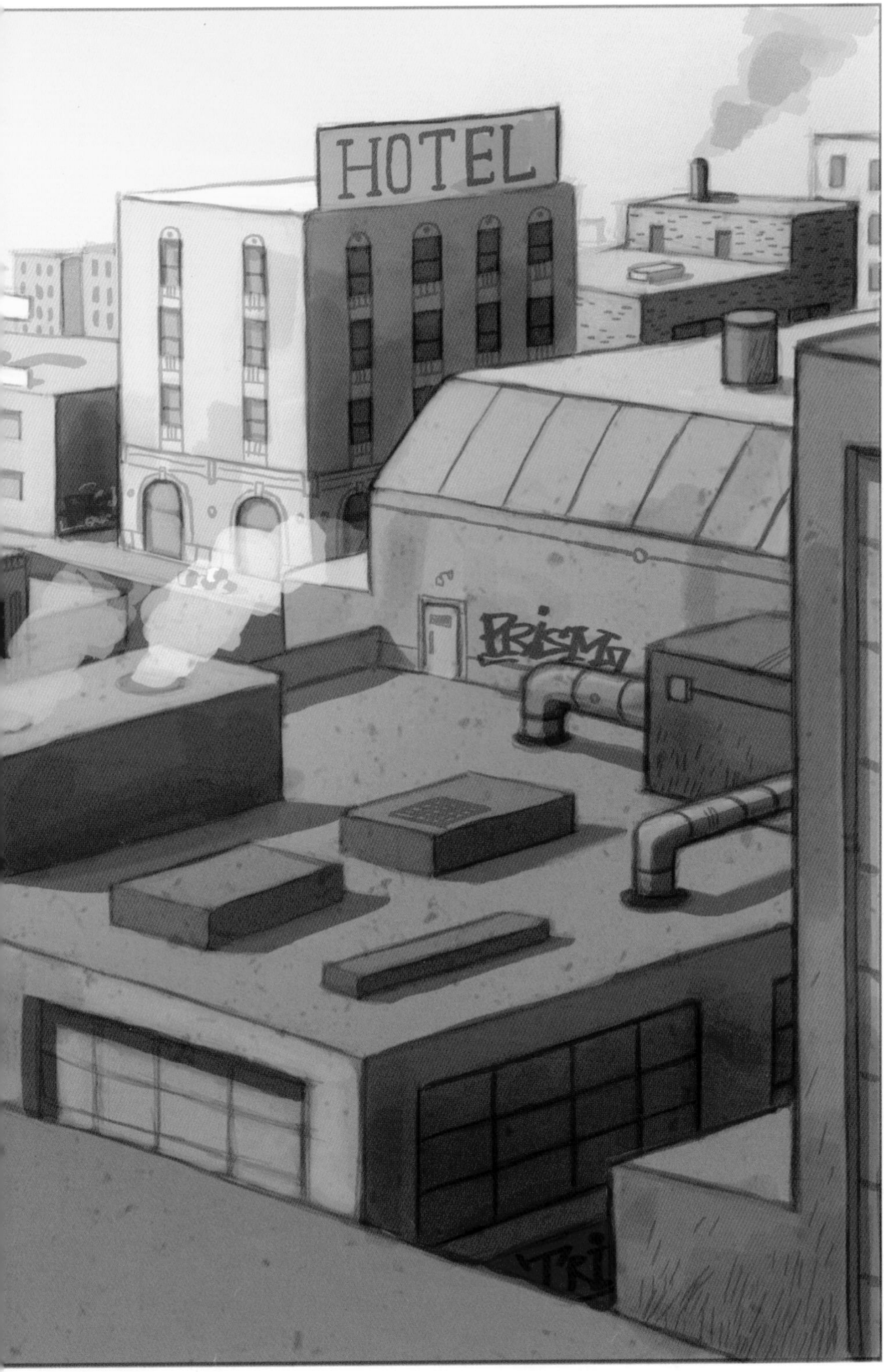
HOTEL

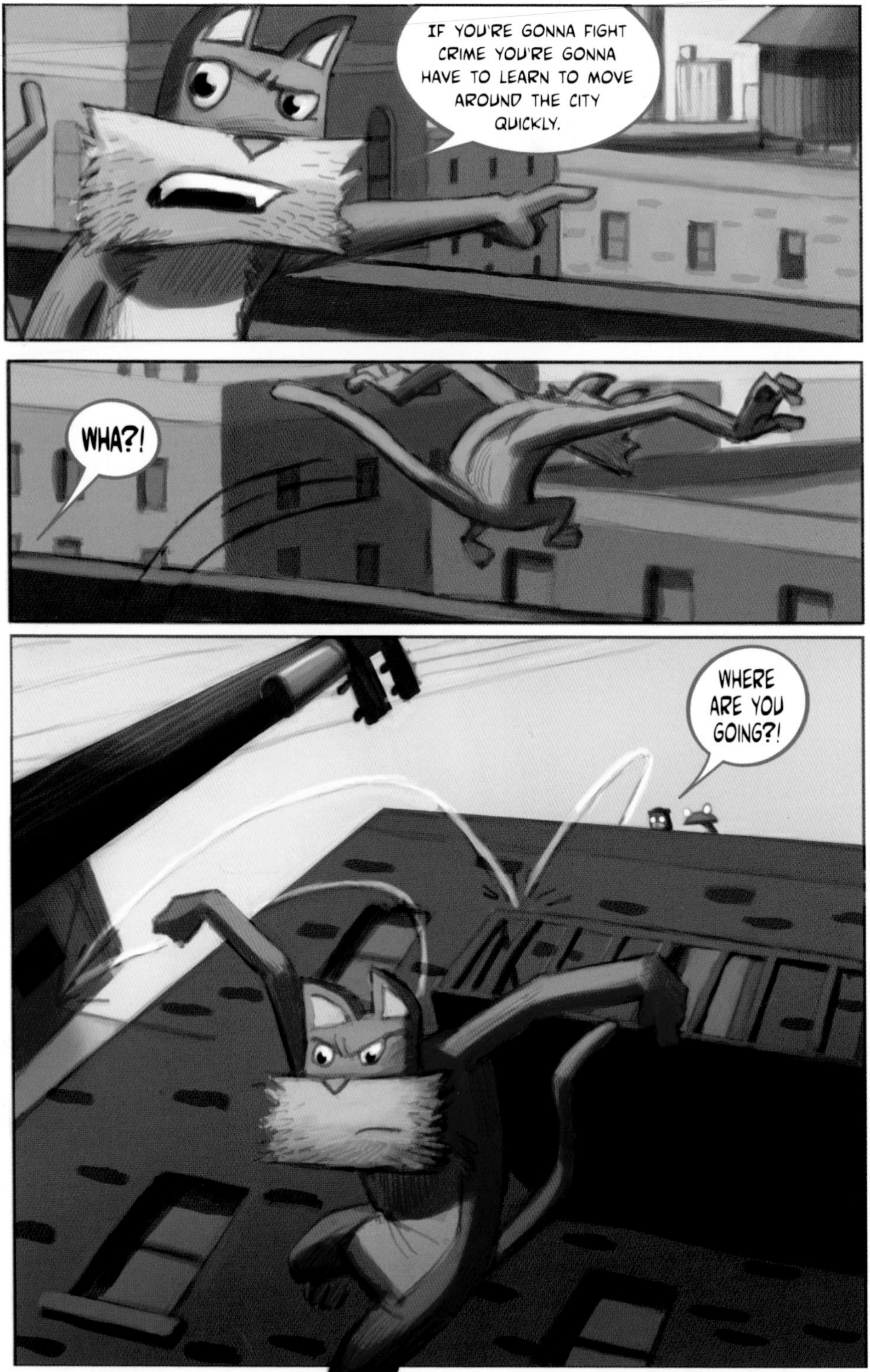
IF YOU'RE GONNA FIGHT CRIME YOU'RE GONNA HAVE TO LEARN TO MOVE AROUND THE CITY QUICKLY.
WHA?!
WHERE ARE YOU GOING?!

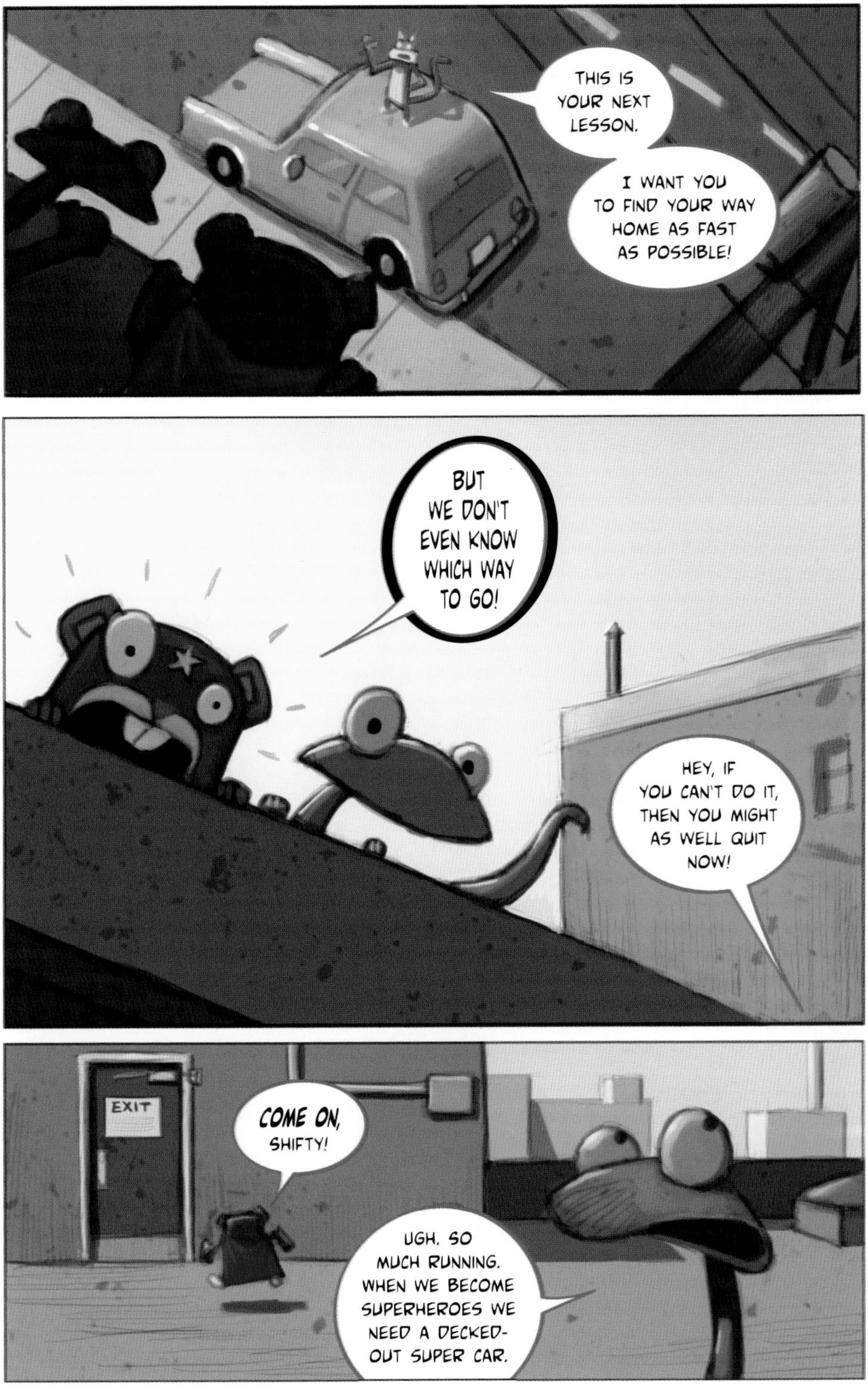
THIS IS YOUR NEXT LESSON.
I WANT YOU TO FIND YOUR WAY HOME AS FAST AS POSSIBLE!
BUT WE DON'T EVEN KNOW WHICH WAY TO GO!
HEY, IF YOU CAN'T DO IT, THEN YOU MIGHT AS WELL QUIT NOW!
EXIT
COME ON, SHIFTY!
UGH. SO MUCH RUNNING. WHEN WE BECOME SUPERHEROES WE NEED A DECKED-OUT SUPER CAR.

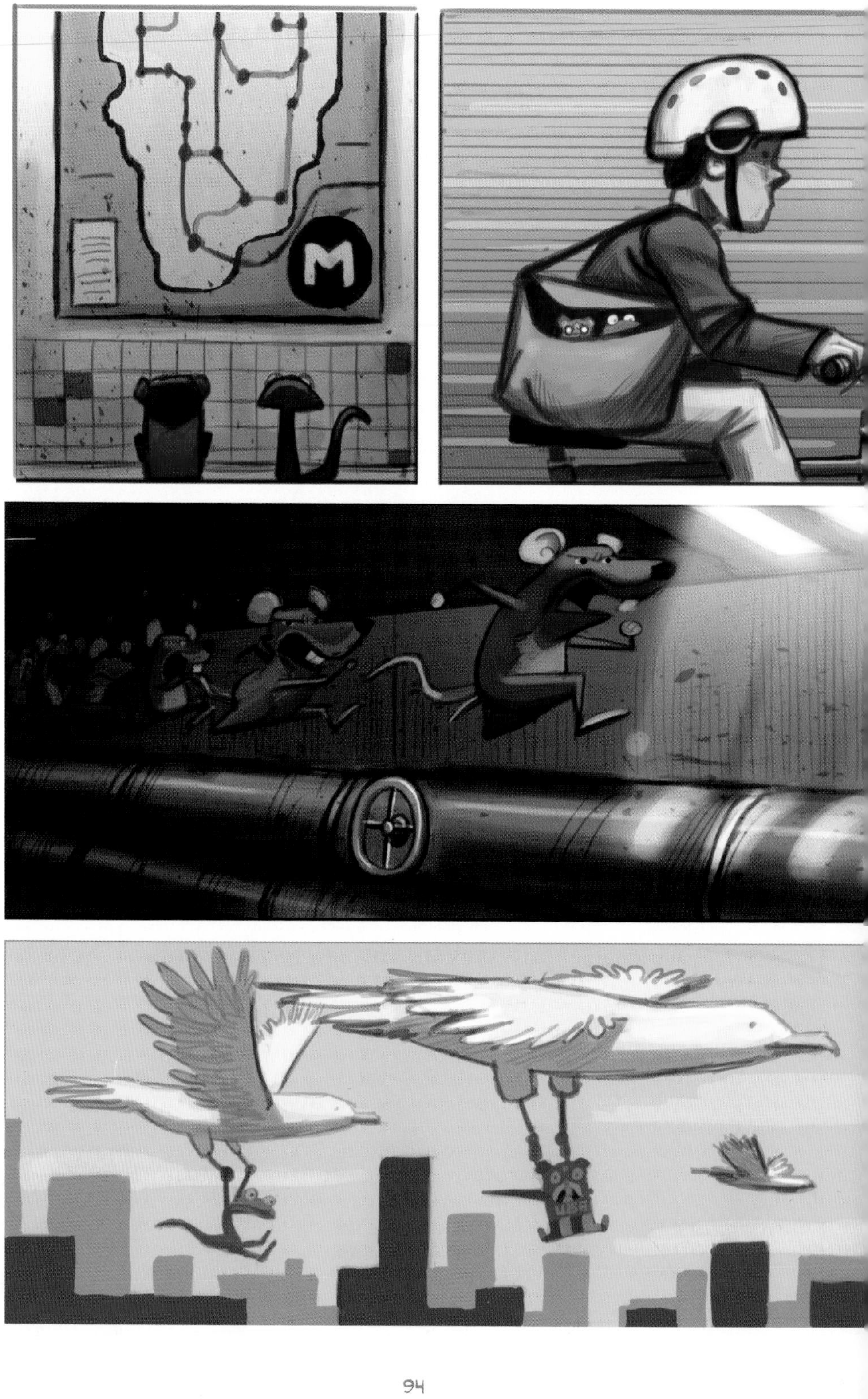
M

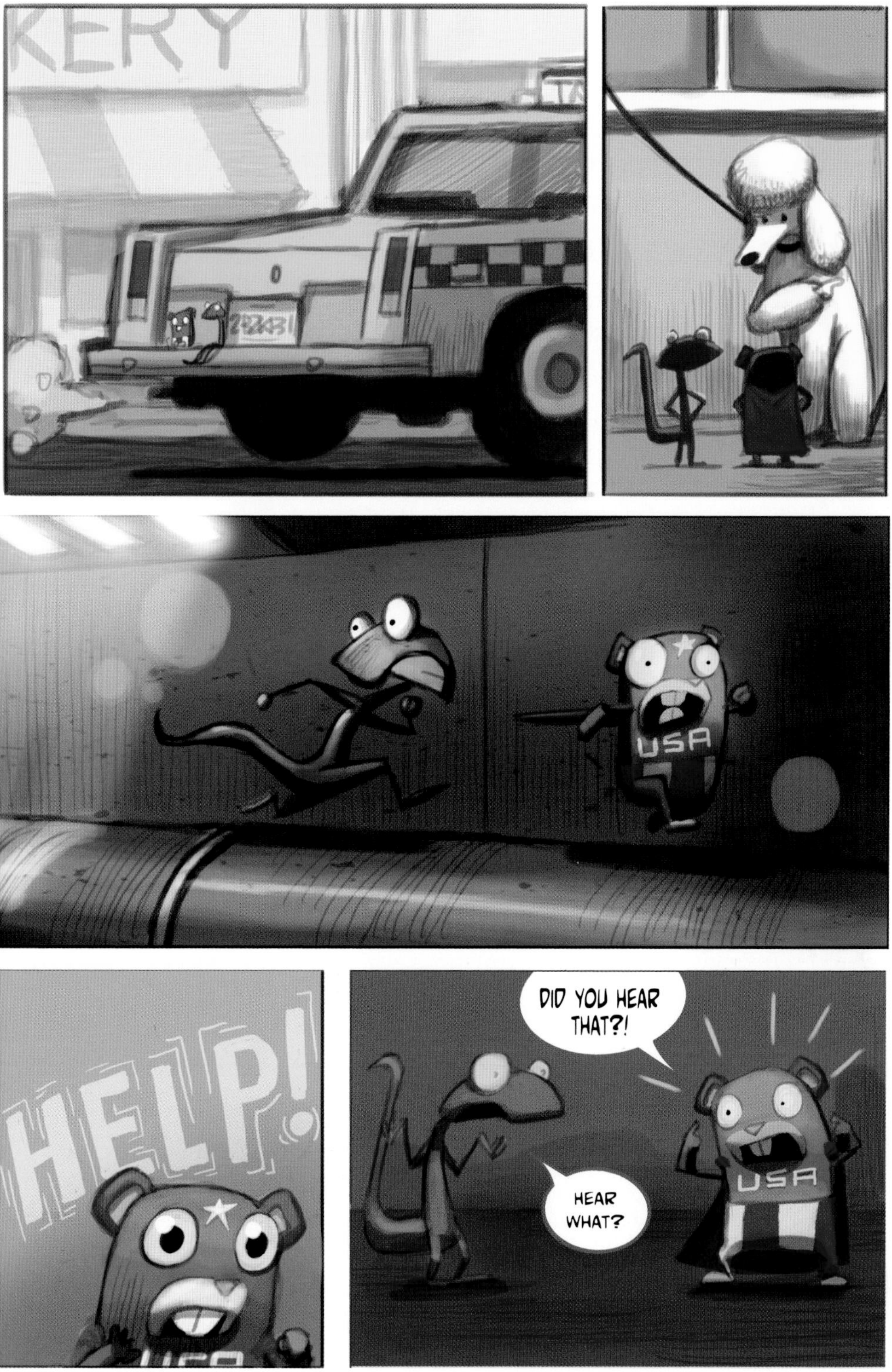
KERY
HELP!
DID YOU HEAR THAT?!
HEAR WHAT?

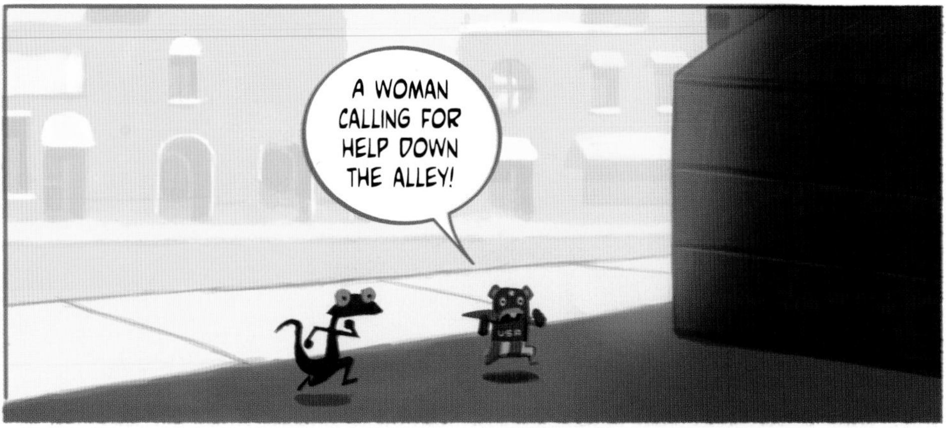
A WOMAN CALLING FOR HELP DOWN THE ALLEY!
USA

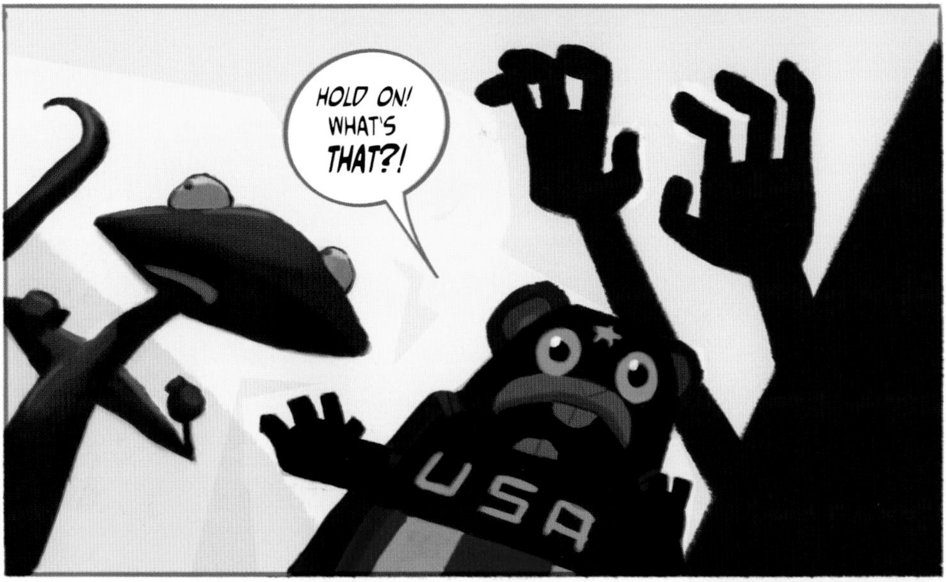
HOLD ON! WHAT'S THAT?!
USA

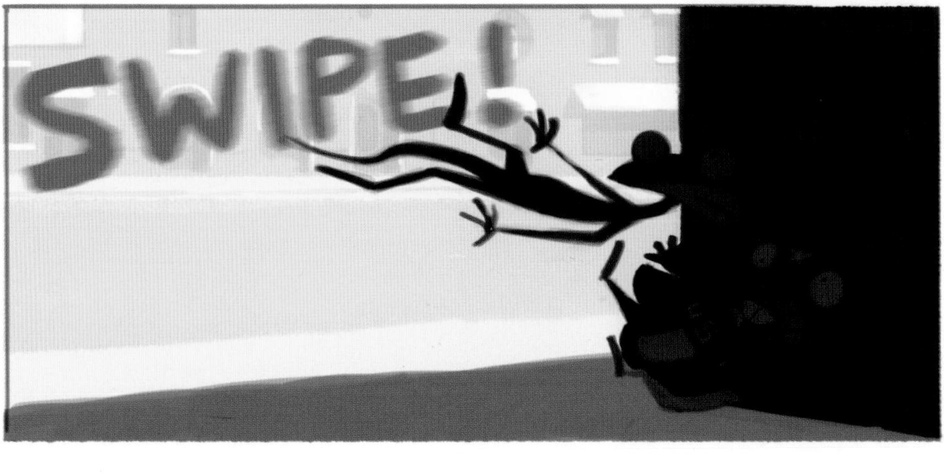
SWIPE!

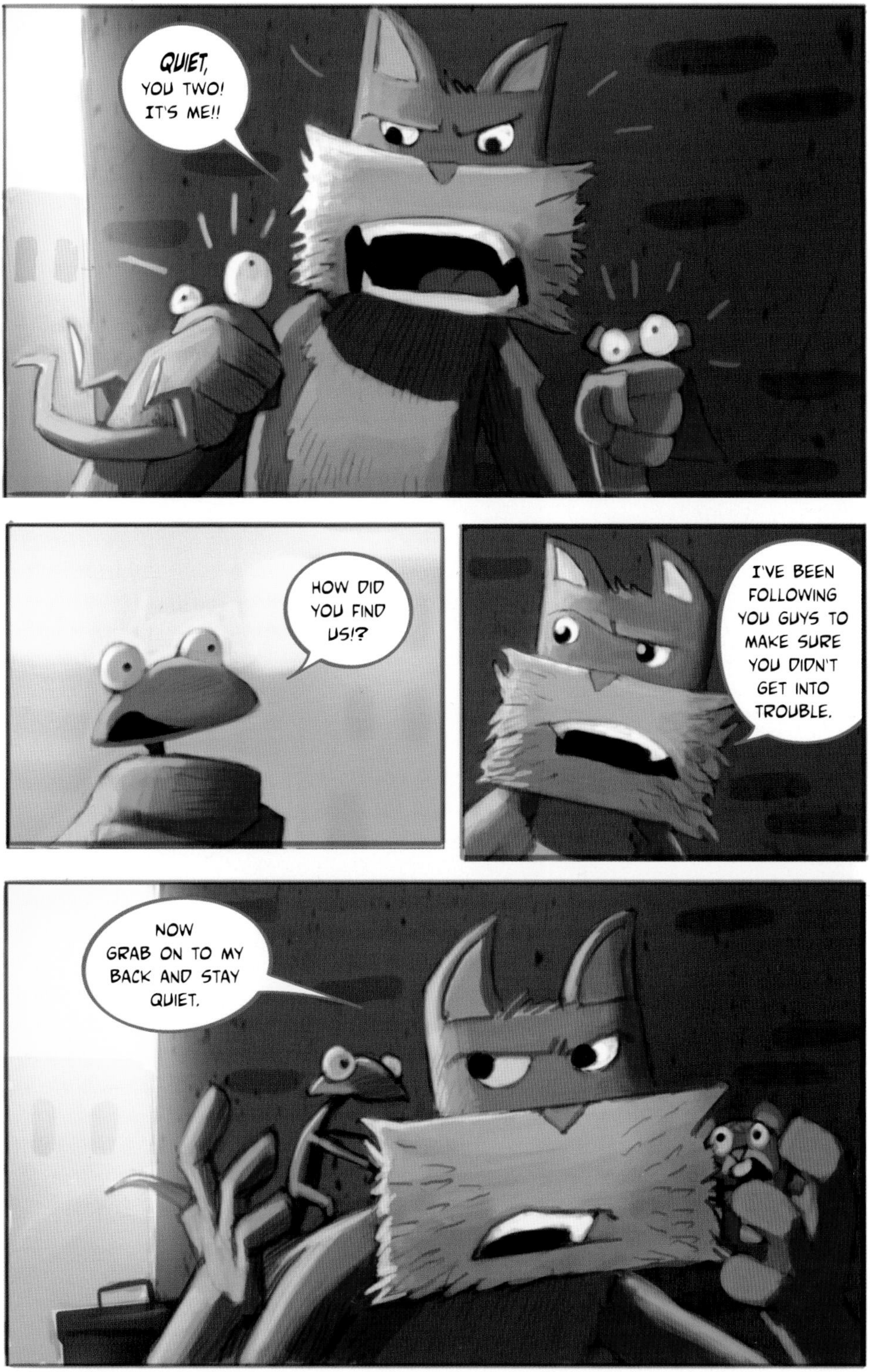
QUIET, YOU TWO! IT'S ME!!
HOW DID YOU FIND US!?
I'VE BEEN FOLLOWING YOU GUYS TO MAKE SURE YOU DIDN'T GET INTO TROUBLE.
NOW GRAB ON TO MY BACK AND STAY QUIET.

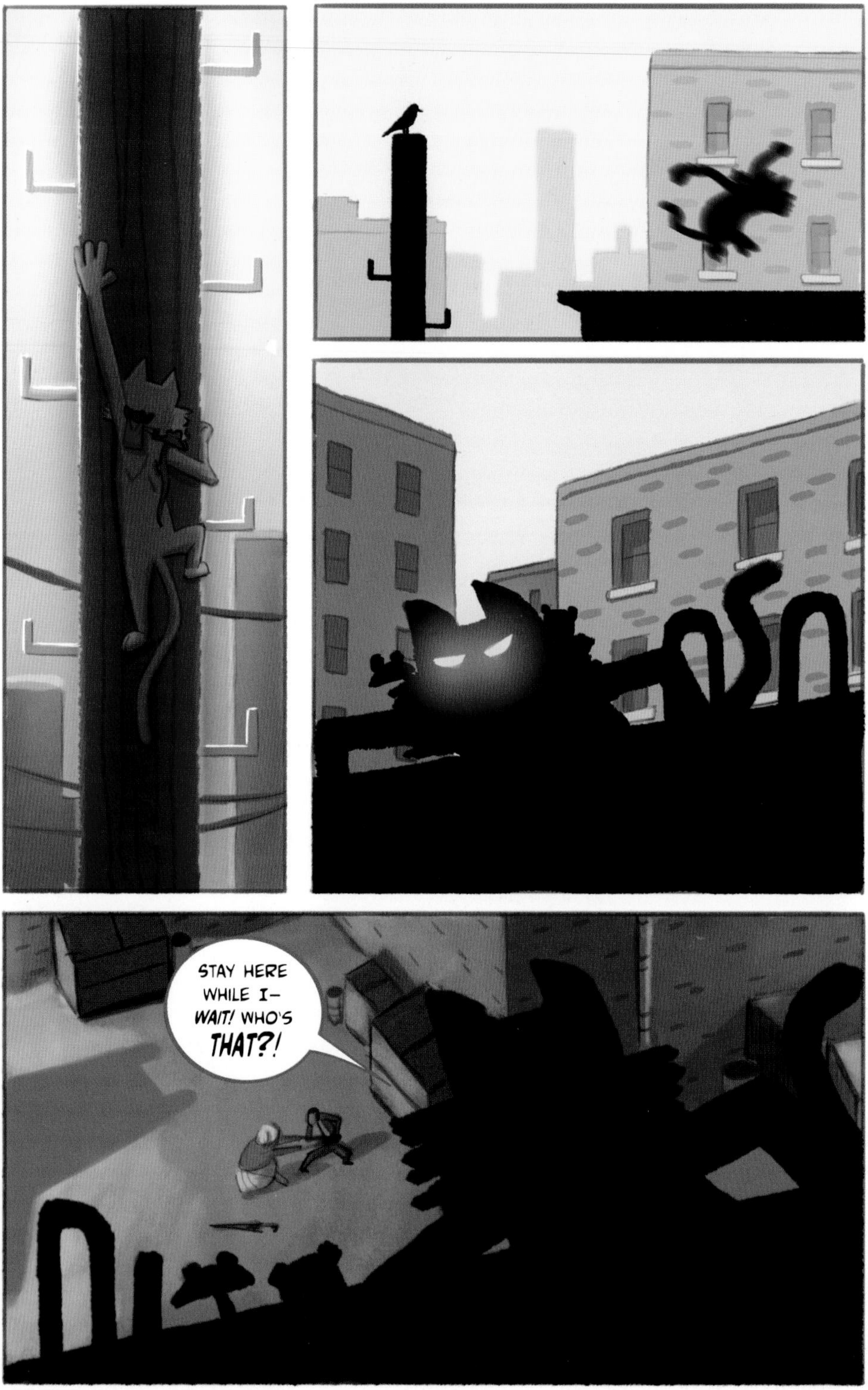
STAY HERE WHILE I— WAIT! WHO'S THAT?!

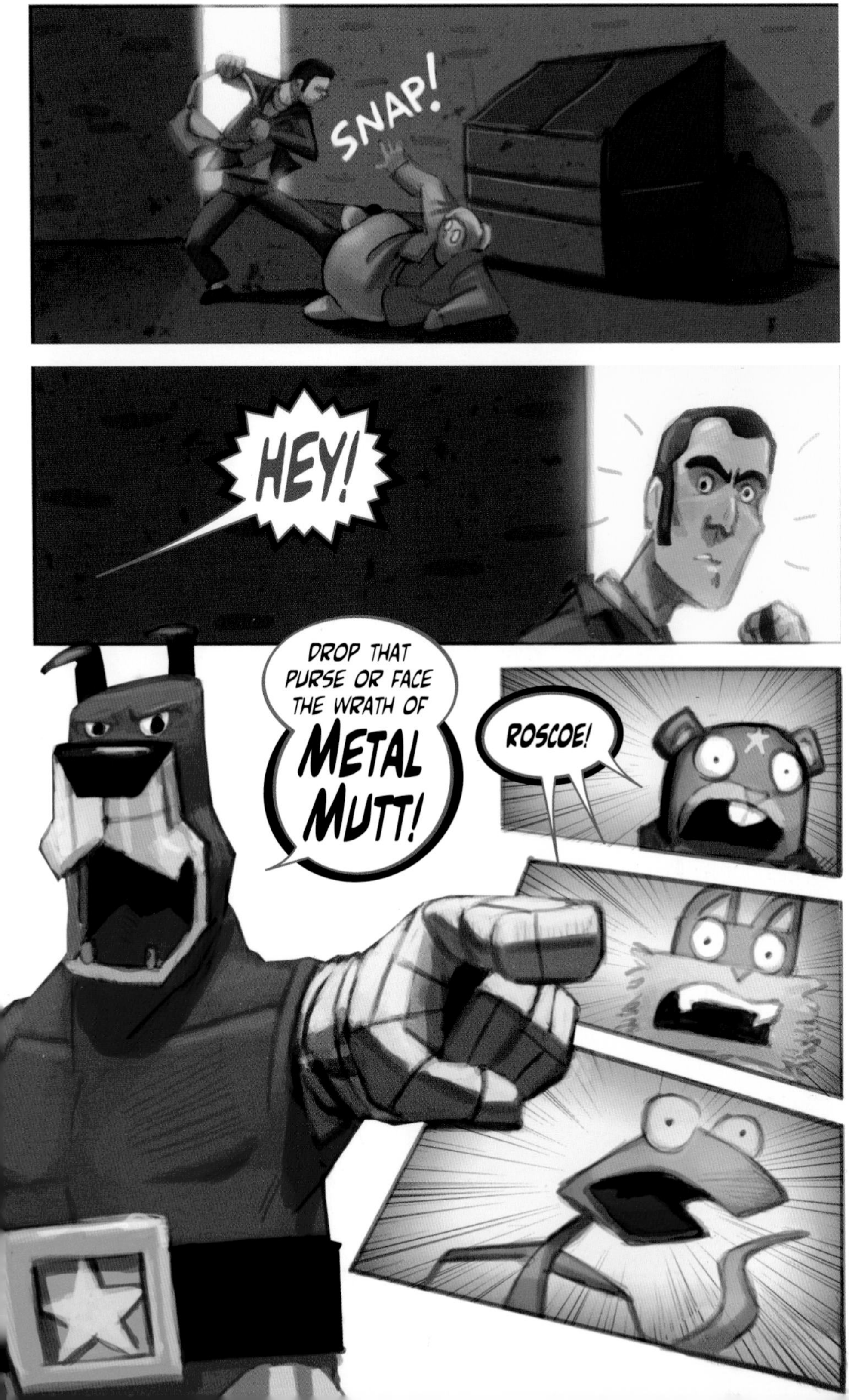
SNAP!
HEY!
DROP THAT PURSE OR FACE THE WRATH OF METAL MUTT!
ROSCOE!

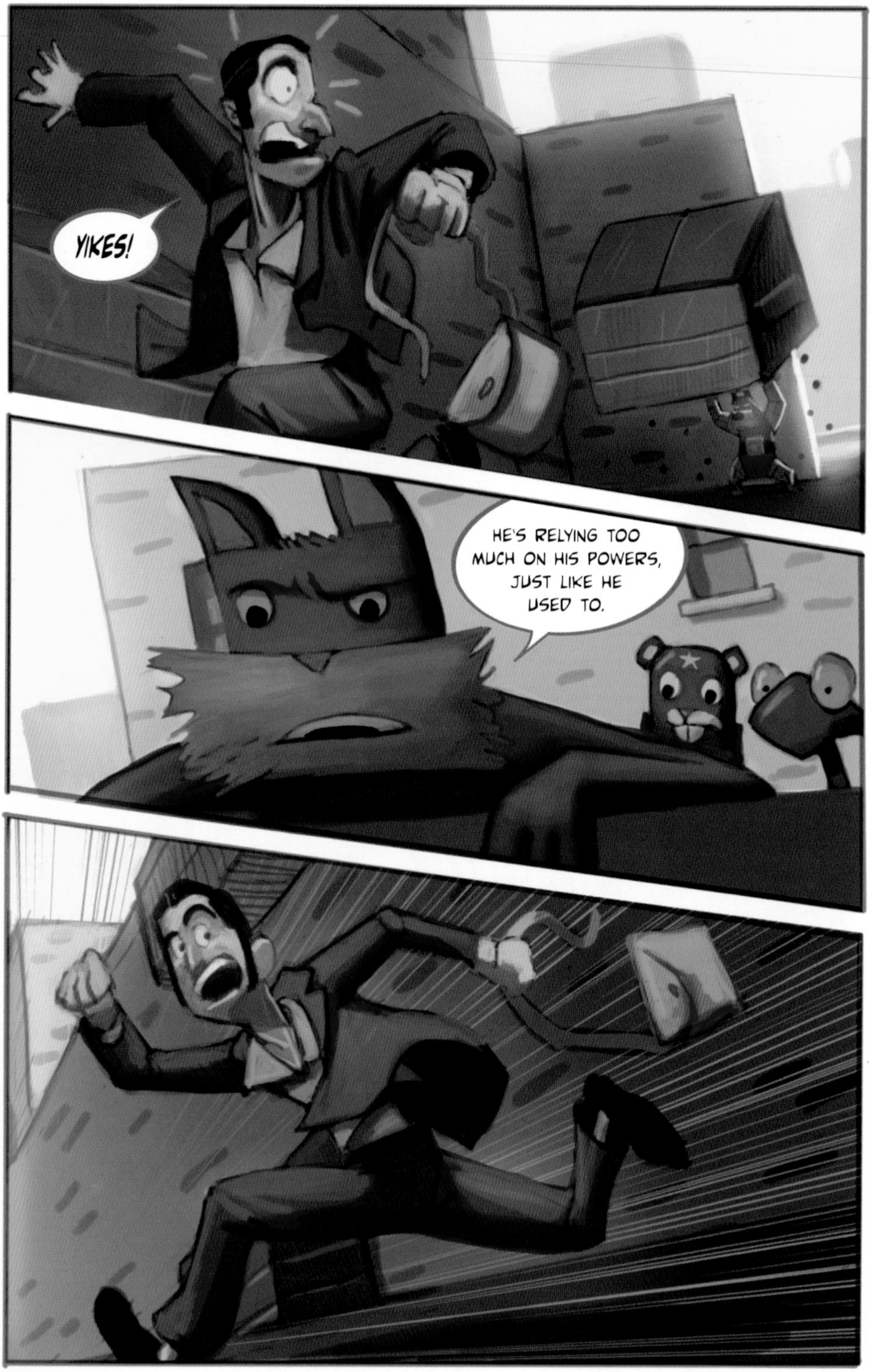
YIKES!
HE'S RELYING TOO MUCH ON HIS POWERS, JUST LIKE HE USED TO.

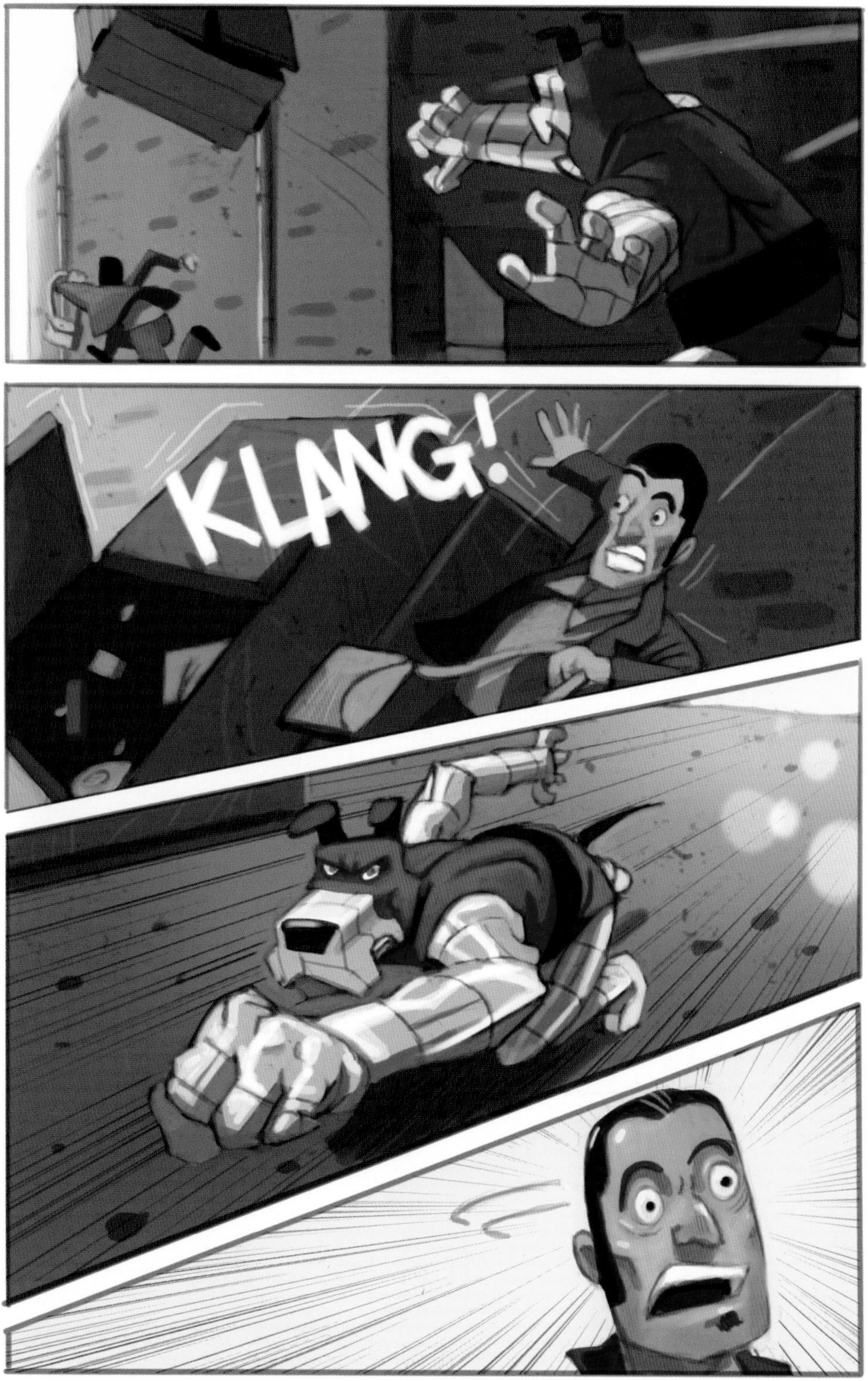
KLANG!

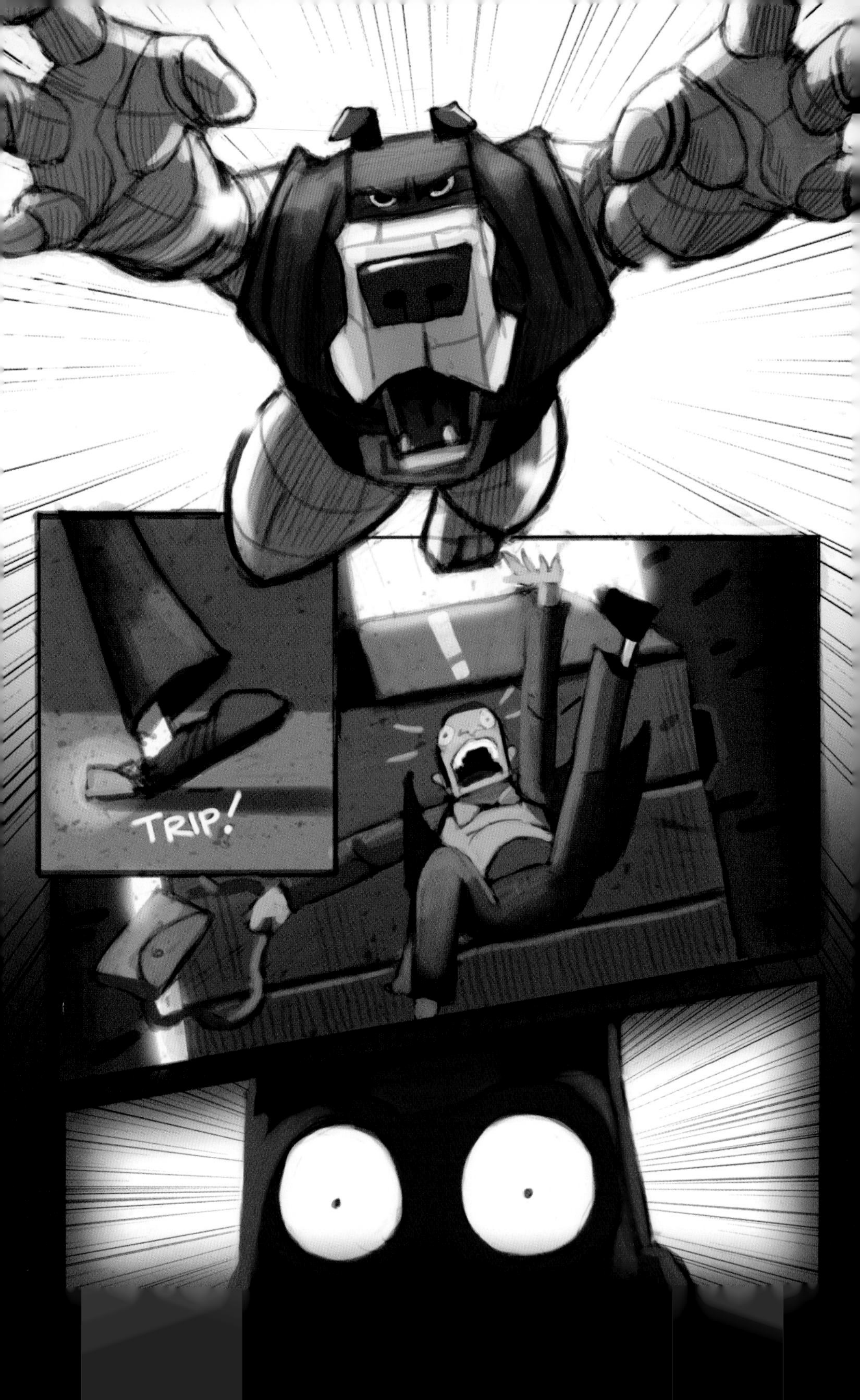
TRIP!

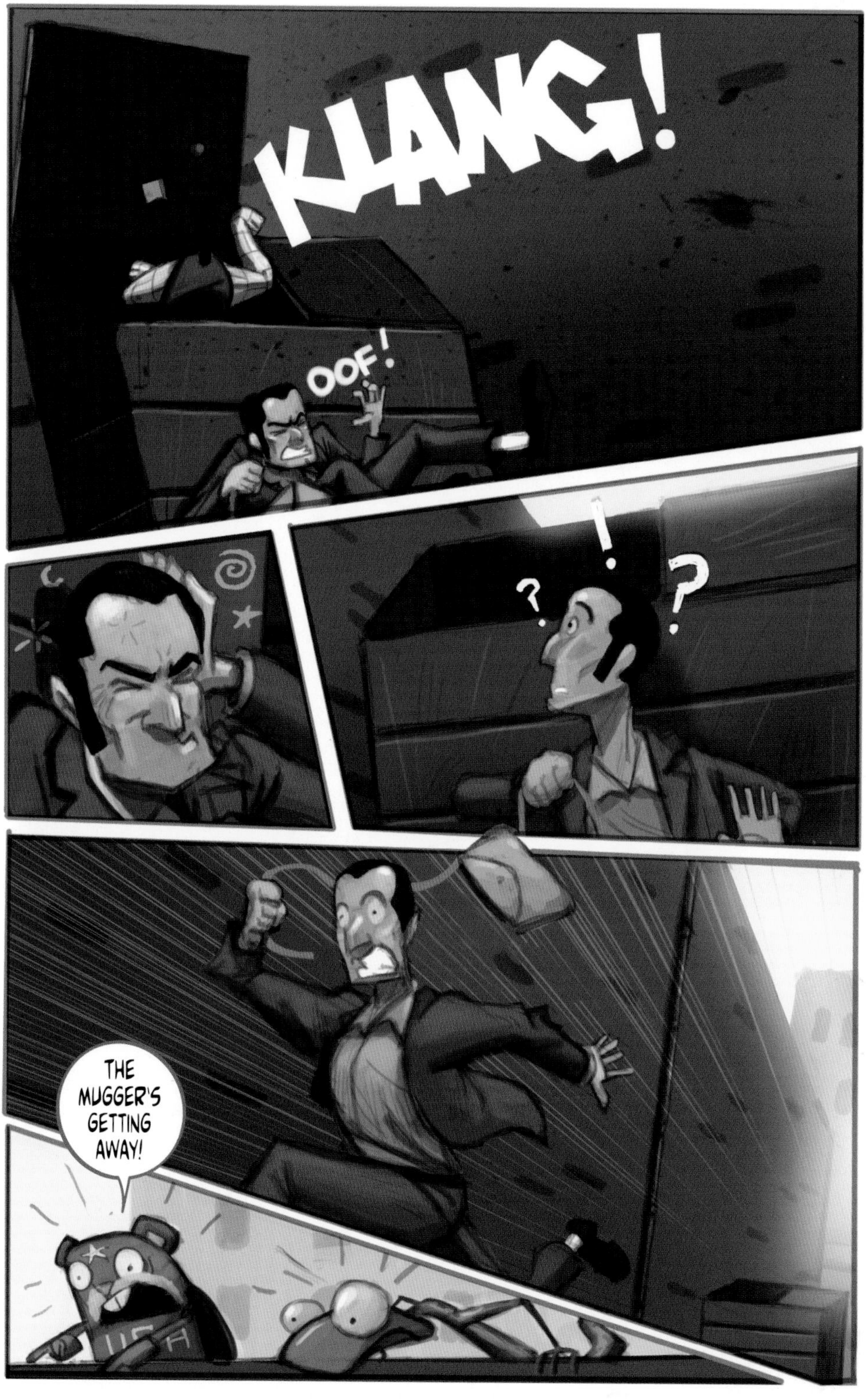
KLANG!
OOF!
?
!
?
THE MUGGER'S GETTING AWAY!

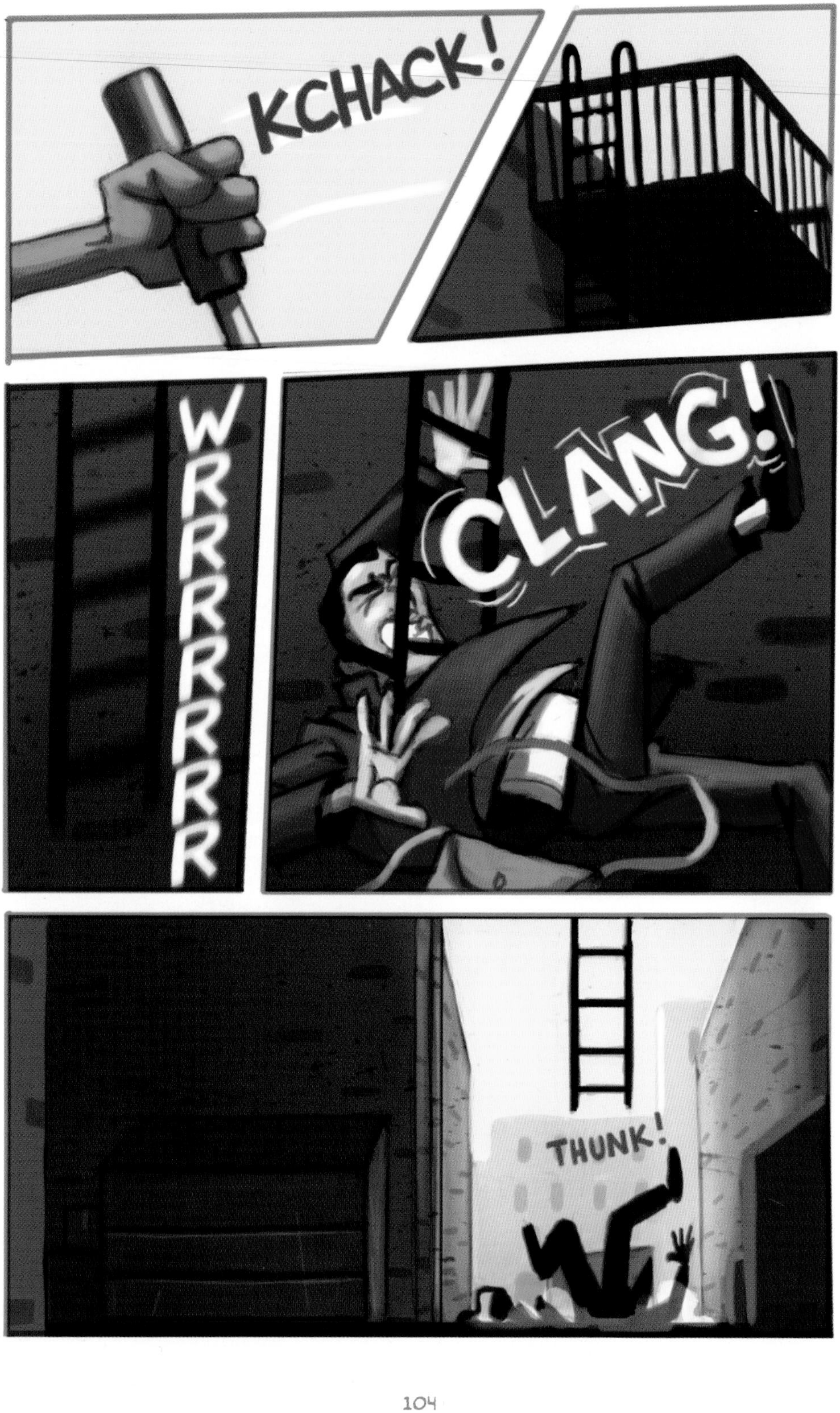
KCHACK!
WRRRRRRR
CLANG!
THUNK!

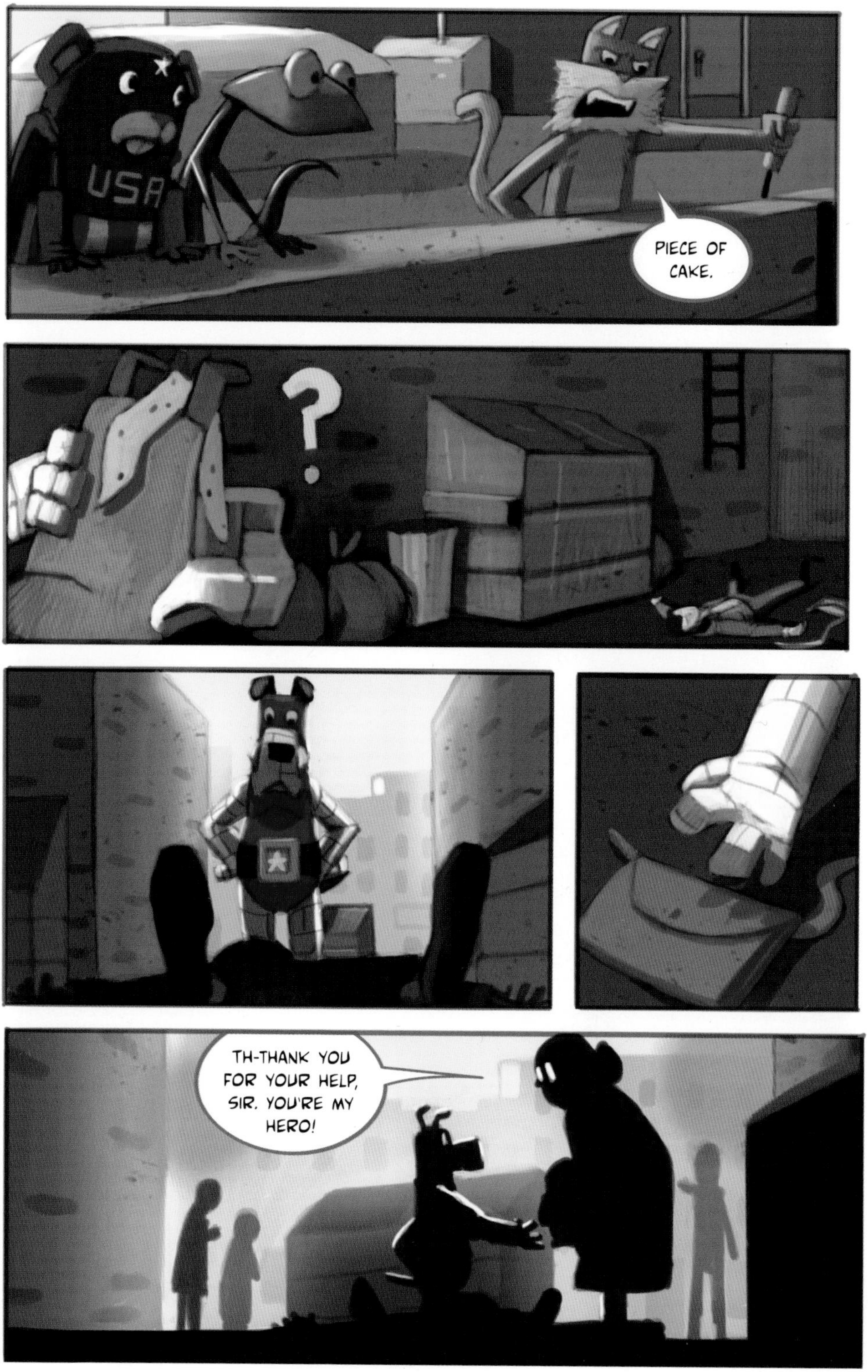
PIECE OF CAKE.
?
TH-THANK YOU FOR YOUR HELP, SIR. YOU'RE MY HERO!

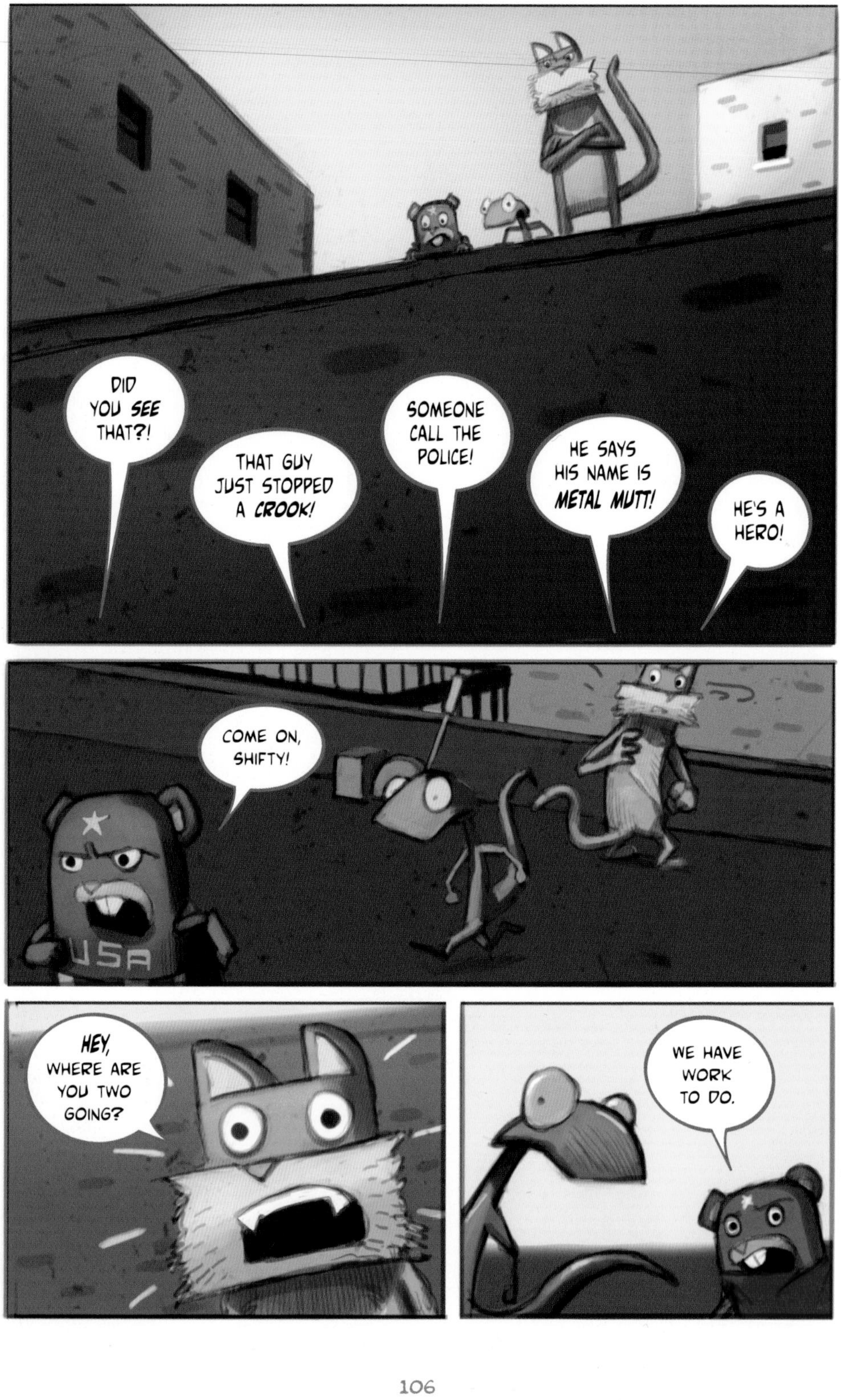
DID YOU SEE THAT?!
THAT GUY JUST STOPPED A CROOK!
SOMEONE CALL THE POLICE!
HE SAYS HIS NAME IS METAL MUTT!
HE'S A HERO!
USA
COME ON, SHIFTY!
HEY, WHERE ARE YOU TWO GOING?
WE HAVE WORK TO DO.

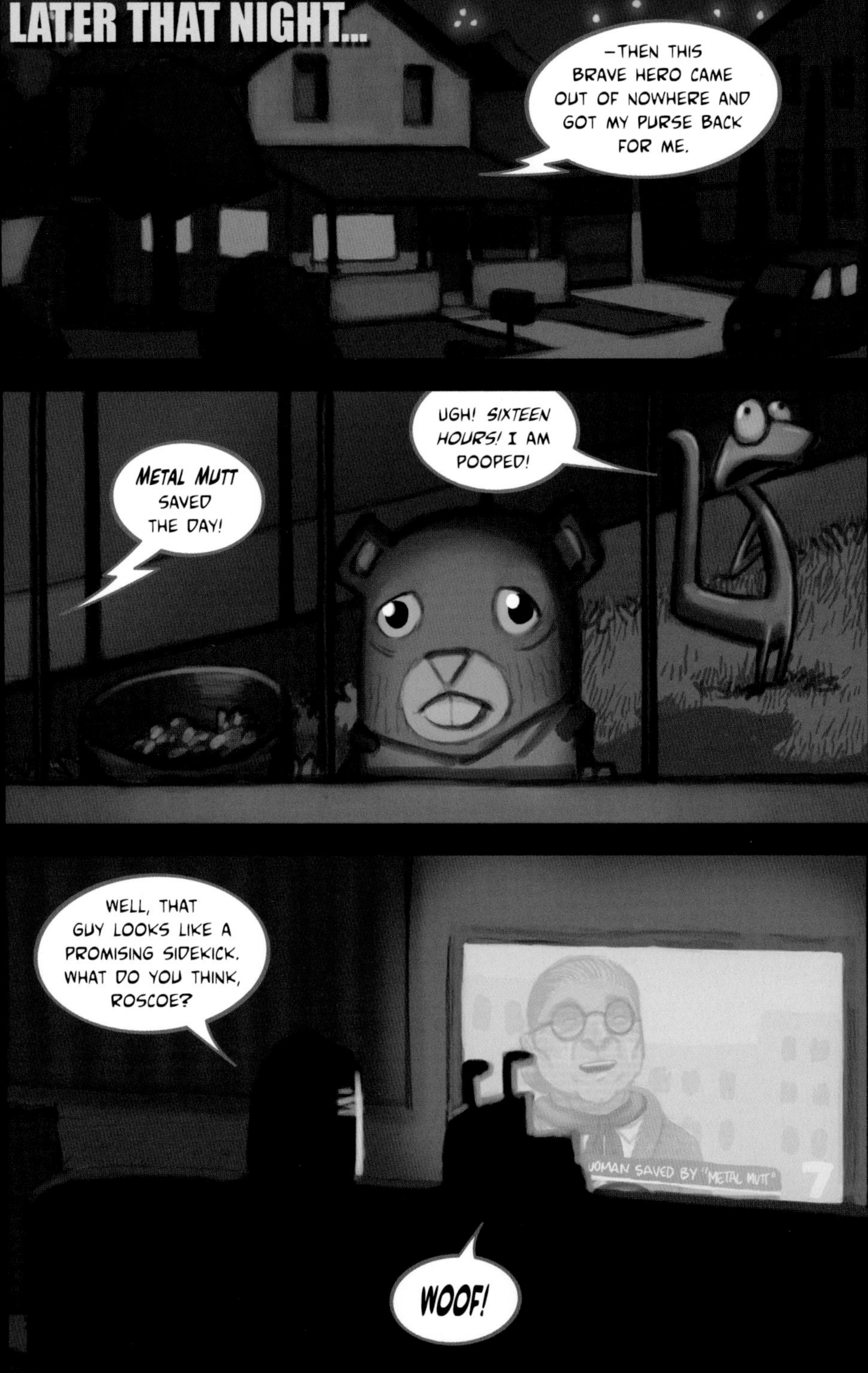
LATER THAT NIGHT...
—THEN THIS BRAVE HERO CAME OUT OF NOWHERE AND GOT MY PURSE BACK FOR ME.
METAL MUTT SAVED THE DAY!
UGH! SIXTEEN HOURS! I AM POOPED!
WELL, THAT GUY LOOKS LIKE A PROMISING SIDEKICK. WHAT DO YOU THINK, ROSCOE?
WOMAN SAVED BY "METAL MUTT"
WOOF!

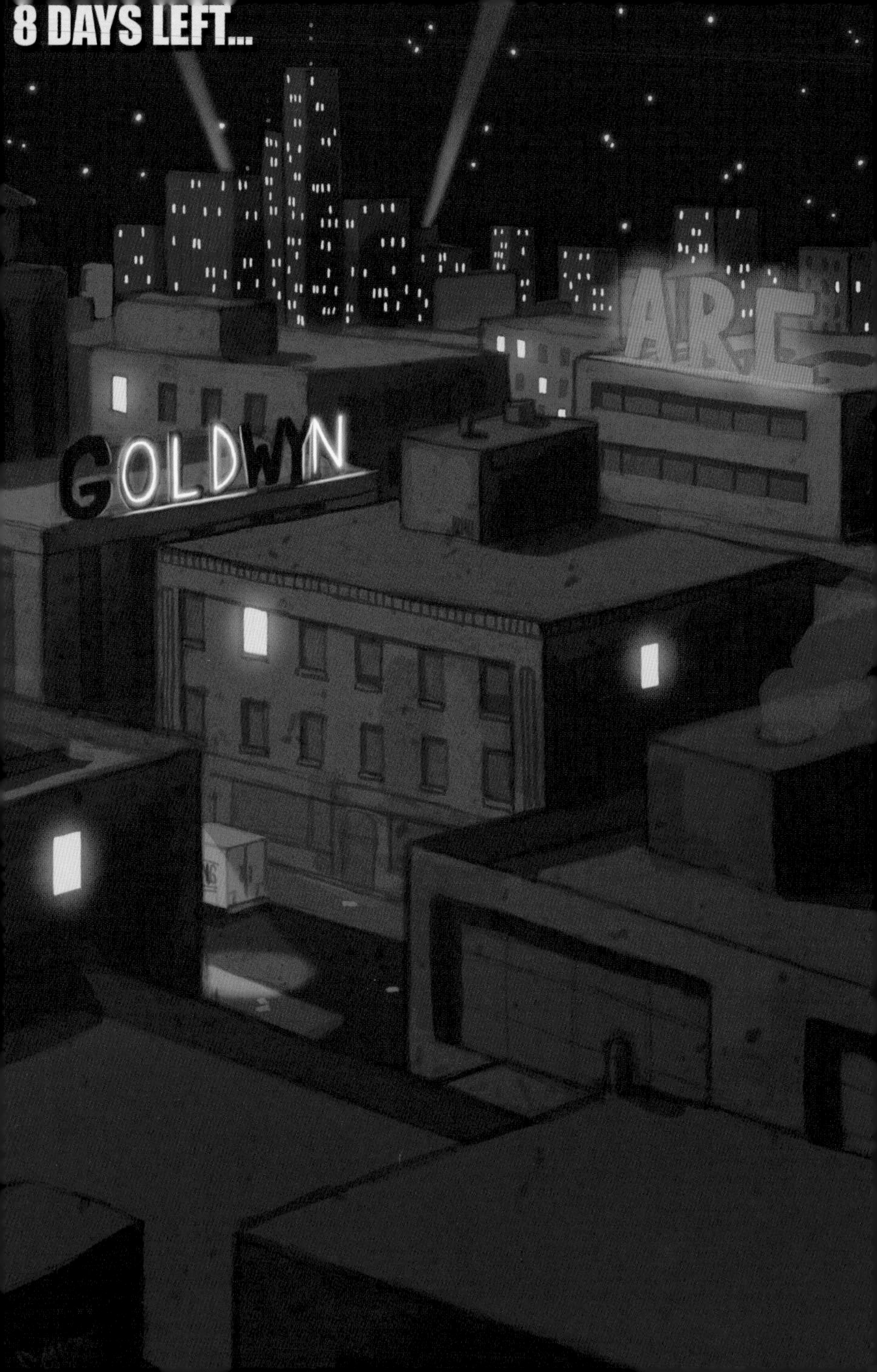
8 DAYS LEFT...
GOLDWYN

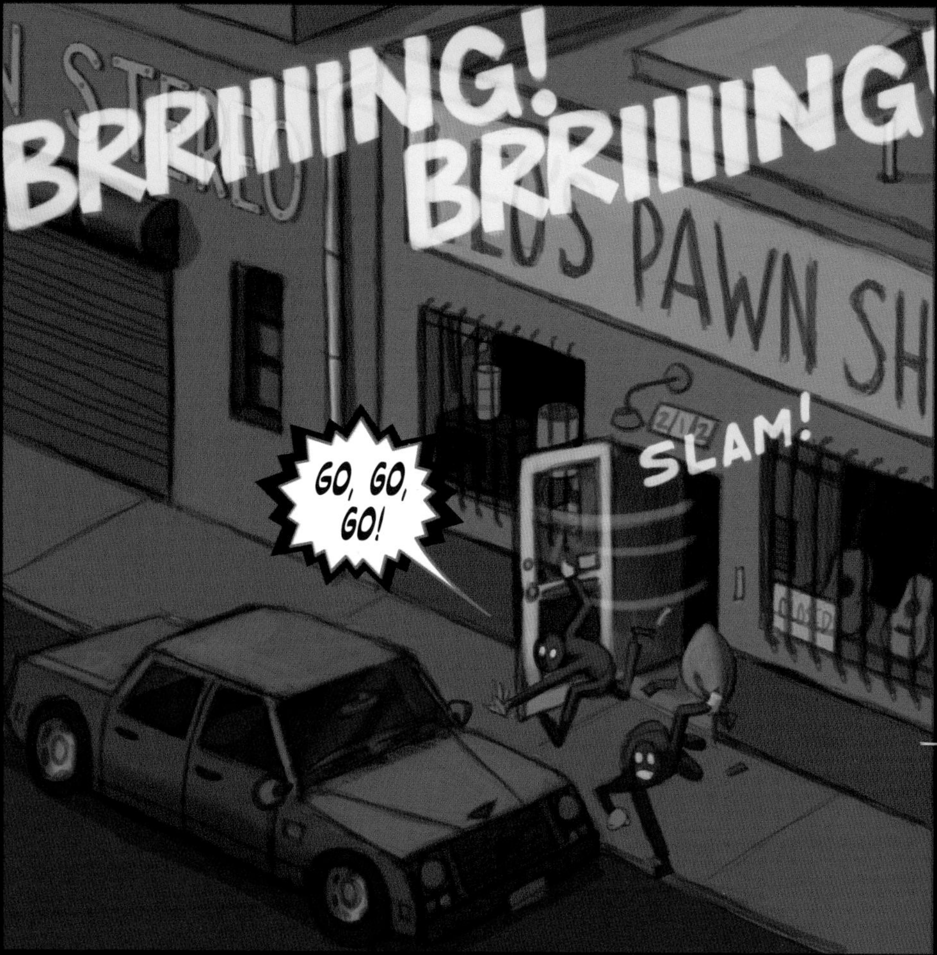
BRRIIING!
BRRIIIING!
GO, GO, GO!
SLAM!

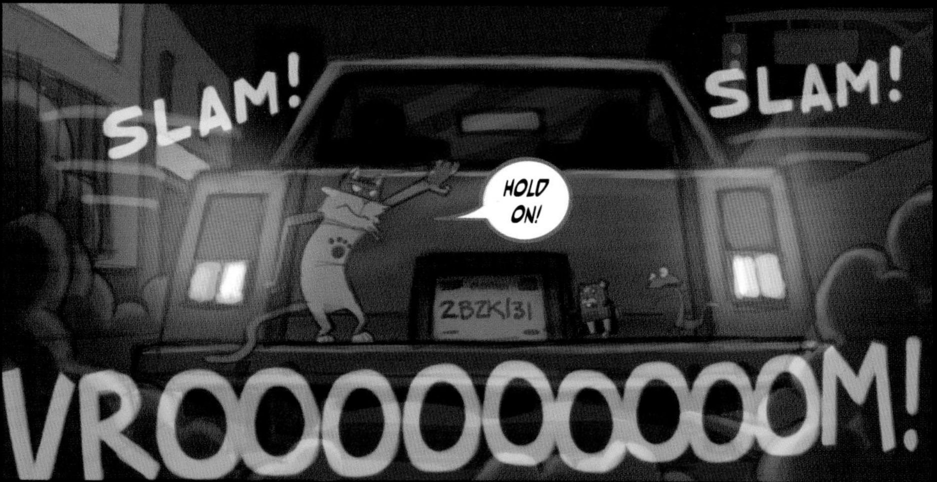
SLAM!
SLAM!
HOLD ON!
VROOOOOOOOOOOM!

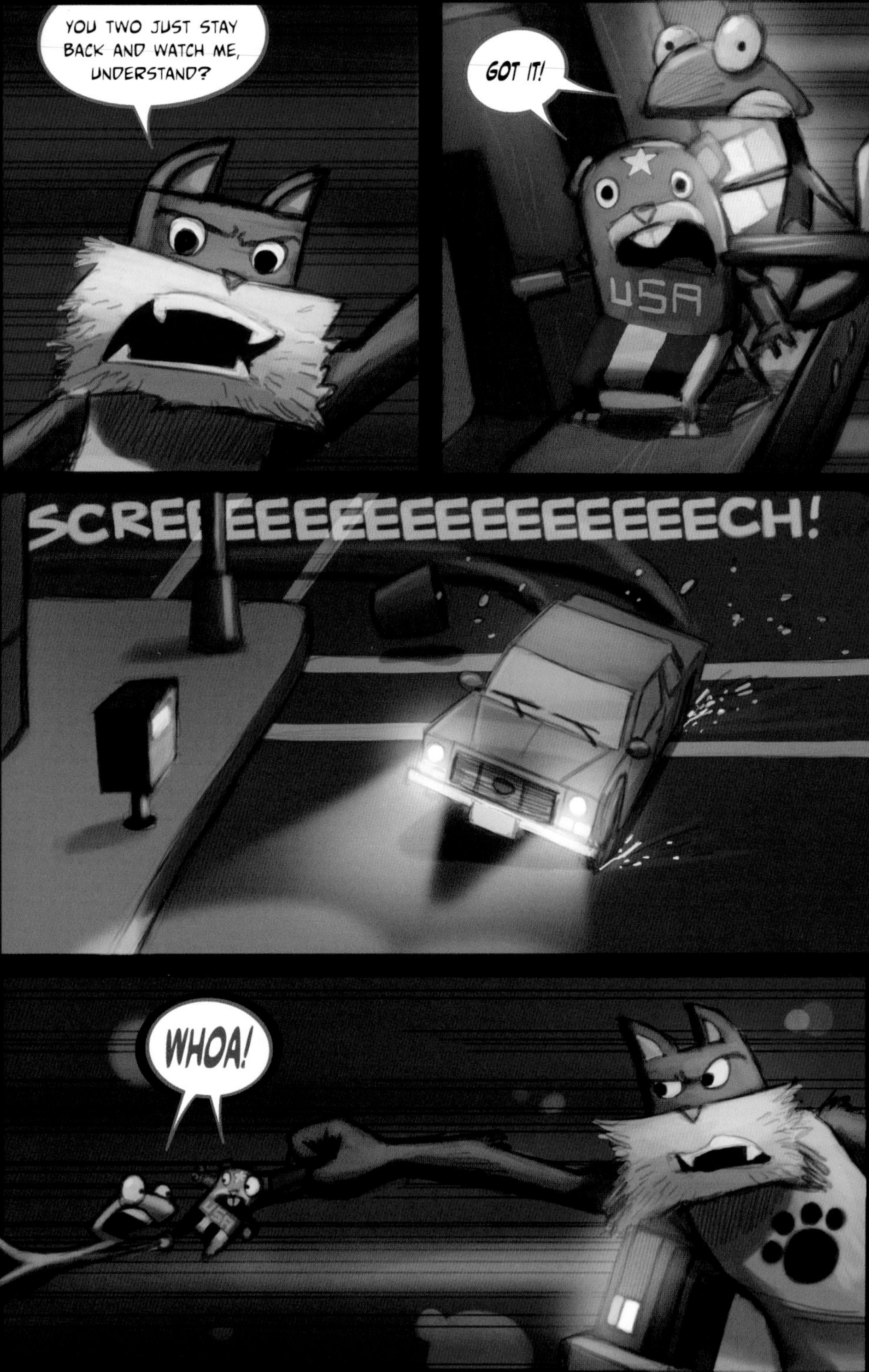
YOU TWO JUST STAY BACK AND WATCH ME, UNDERSTAND?
GOT IT!
USA
SCREEEEEEEEEEEEEEEEEECH!
WHOA!

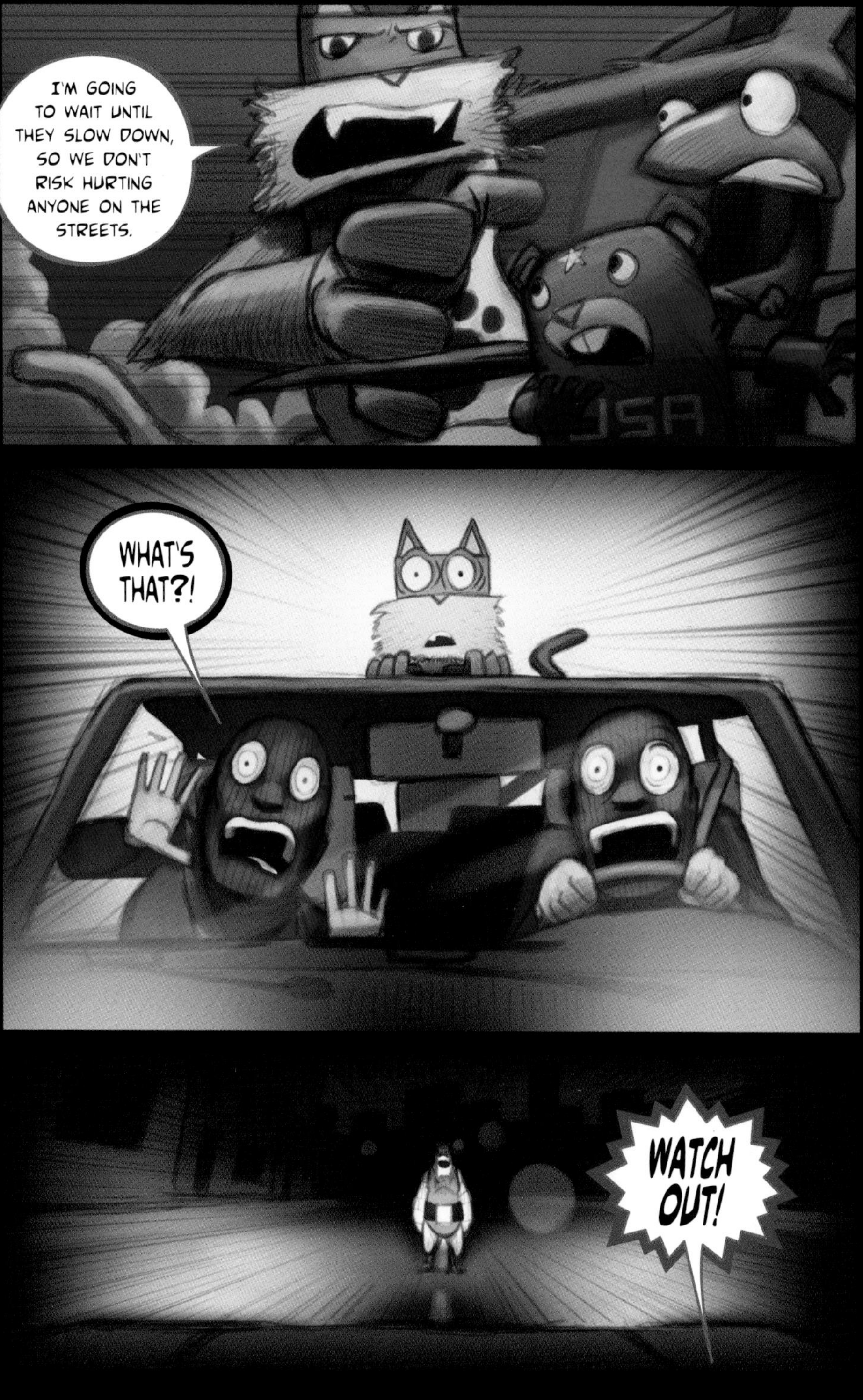
I'M GOING TO WAIT UNTIL THEY SLOW DOWN, SO WE DON'T RISK HURTING ANYONE ON THE STREETS.
USA
WHAT'S THAT?!
WATCH OUT!

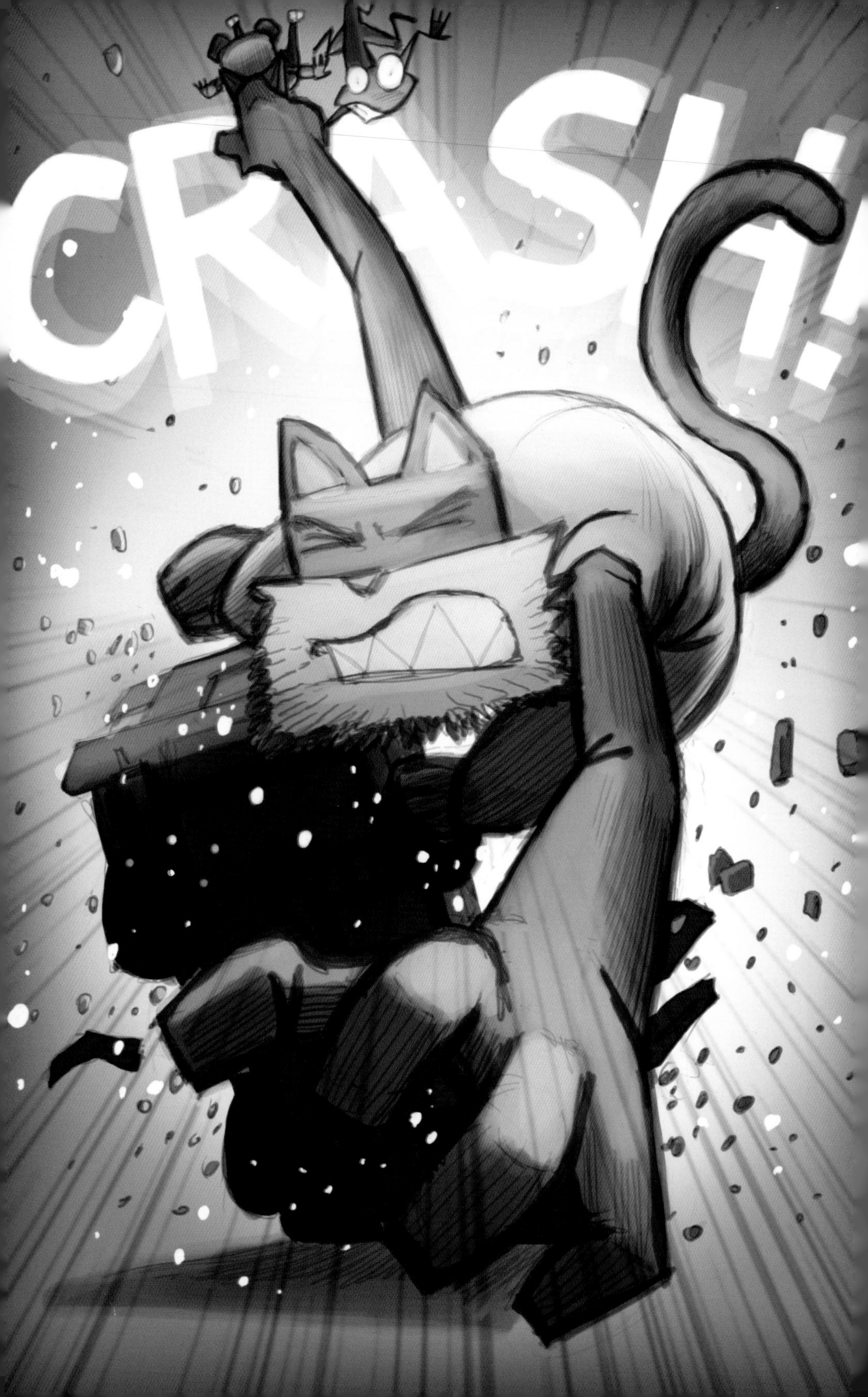
CRASH!

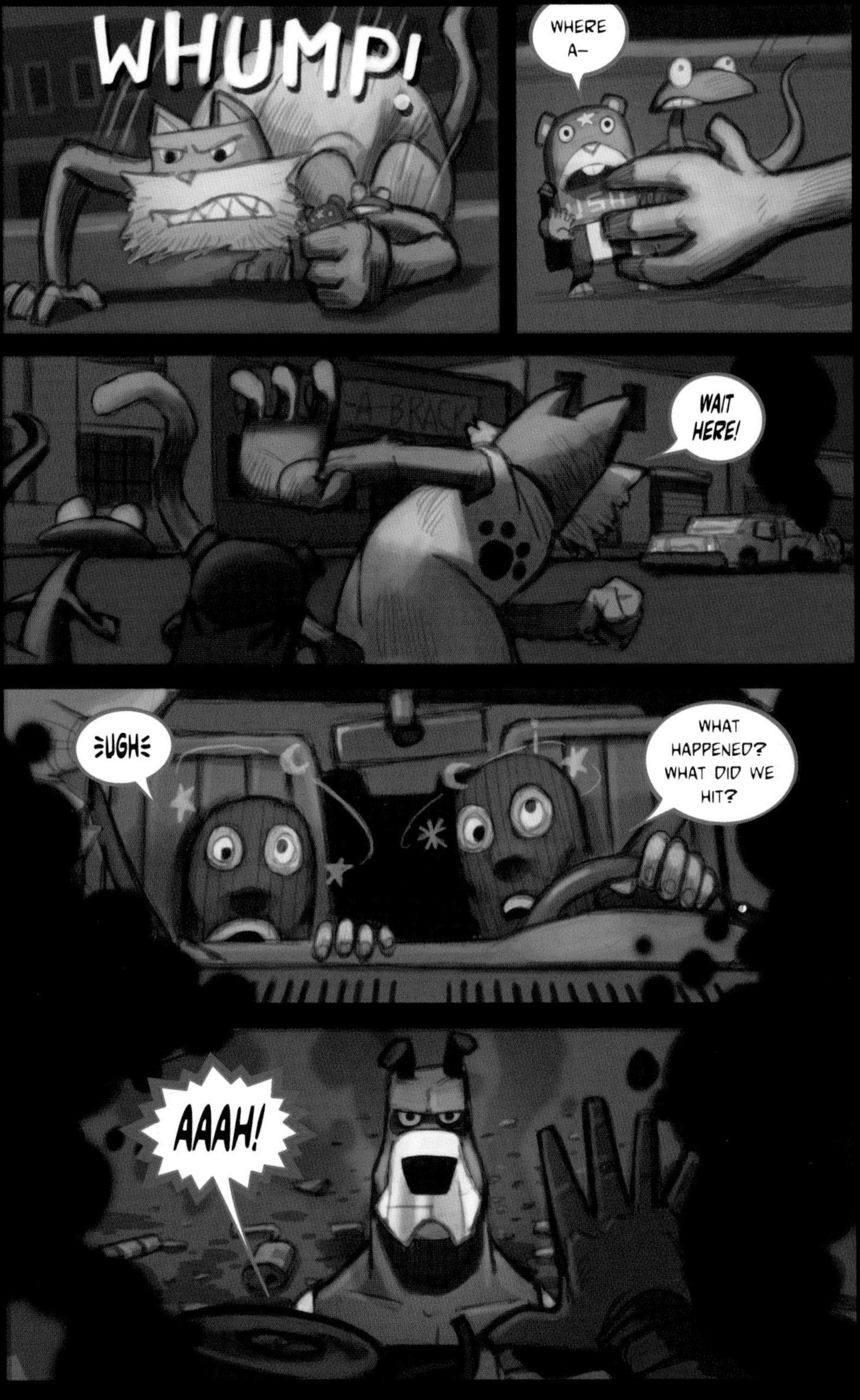
WHUMP!
WHERE A—
WAIT HERE!
UGH
WHAT HAPPENED? WHAT DID WE HIT?
AAAH!

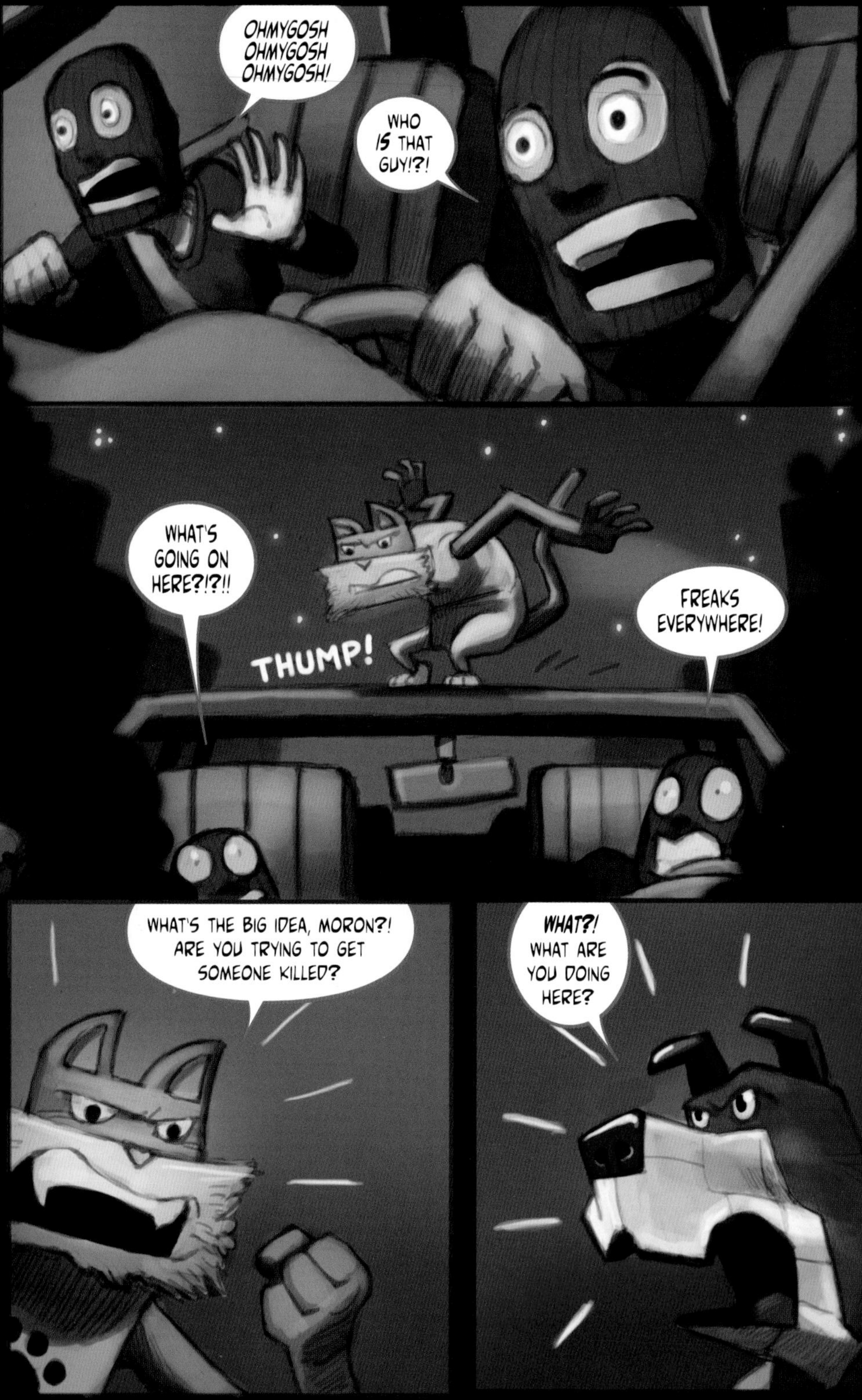
OHMYGOSH OHMYGOSH OHMYGOSH!
WHO IS THAT GUY!?!
WHAT'S GOING ON HERE?!?!!
THUMP!
FREAKS EVERYWHERE!
WHAT'S THE BIG IDEA, MORON?! ARE YOU TRYING TO GET SOMEONE KILLED?
WHAT?! WHAT ARE YOU DOING HERE?

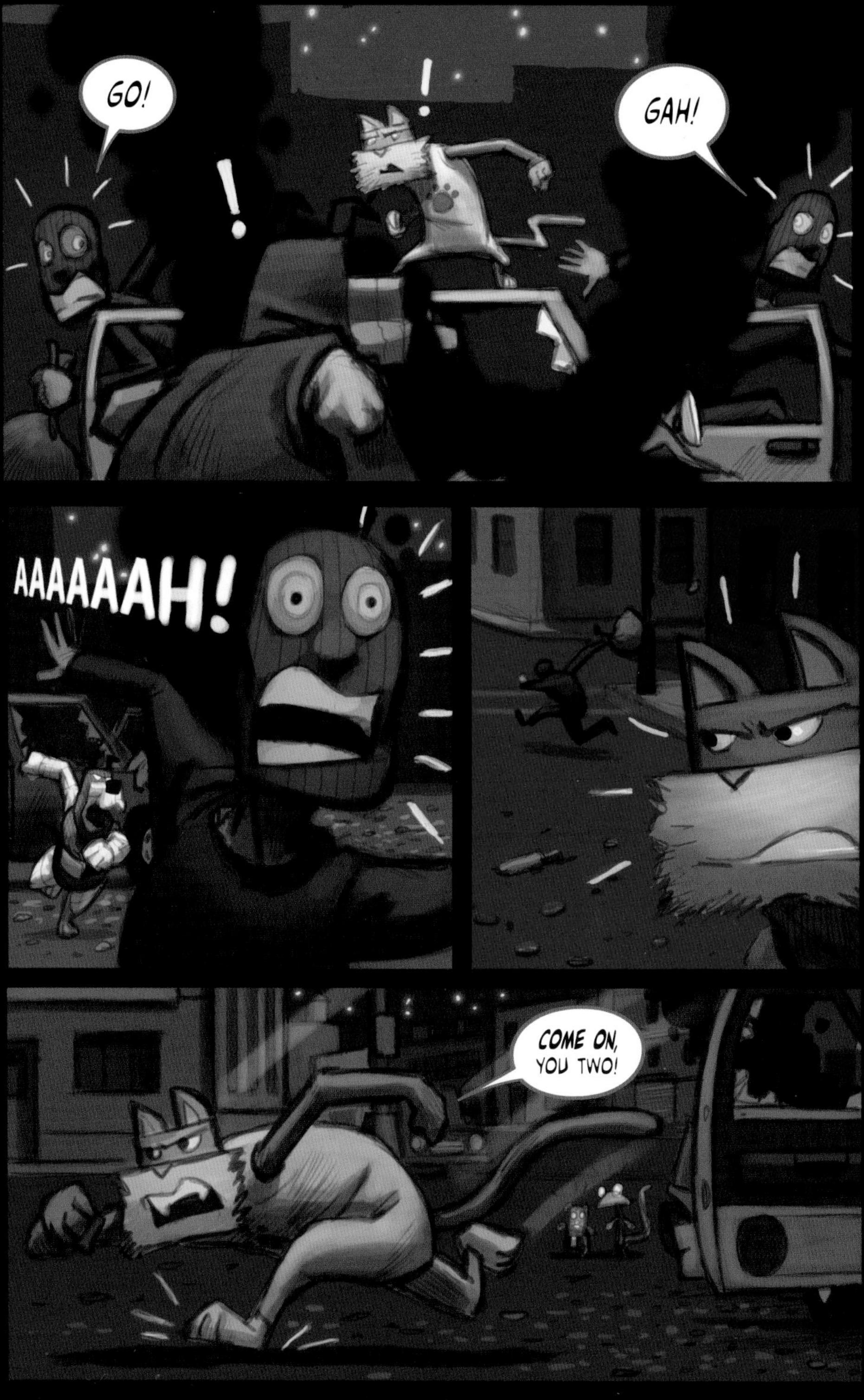
GO!
!
!
GAH!
AAAAAAH!
COME ON, YOU TWO!

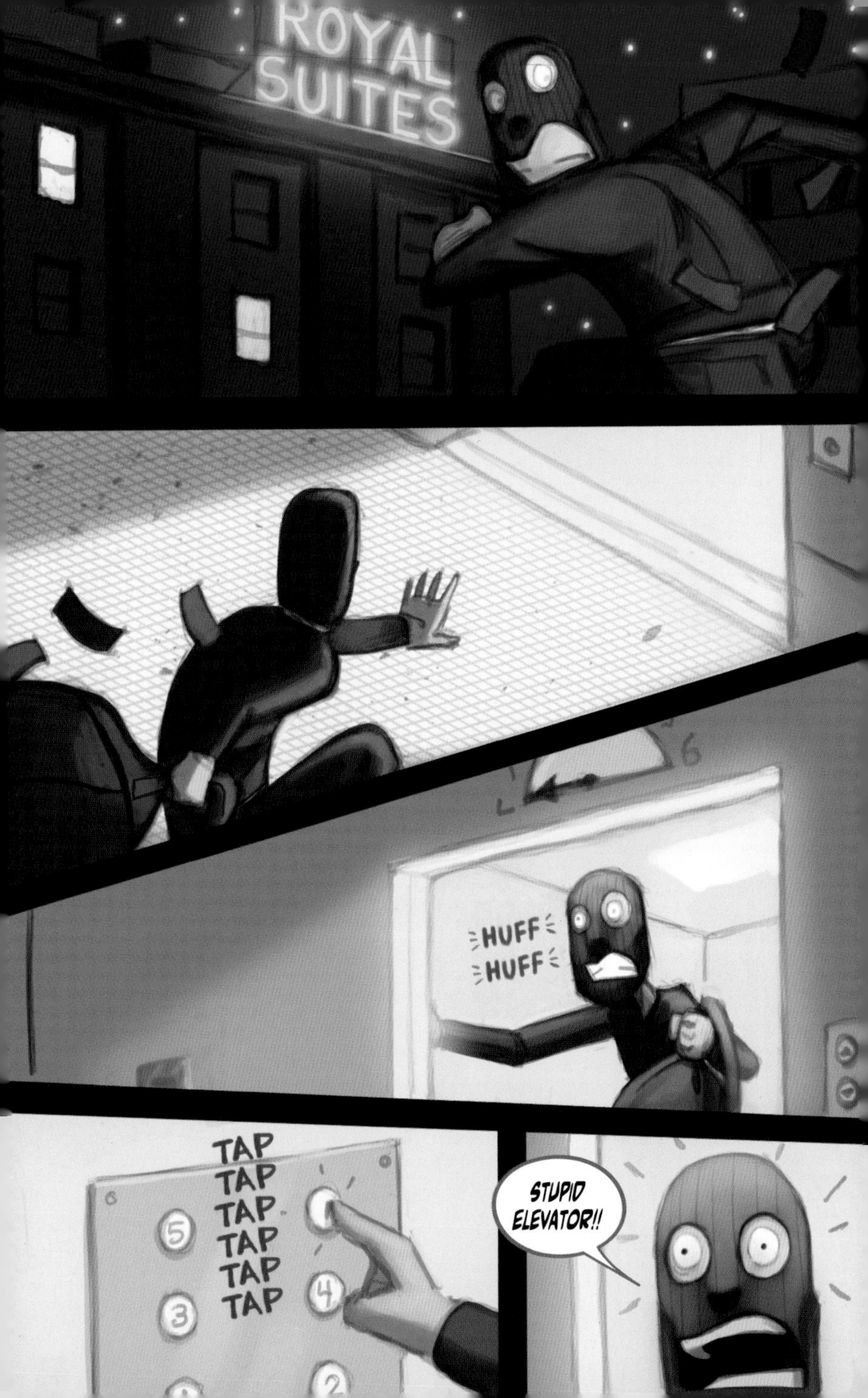
ROYAL SUITES
HUFF
HUFF
TAP
TAP
TAP
TAP
TAP
TAP
STUPID ELEVATOR!!

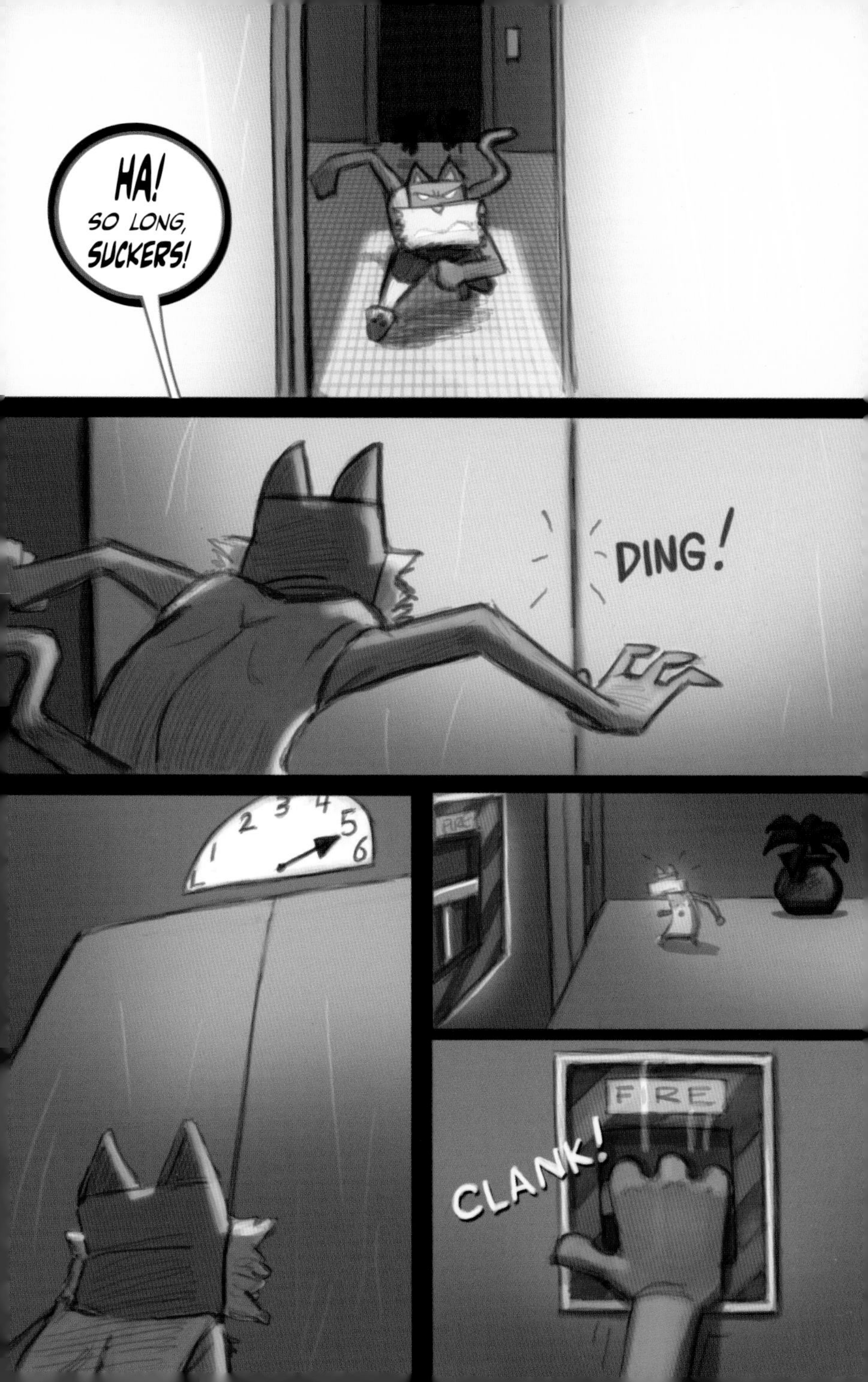
HA! SO LONG, SUCKERS!
DING!
FIRE
FIRE
CLANK!

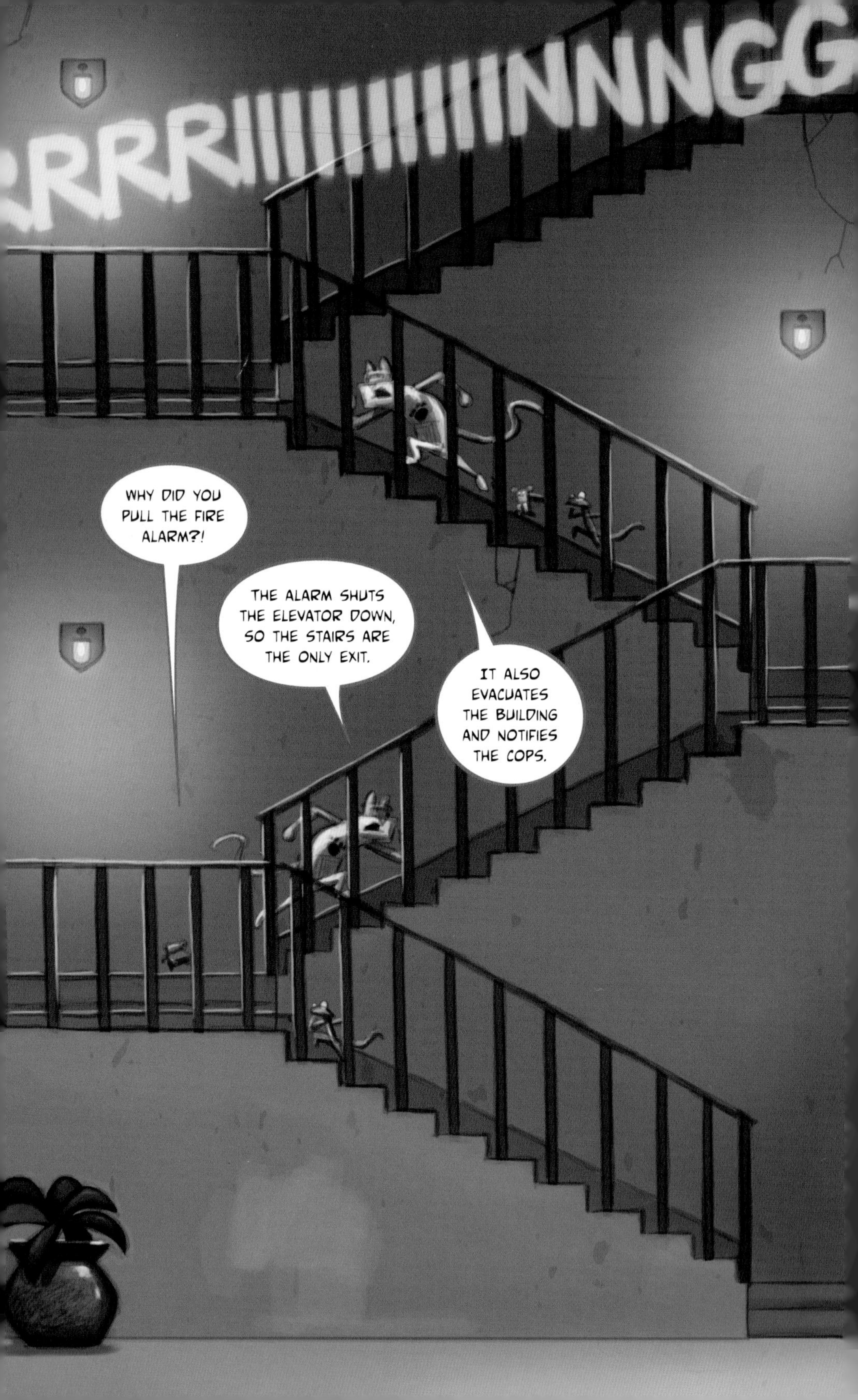
RRRIIIIIIIIIIIIINNNNGG
WHY DID YOU PULL THE FIRE ALARM?!
THE ALARM SHUTS THE ELEVATOR DOWN, SO THE STAIRS ARE THE ONLY EXIT.
IT ALSO EVACUATES THE BUILDING AND NOTIFIES THE COPS.

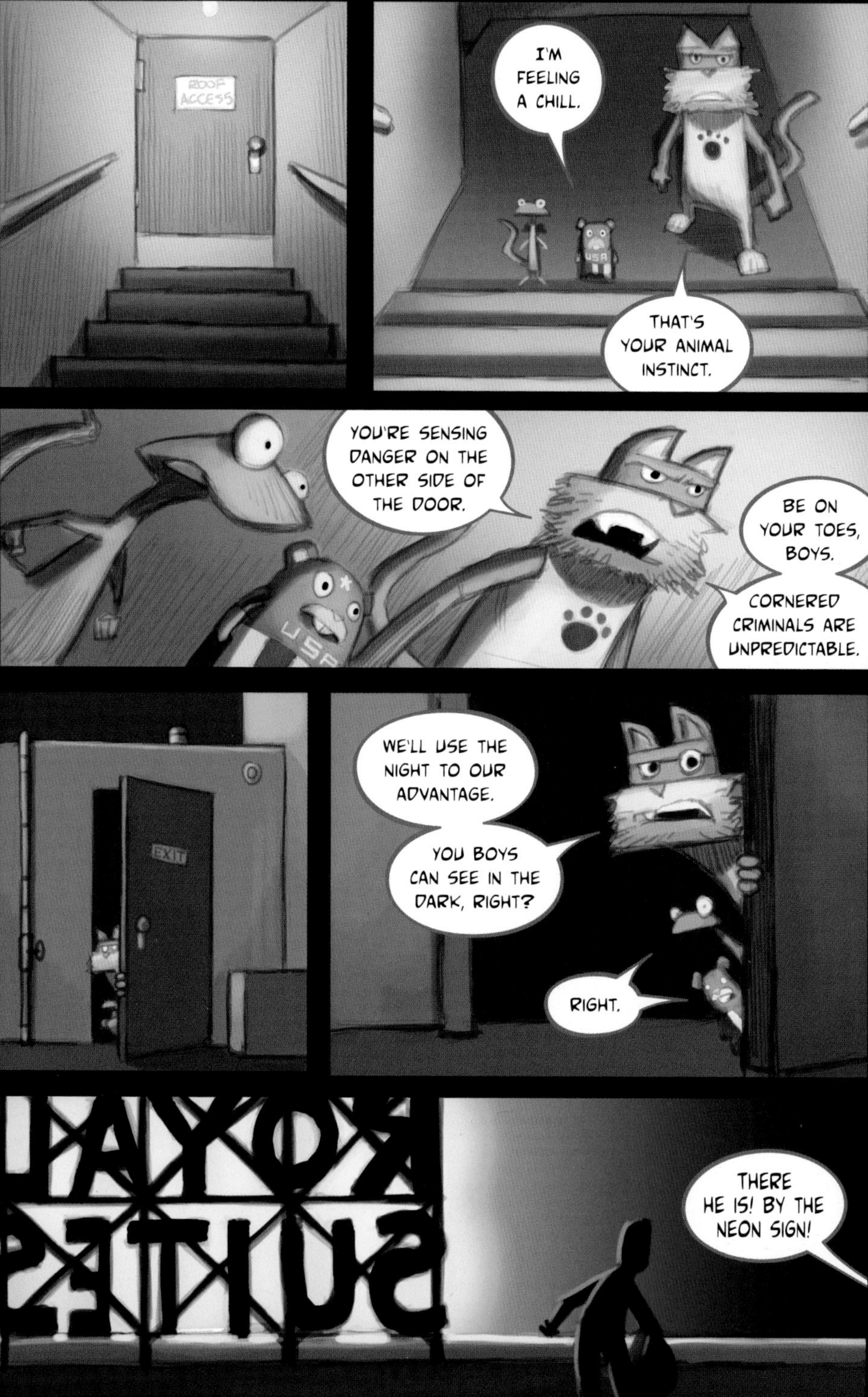
ROOF ACCESS
I'M FEELING A CHILL.
THAT'S YOUR ANIMAL INSTINCT.
YOU'RE SENSING DANGER ON THE OTHER SIDE OF THE DOOR.
BE ON YOUR TOES, BOYS.
CORNERED CRIMINALS ARE UNPREDICTABLE.
EXIT
WE'LL USE THE NIGHT TO OUR ADVANTAGE.
YOU BOYS CAN SEE IN THE DARK, RIGHT?
RIGHT.
THERE HE IS! BY THE NEON SIGN!

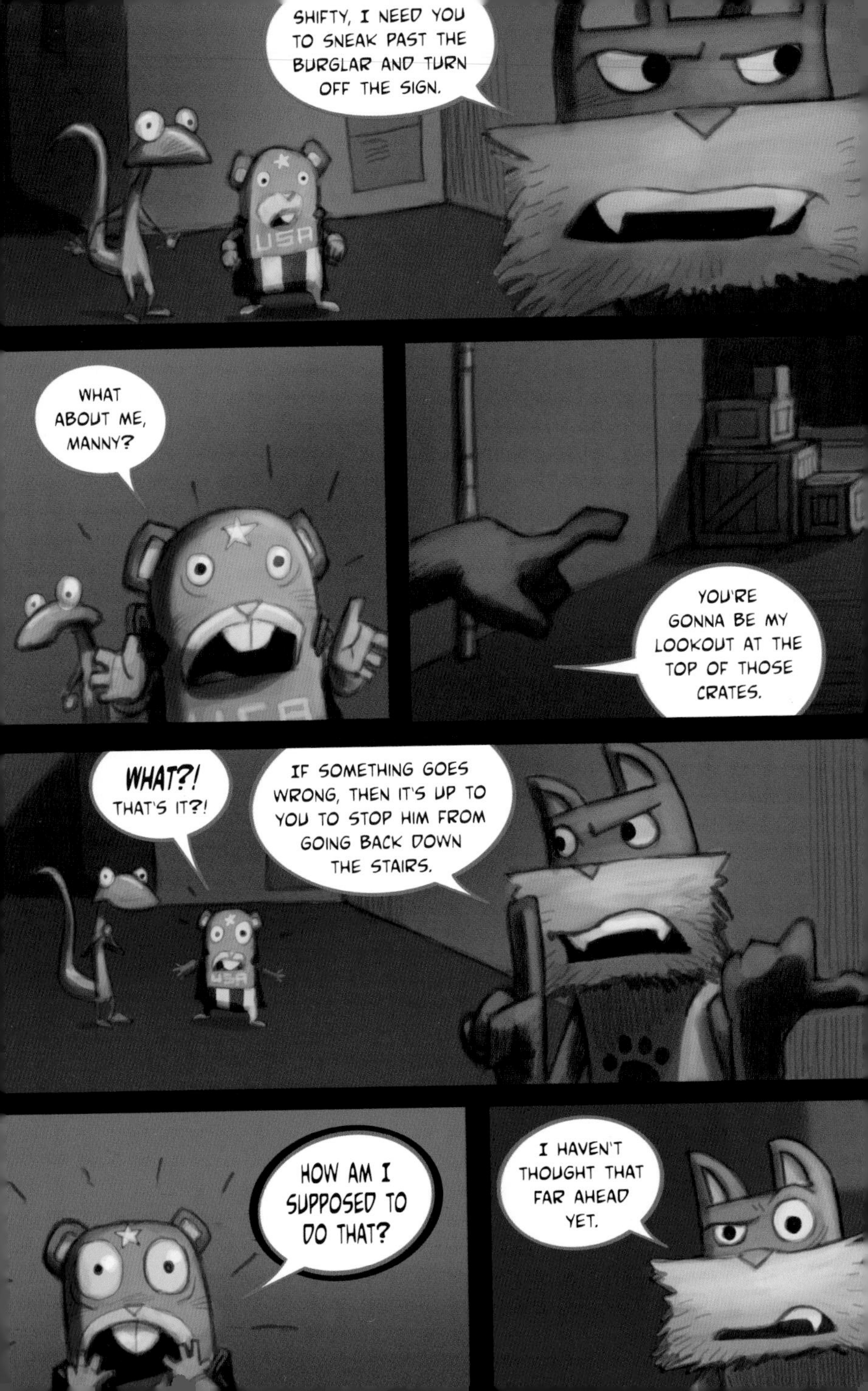
SHIFTY, I NEED YOU TO SNEAK PAST THE BURGLAR AND TURN OFF THE SIGN.
WHAT ABOUT ME, MANNY?
YOU'RE GONNA BE MY LOOKOUT AT THE TOP OF THOSE CRATES.
WHAT?! THAT'S IT?!
IF SOMETHING GOES WRONG, THEN IT'S UP TO YOU TO STOP HIM FROM GOING BACK DOWN THE STAIRS.
HOW AM I SUPPOSED TO DO THAT?
I HAVEN'T THOUGHT THAT FAR AHEAD YET.

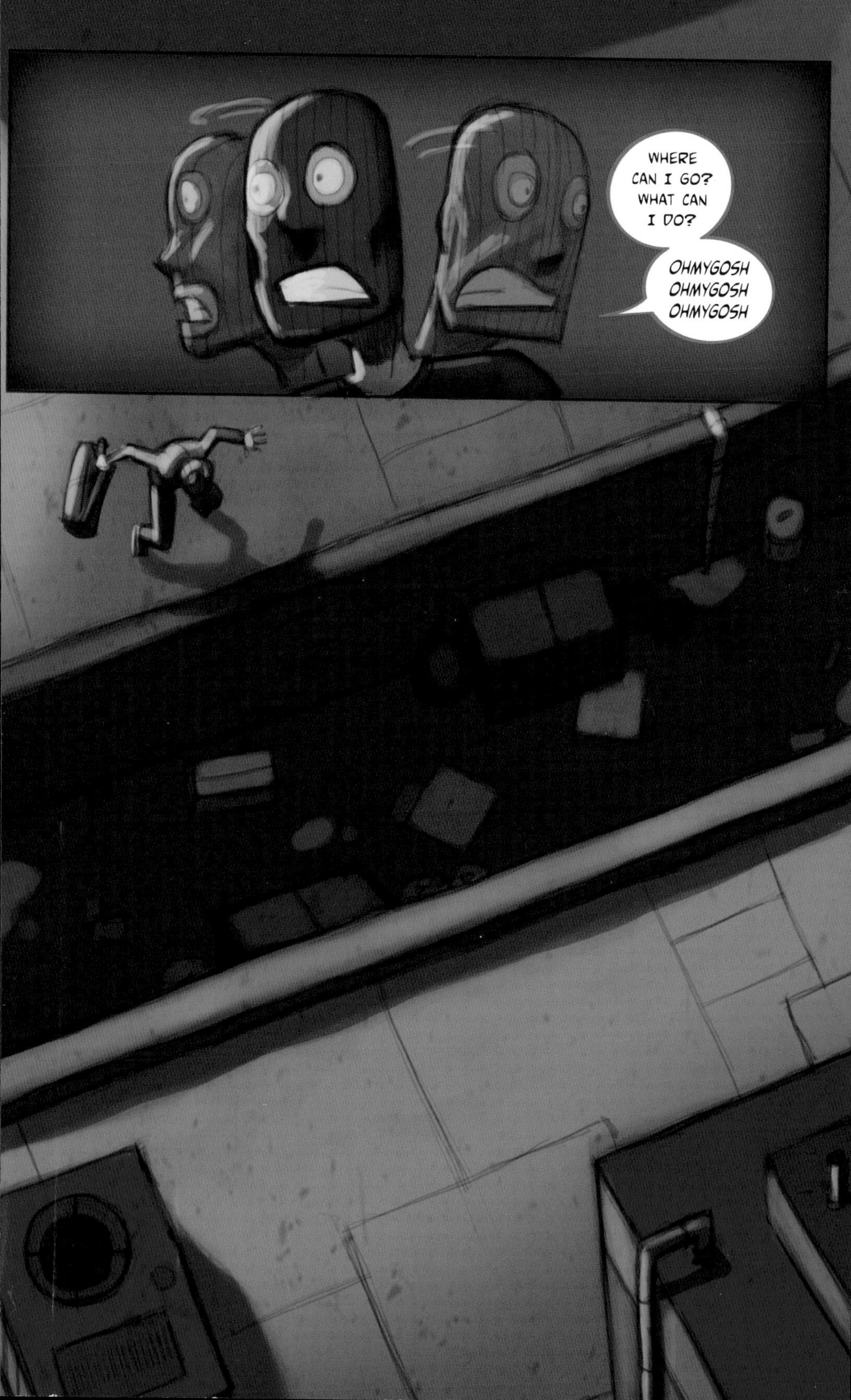
WHERE CAN I GO? WHAT CAN I DO?
OHMYGOSH OHMYGOSH OHMYGOSH

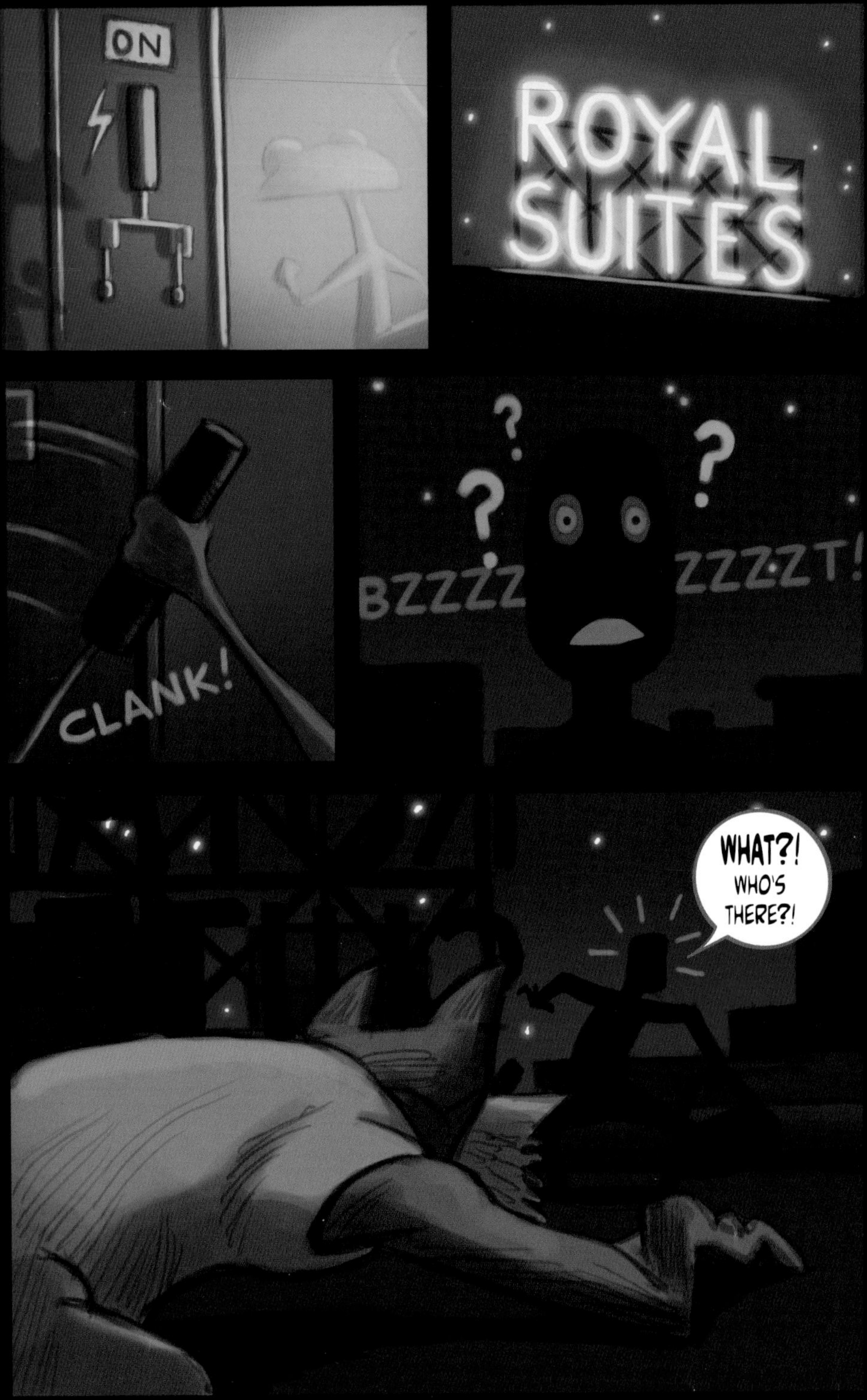
ON
ROYAL SUITES
CLANK!
?
?
?
BZZZZ
ZZZZZT!
WHAT?!
WHO'S THERE?!

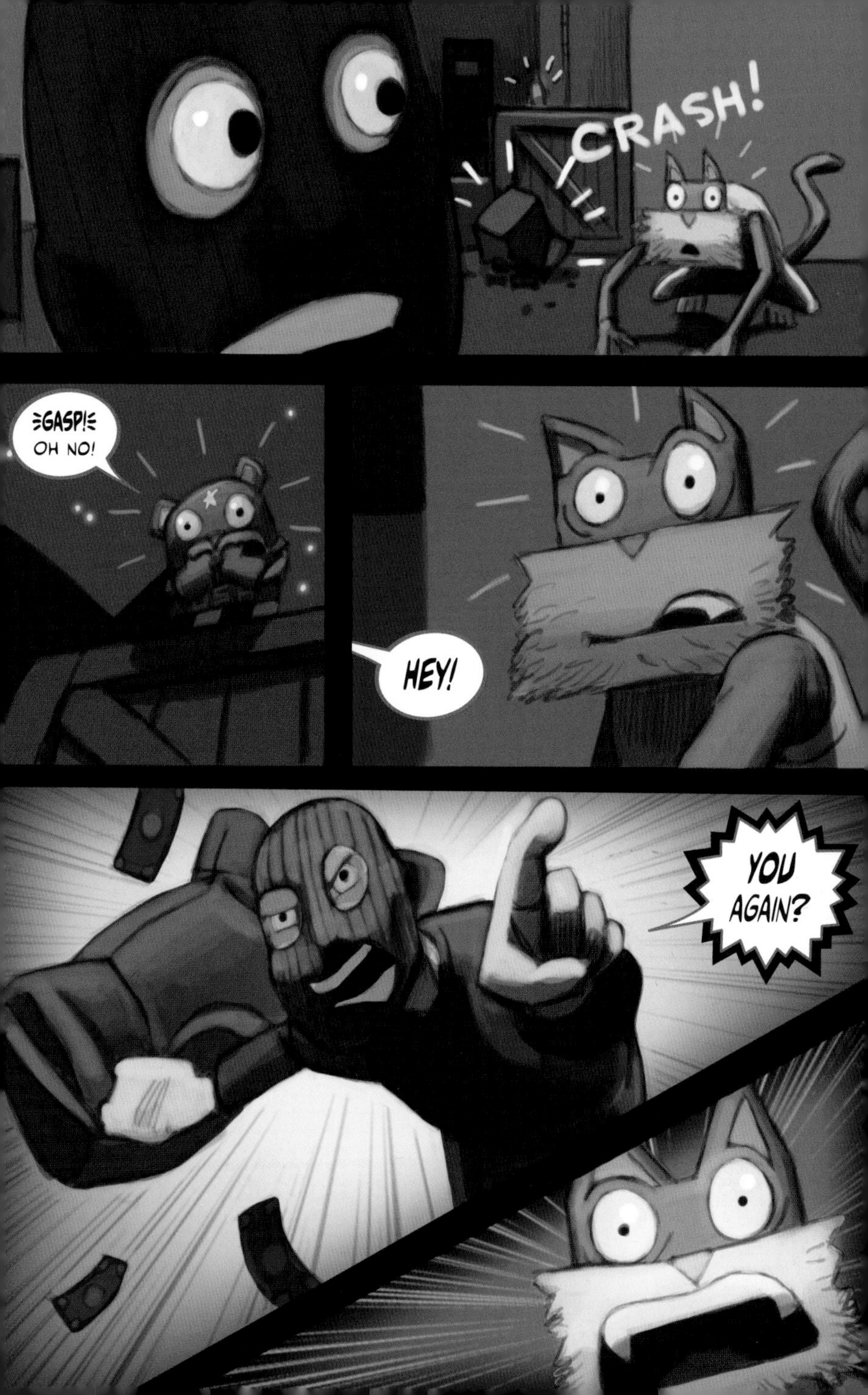
CRASH!
GASP! OH NO!
HEY!
YOU AGAIN?

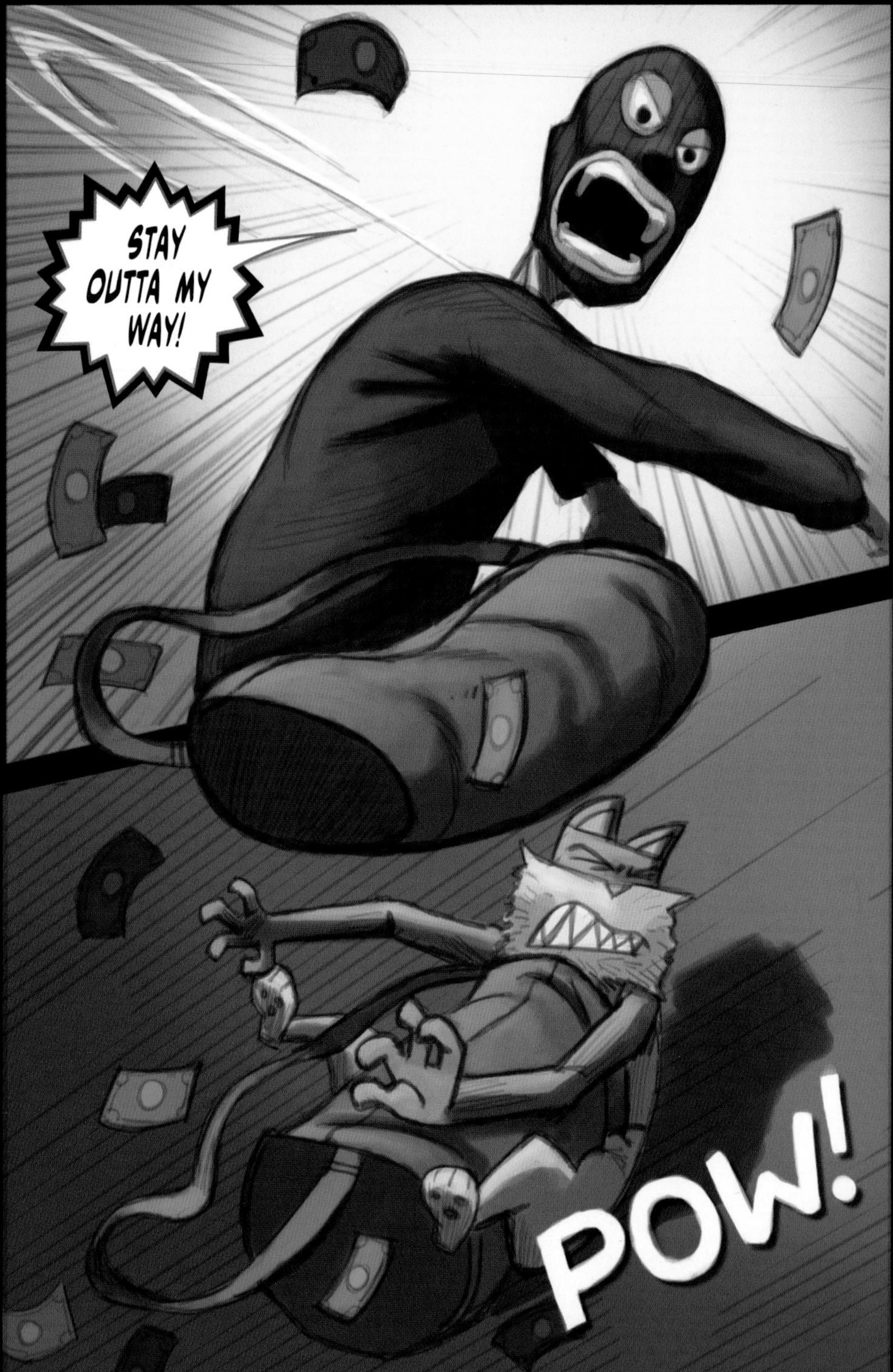
STAY OUTTA MY WAY!
POW!

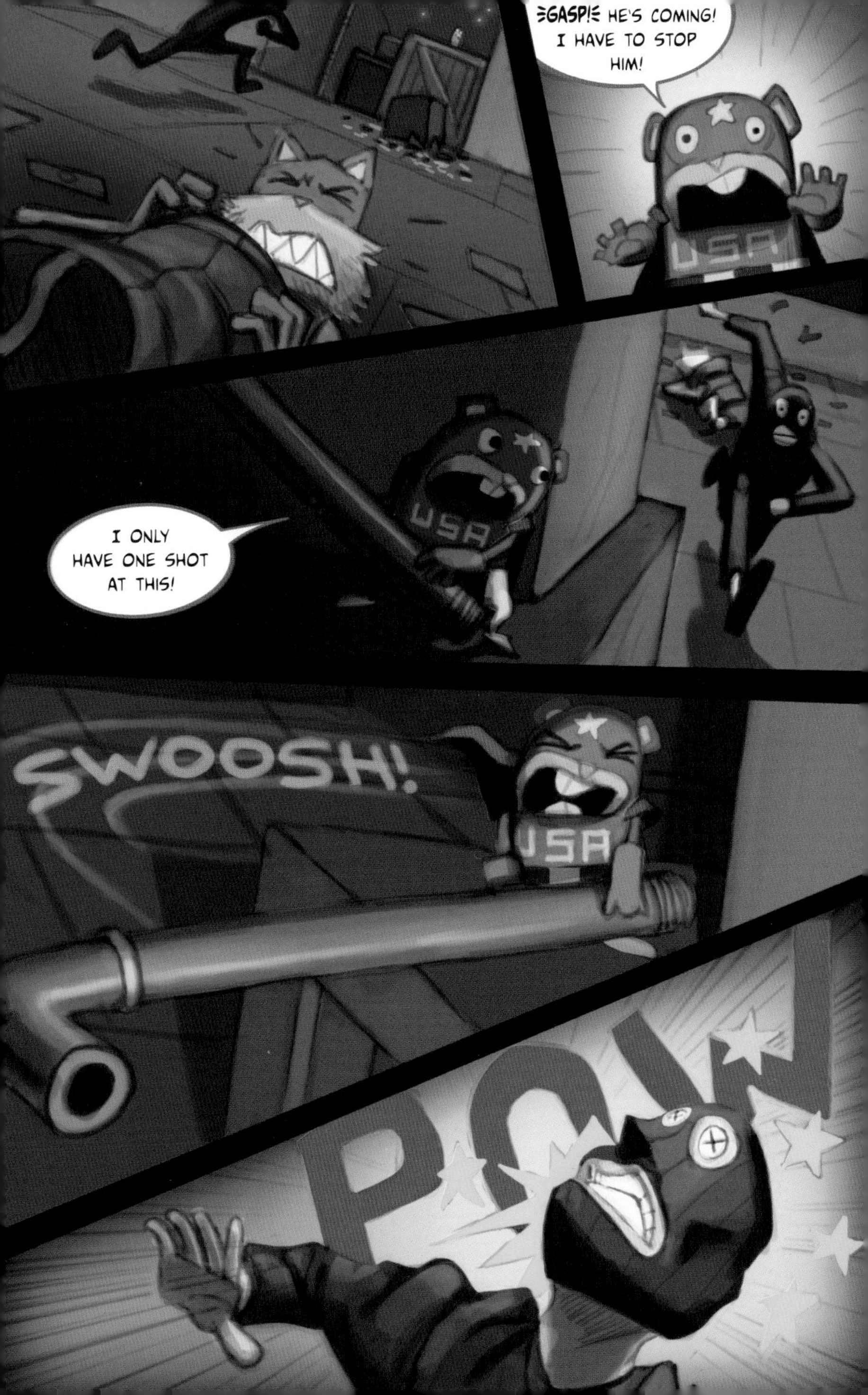

≡GASP!≡ HE'S COMING! I HAVE TO STOP HIM!
USA
I ONLY HAVE ONE SHOT AT THIS!
USA
SWOOSH!
USA

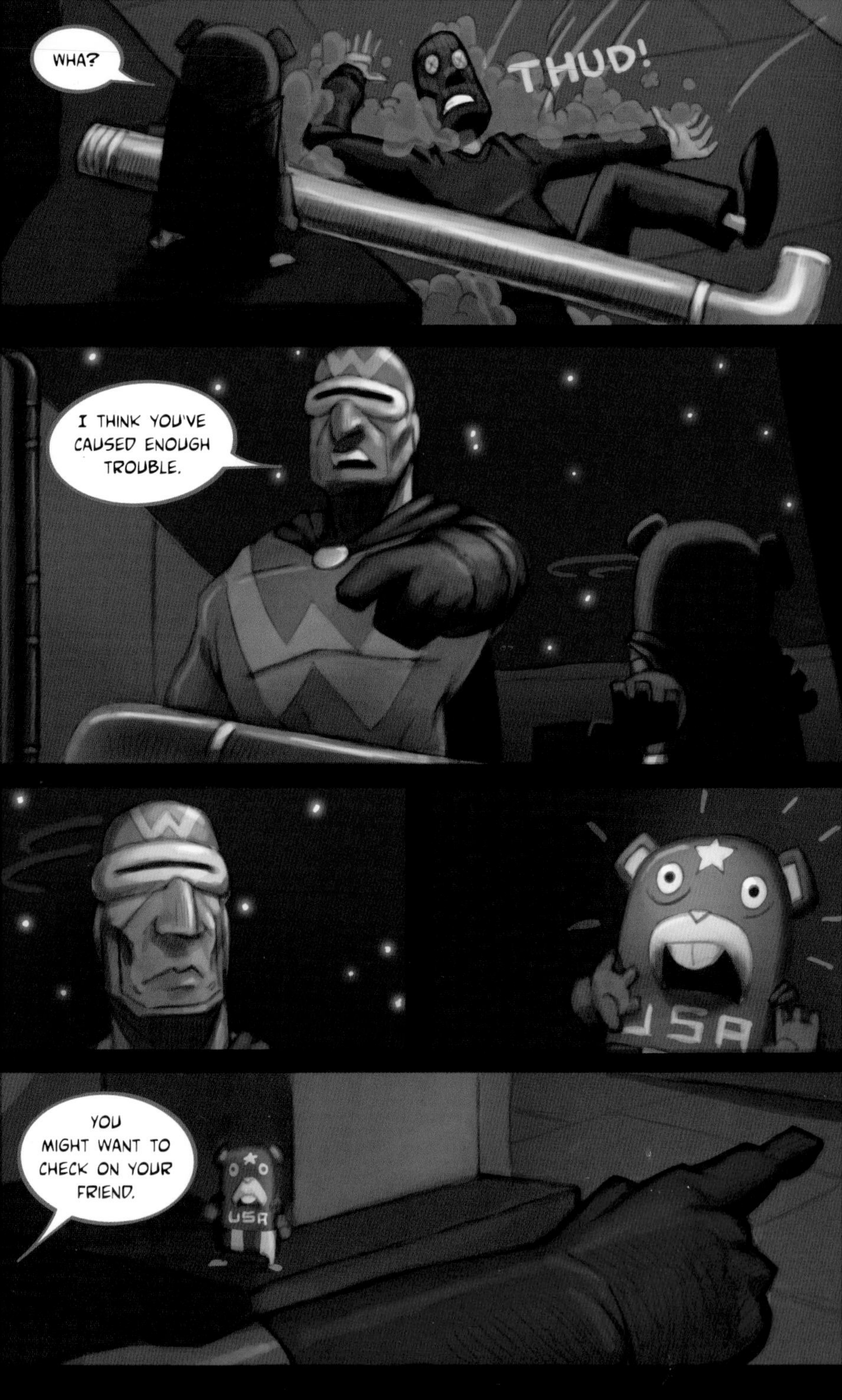
WHA?
THUD!
I THINK YOU'VE CAUSED ENOUGH TROUBLE.
USA
YOU MIGHT WANT TO CHECK ON YOUR FRIEND.
USA

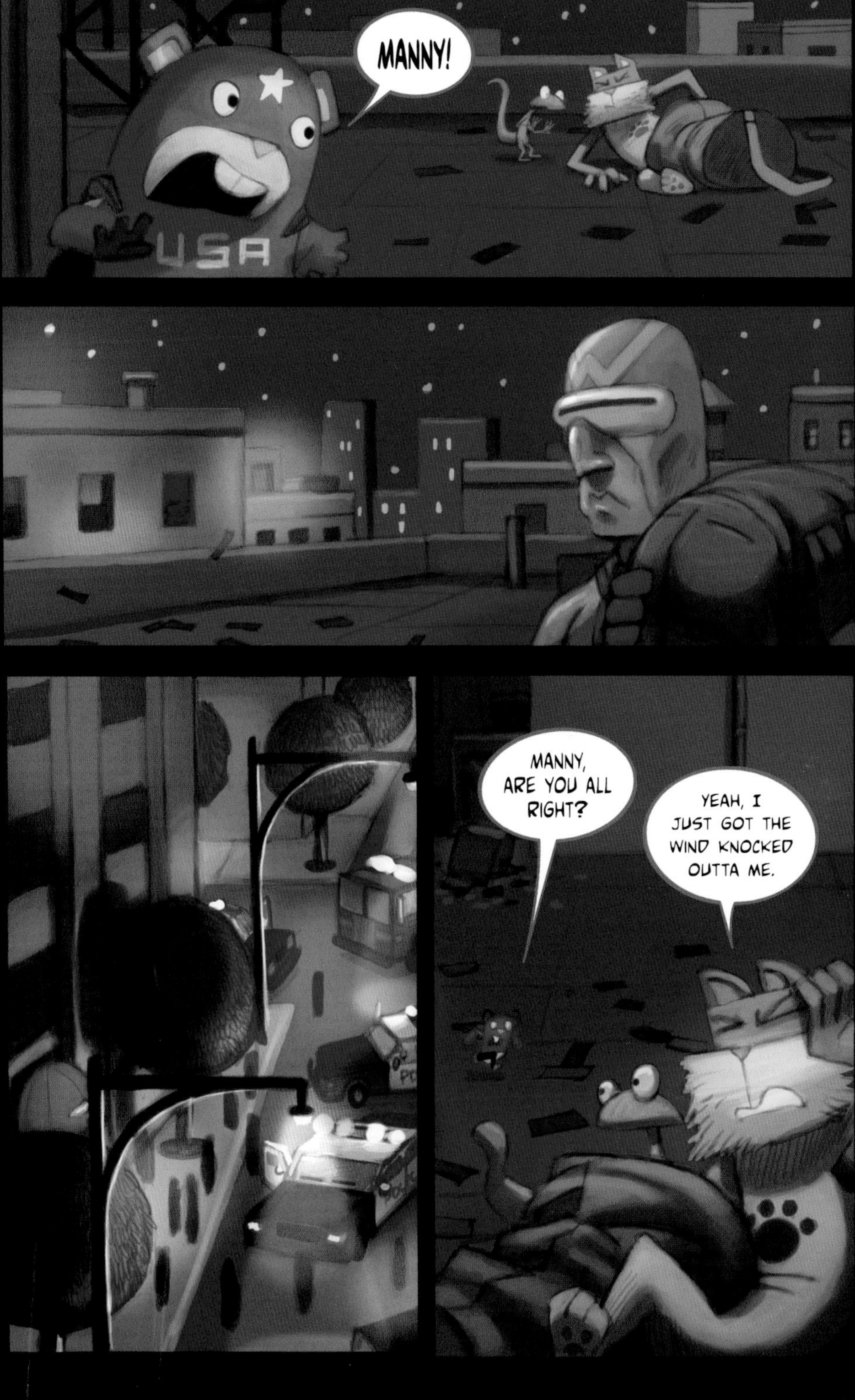
MANNY!
MANNY, ARE YOU ALL RIGHT?
YEAH, I JUST GOT THE WIND KNOCKED OUTTA ME.

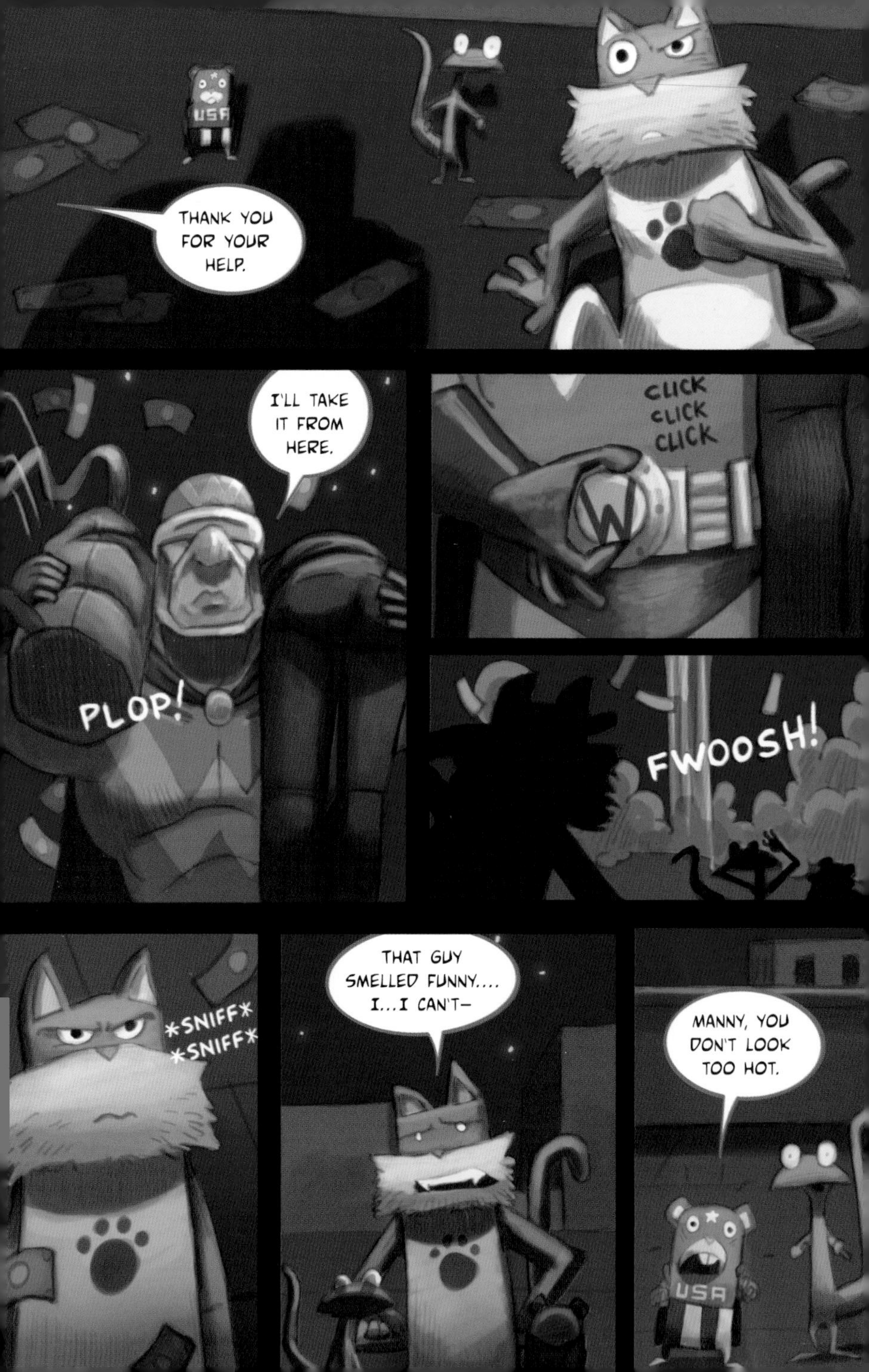
THANK YOU FOR YOUR HELP.
I'LL TAKE IT FROM HERE.
CLICK CLICK CLICK
PLOP!
FWOOSH!
SNIFF *SNIFF*
THAT GUY SMELLED FUNNY.... I...I CAN'T–
MANNY, YOU DON'T LOOK TOO HOT.

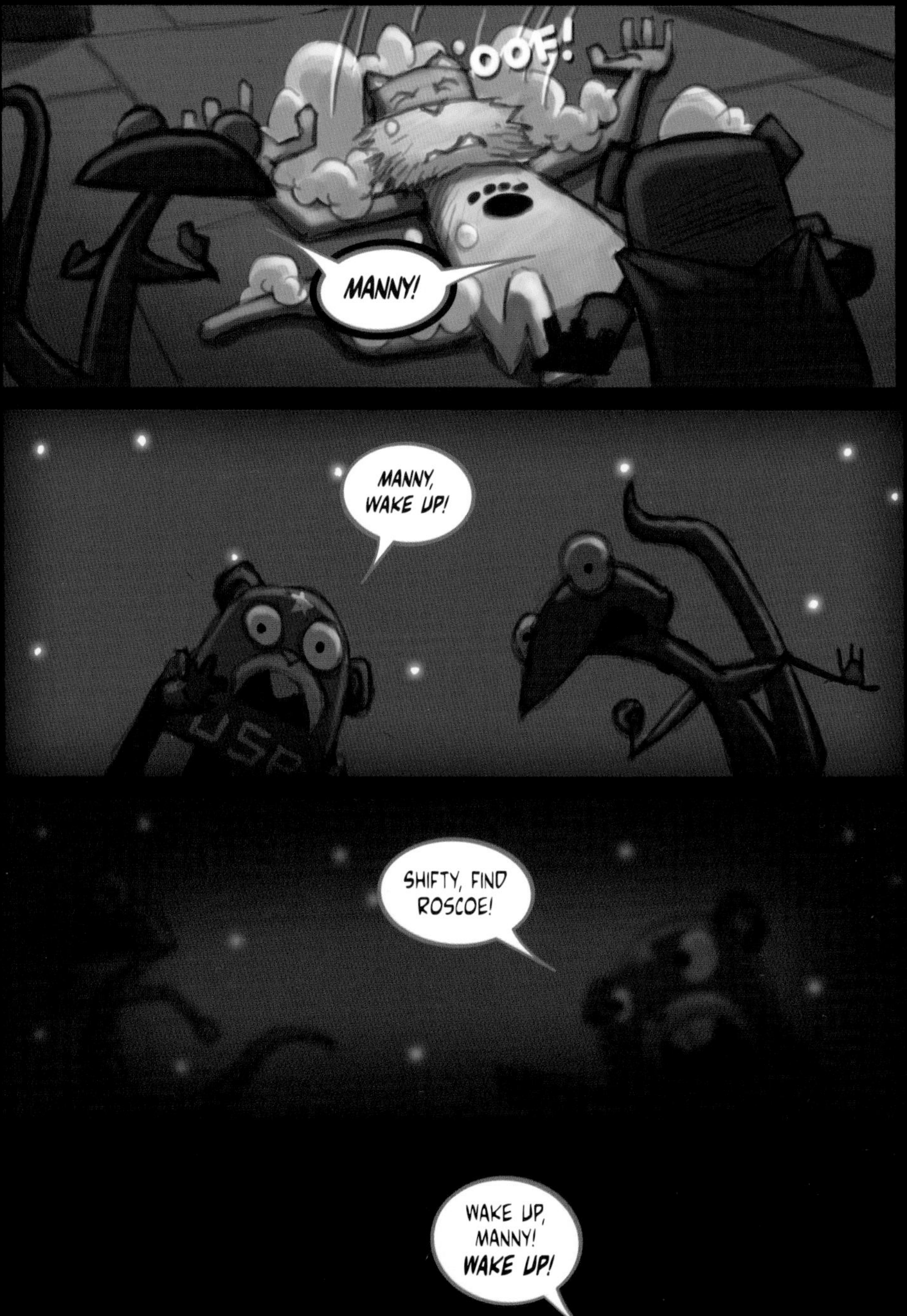
OOF!
MANNY!
MANNY, WAKE UP!
SHIFTY, FIND ROSCOE!
WAKE UP, MANNY! WAKE UP!

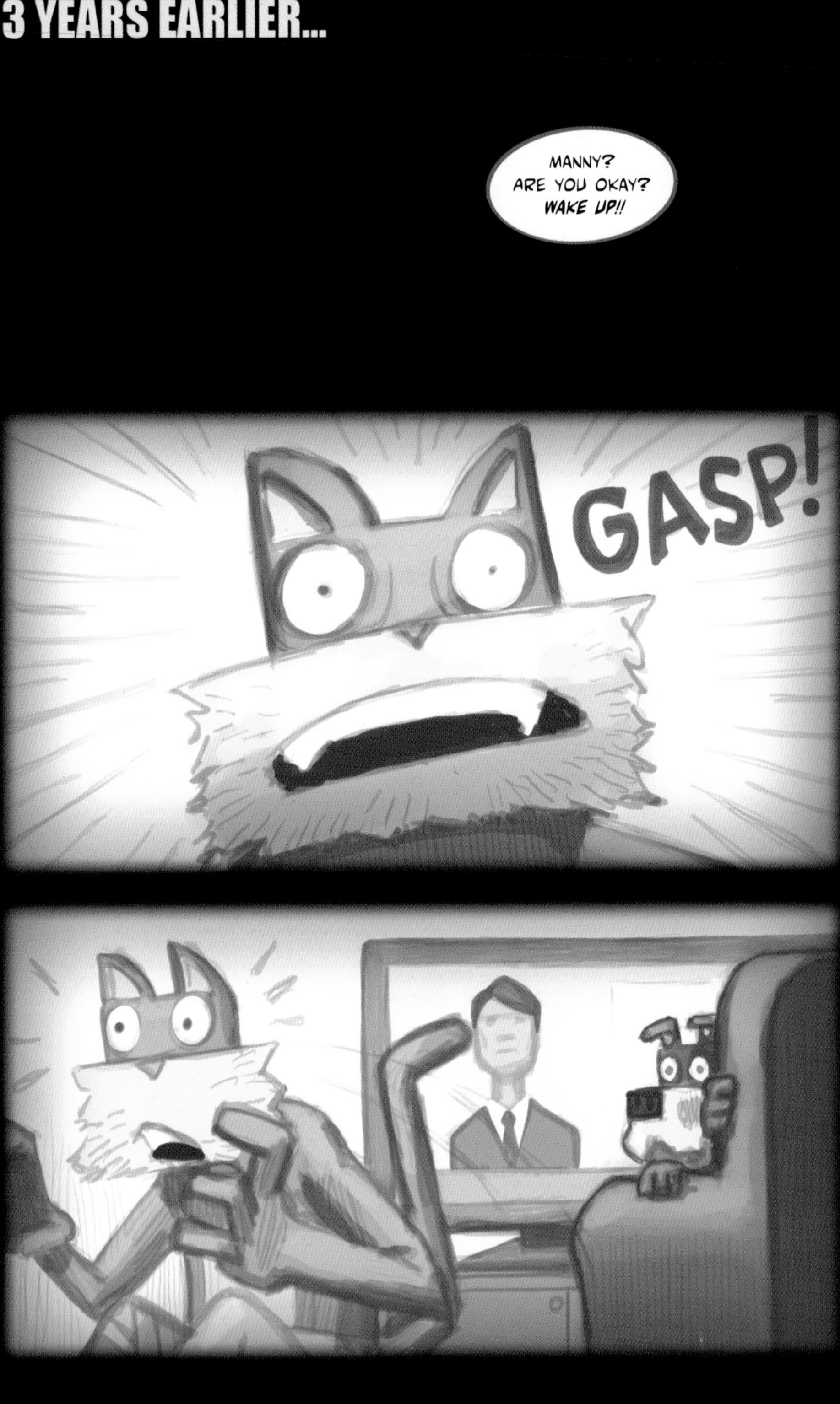
3 YEARS EARLIER...
MANNY? ARE YOU OKAY? WAKE UP!!
GASP!

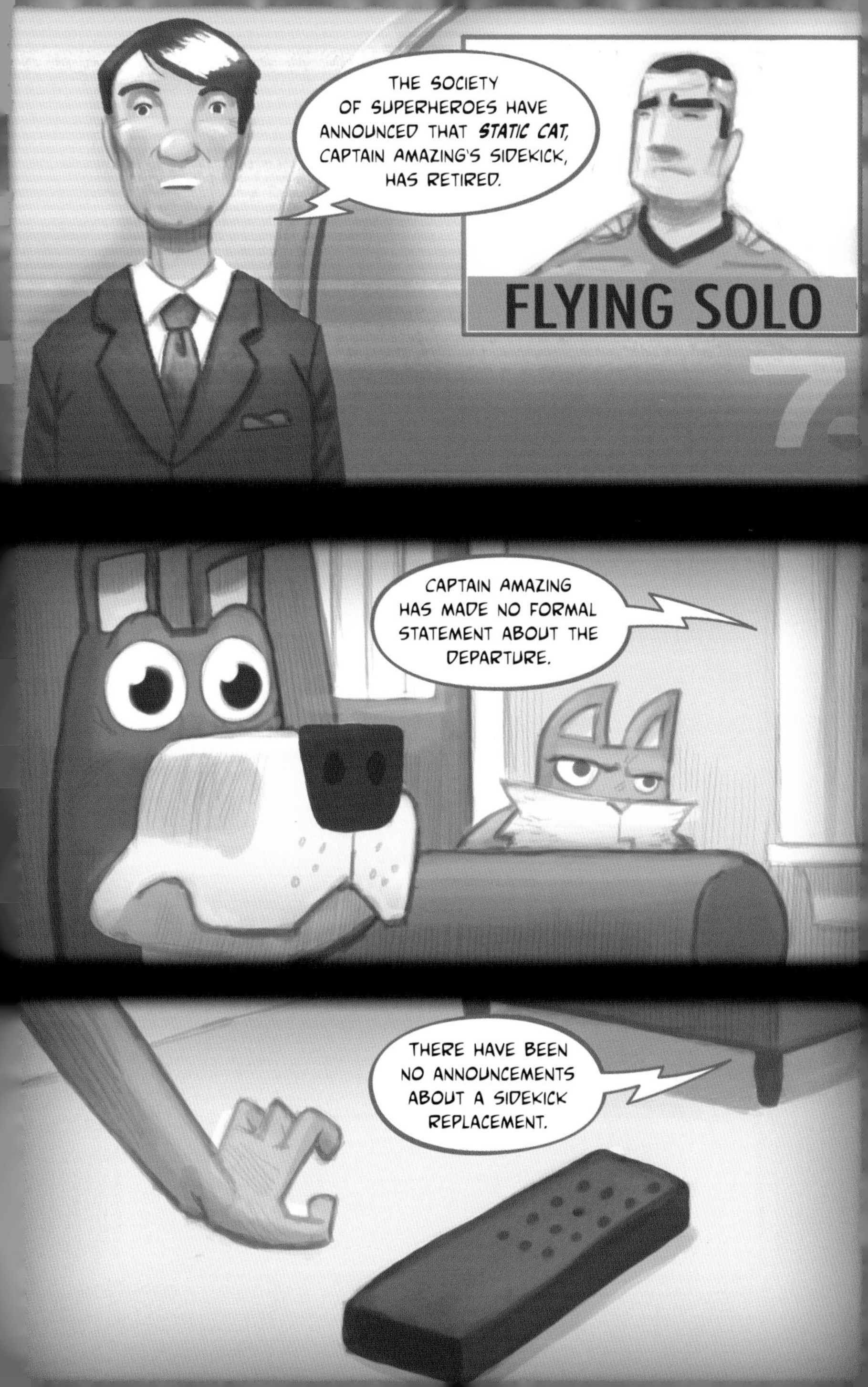
THE SOCIETY OF SUPERHEROES HAVE ANNOUNCED THAT STATIC CAT, CAPTAIN AMAZING'S SIDEKICK, HAS RETIRED.
FLYING SOLO
CAPTAIN AMAZING HAS MADE NO FORMAL STATEMENT ABOUT THE DEPARTURE.
THERE HAVE BEEN NO ANNOUNCEMENTS ABOUT A SIDEKICK REPLACEMENT.

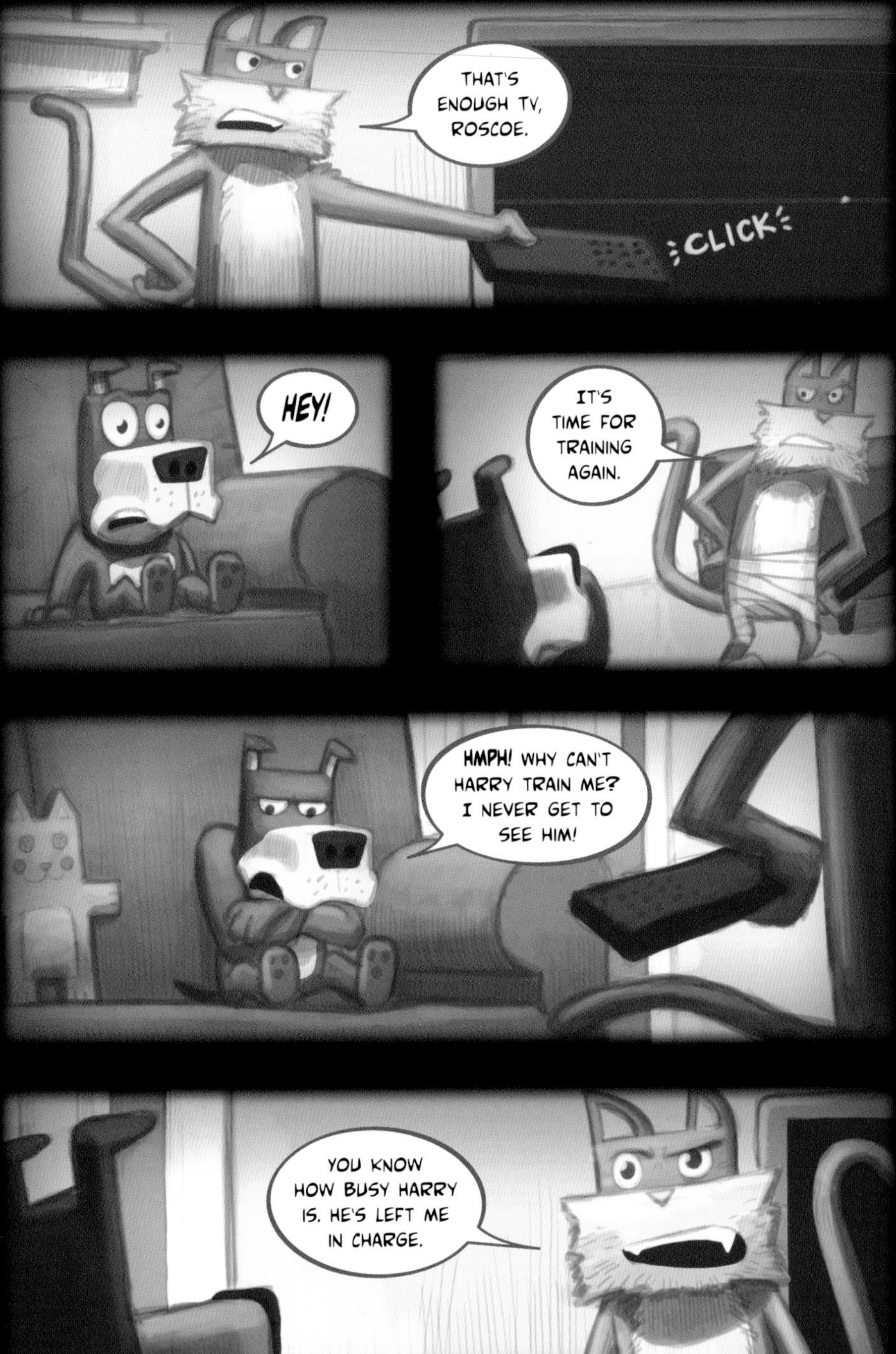
THAT'S ENOUGH TV, ROSCOE.
CLICK
HEY!
IT'S TIME FOR TRAINING AGAIN.
HMPH! WHY CAN'T HARRY TRAIN ME? I NEVER GET TO SEE HIM!
YOU KNOW HOW BUSY HARRY IS. HE'S LEFT ME IN CHARGE.

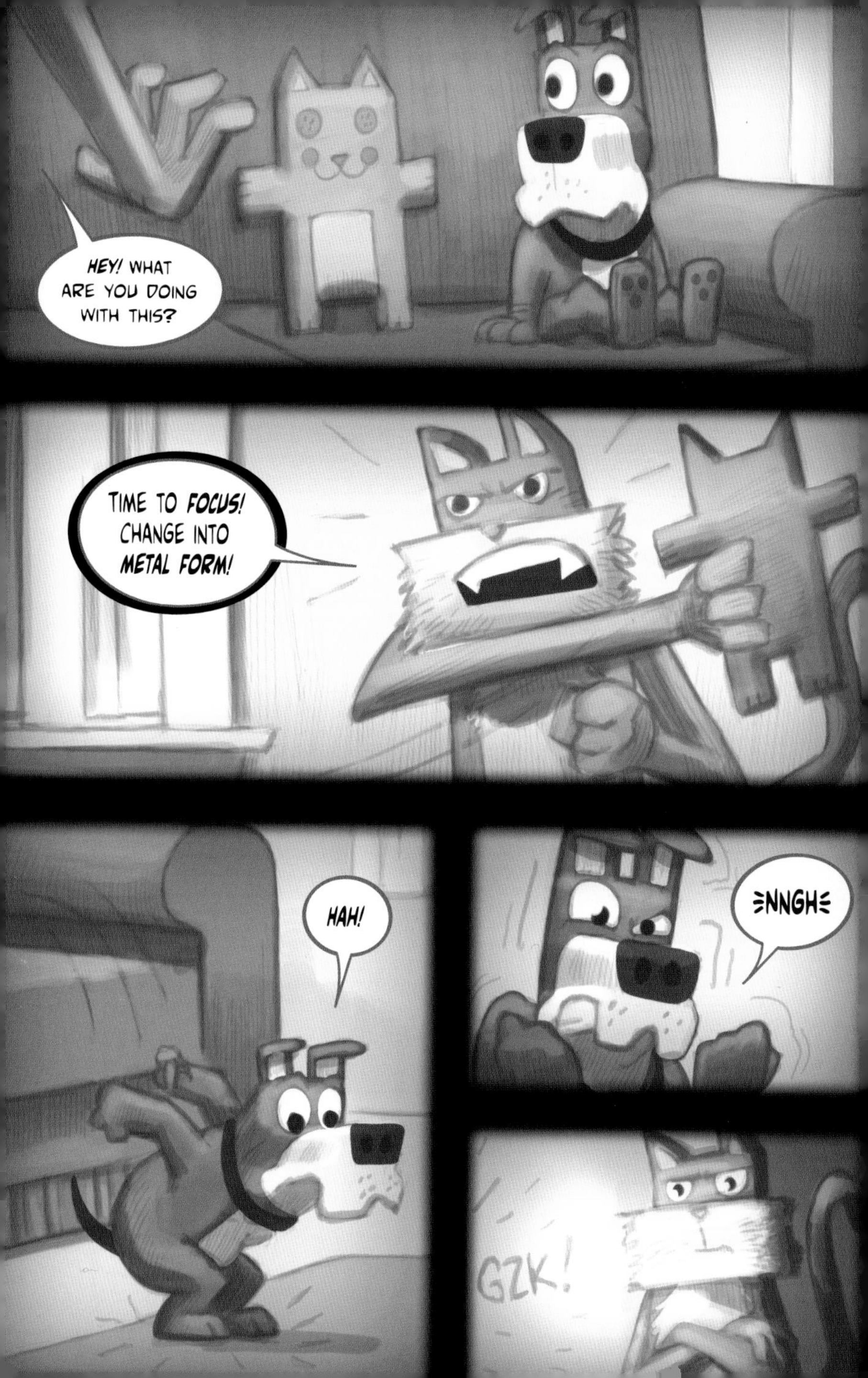
HEY! WHAT ARE YOU DOING WITH THIS?
TIME TO FOCUS! CHANGE INTO METAL FORM!
HAH!
NNGH
GZK!

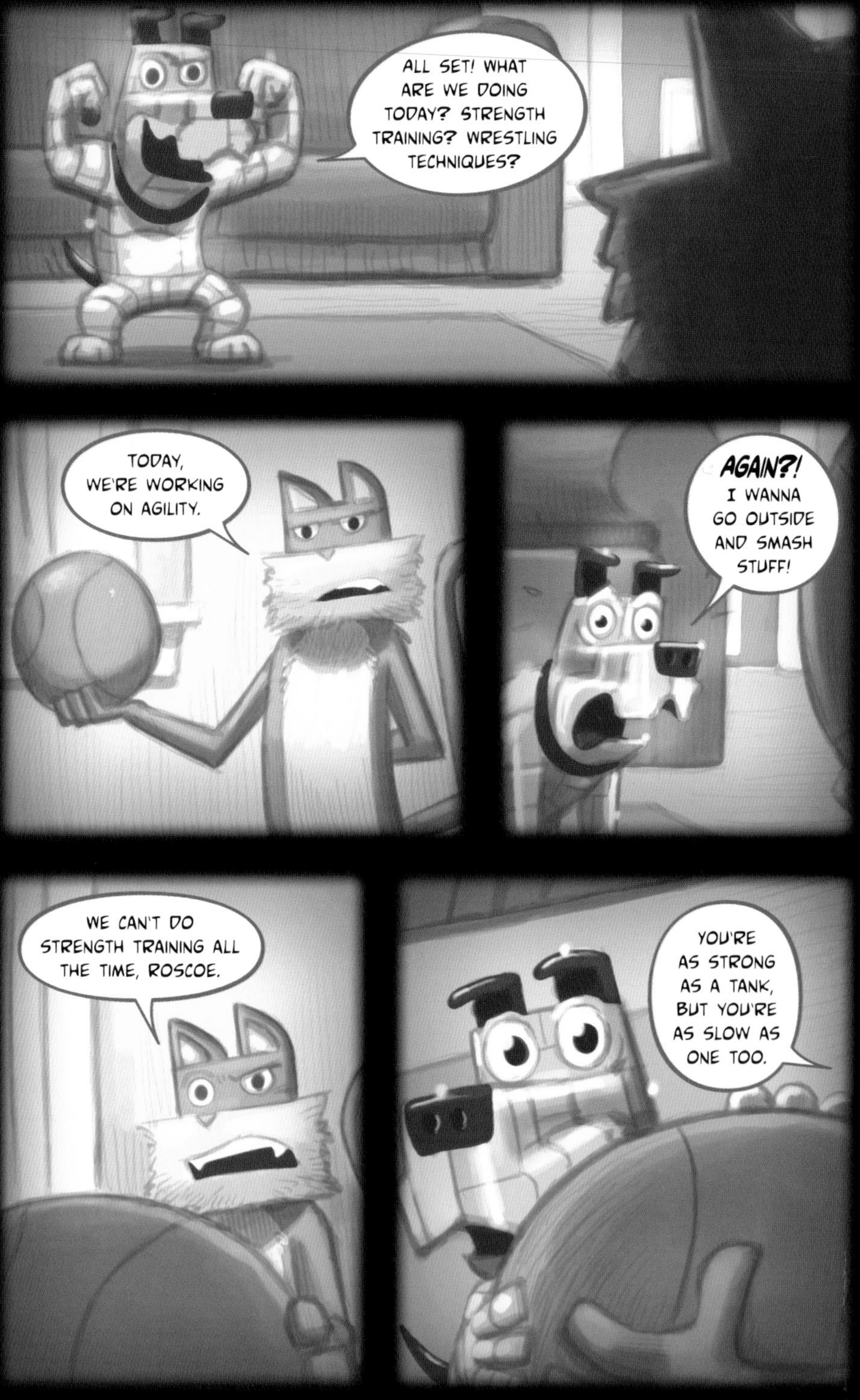
ALL SET! WHAT ARE WE DOING TODAY? STRENGTH TRAINING? WRESTLING TECHNIQUES?
TODAY, WE'RE WORKING ON AGILITY.
AGAIN?! I WANNA GO OUTSIDE AND SMASH STUFF!
WE CAN'T DO STRENGTH TRAINING ALL THE TIME, ROSCOE.
YOU'RE AS STRONG AS A TANK, BUT YOU'RE AS SLOW AS ONE TOO.

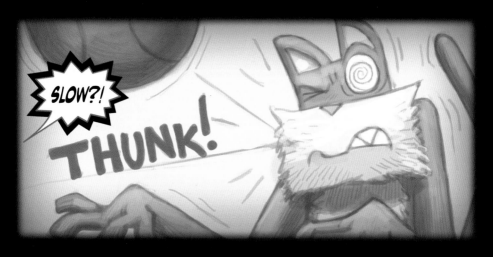

SLOW?!

THUNK!

HA HA HA! UNHAND THAT CITIZEN, FIENDISH FELINE!

STOP GOOFING OFF, ROSCOE! YOU'RE HURTING MY HIP!

NEVER, EVILDOER! FOR I AM *METAL PUP!*

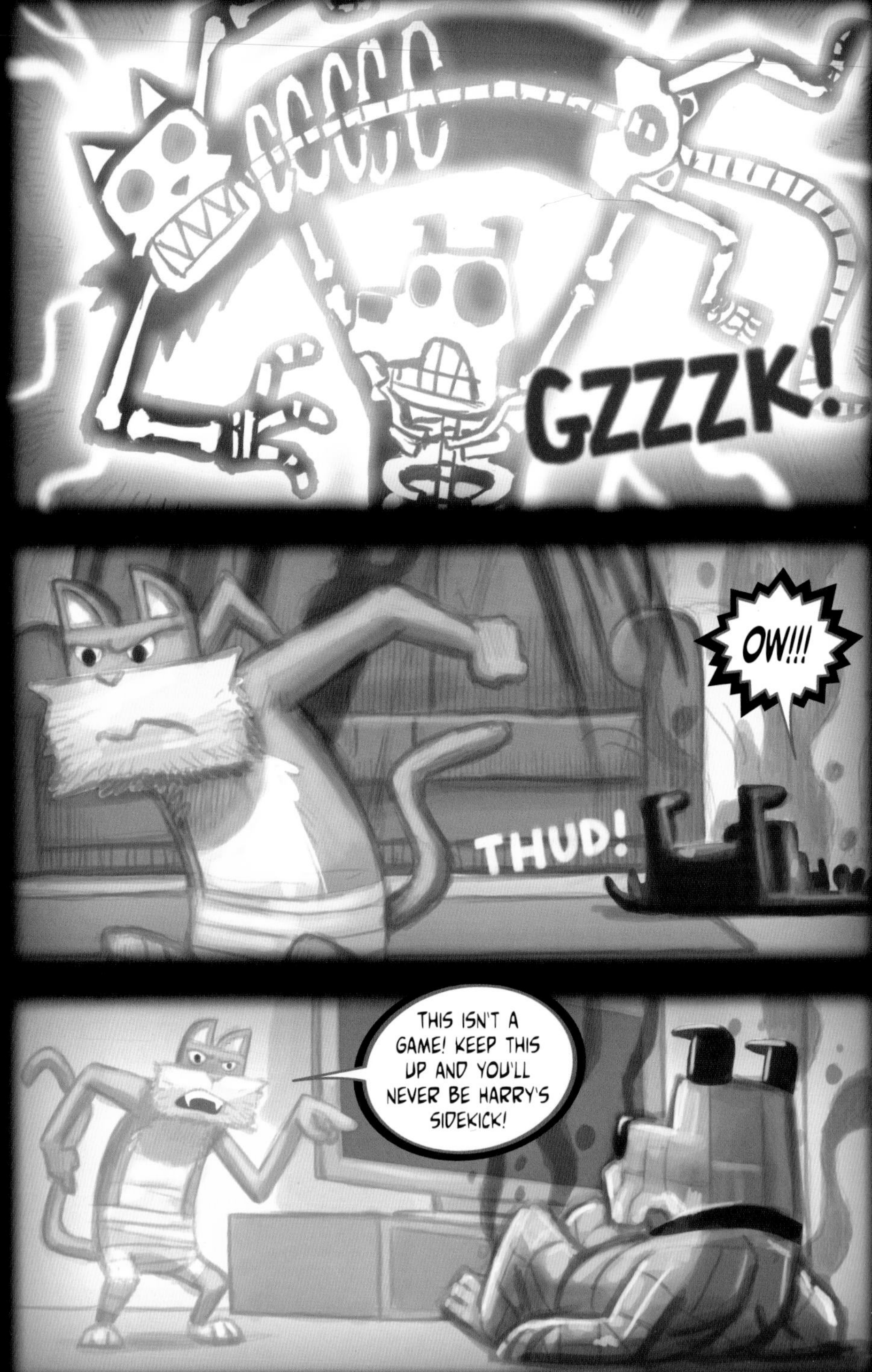
GZZZK!
OW!!!
THUD!
THIS ISN'T A GAME! KEEP THIS UP AND YOU'LL NEVER BE HARRY'S SIDEKICK!

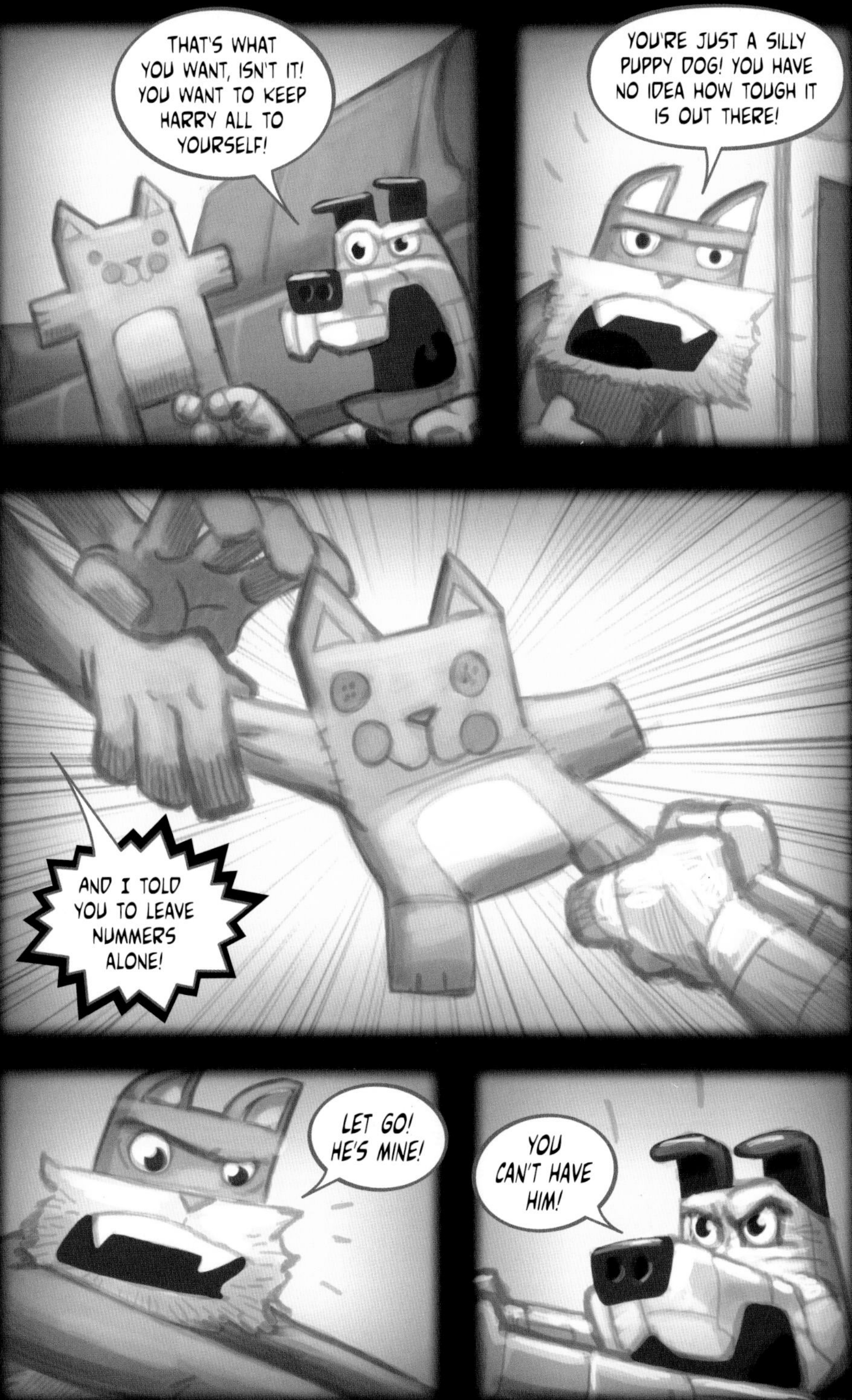
THAT'S WHAT YOU WANT, ISN'T IT! YOU WANT TO KEEP HARRY ALL TO YOURSELF!
YOU'RE JUST A SILLY PUPPY DOG! YOU HAVE NO IDEA HOW TOUGH IT IS OUT THERE!
AND I TOLD YOU TO LEAVE NUMMERS ALONE!
LET GO! HE'S MINE!
YOU CAN'T HAVE HIM!

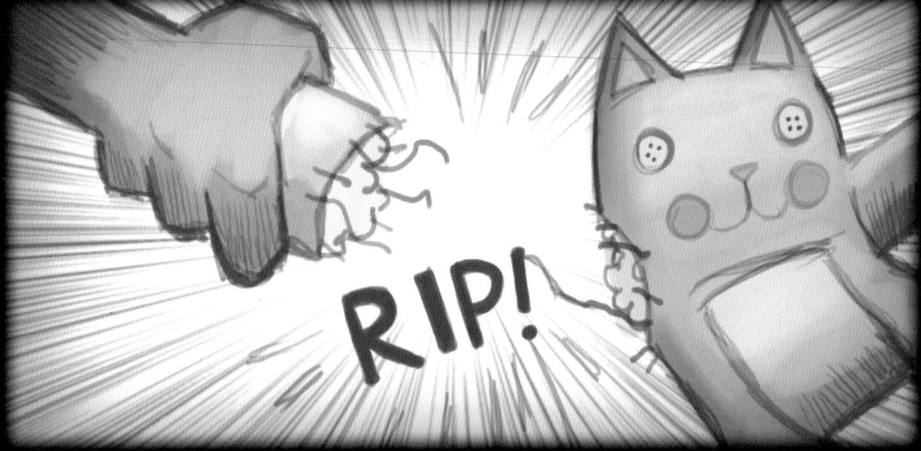
RIP!

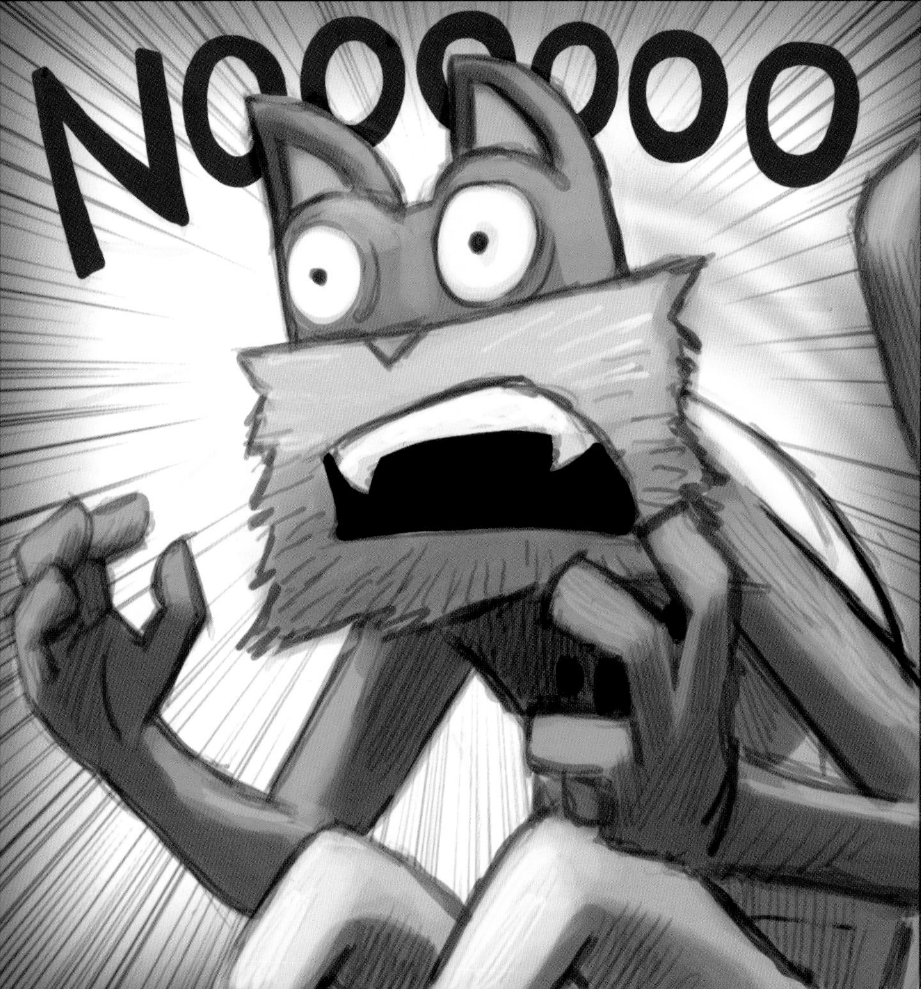
NOOOOOO

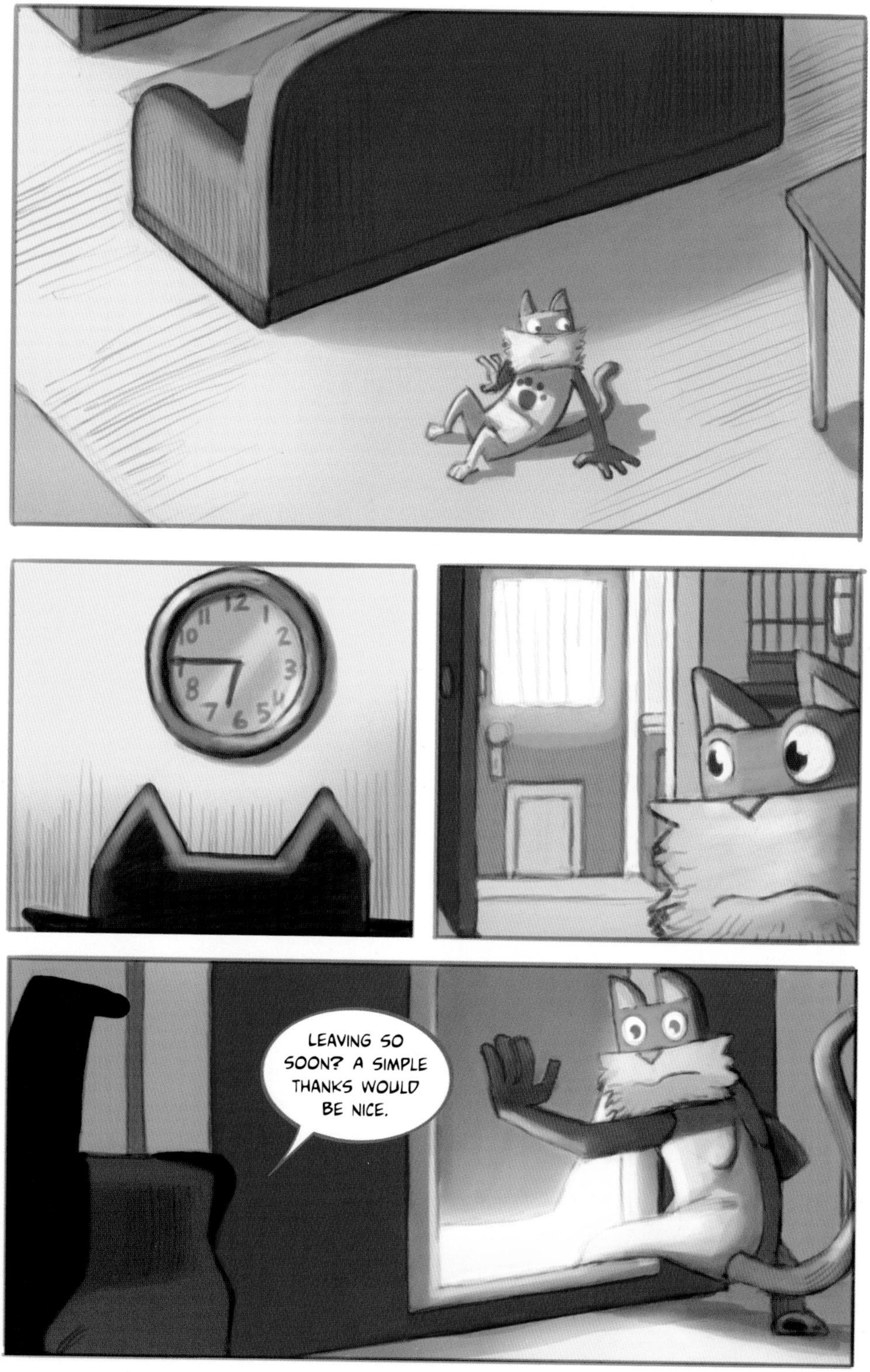
LEAVING SO SOON? A SIMPLE THANKS WOULD BE NICE.

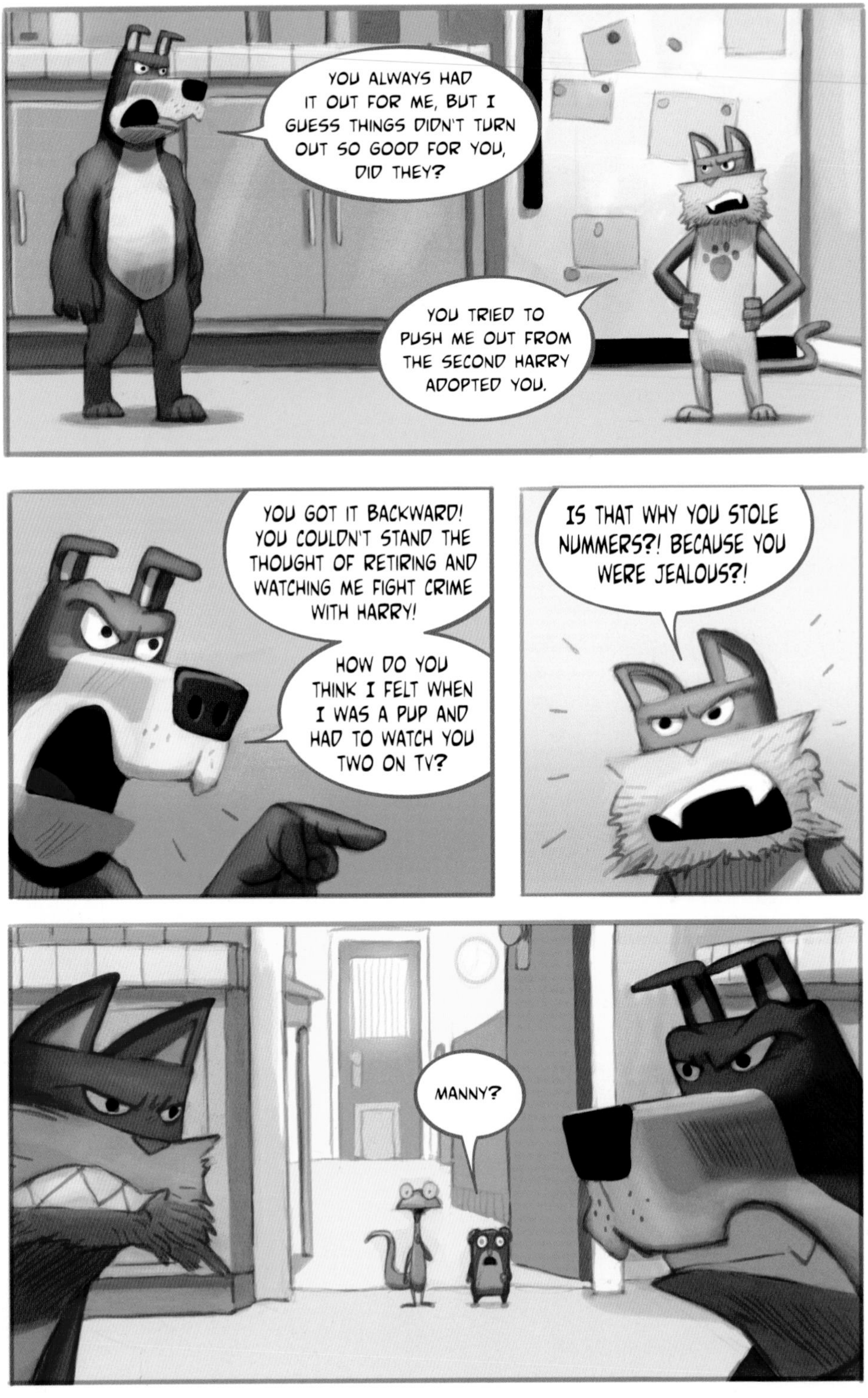
YOU ALWAYS HAD IT OUT FOR ME, BUT I GUESS THINGS DIDN'T TURN OUT SO GOOD FOR YOU, DID THEY?
YOU TRIED TO PUSH ME OUT FROM THE SECOND HARRY ADOPTED YOU.
YOU GOT IT BACKWARD! YOU COULDN'T STAND THE THOUGHT OF RETIRING AND WATCHING ME FIGHT CRIME WITH HARRY!
HOW DO YOU THINK I FELT WHEN I WAS A PUP AND HAD TO WATCH YOU TWO ON TV?
IS THAT WHY YOU STOLE NUMMERS?! BECAUSE YOU WERE JEALOUS?!
MANNY?

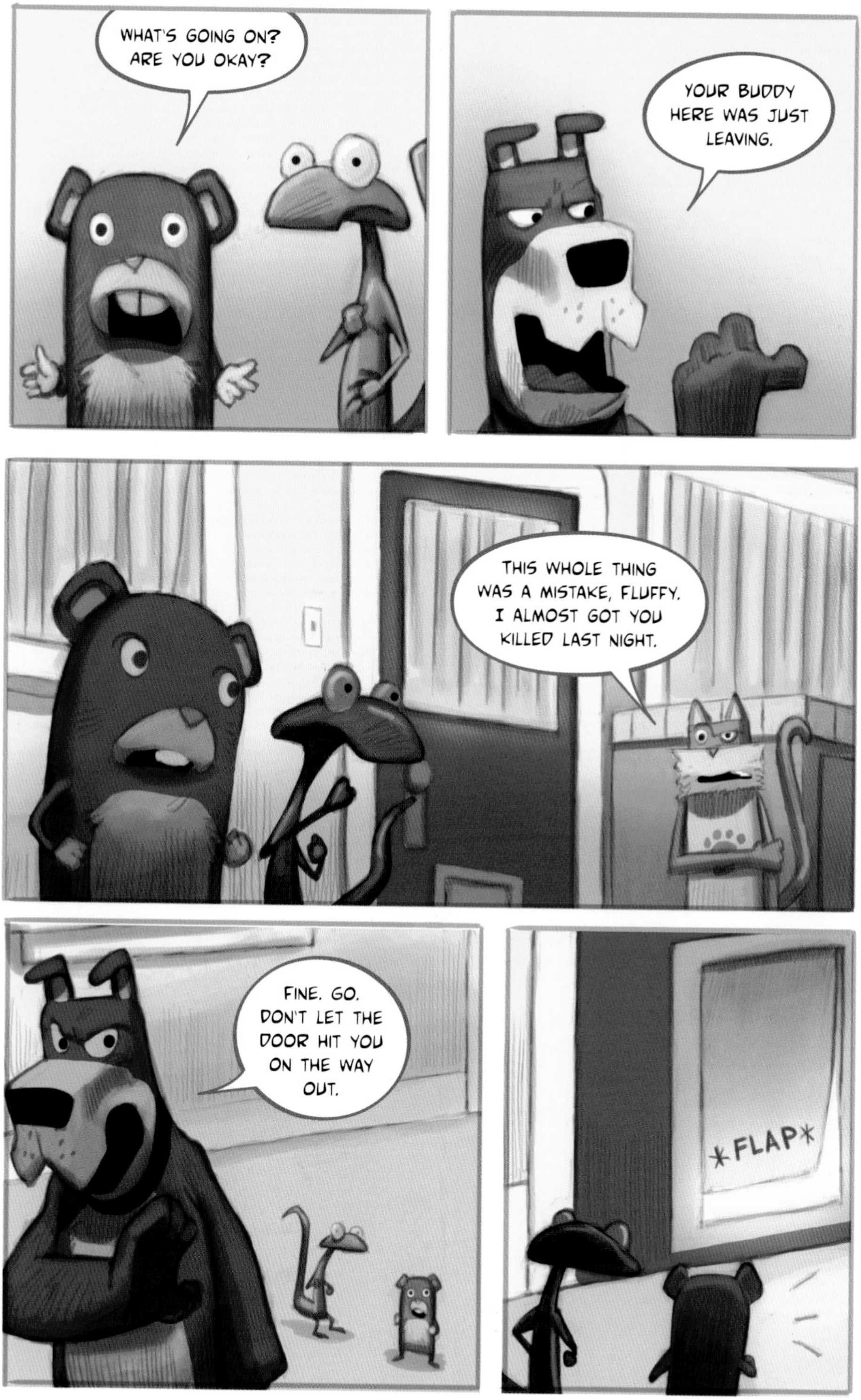
WHAT'S GOING ON? ARE YOU OKAY?
YOUR BUDDY HERE WAS JUST LEAVING.
THIS WHOLE THING WAS A MISTAKE, FLUFFY. I ALMOST GOT YOU KILLED LAST NIGHT.
FINE. GO. DON'T LET THE DOOR HIT YOU ON THE WAY OUT.
FLAP

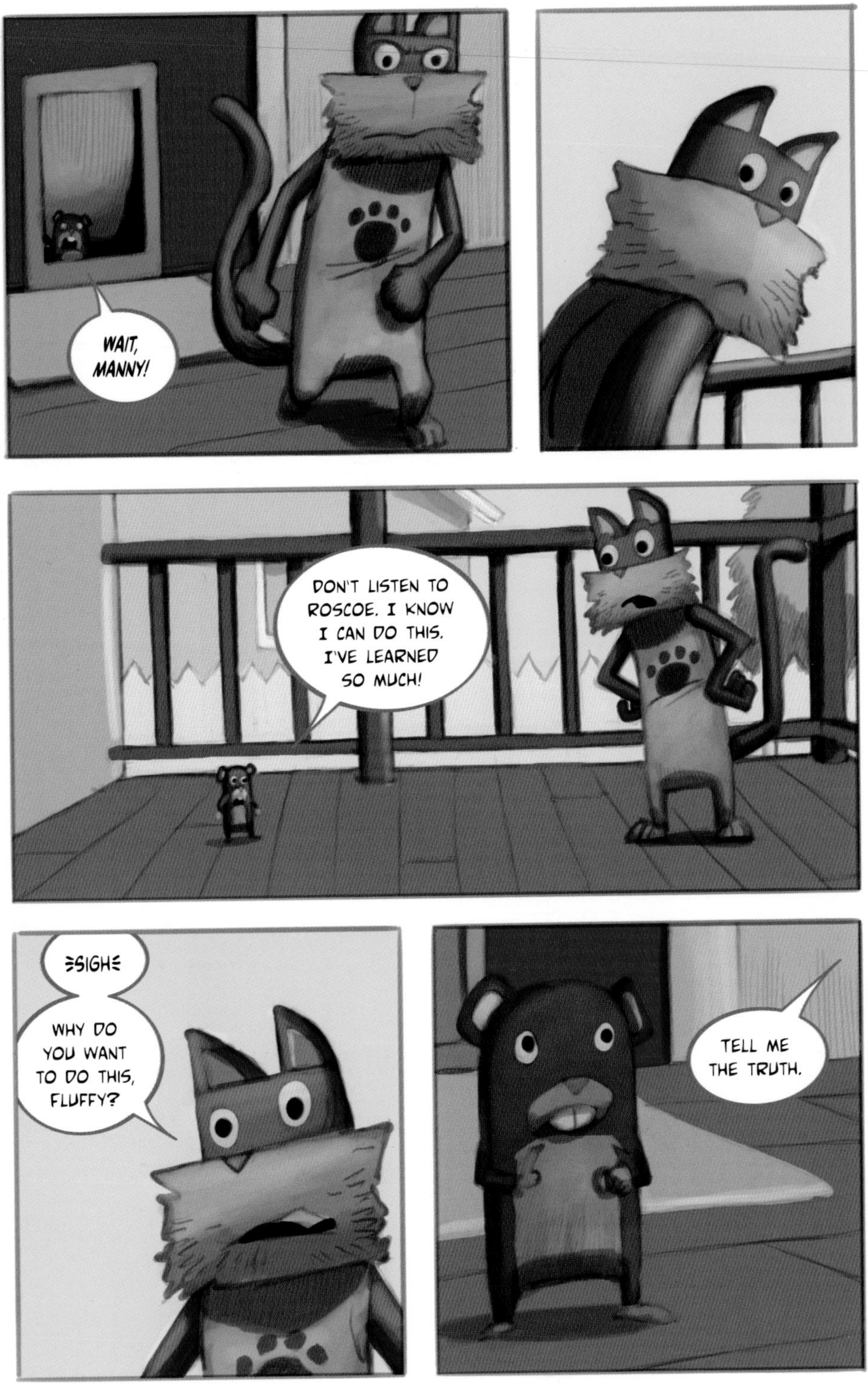
WAIT, MANNY!
DON'T LISTEN TO ROSCOE. I KNOW I CAN DO THIS. I'VE LEARNED SO MUCH!
≡SIGH≡
WHY DO YOU WANT TO DO THIS, FLUFFY?
TELL ME THE TRUTH.

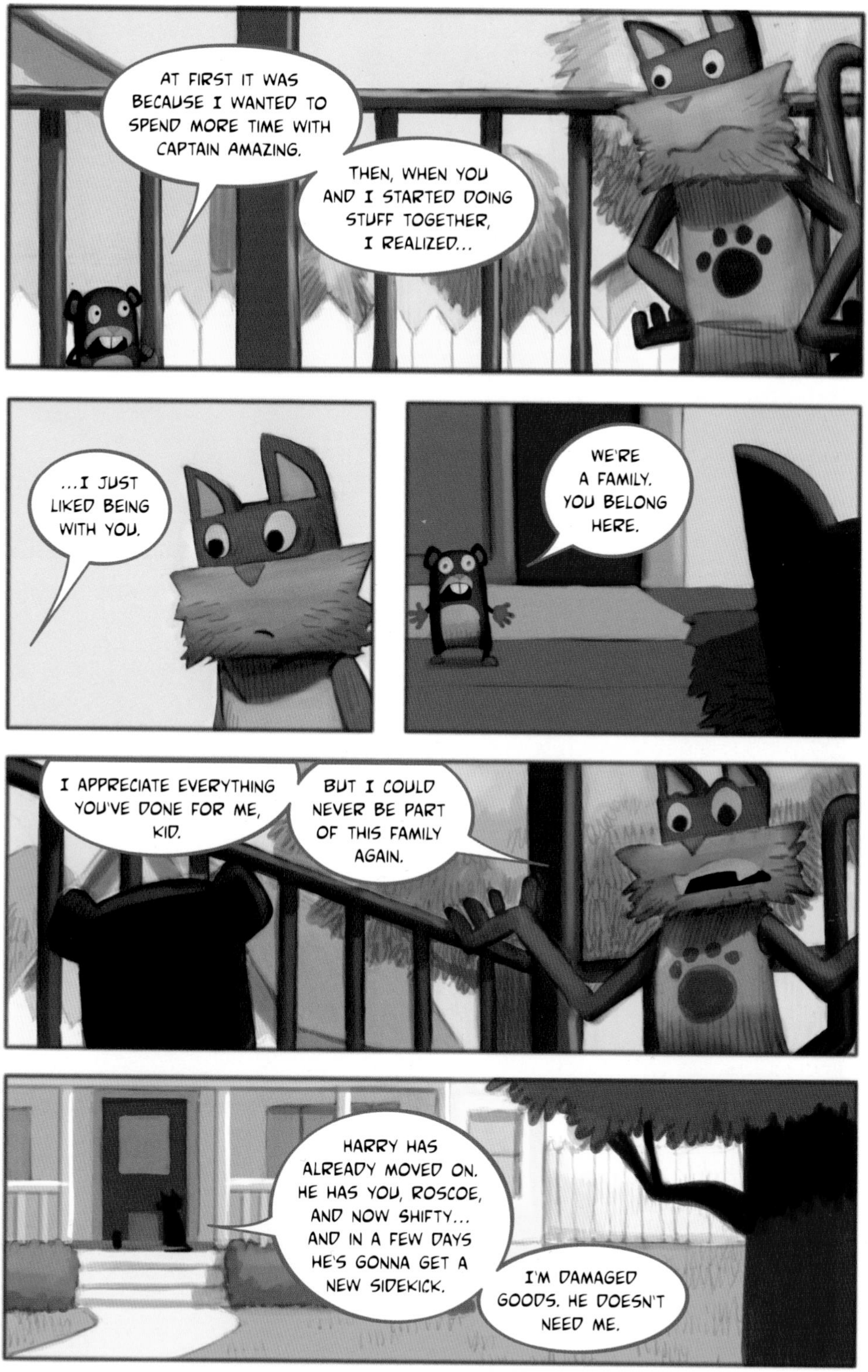
AT FIRST IT WAS BECAUSE I WANTED TO SPEND MORE TIME WITH CAPTAIN AMAZING.
THEN, WHEN YOU AND I STARTED DOING STUFF TOGETHER, I REALIZED...
...I JUST LIKED BEING WITH YOU.
WE'RE A FAMILY. YOU BELONG HERE.
I APPRECIATE EVERYTHING YOU'VE DONE FOR ME, KID.
BUT I COULD NEVER BE PART OF THIS FAMILY AGAIN.
HARRY HAS ALREADY MOVED ON. HE HAS YOU, ROSCOE, AND NOW SHIFTY... AND IN A FEW DAYS HE'S GONNA GET A NEW SIDEKICK.
I'M DAMAGED GOODS. HE DOESN'T NEED ME.

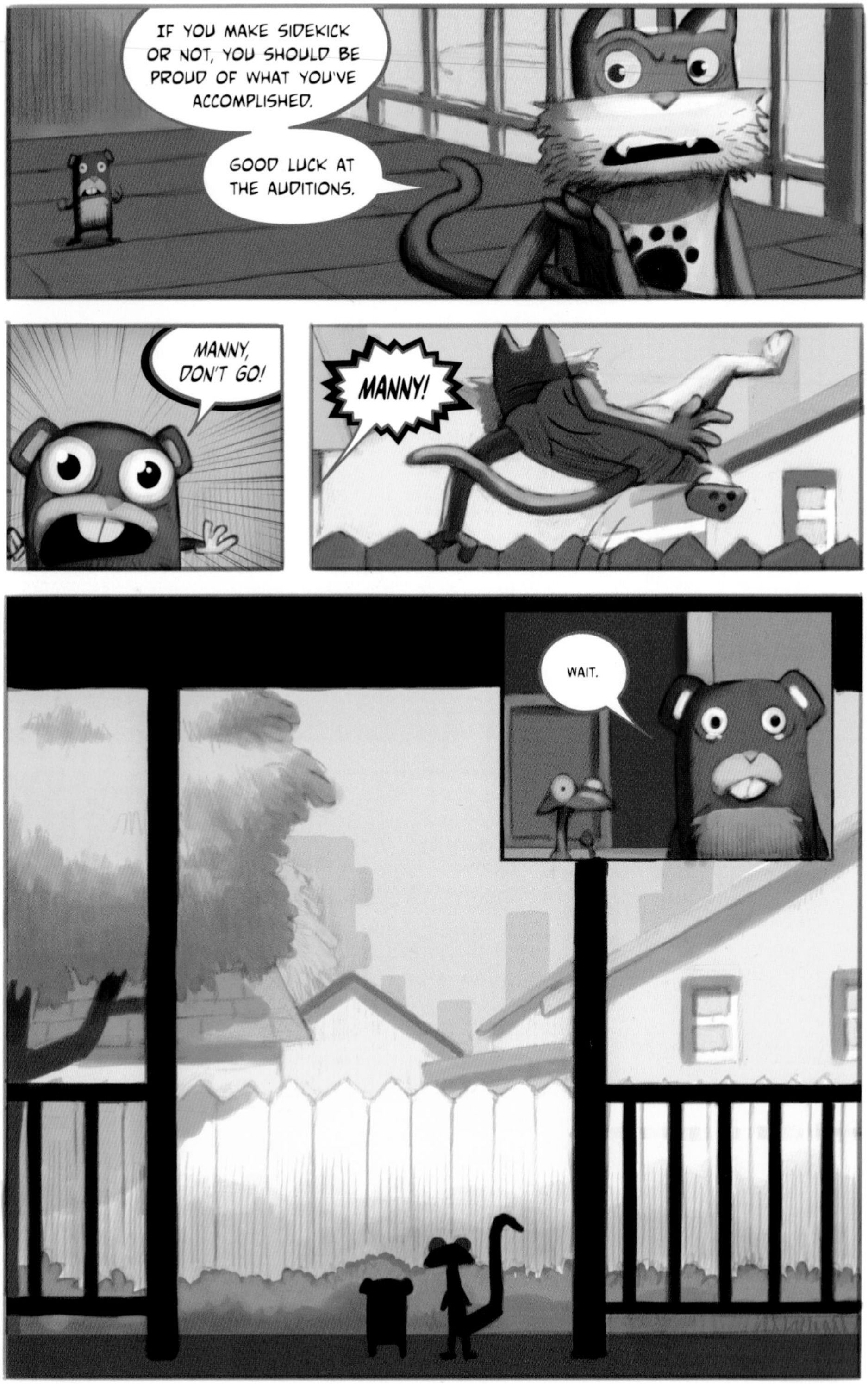
IF YOU MAKE SIDEKICK OR NOT, YOU SHOULD BE PROUD OF WHAT YOU'VE ACCOMPLISHED.
GOOD LUCK AT THE AUDITIONS.
MANNY, DON'T GO!
MANNY!
WAIT.

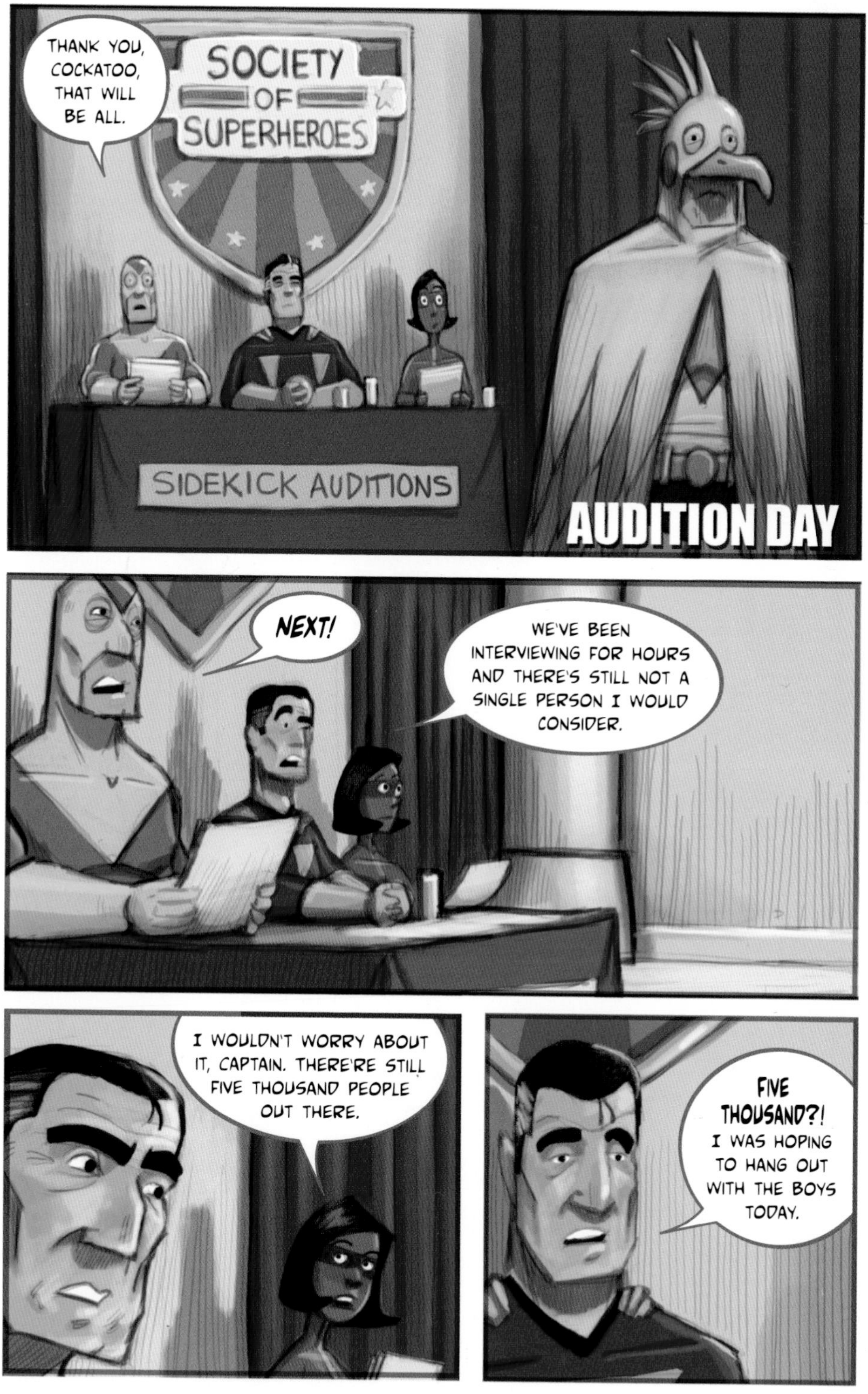
THANK YOU, COCKATOO, THAT WILL BE ALL.
SOCIETY OF SUPERHEROES
SIDEKICK AUDITIONS
AUDITION DAY
NEXT!
WE'VE BEEN INTERVIEWING FOR HOURS AND THERE'S STILL NOT A SINGLE PERSON I WOULD CONSIDER.
I WOULDN'T WORRY ABOUT IT, CAPTAIN. THERE'RE STILL FIVE THOUSAND PEOPLE OUT THERE.
FIVE THOUSAND?! I WAS HOPING TO HANG OUT WITH THE BOYS TODAY.

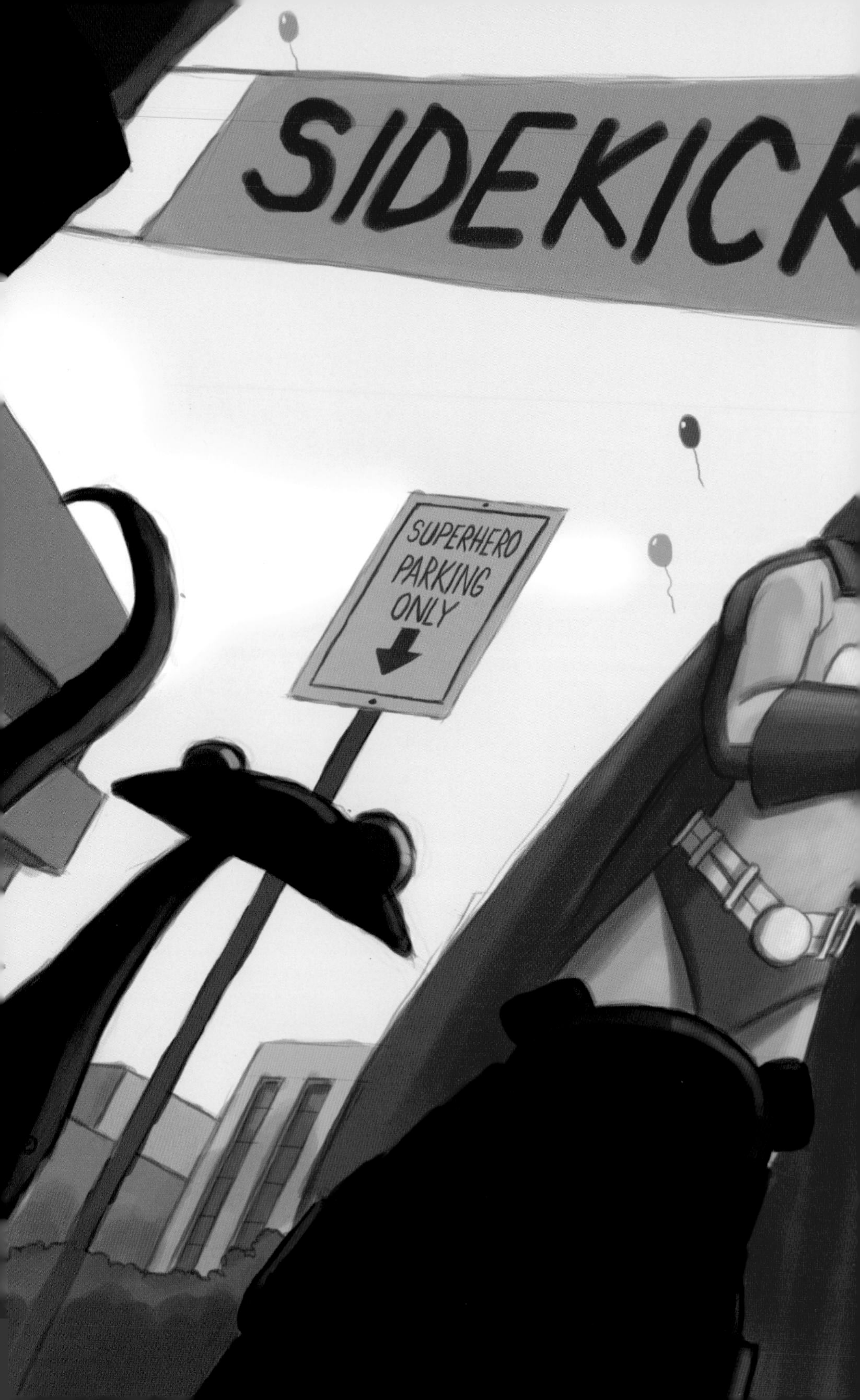
SIDEKICK
SUPERHERO
PARKING
ONLY

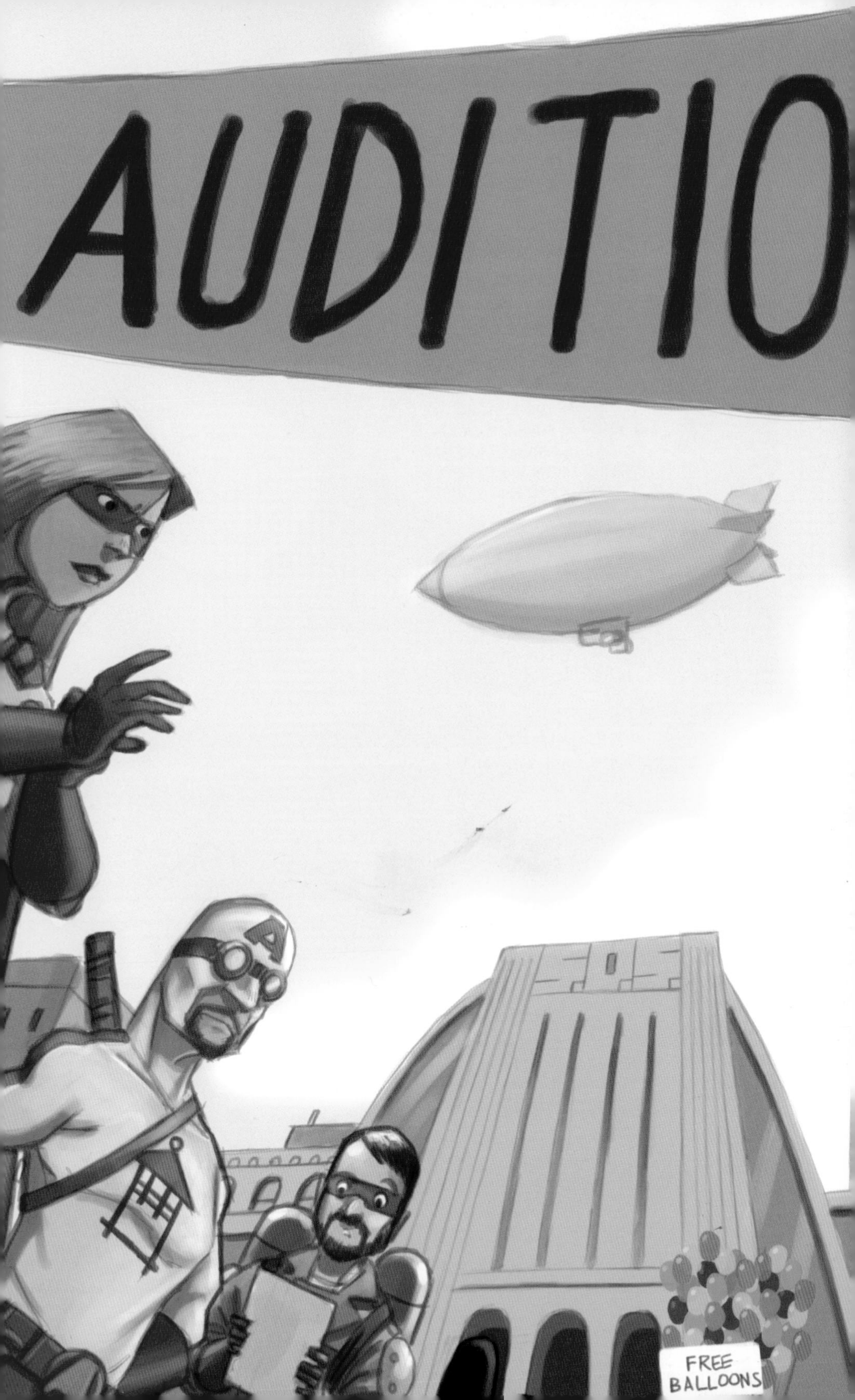
AUDITIO
FREE
BALLOONS

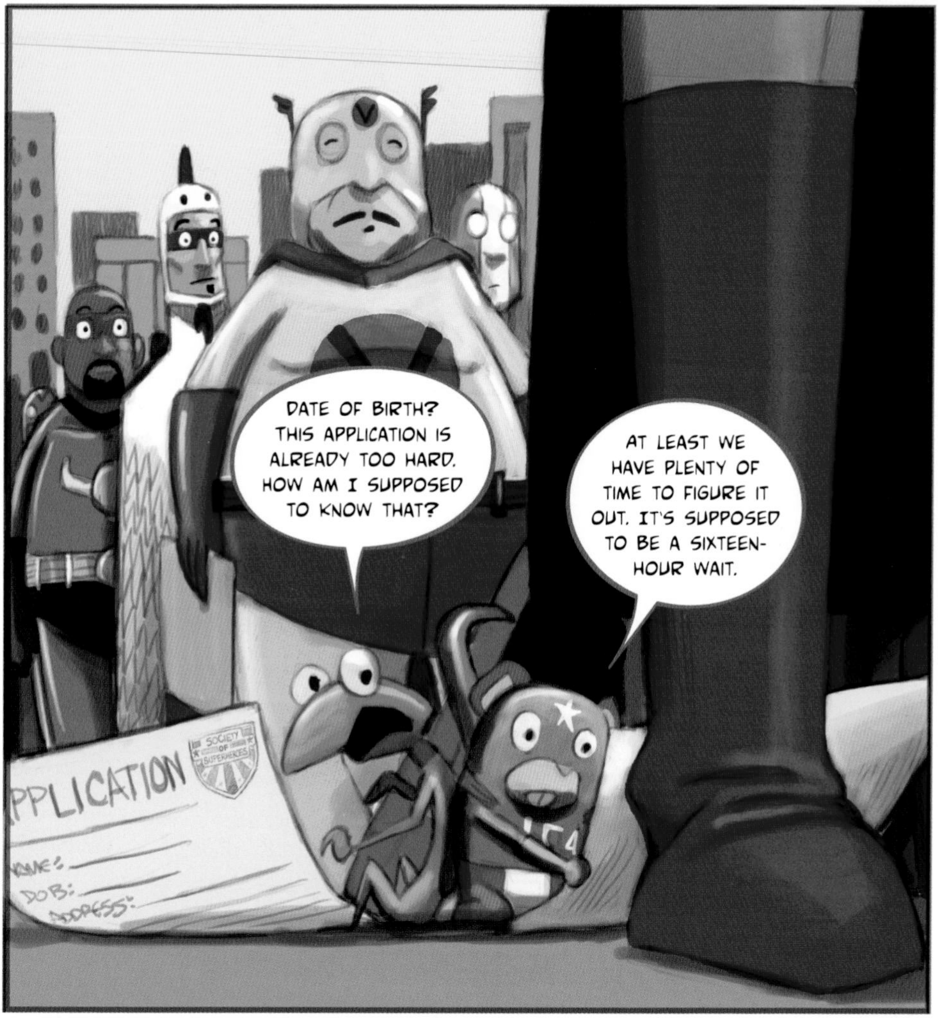
DATE OF BIRTH? THIS APPLICATION IS ALREADY TOO HARD. HOW AM I SUPPOSED TO KNOW THAT?
AT LEAST WE HAVE PLENTY OF TIME TO FIGURE IT OUT. IT'S SUPPOSED TO BE A SIXTEEN-HOUR WAIT.
APPLICATION
SOCIETY OF SUPERHEROES
NAME:
DOB:
ADDRESS:

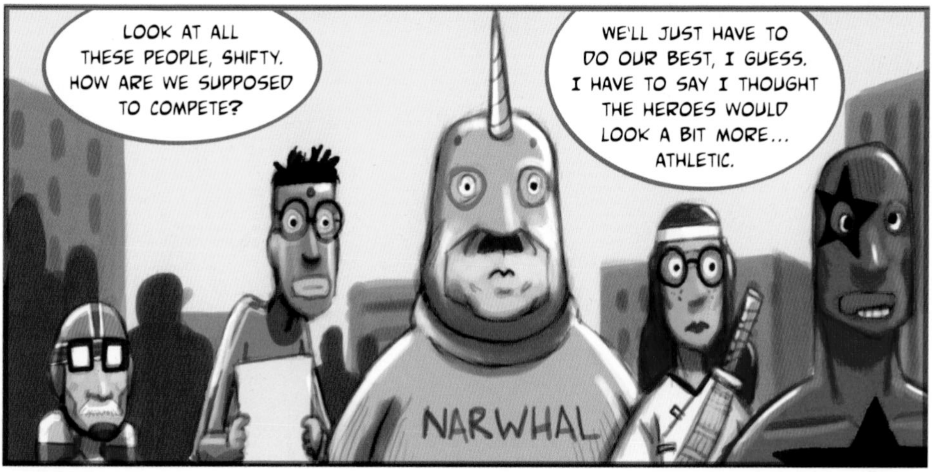
LOOK AT ALL THESE PEOPLE, SHIFTY. HOW ARE WE SUPPOSED TO COMPETE?
WE'LL JUST HAVE TO DO OUR BEST, I GUESS. I HAVE TO SAY I THOUGHT THE HEROES WOULD LOOK A BIT MORE... ATHLETIC.
NARWHAL

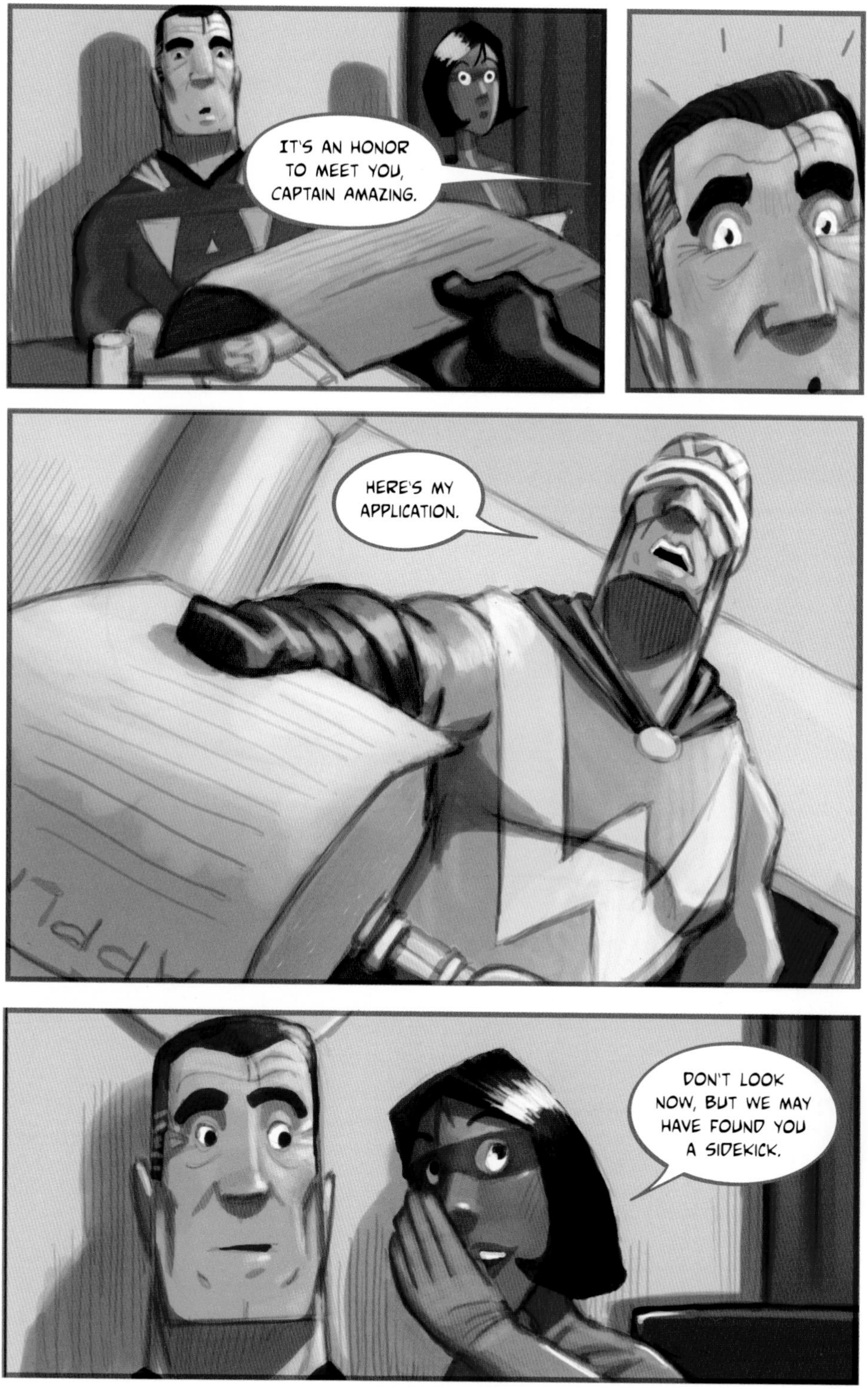
IT'S AN HONOR TO MEET YOU, CAPTAIN AMAZING.
HERE'S MY APPLICATION.
DON'T LOOK NOW, BUT WE MAY HAVE FOUND YOU A SIDEKICK.

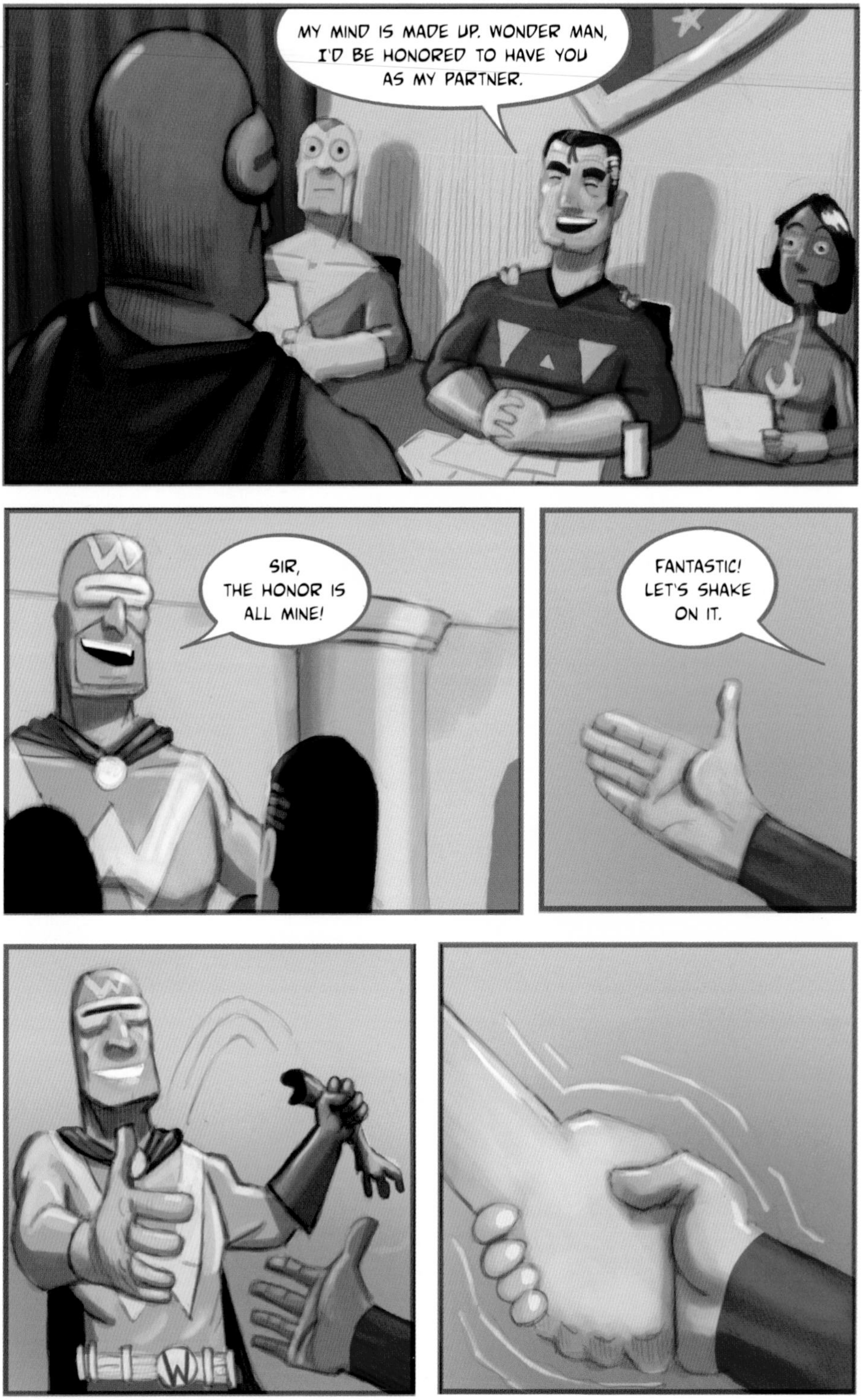
MY MIND IS MADE UP. WONDER MAN, I'D BE HONORED TO HAVE YOU AS MY PARTNER.
SIR, THE HONOR IS ALL MINE!
FANTASTIC! LET'S SHAKE ON IT.

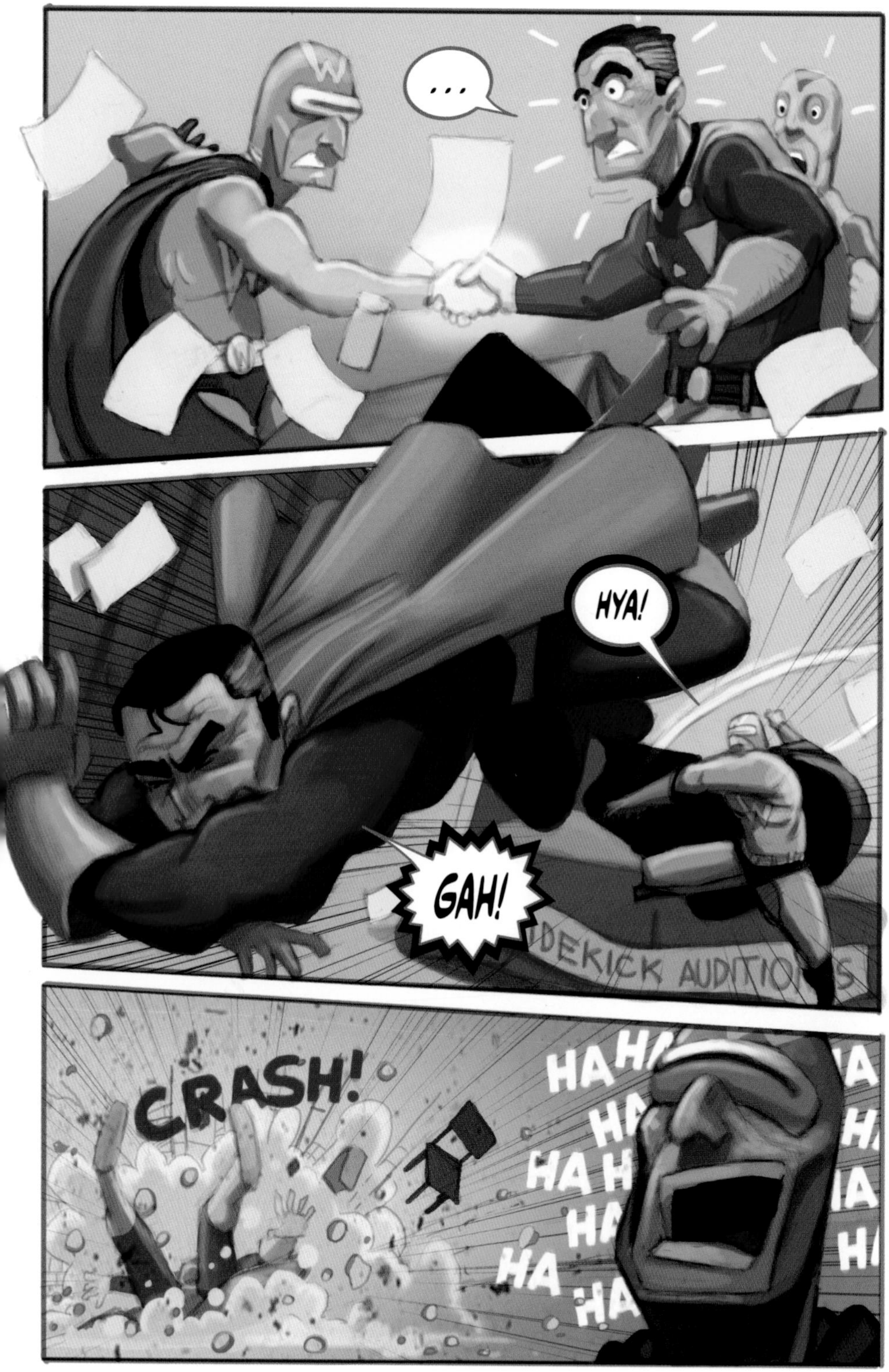
...
HYA!
GAH!
DEKICK AUDITIO S
CRASH!
HA HA HA HA HA HA HA HA

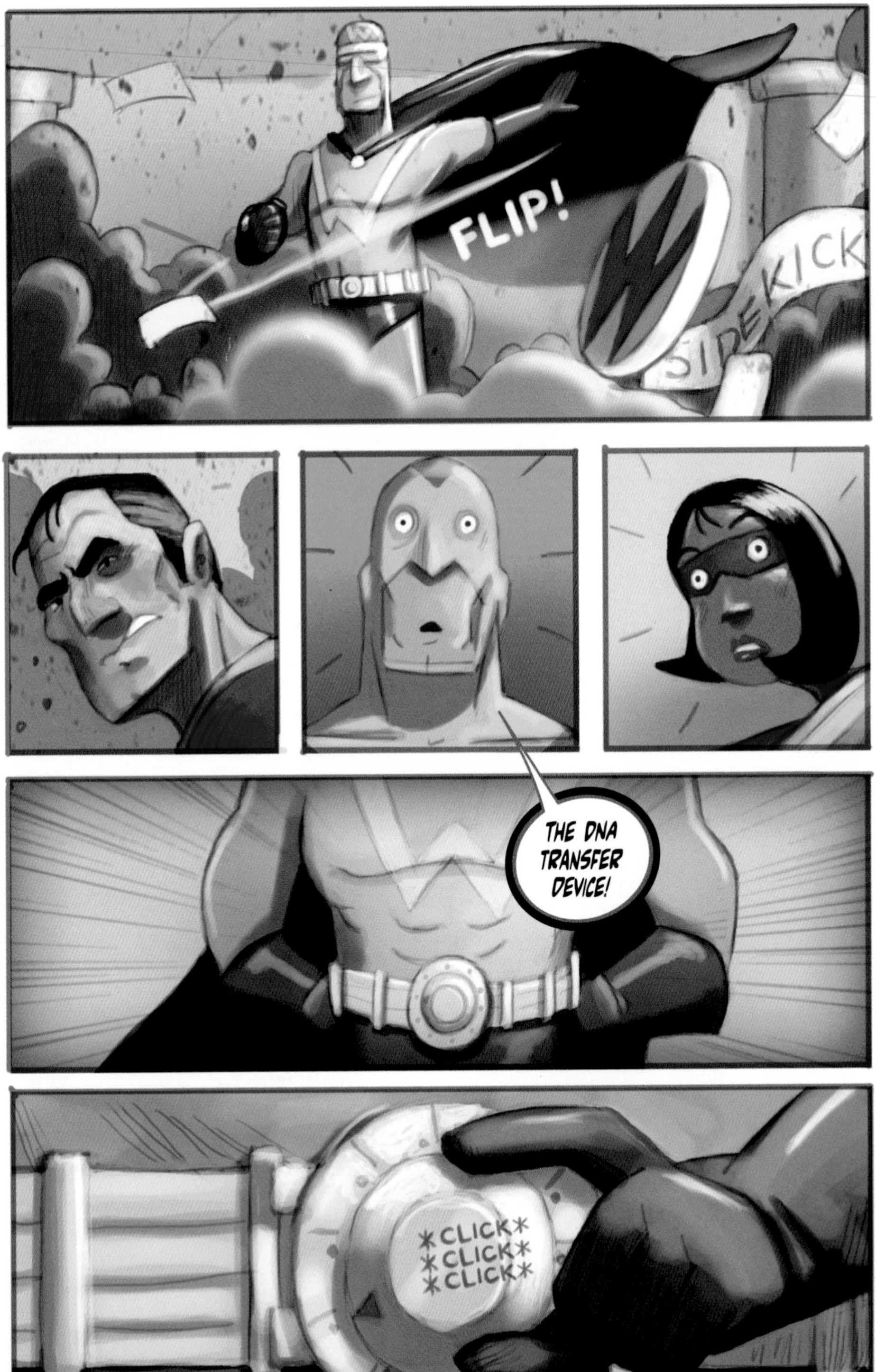
FLIP!
SIDEKICK
THE DNA TRANSFER DEVICE!
CLICK
CLICK
CLICK

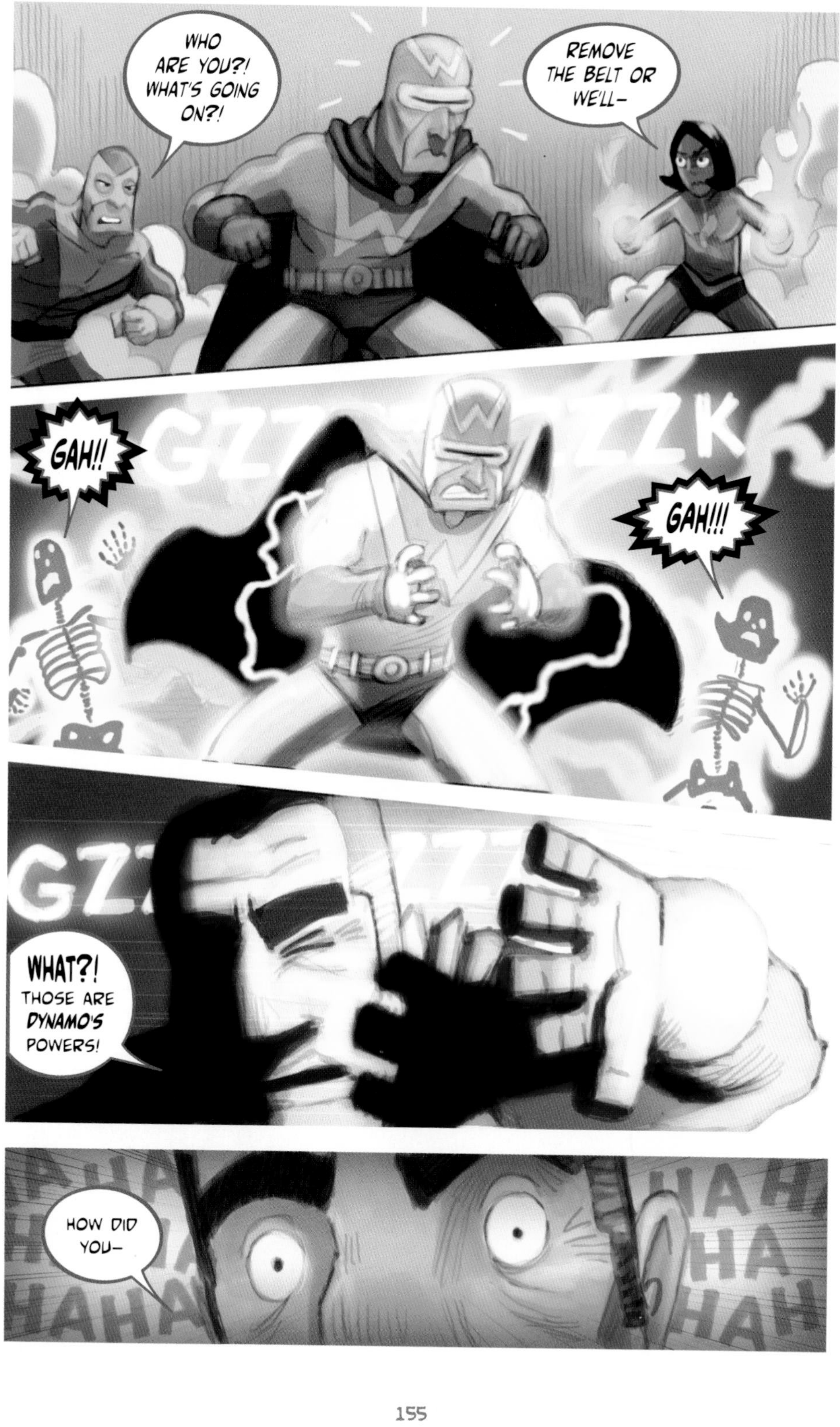
WHO ARE YOU?! WHAT'S GOING ON?!
REMOVE THE BELT OR WE'LL–
GAH!!
GAH!!!
WHAT?! THOSE ARE DYNAMO'S POWERS!
HOW DID YOU–

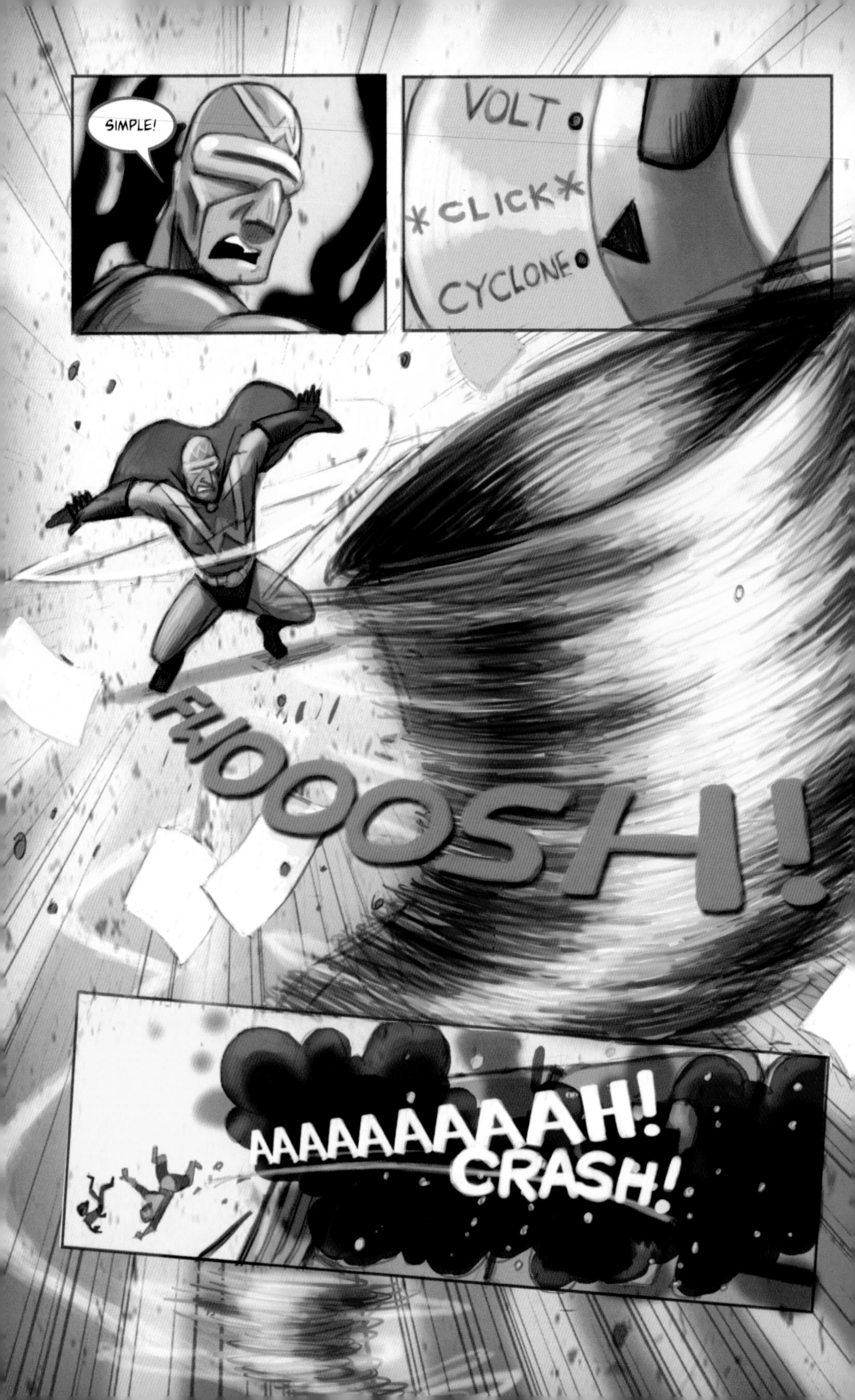
SIMPLE!
VOLT
CLICK
CYCLONE
FWOOOSH!!
AAAAAAAAAH!
CRASH!

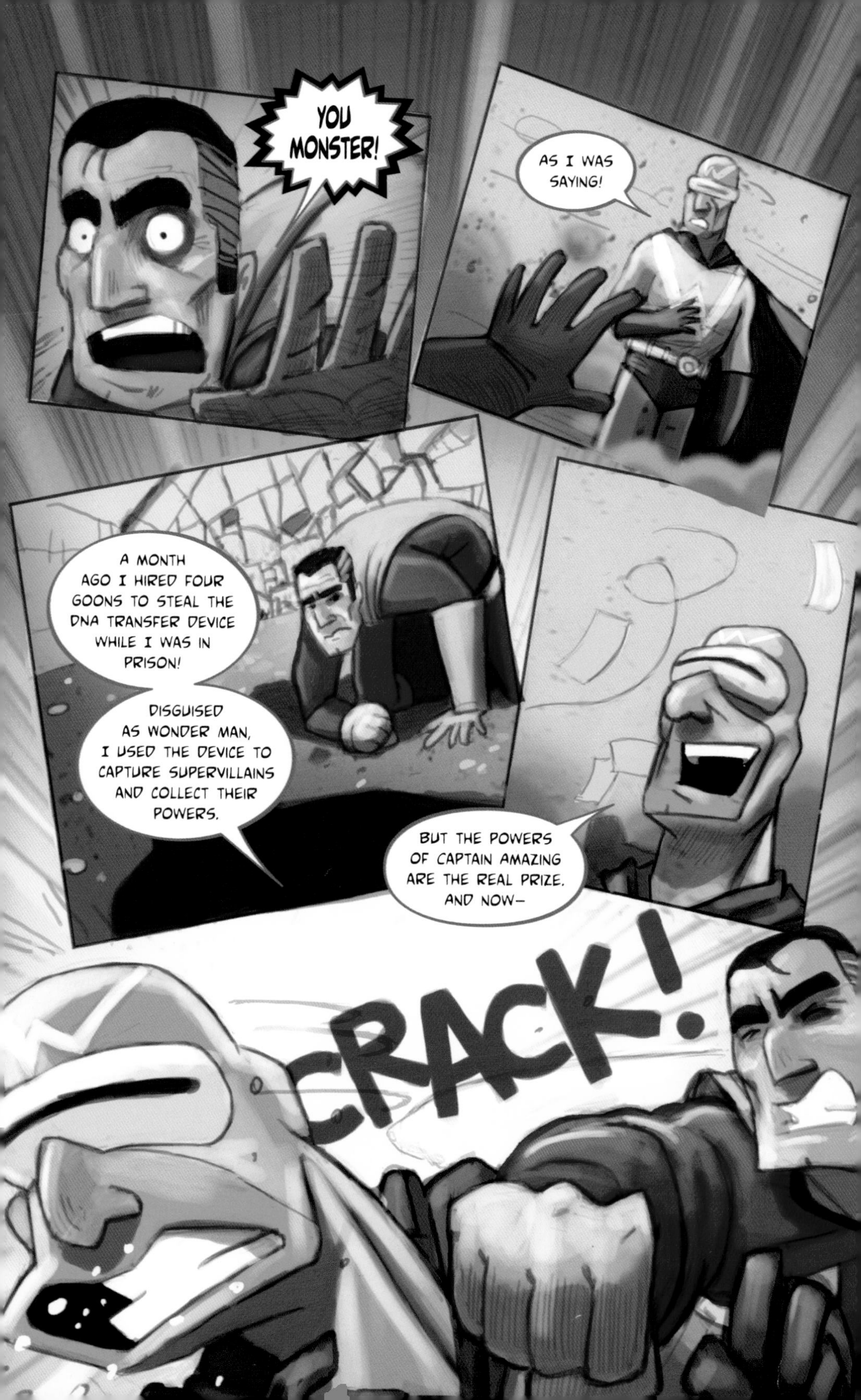

YOU MONSTER!
AS I WAS SAYING!
A MONTH AGO I HIRED FOUR GOONS TO STEAL THE DNA TRANSFER DEVICE WHILE I WAS IN PRISON!
DISGUISED AS WONDER MAN, I USED THE DEVICE TO CAPTURE SUPERVILLAINS AND COLLECT THEIR POWERS.
BUT THE POWERS OF CAPTAIN AMAZING ARE THE REAL PRIZE. AND NOW—
CRACK!

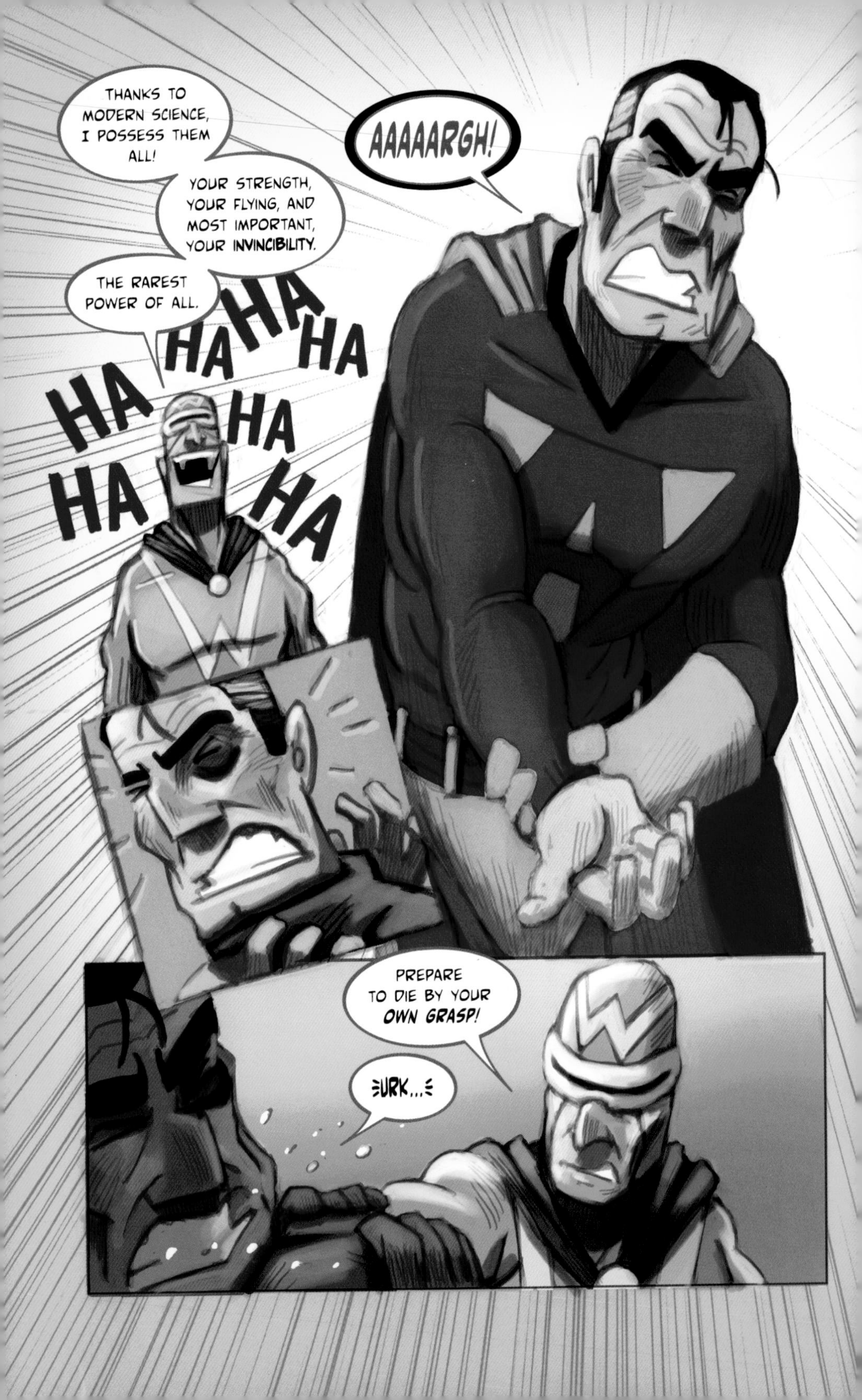
THANKS TO MODERN SCIENCE, I POSSESS THEM ALL!
YOUR STRENGTH, YOUR FLYING, AND MOST IMPORTANT, YOUR INVINCIBILITY.
THE RAREST POWER OF ALL.
AAAAARGH!
HA HA HA HA HA HA HA HA
PREPARE TO DIE BY YOUR OWN GRASP!
URK...

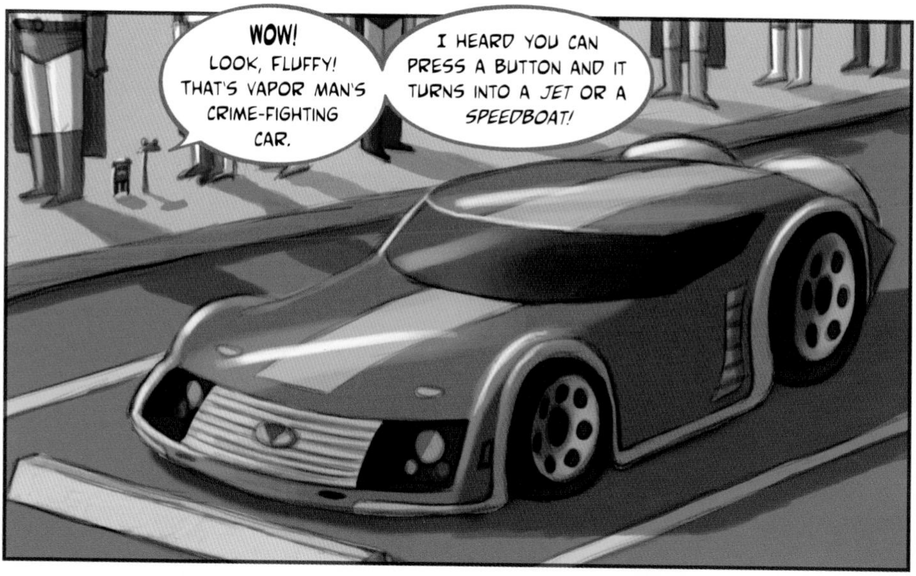
WOW! LOOK, FLUFFY! THAT'S VAPOR MAN'S CRIME-FIGHTING CAR.
I HEARD YOU CAN PRESS A BUTTON AND IT TURNS INTO A *JET* OR A *SPEEDBOAT!*

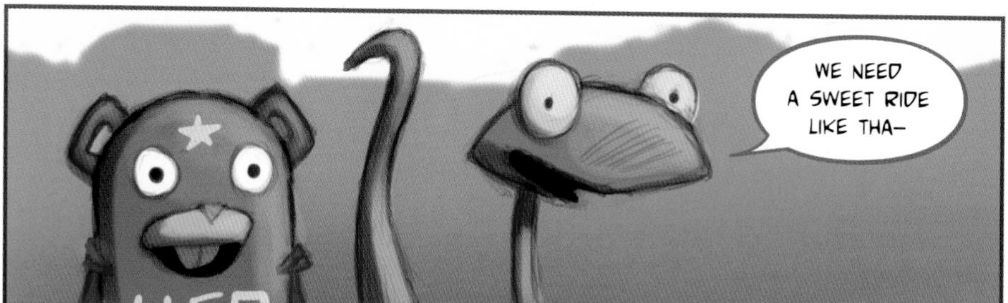
WE NEED A SWEET RIDE LIKE THA—

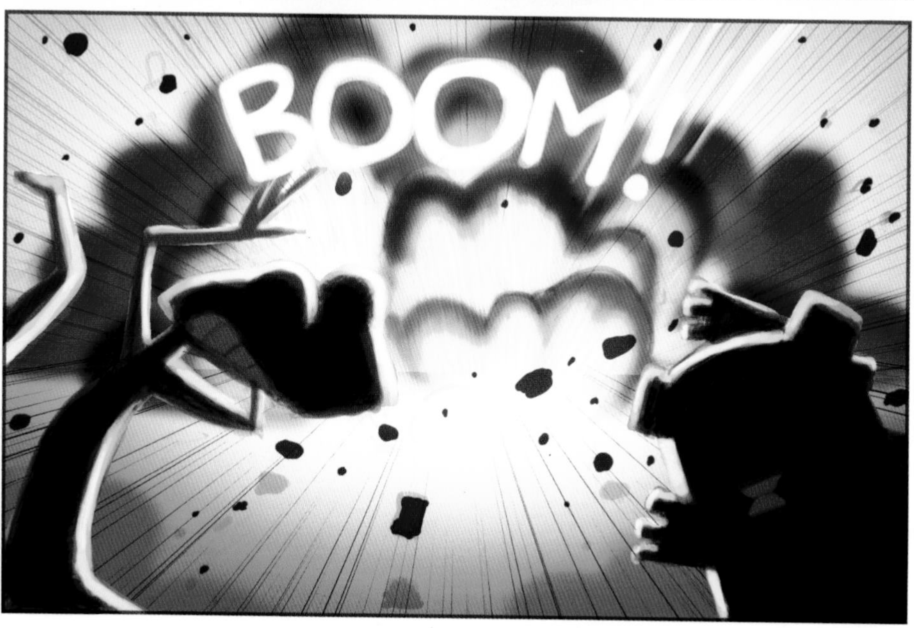
BOOM!

THE... THE CAR...

CLEAR THE AREA! WE HAVE AN EMERGENCY!

WONDER MAN IS UP THERE! HE STOLE CAPTAIN AMAZING'S POWERS! THERE WAS NOTHING WE COULD DO TO HELP!

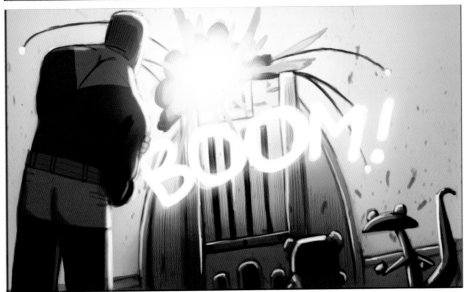

BOOM!

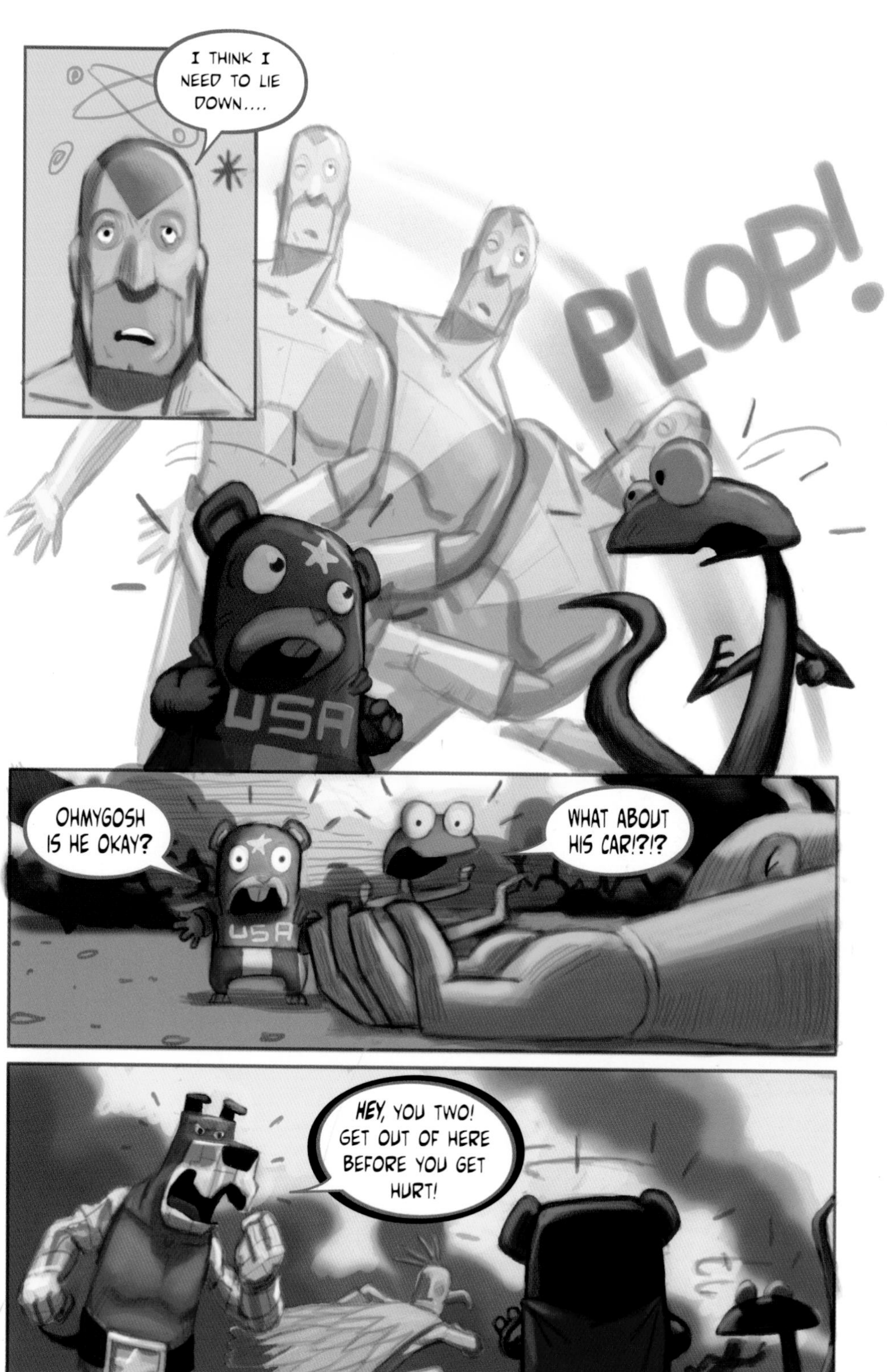
I THINK I NEED TO LIE DOWN....
PLOP!
OHMYGOSH IS HE OKAY?
WHAT ABOUT HIS CAR!?!?
HEY, YOU TWO! GET OUT OF HERE BEFORE YOU GET HURT!

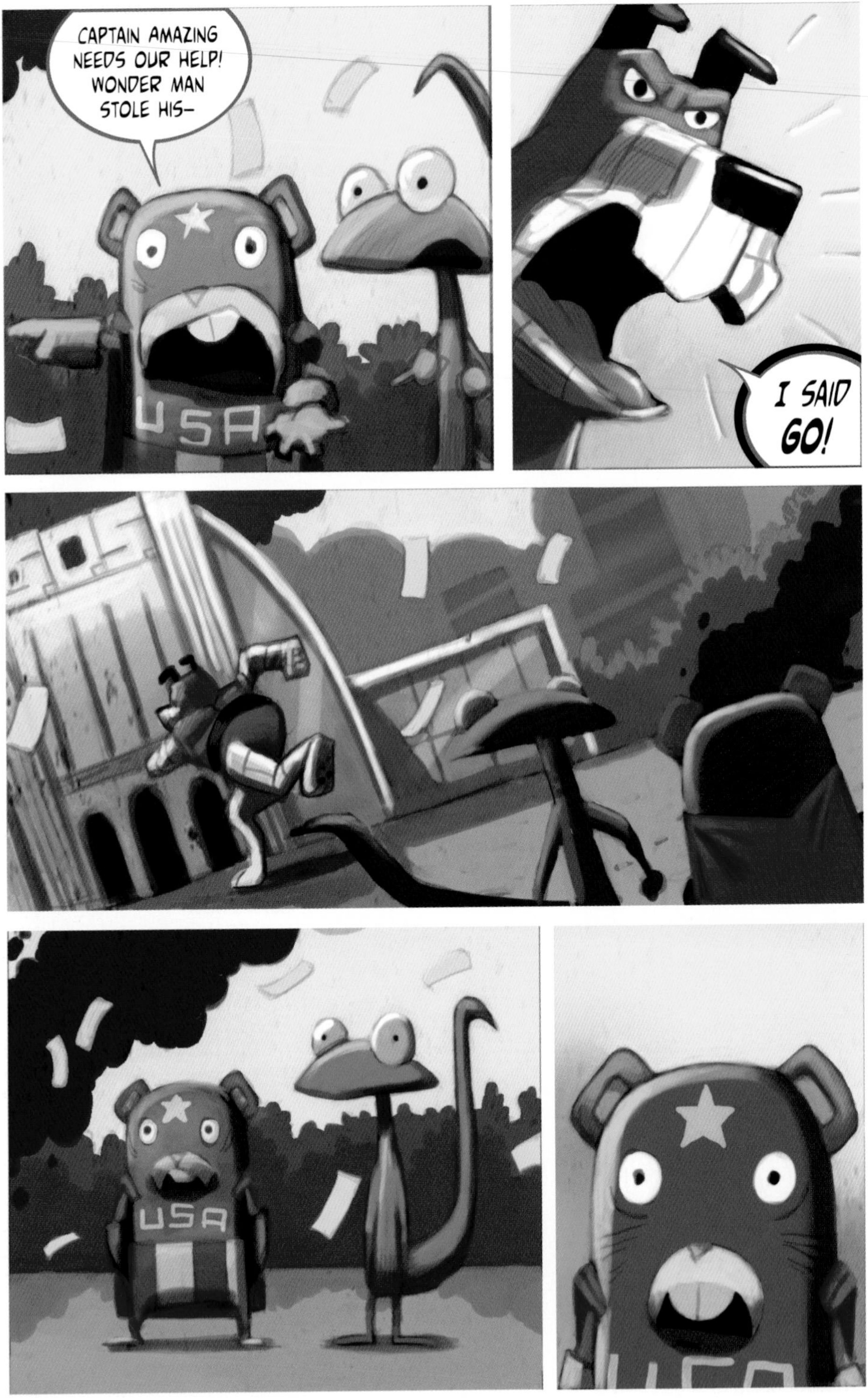
CAPTAIN AMAZING NEEDS OUR HELP! WONDER MAN STOLE HIS—
I SAID GO!

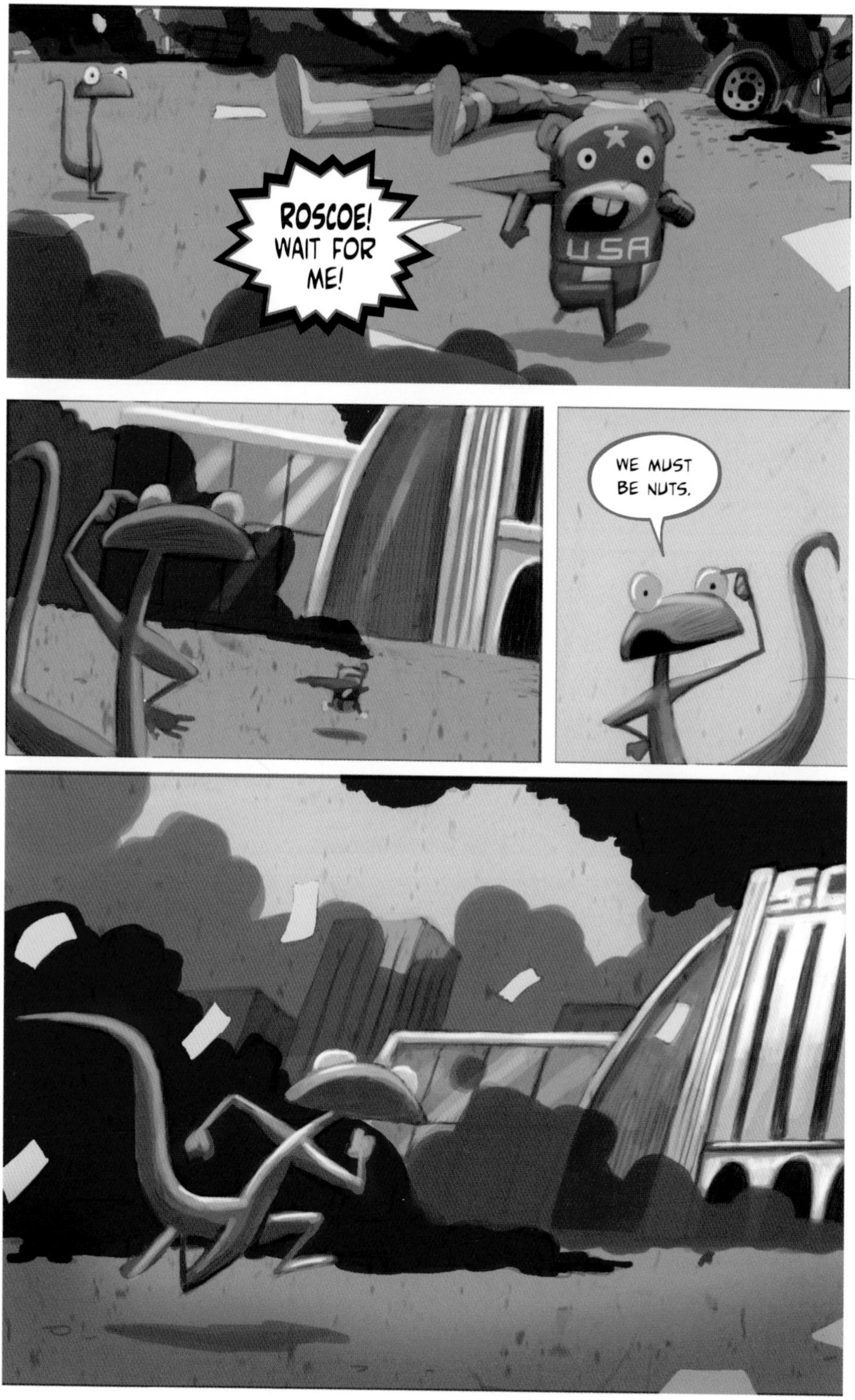
ROSCOE! WAIT FOR ME!
WE MUST BE NUTS.

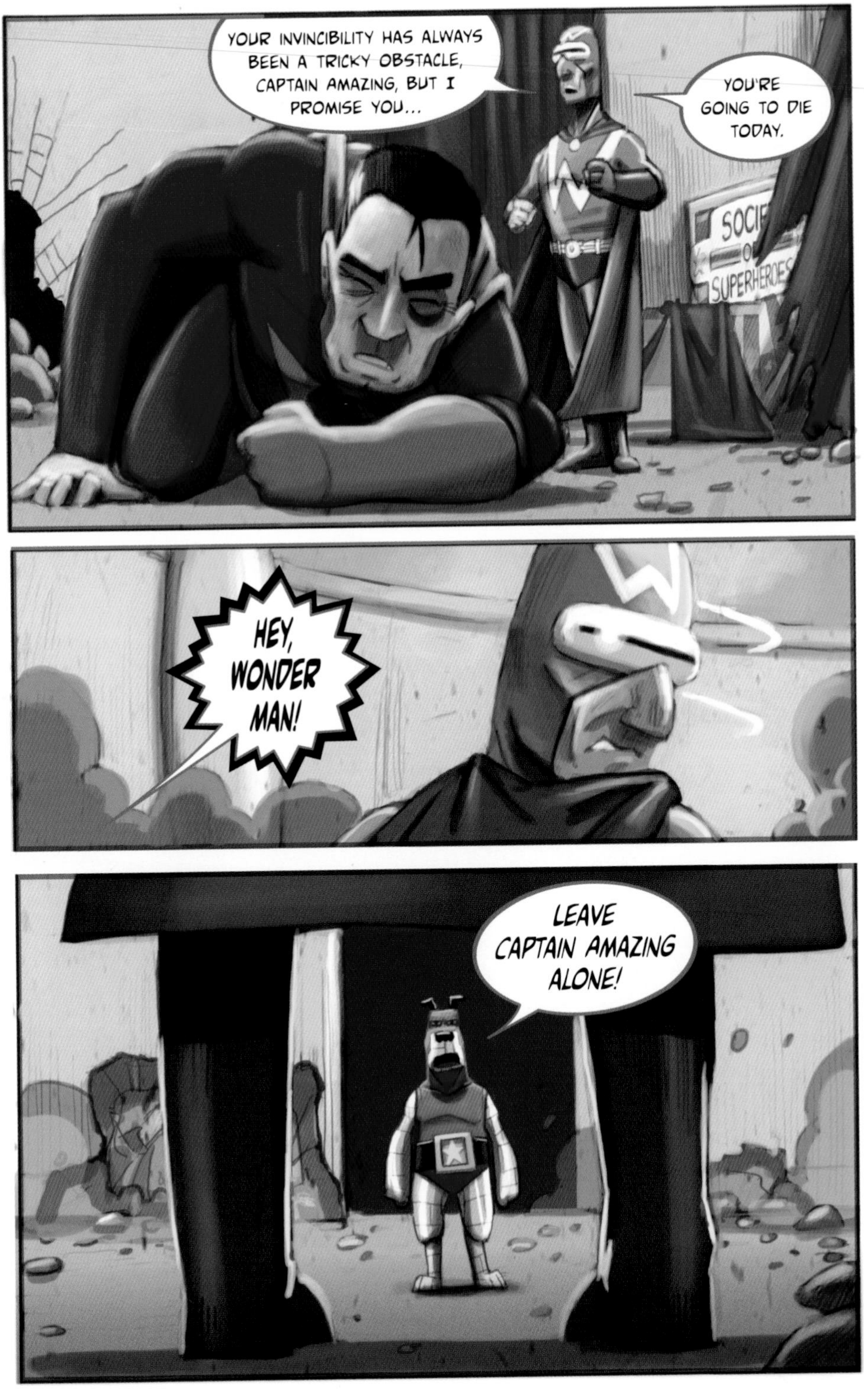
YOUR INVINCIBILITY HAS ALWAYS BEEN A TRICKY OBSTACLE, CAPTAIN AMAZING, BUT I PROMISE YOU...
YOU'RE GOING TO DIE TODAY.
SOCI
O
SUPERHEROES
HEY, WONDER MAN!
LEAVE CAPTAIN AMAZING ALONE!

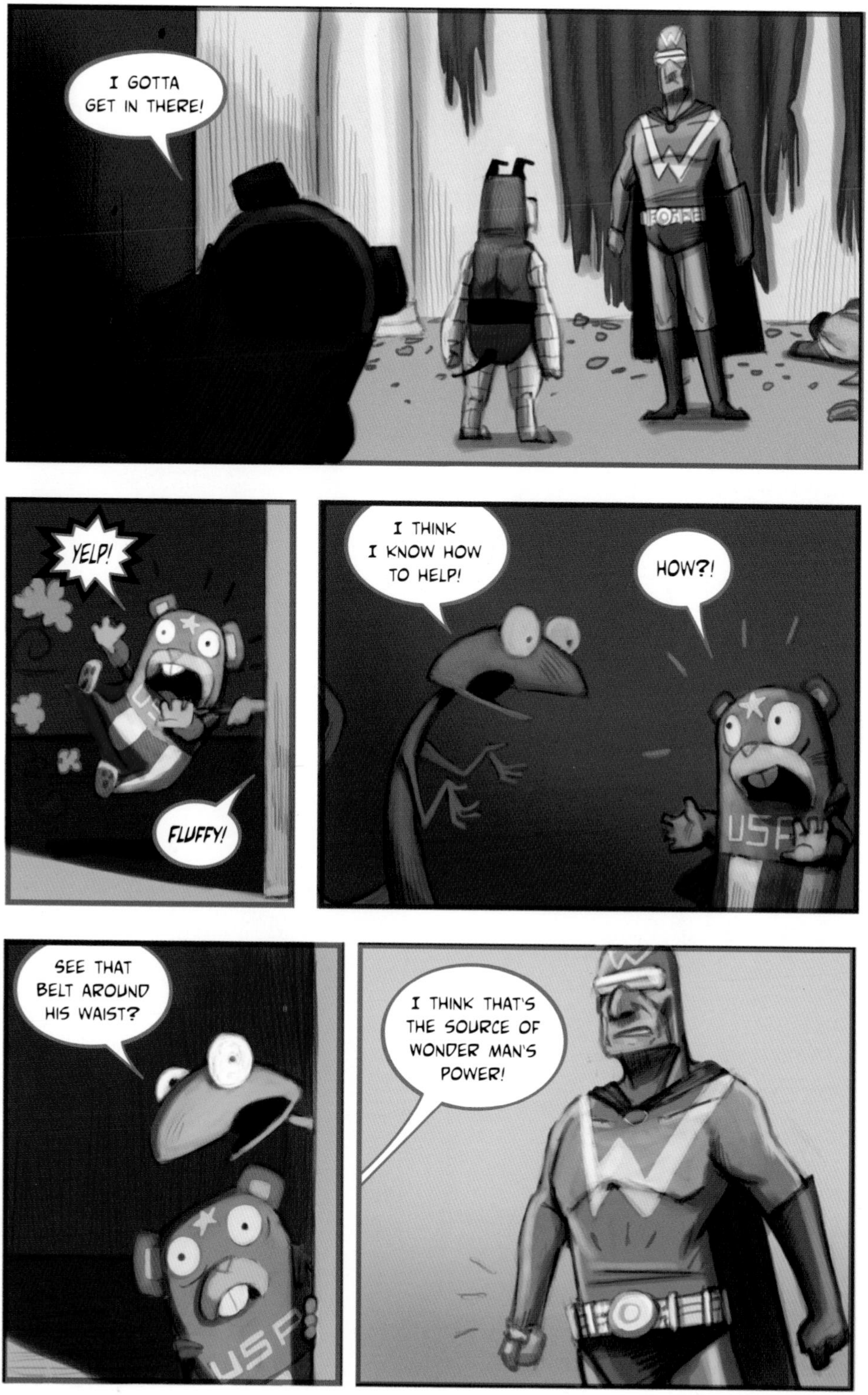
I GOTTA GET IN THERE!
YELP!
FLUFFY!
I THINK I KNOW HOW TO HELP!
HOW?!
SEE THAT BELT AROUND HIS WAIST?
I THINK THAT'S THE SOURCE OF WONDER MAN'S POWER!

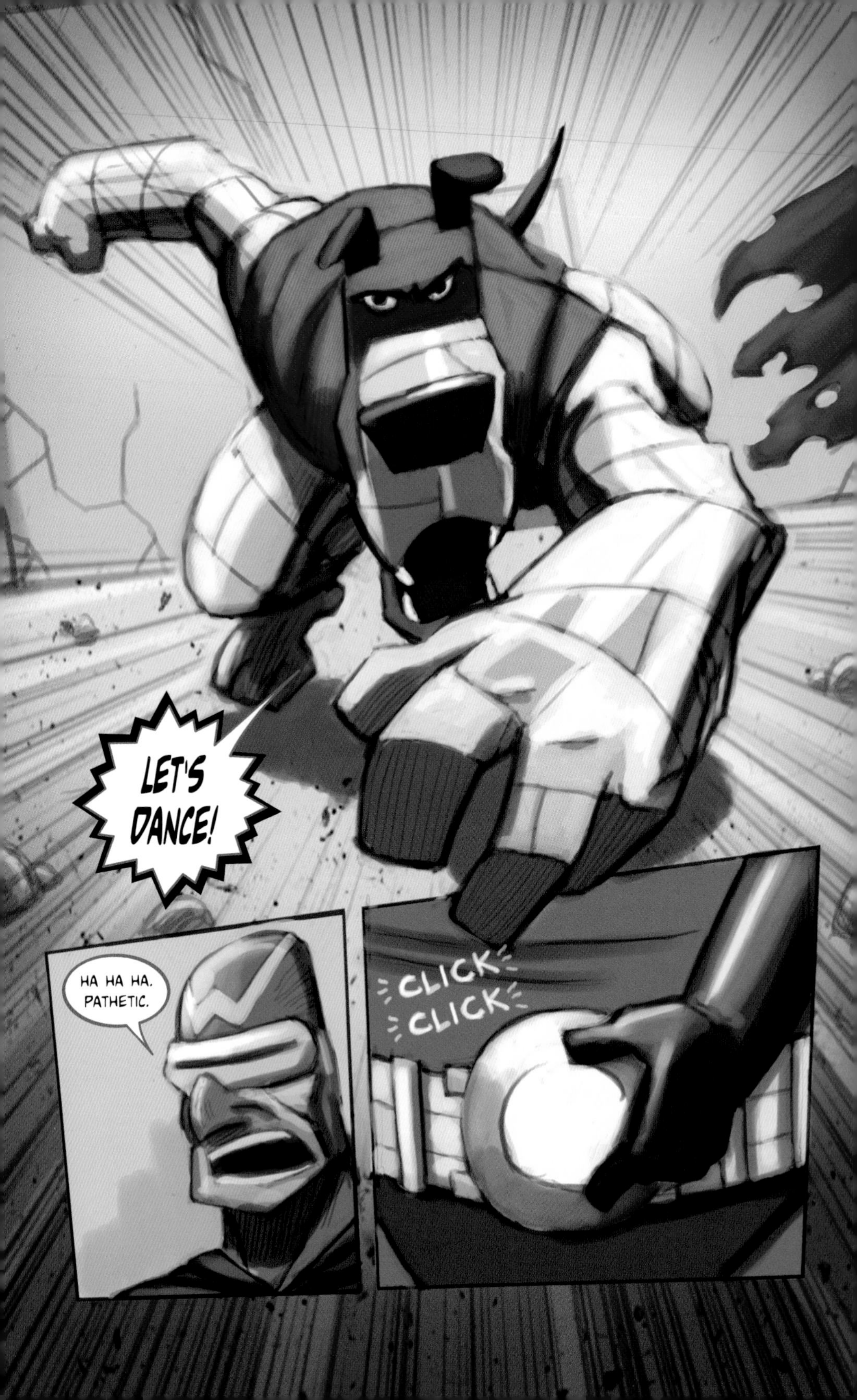
LET'S DANCE!
HA HA HA. PATHETIC.
CLICK CLICK

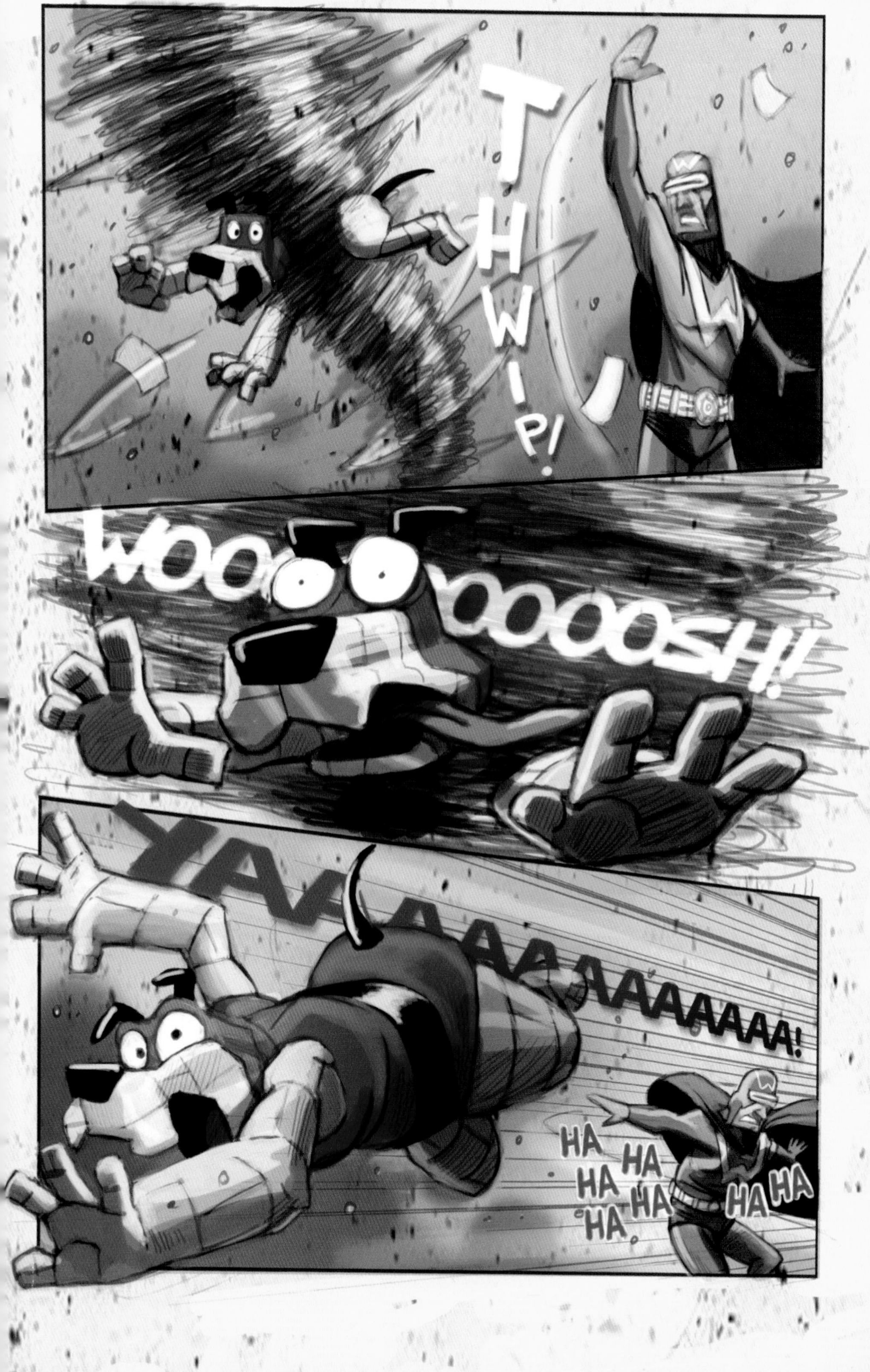
THWIP!
WOOOOOOOSH!!
YAAAAAAAAAAAAA!
HA HA HA HA HA HA HA HA

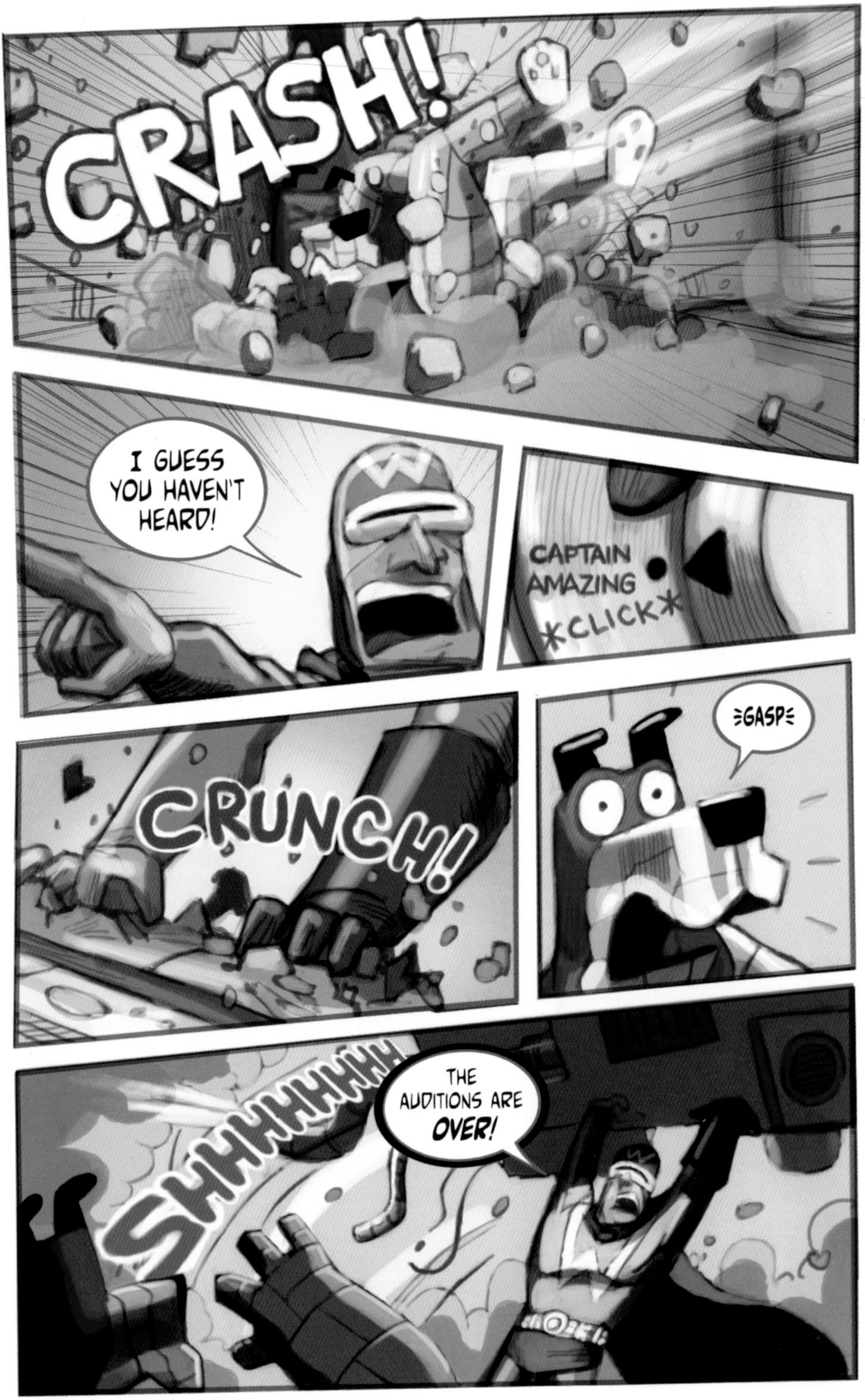
CRASH!
I GUESS YOU HAVEN'T HEARD!
CAPTAIN AMAZING
CLICK
CRUNCH!
GASP
SHHHHHHH
THE AUDITIONS ARE OVER!

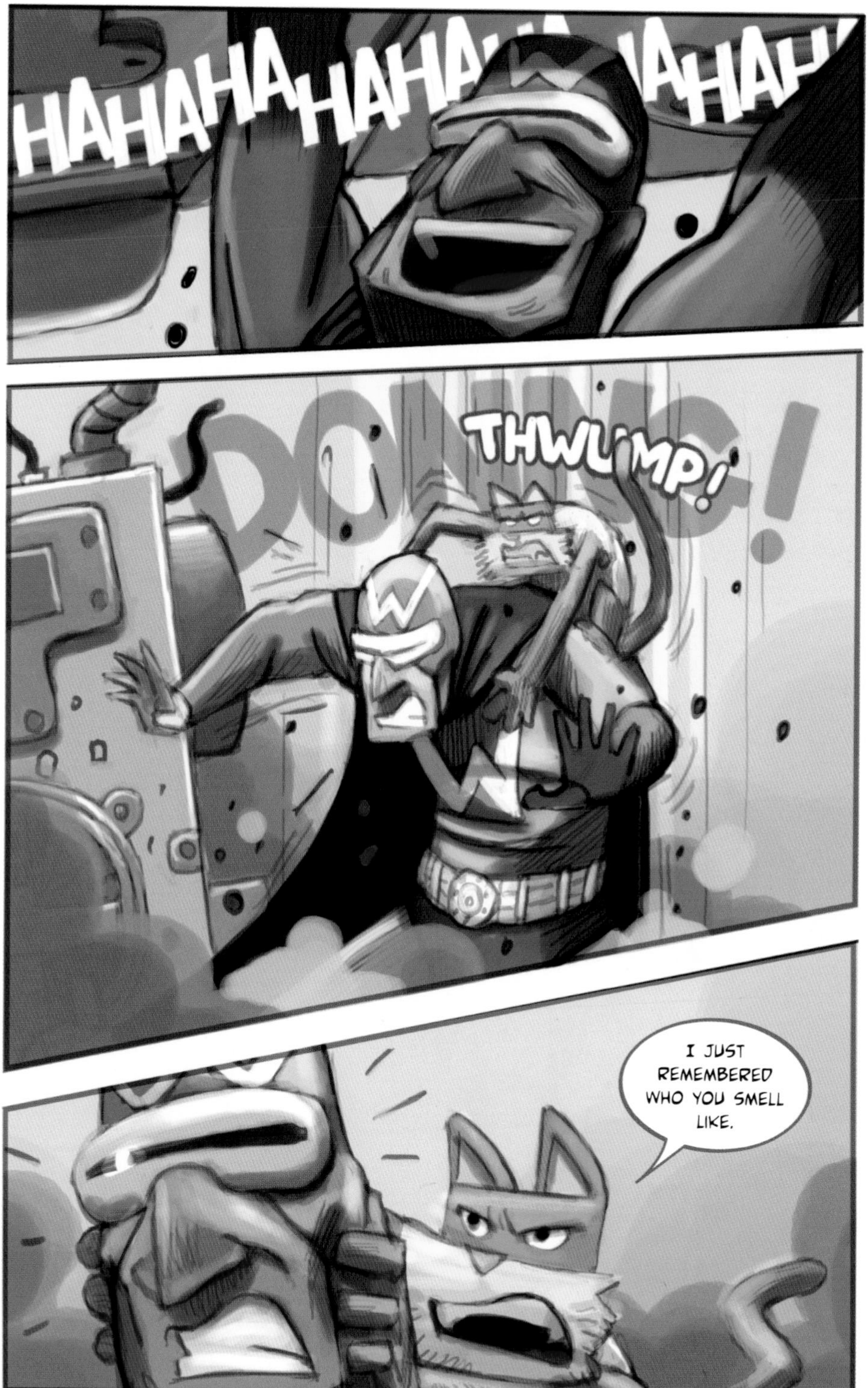
HAHAHA HAHAHA
THWUMP!
I JUST REMEMBERED WHO YOU SMELL LIKE.

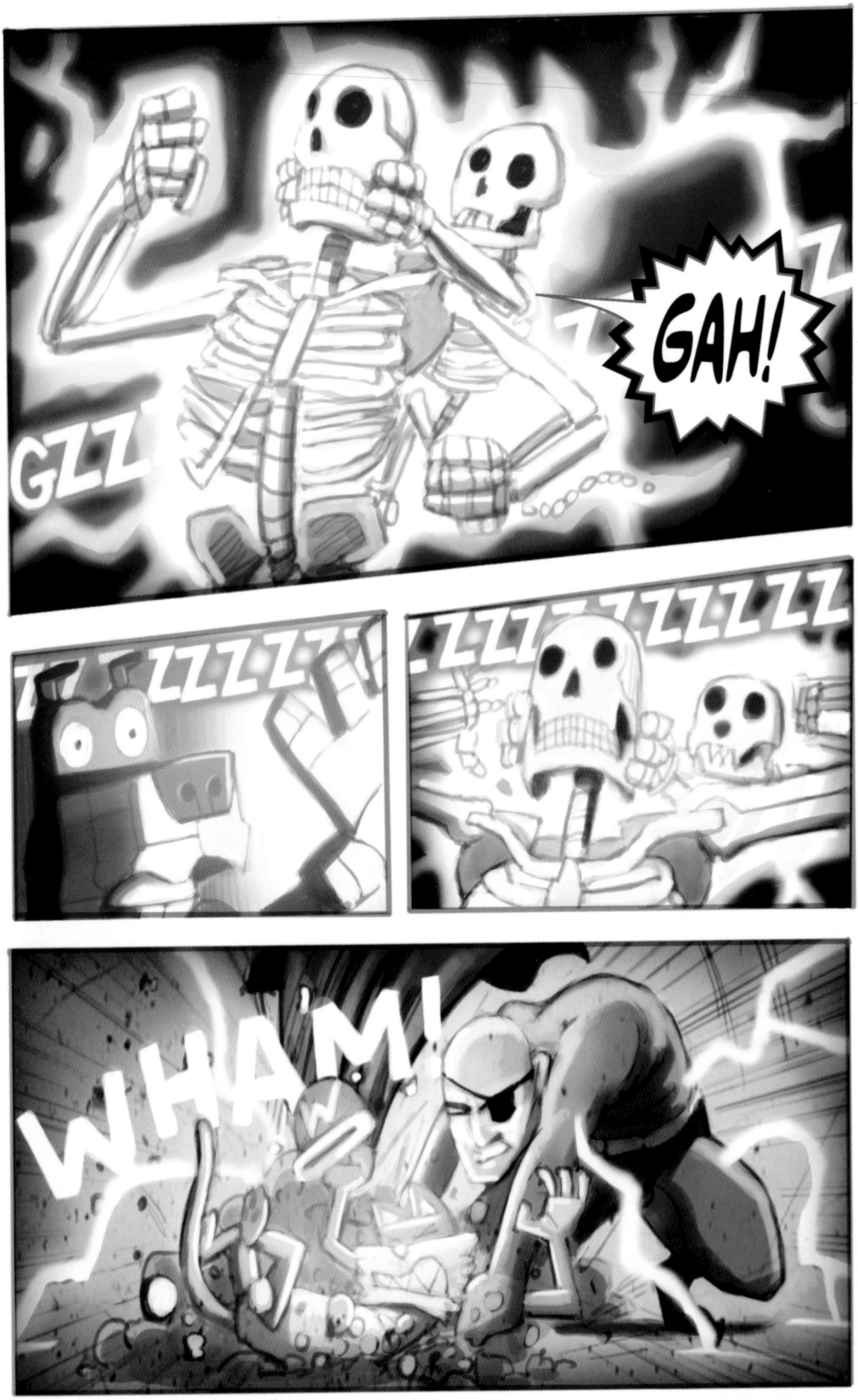
GZZZ
GAH!
WHAM!

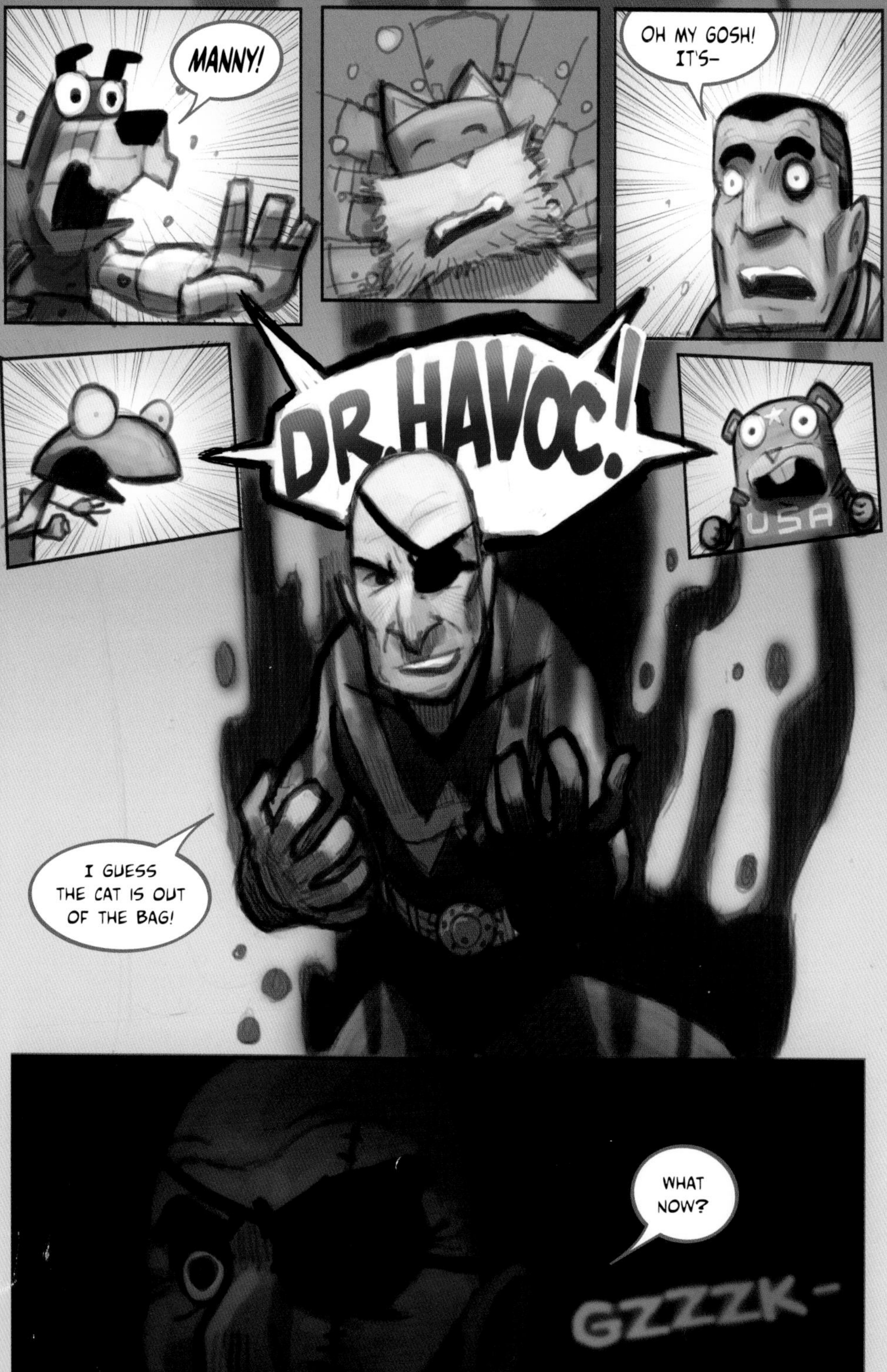
MANNY!
OH MY GOSH! IT'S–
DR. HAVOC!
I GUESS THE CAT IS OUT OF THE BAG!
WHAT NOW?
GZZZK-

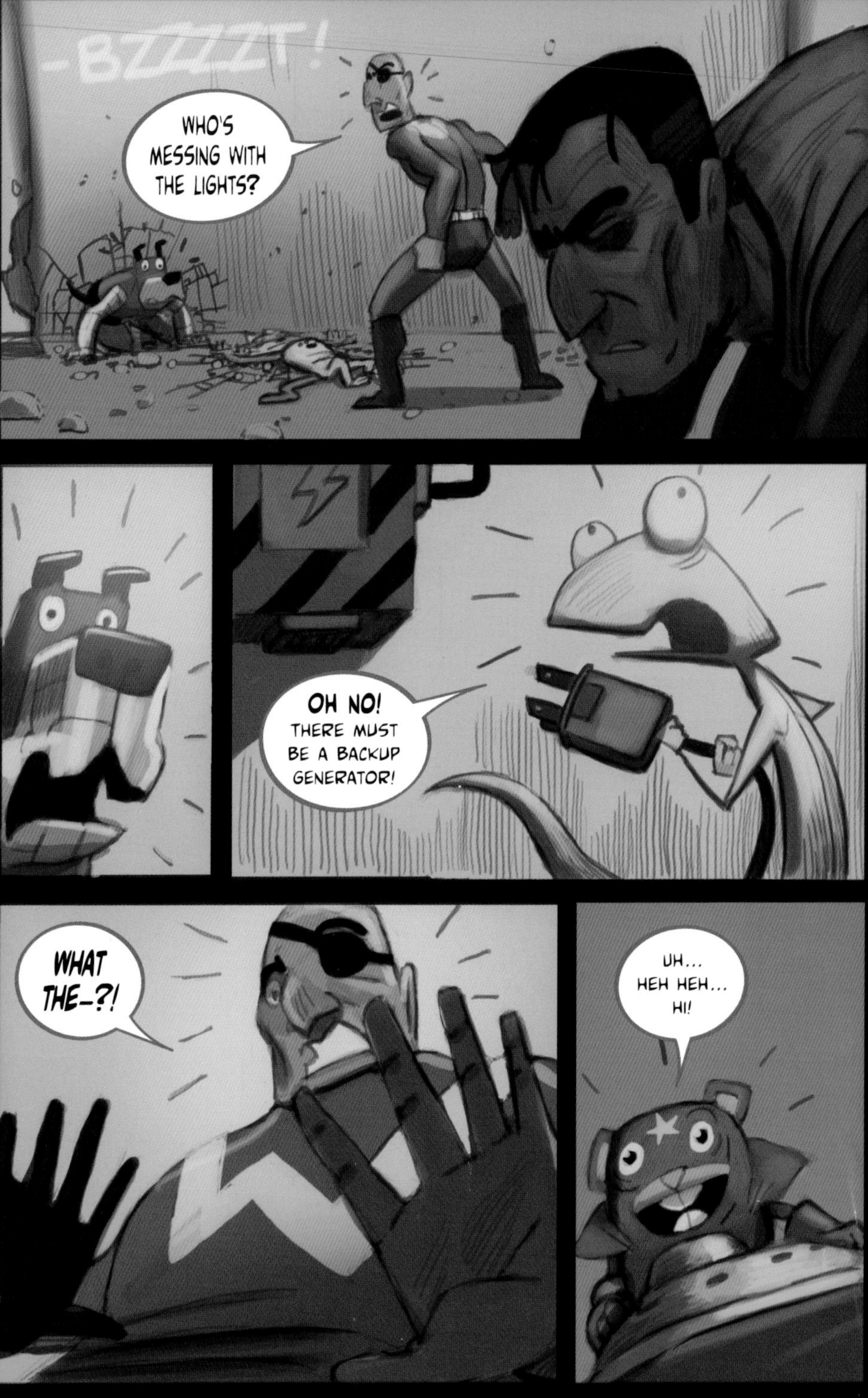

-BZZZZT!
WHO'S MESSING WITH THE LIGHTS?
OH NO! THERE MUST BE A BACKUP GENERATOR!
WHAT THE-?!
UH... HEH HEH... HI!

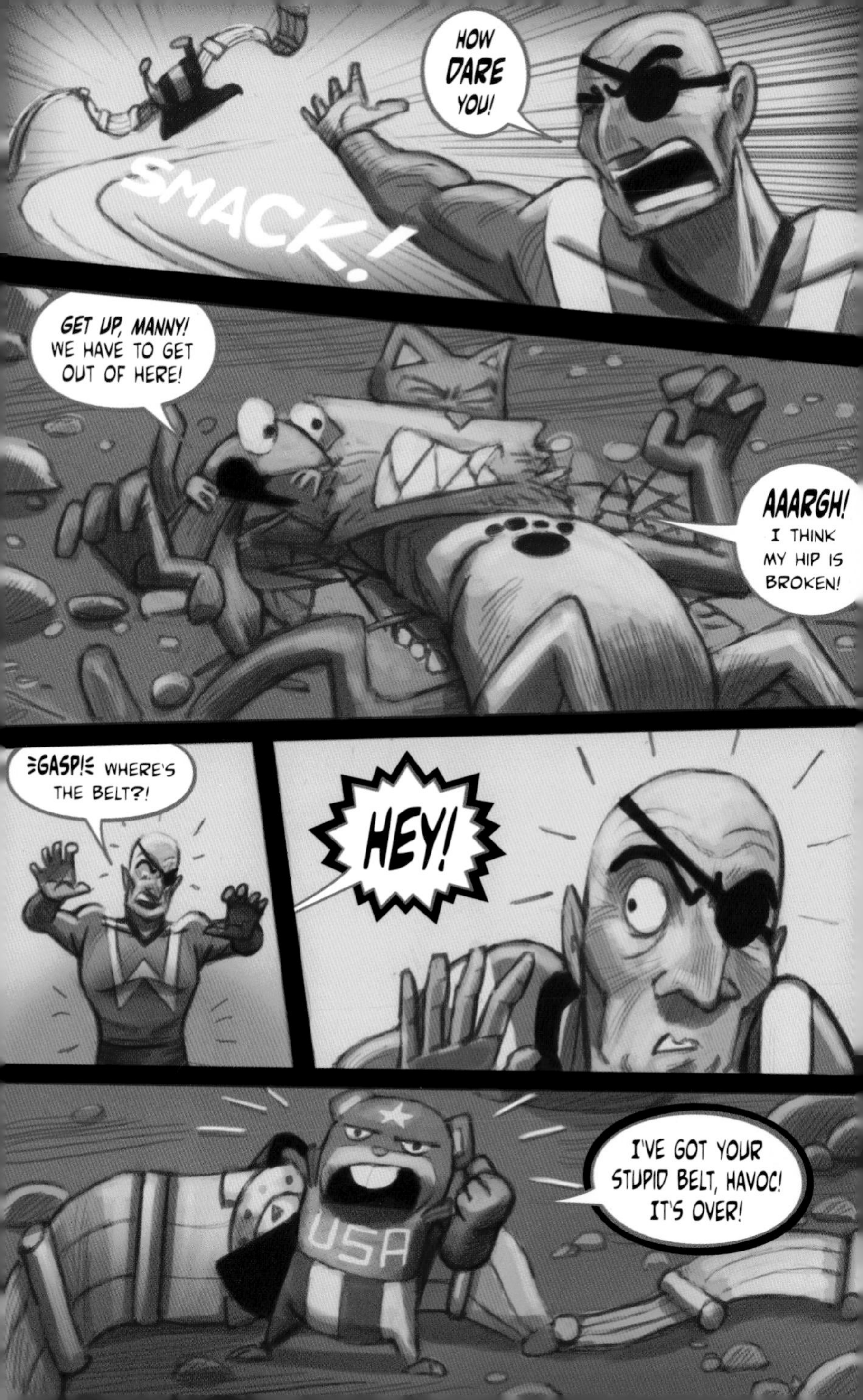
HOW DARE YOU!
SMACK!
GET UP, MANNY! WE HAVE TO GET OUT OF HERE!
AAARGH! I THINK MY HIP IS BROKEN!
GASP! WHERE'S THE BELT?!
HEY!
I'VE GOT YOUR STUPID BELT, HAVOC! IT'S OVER!
USA

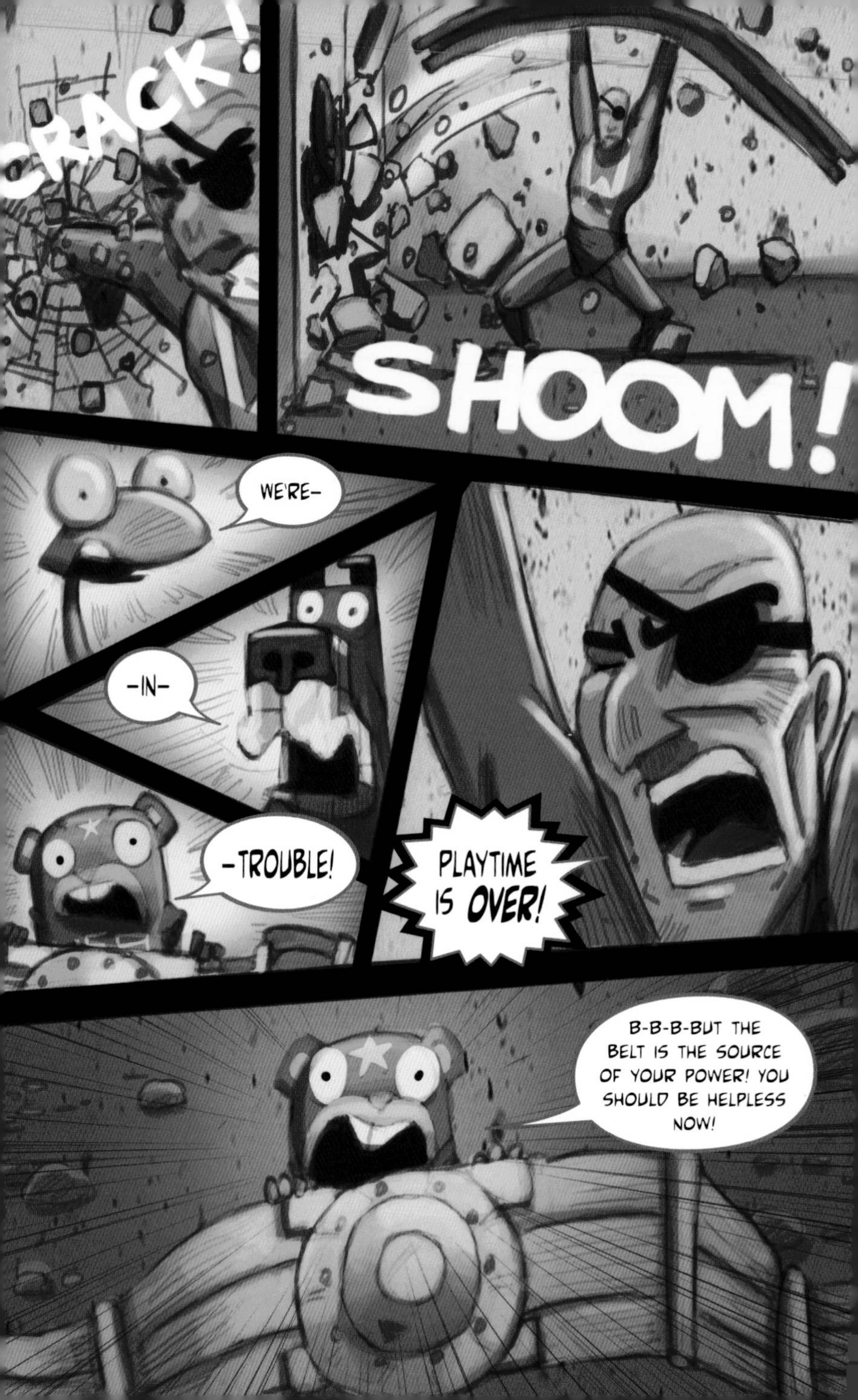
CRACK!
SHOOM!
WE'RE-
-IN-
-TROUBLE!
PLAYTIME IS OVER!
B-B-B-BUT THE BELT IS THE SOURCE OF YOUR POWER! YOU SHOULD BE HELPLESS NOW!

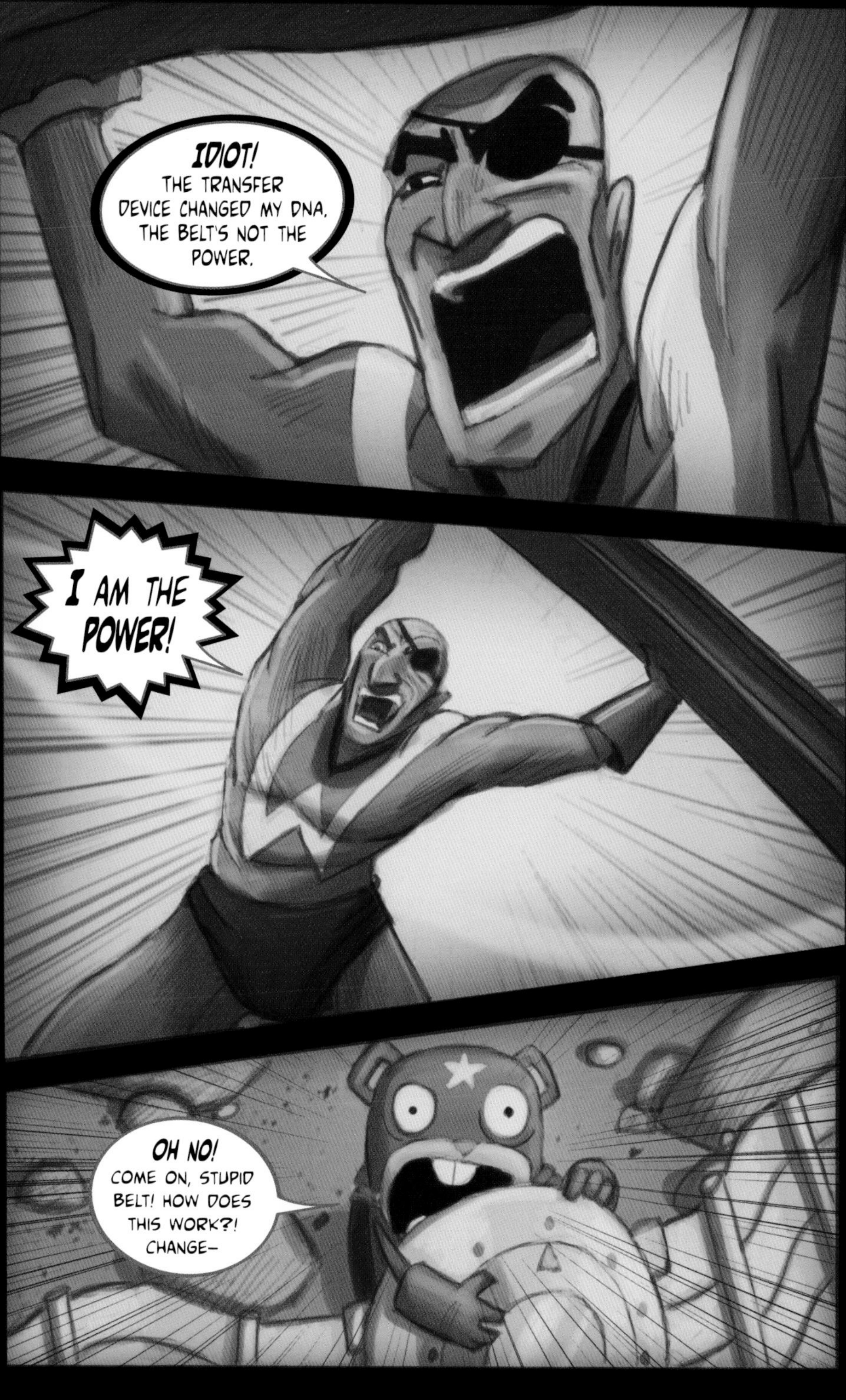
IDIOT! THE TRANSFER DEVICE CHANGED MY DNA. THE BELT'S NOT THE POWER.
I AM THE POWER!
OH NO! COME ON, STUPID BELT! HOW DOES THIS WORK?! CHANGE—

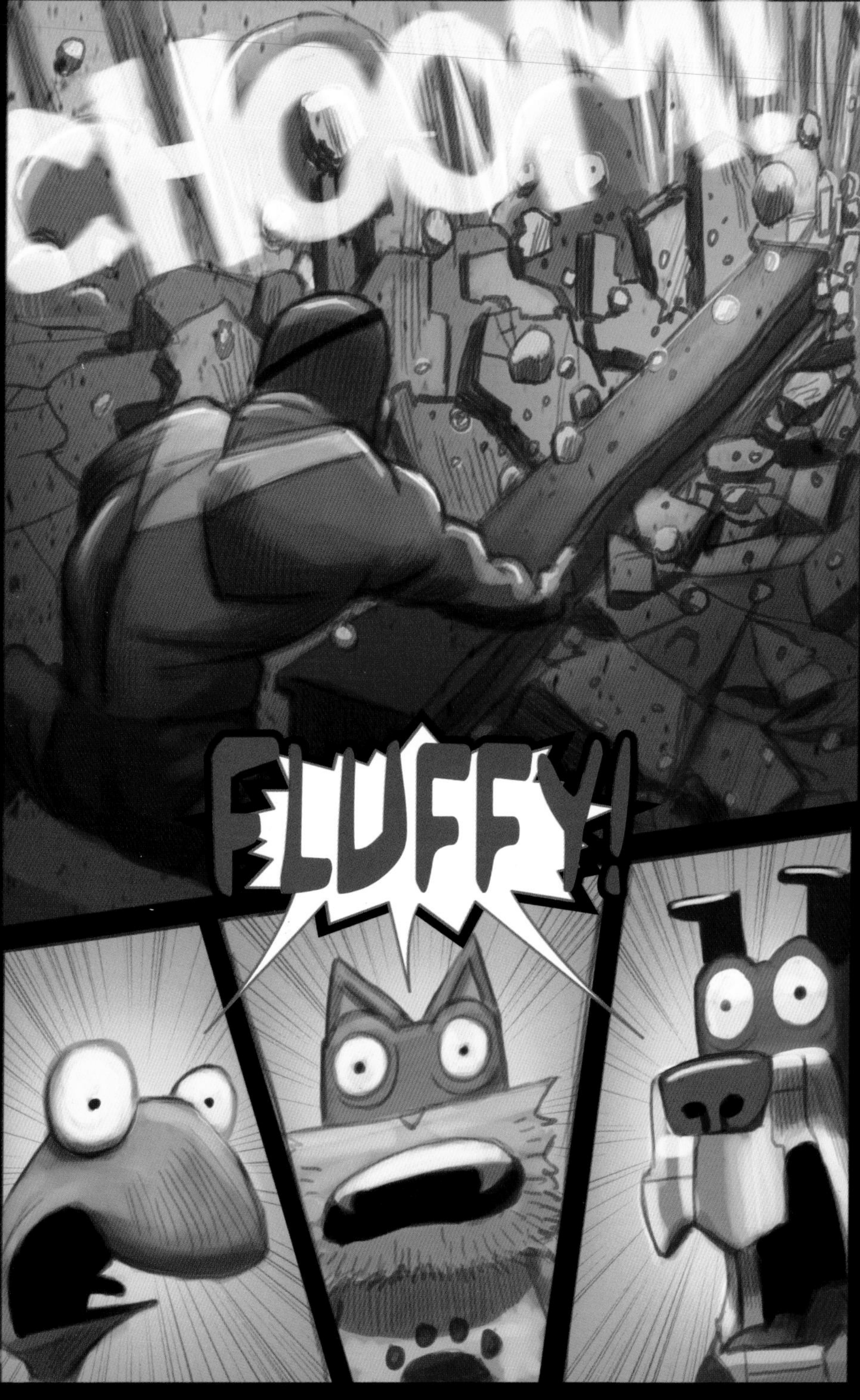
CHOOOM!
FLUFFY!

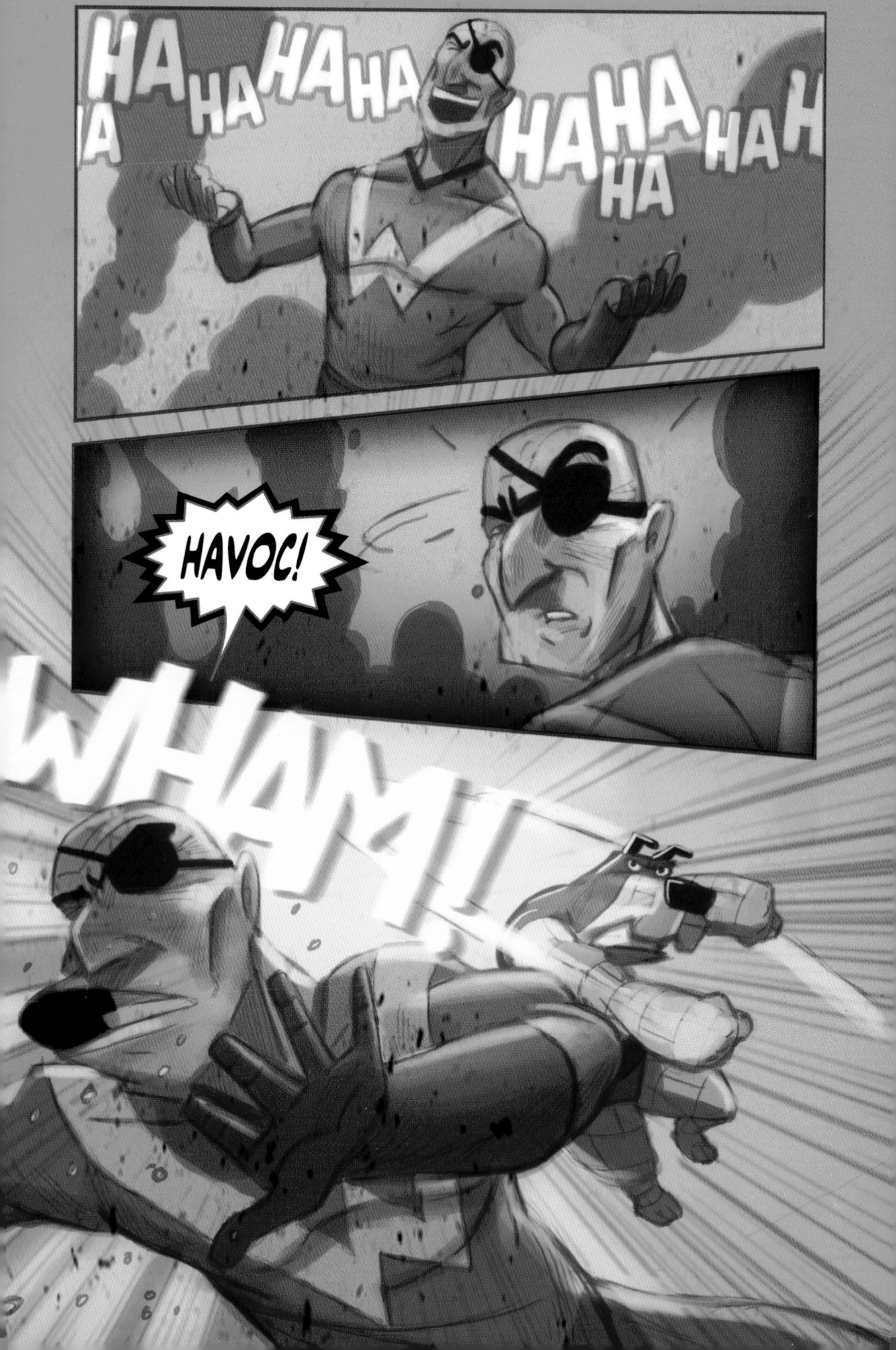
HA HA HA HA HA HA HA HA HA HA HA H
HAVOC!
WHAM!

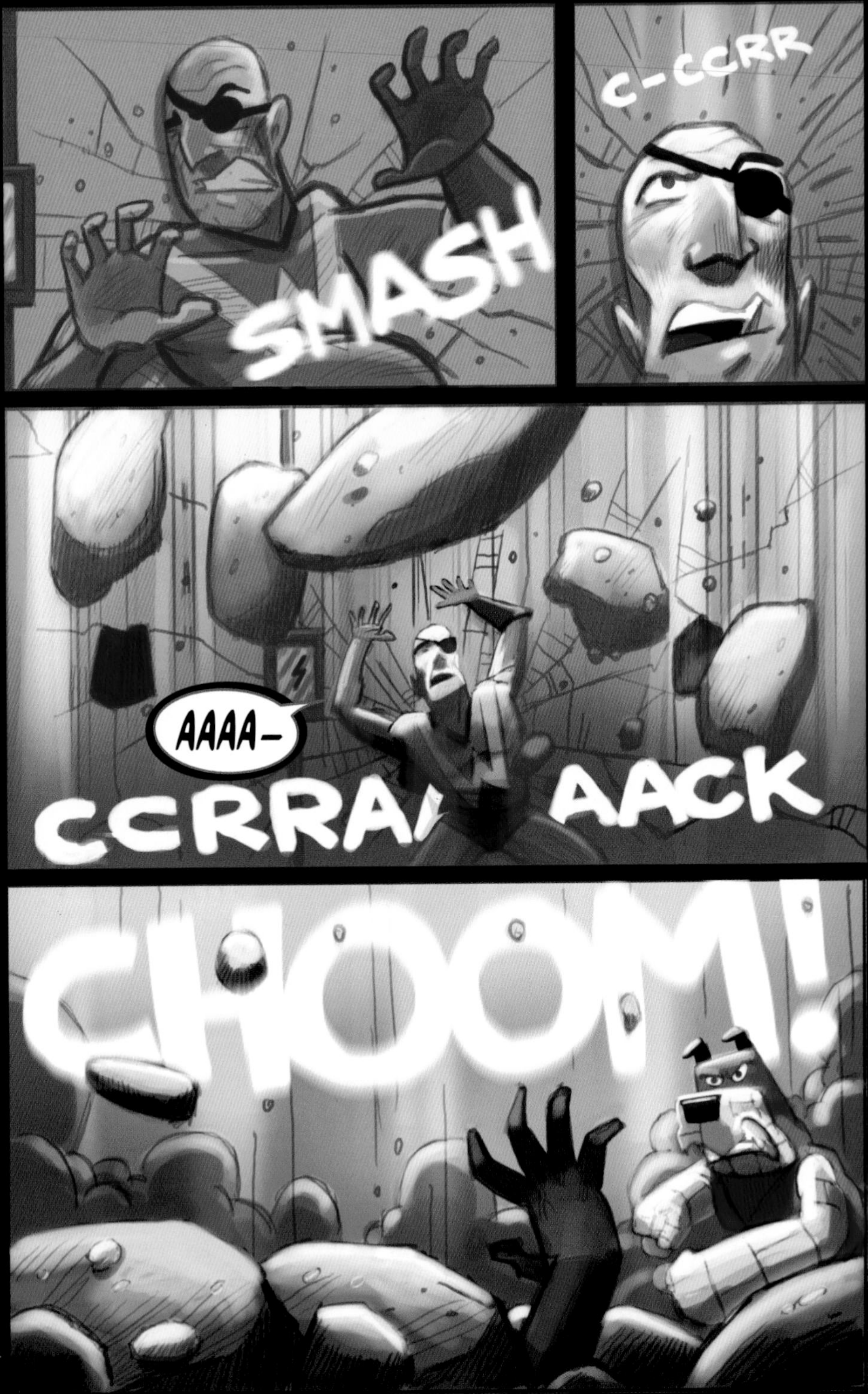
SMASH
C-CCRR
AAAA-
CCRRA AACK
CHOOM!

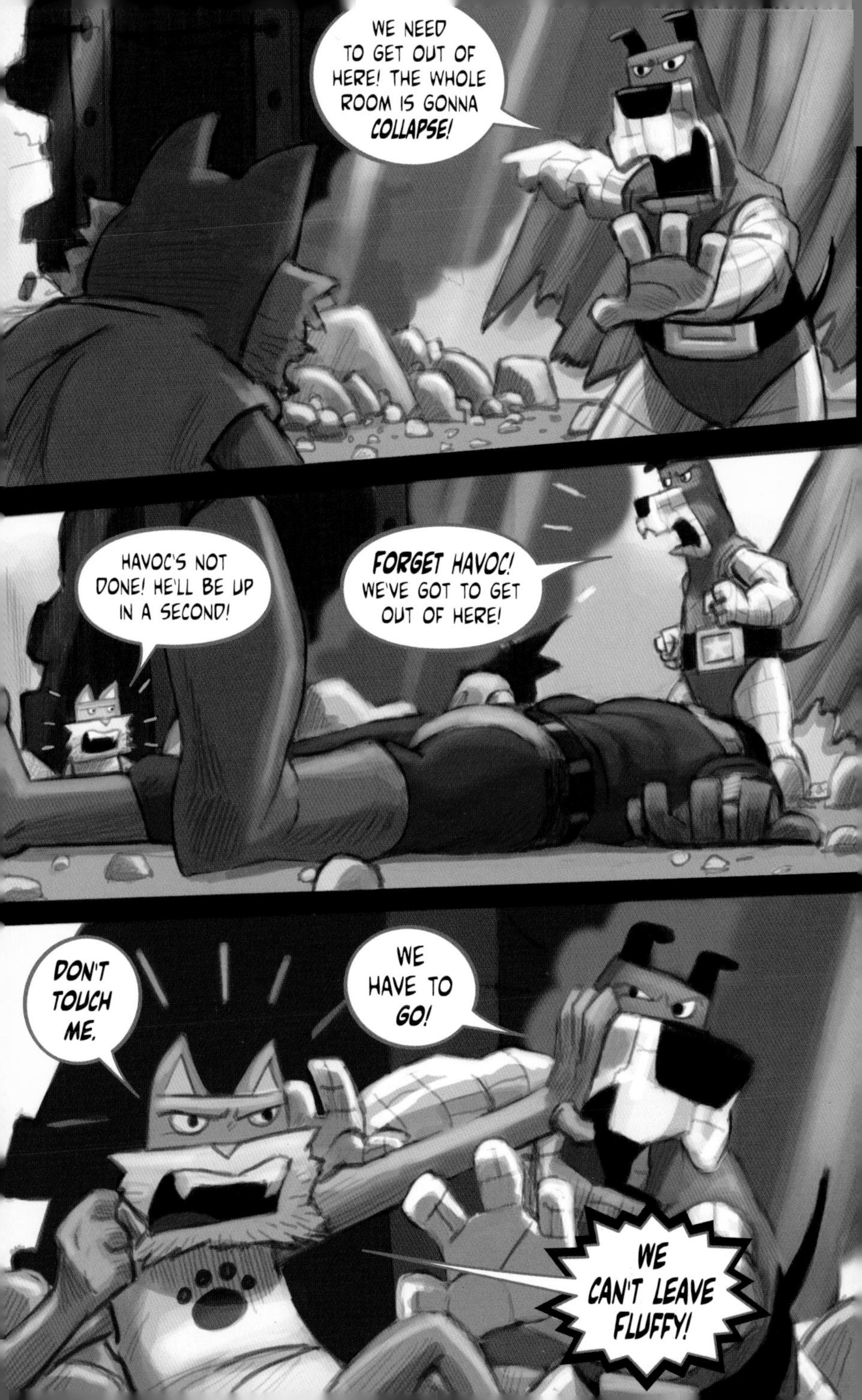
WE NEED TO GET OUT OF HERE! THE WHOLE ROOM IS GONNA COLLAPSE!
HAVOC'S NOT DONE! HE'LL BE UP IN A SECOND!
FORGET HAVOC! WE'VE GOT TO GET OUT OF HERE!
DON'T TOUCH ME.
WE HAVE TO GO!
WE CAN'T LEAVE FLUFFY!

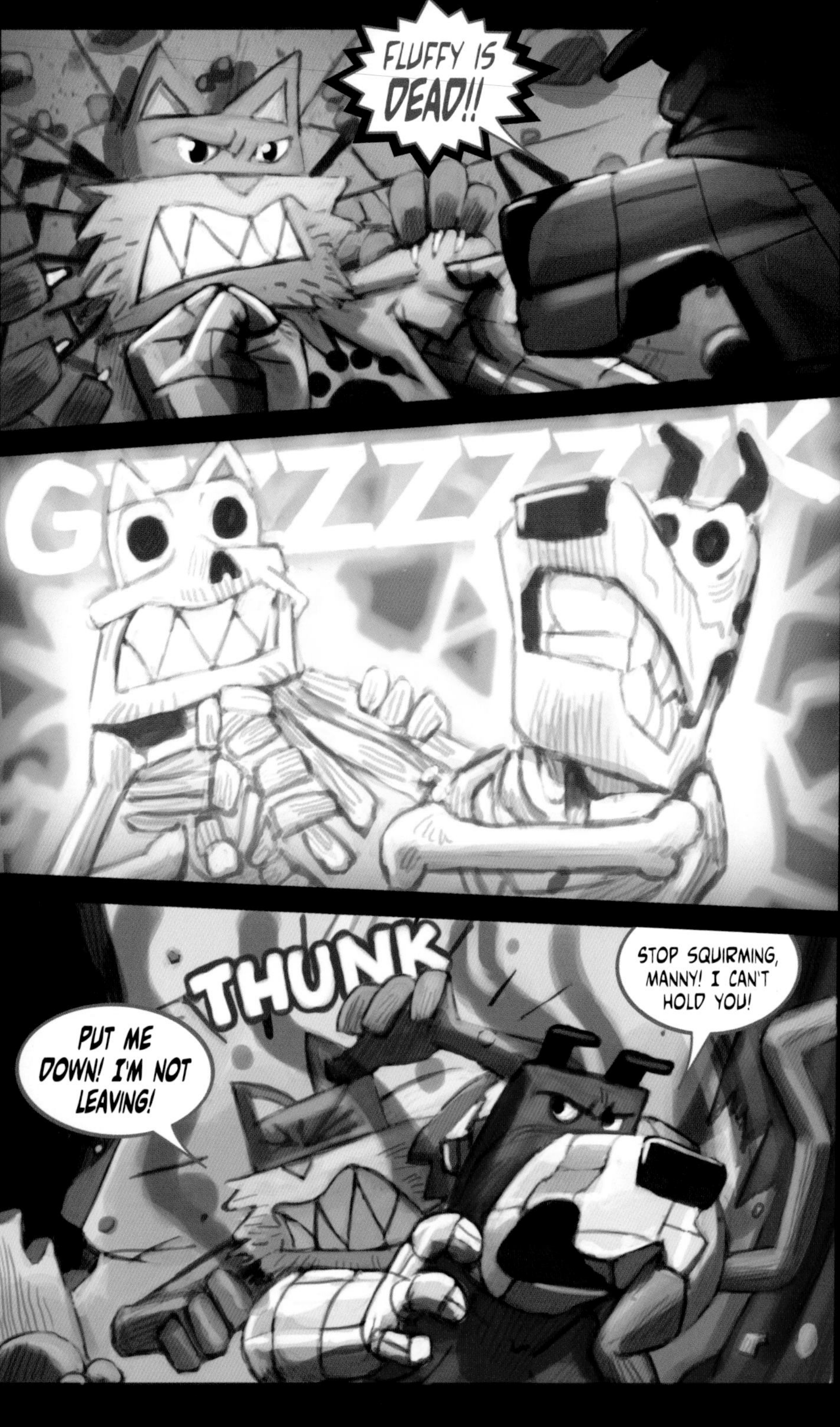
FLUFFY IS DEAD!!
THUNK
STOP SQUIRMING, MANNY! I CAN'T HOLD YOU!
PUT ME DOWN! I'M NOT LEAVING!

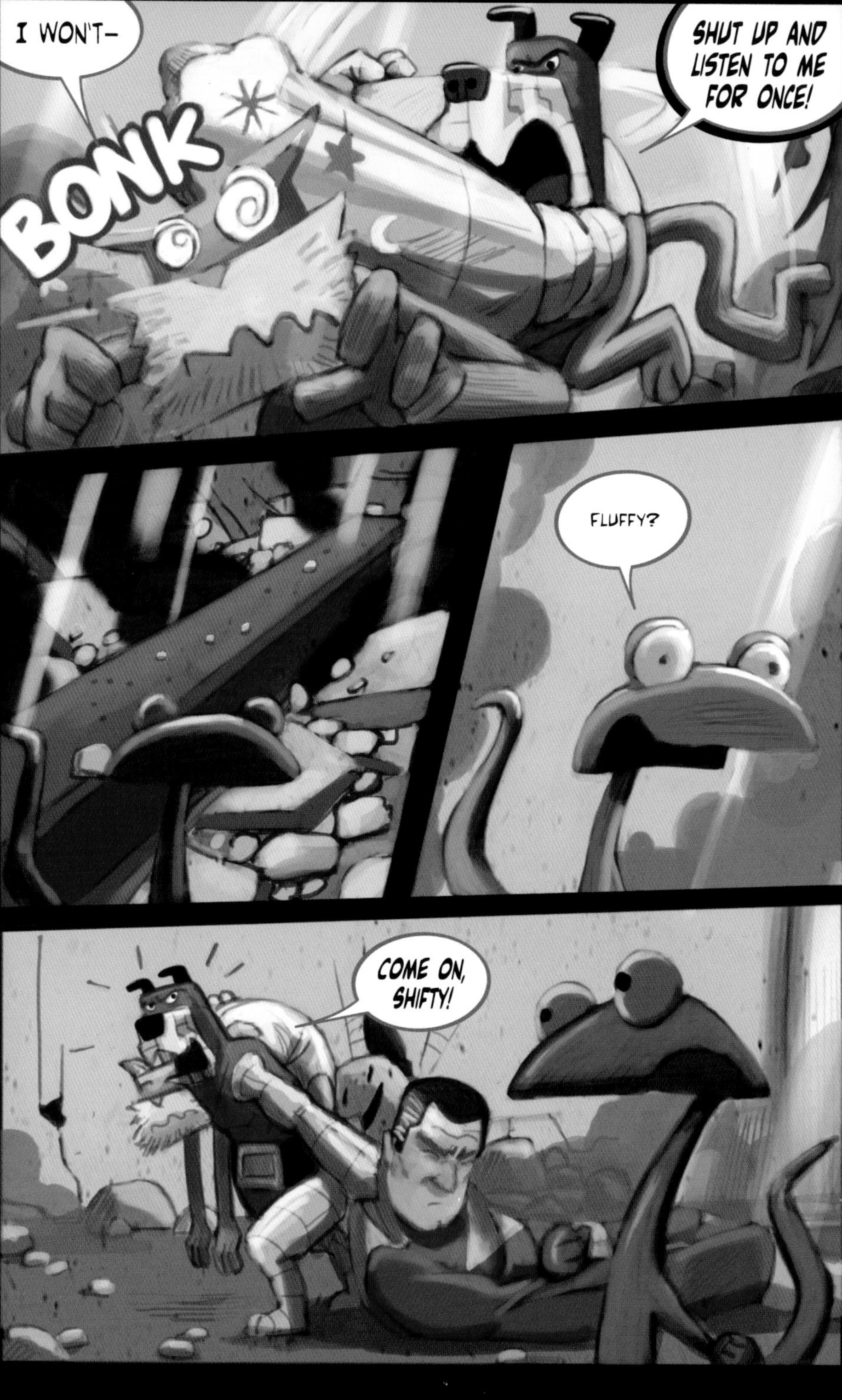
I WON'T-
BONK
SHUT UP AND LISTEN TO ME FOR ONCE!
FLUFFY?
COME ON, SHIFTY!

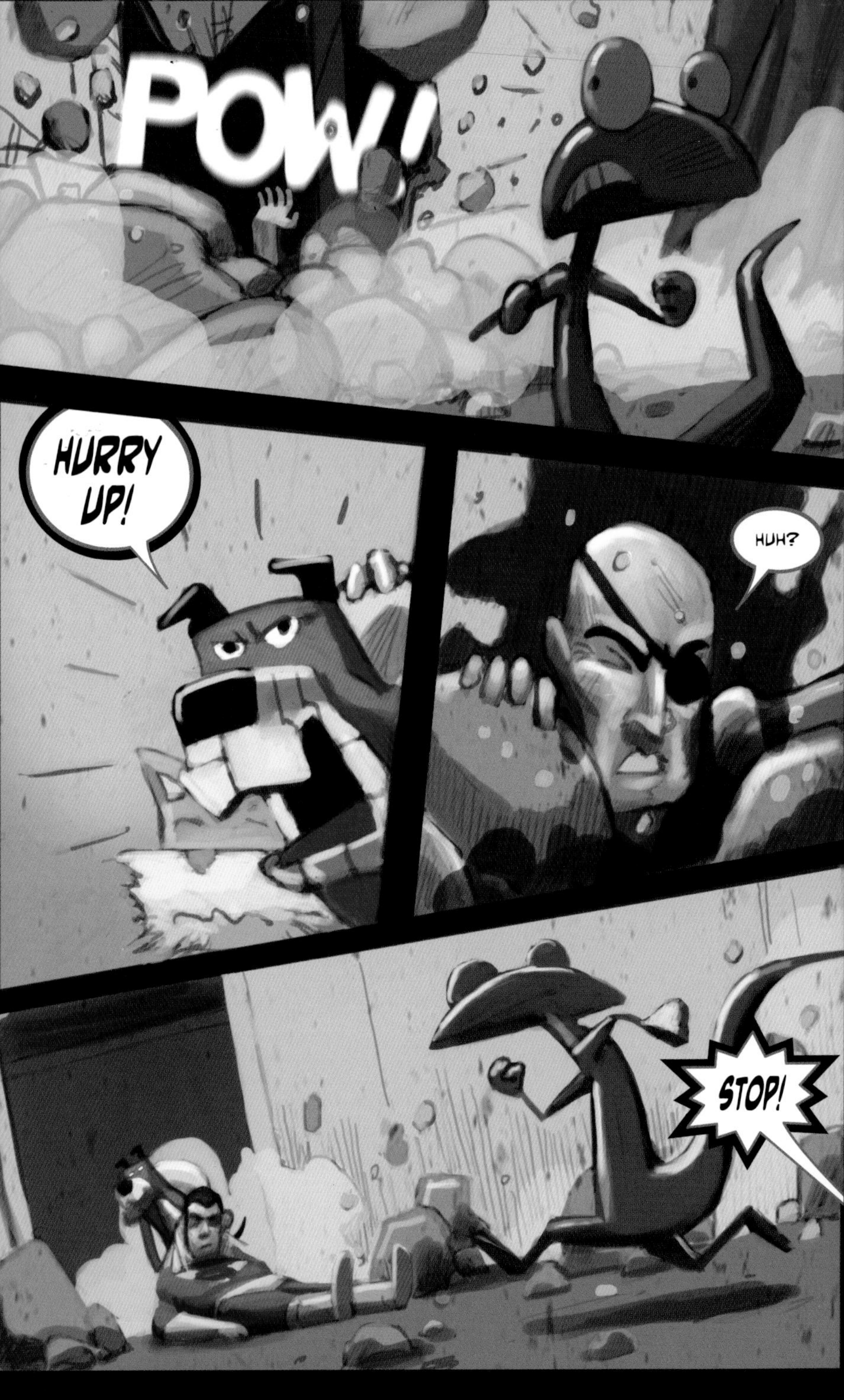
POW!
HURRY UP!
HUH?
STOP!

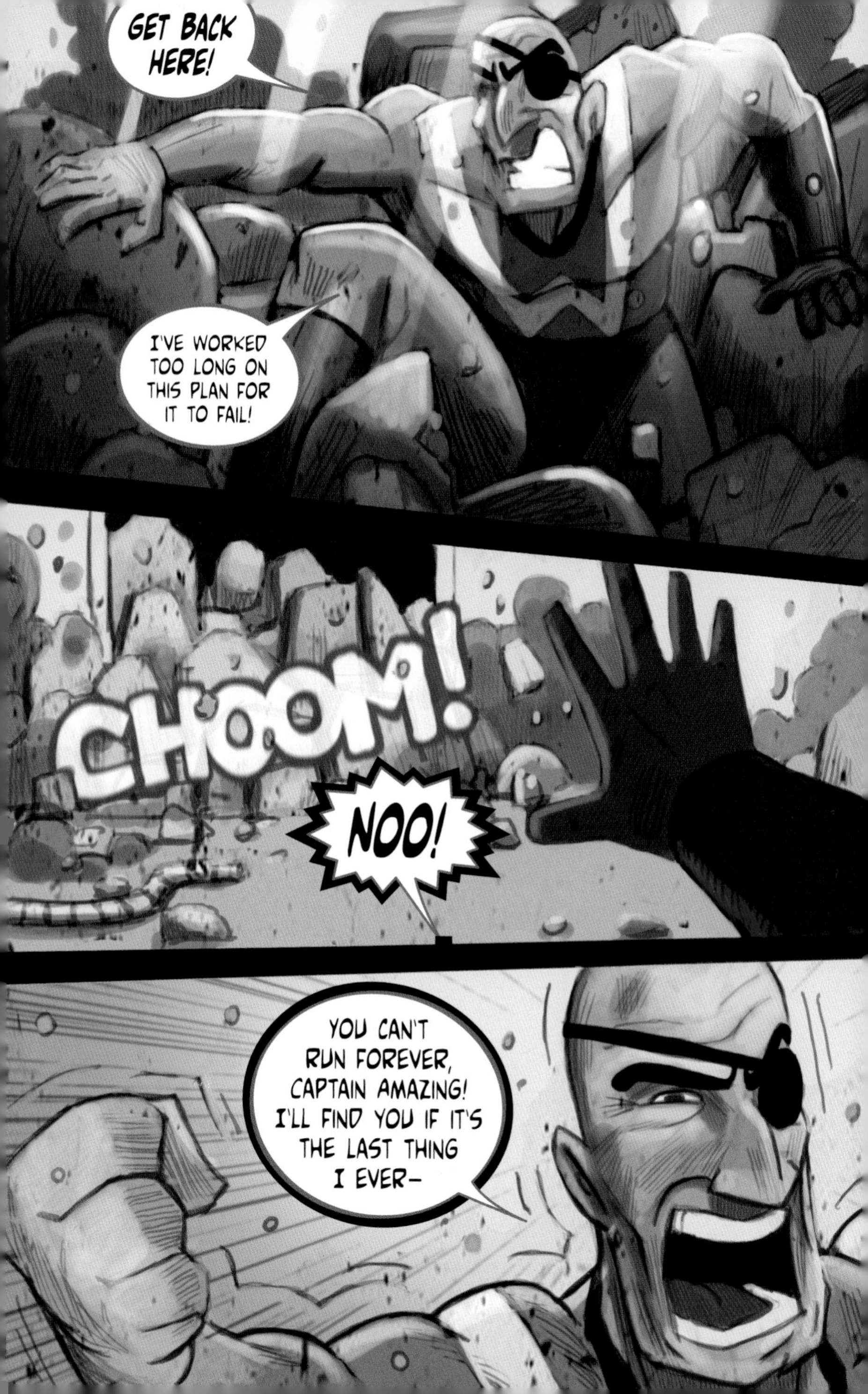
GET BACK HERE!
I'VE WORKED TOO LONG ON THIS PLAN FOR IT TO FAIL!
CHOOM!
NOO!
YOU CAN'T RUN FOREVER, CAPTAIN AMAZING! I'LL FIND YOU IF IT'S THE LAST THING I EVER–

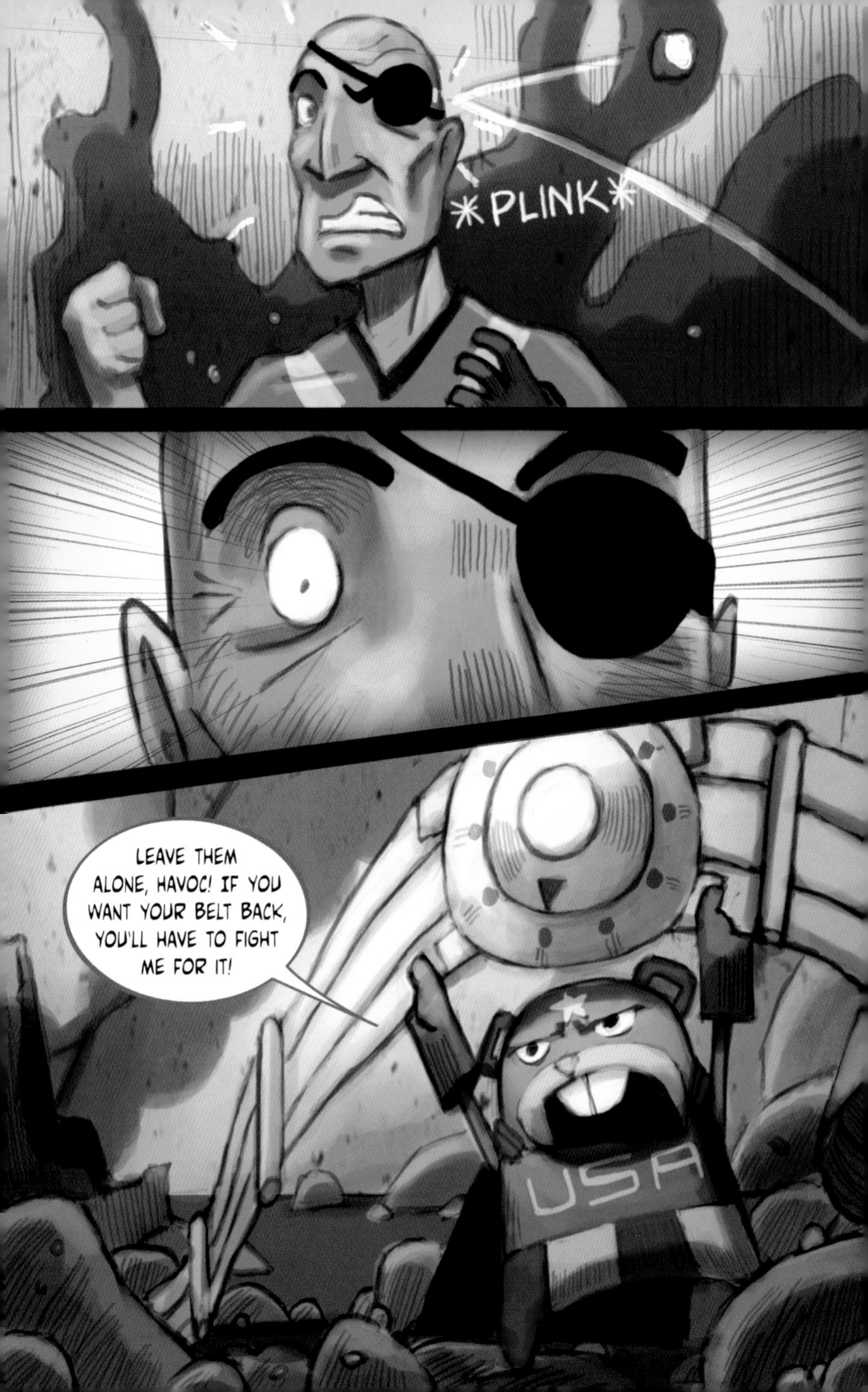
PLINK
LEAVE THEM ALONE, HAVOC! IF YOU WANT YOUR BELT BACK, YOU'LL HAVE TO FIGHT ME FOR IT!
USA

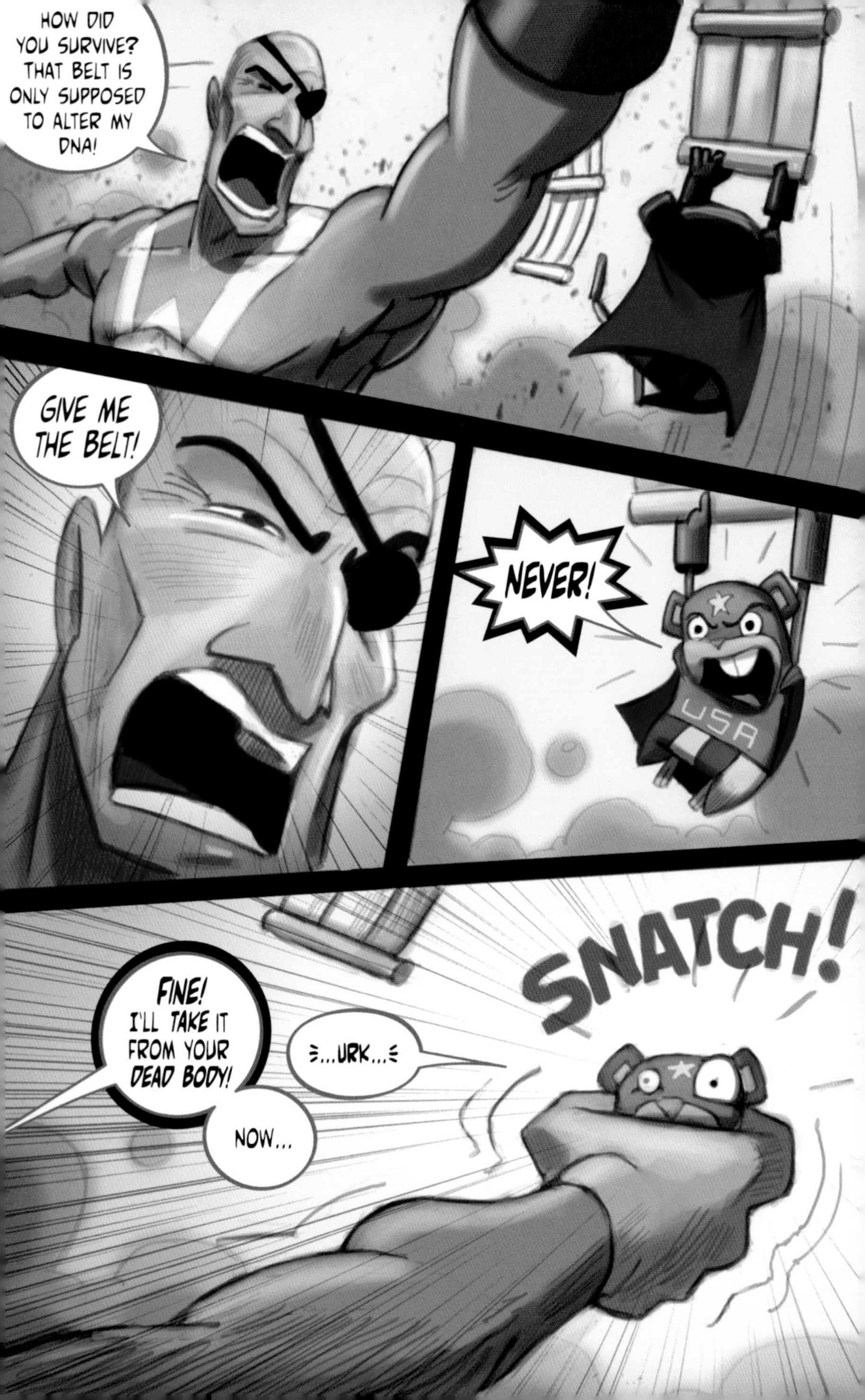
HOW DID YOU SURVIVE? THAT BELT IS ONLY SUPPOSED TO ALTER MY DNA!
GIVE ME THE BELT!
NEVER!
SNATCH!
...URK...
NOW...
FINE! I'LL TAKE IT FROM YOUR DEAD BODY!

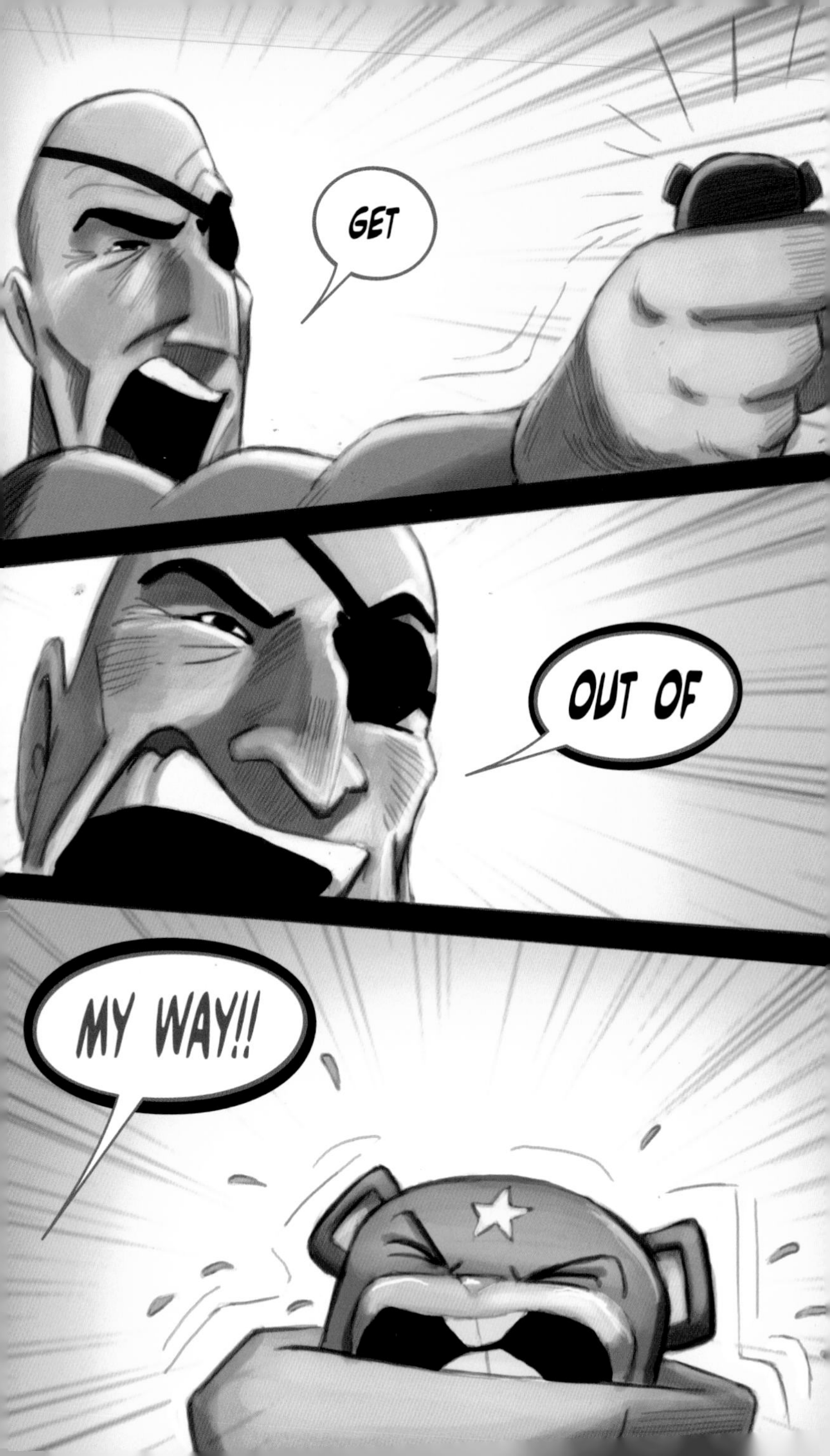
GET
OUT OF
MY WAY!!

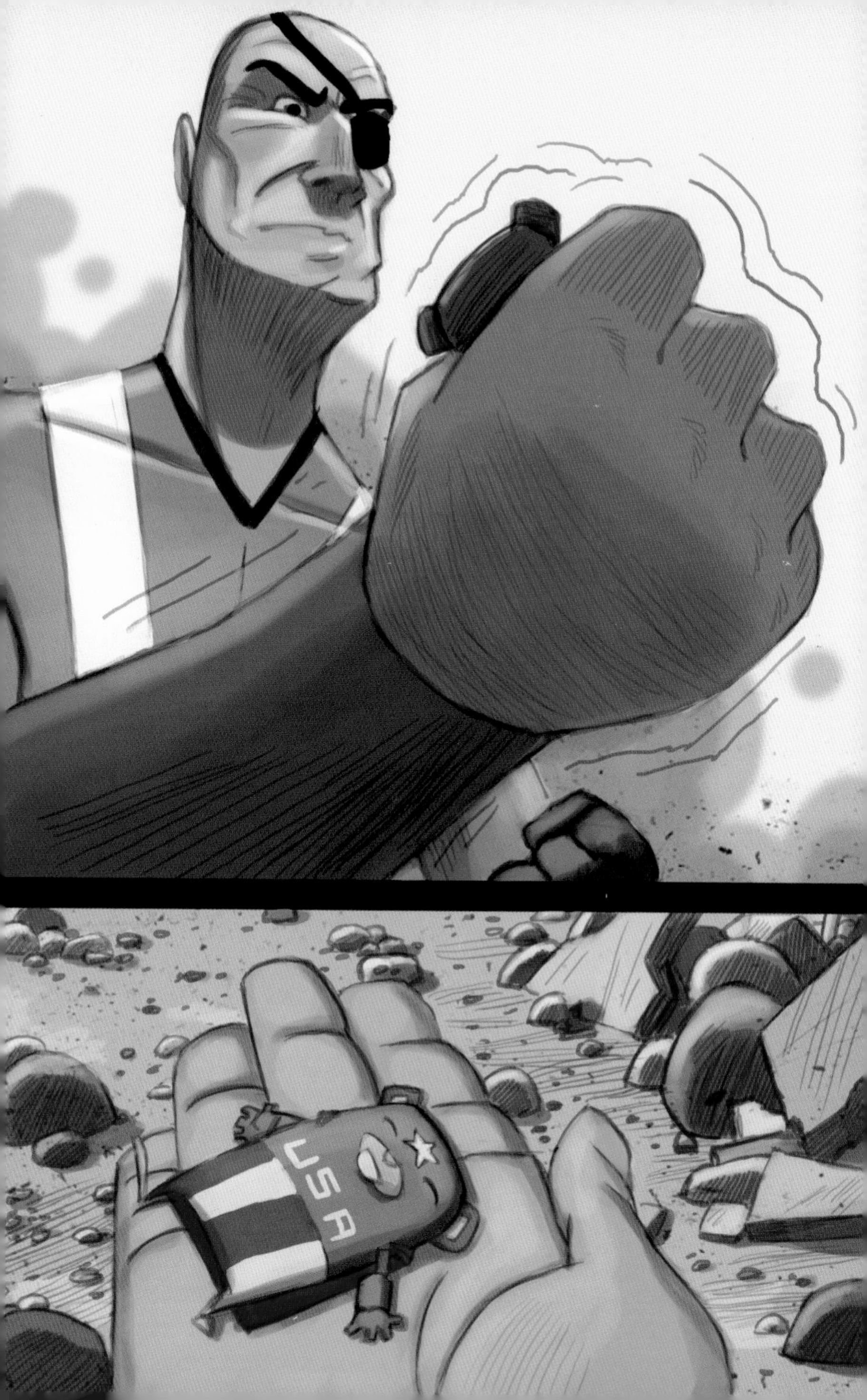
USA

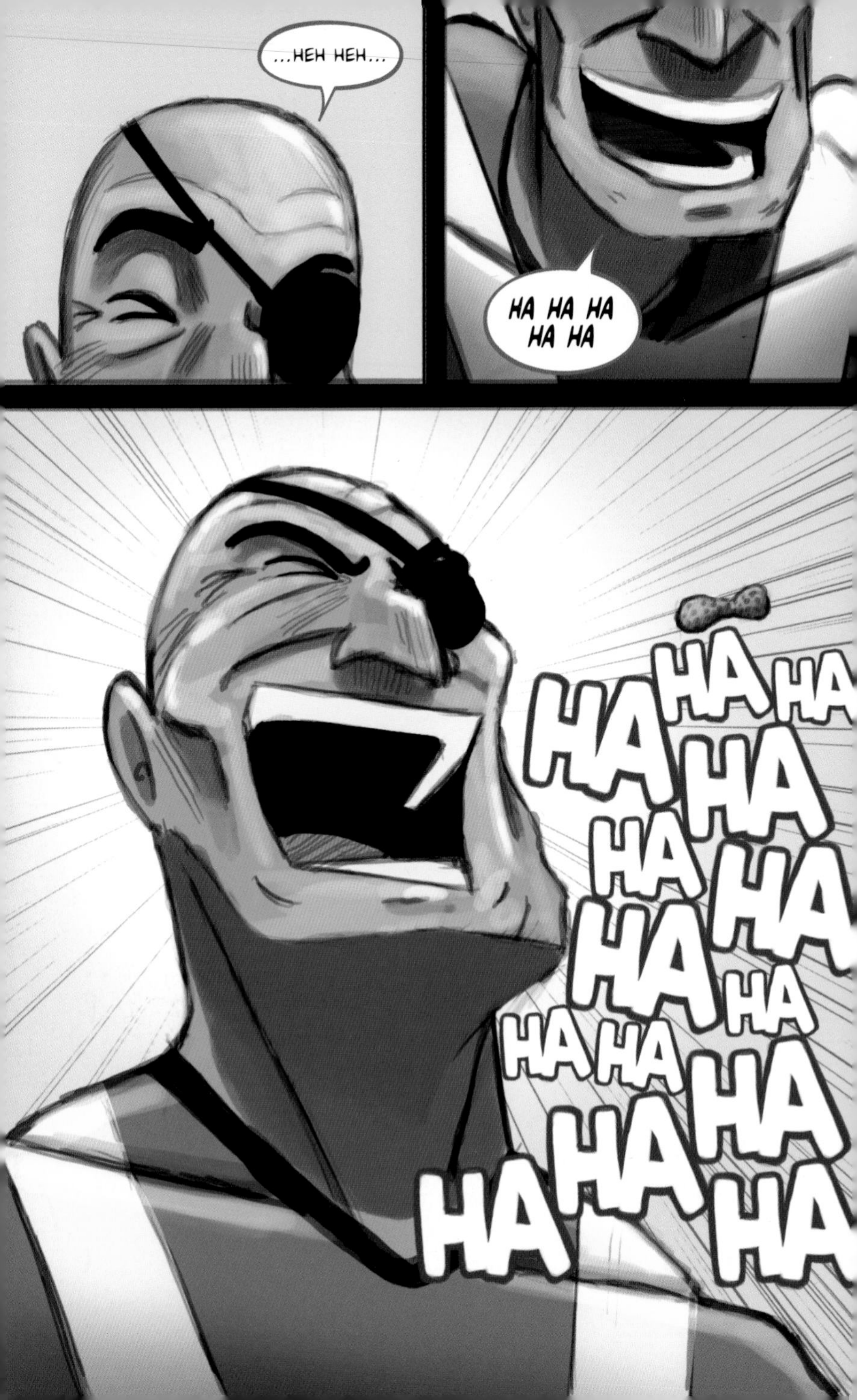
...HEH HEH...
HA HA HA
HA HA
HA HA HA
HA
HA HA
HA HA
HA HA HA
HA HA
HA HA

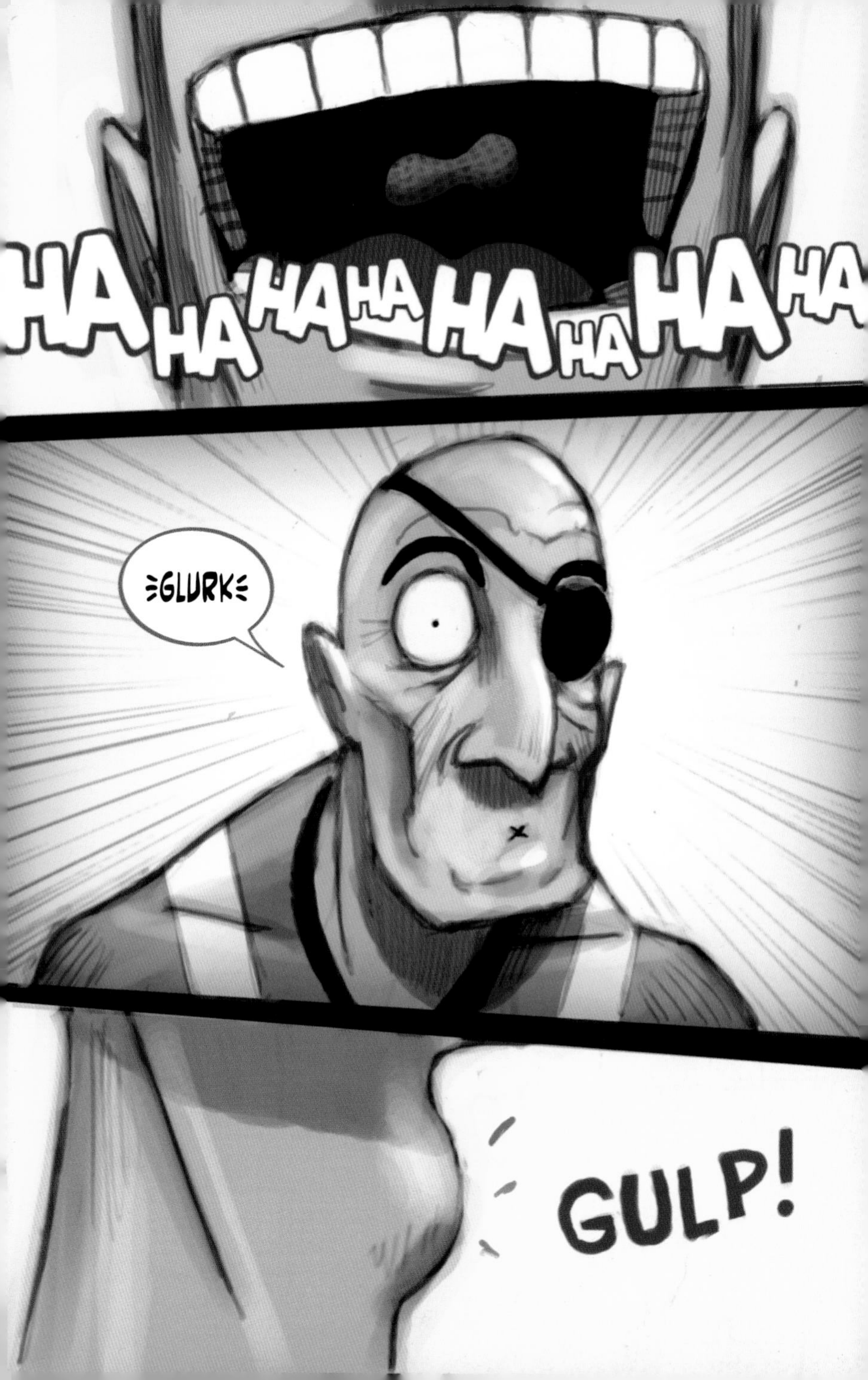
HA HA HA HA HA HA HA HA
GLURK
GULP!

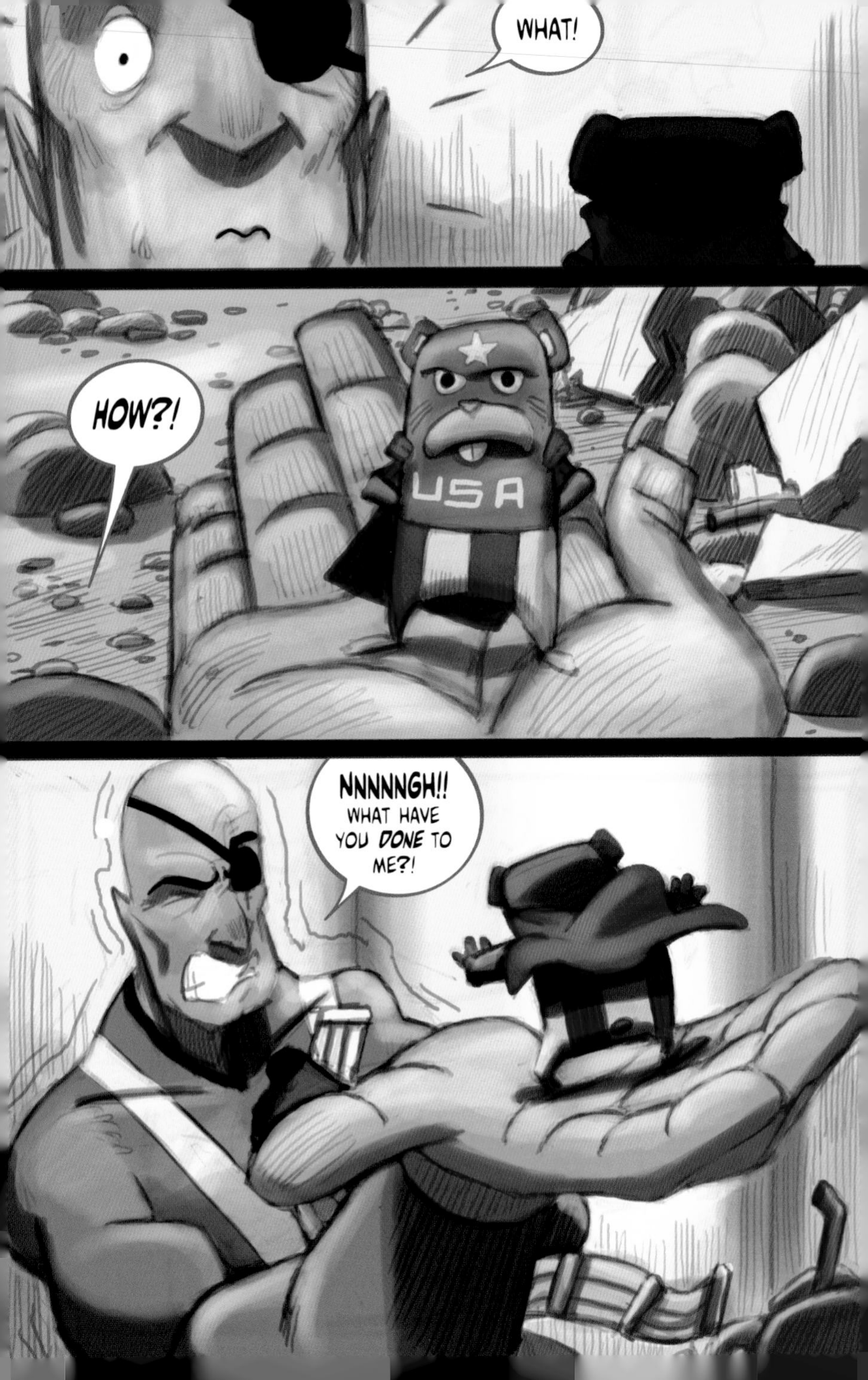
WHAT!
HOW?!
USA
NNNNNGH!! WHAT HAVE YOU DONE TO ME?!

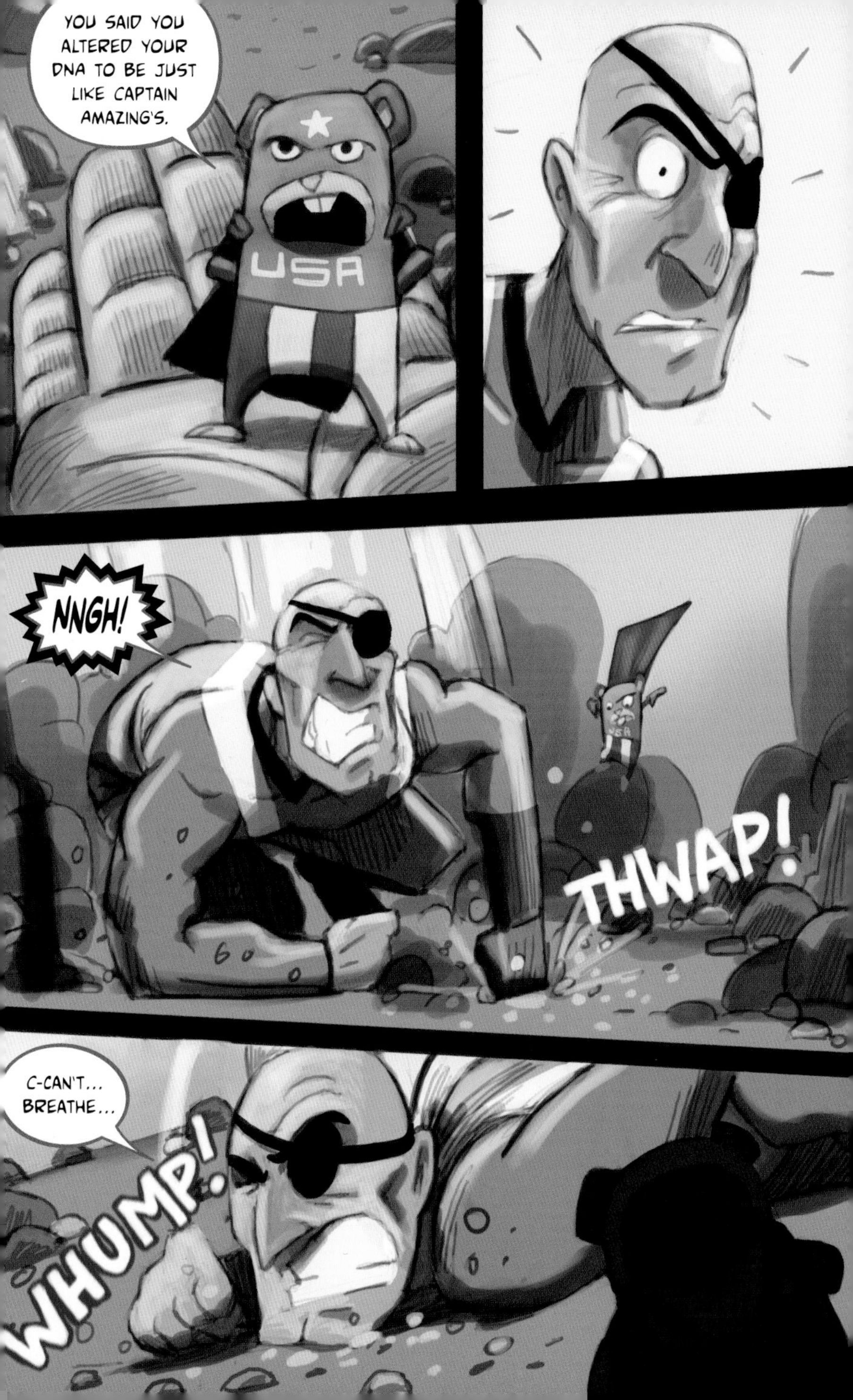
YOU SAID YOU ALTERED YOUR DNA TO BE JUST LIKE CAPTAIN AMAZING'S.
USA
NNGH!
THWAP!
C-CAN'T... BREATHE...
WHUMP!

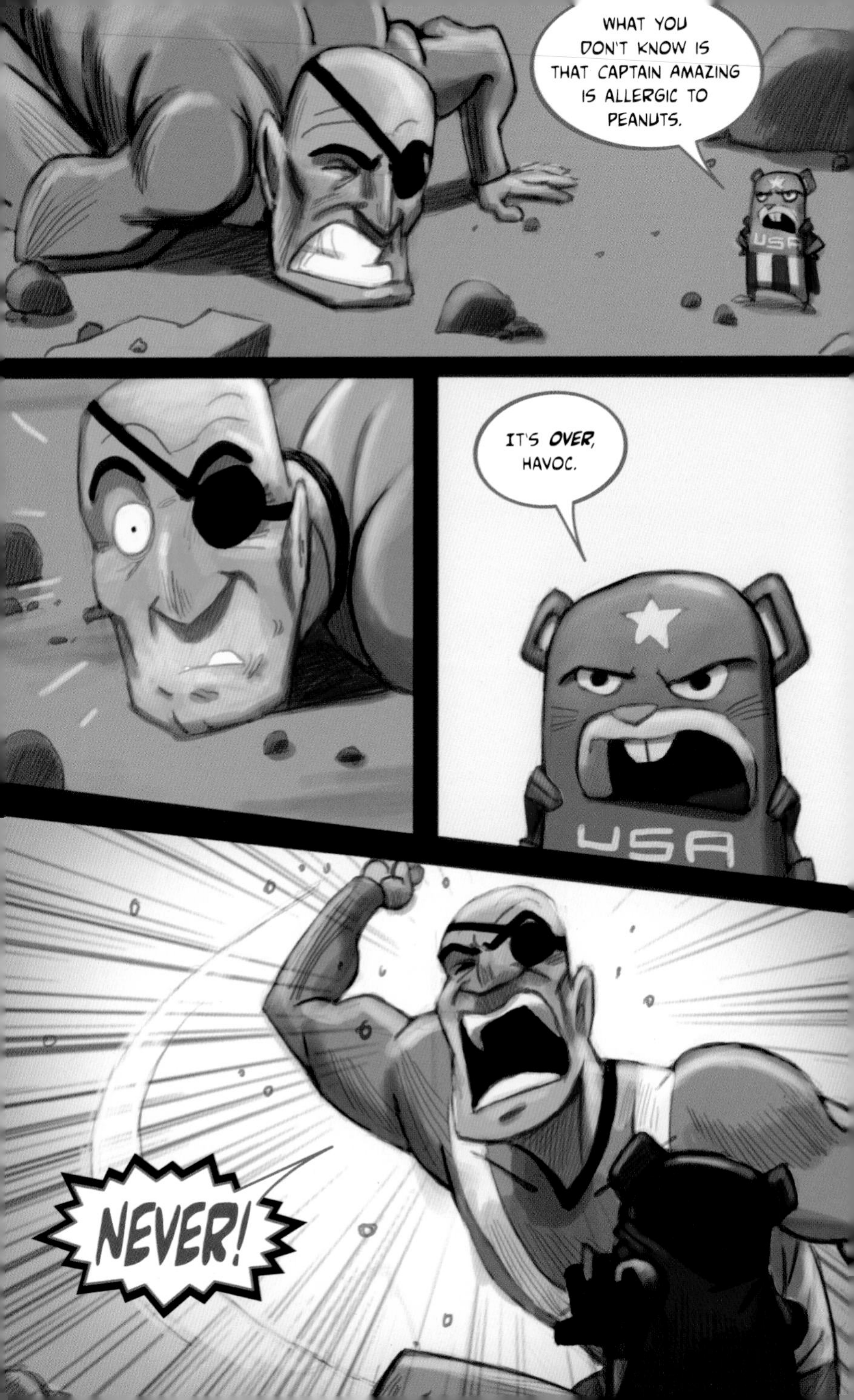
WHAT YOU DON'T KNOW IS THAT CAPTAIN AMAZING IS ALLERGIC TO PEANUTS.
IT'S *OVER,* HAVOC.
NEVER!

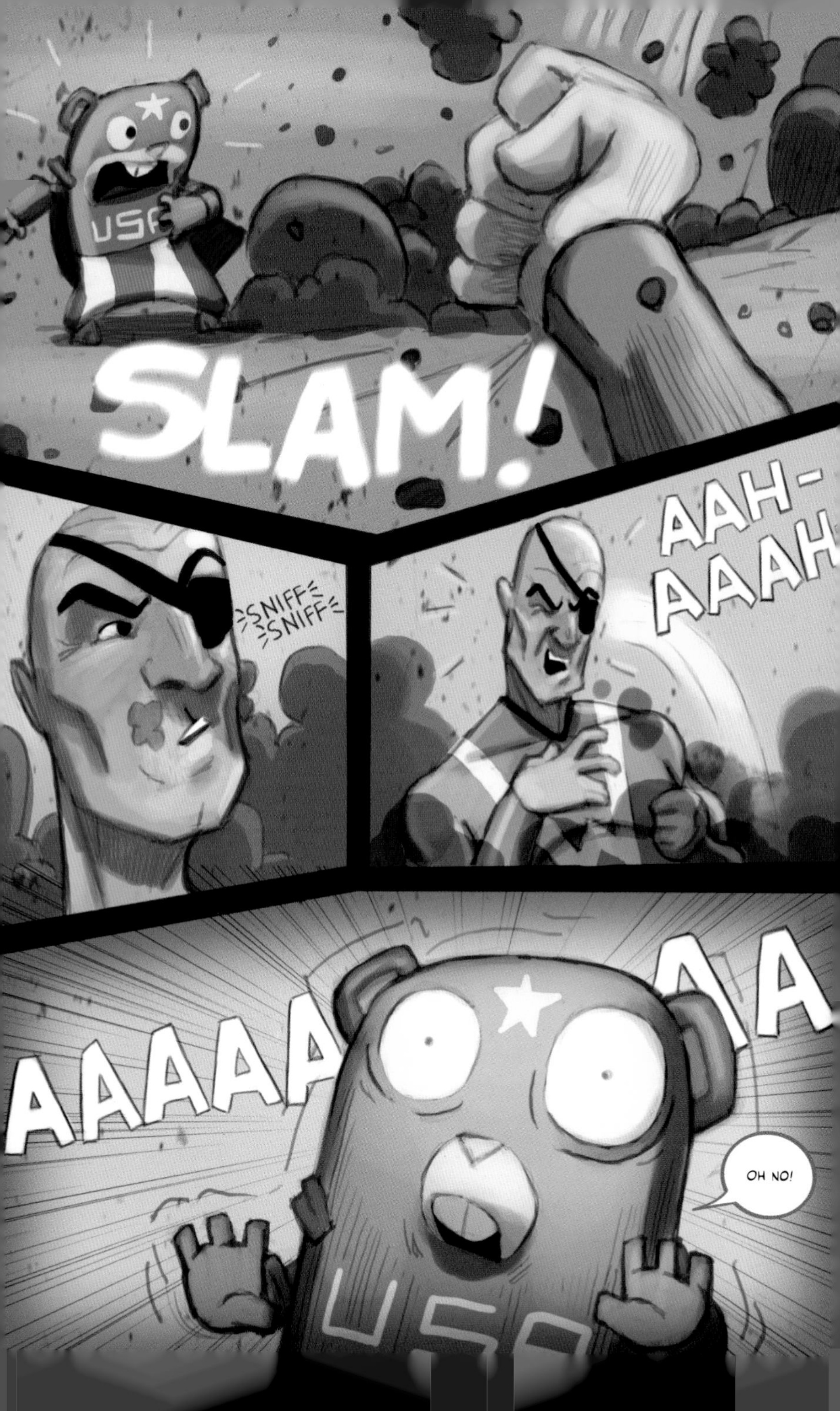
SLAM!
SNIFF
SNIFF
AAH-
AAAH
AAAAAAA
OH NO!

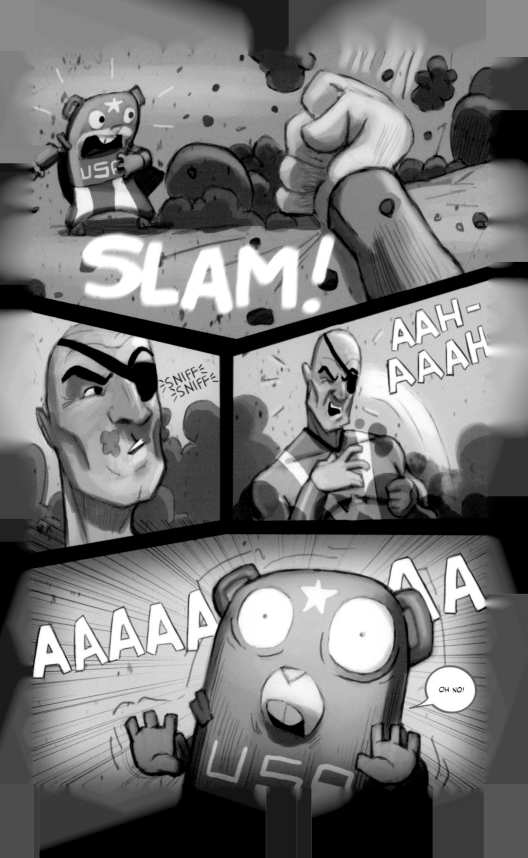

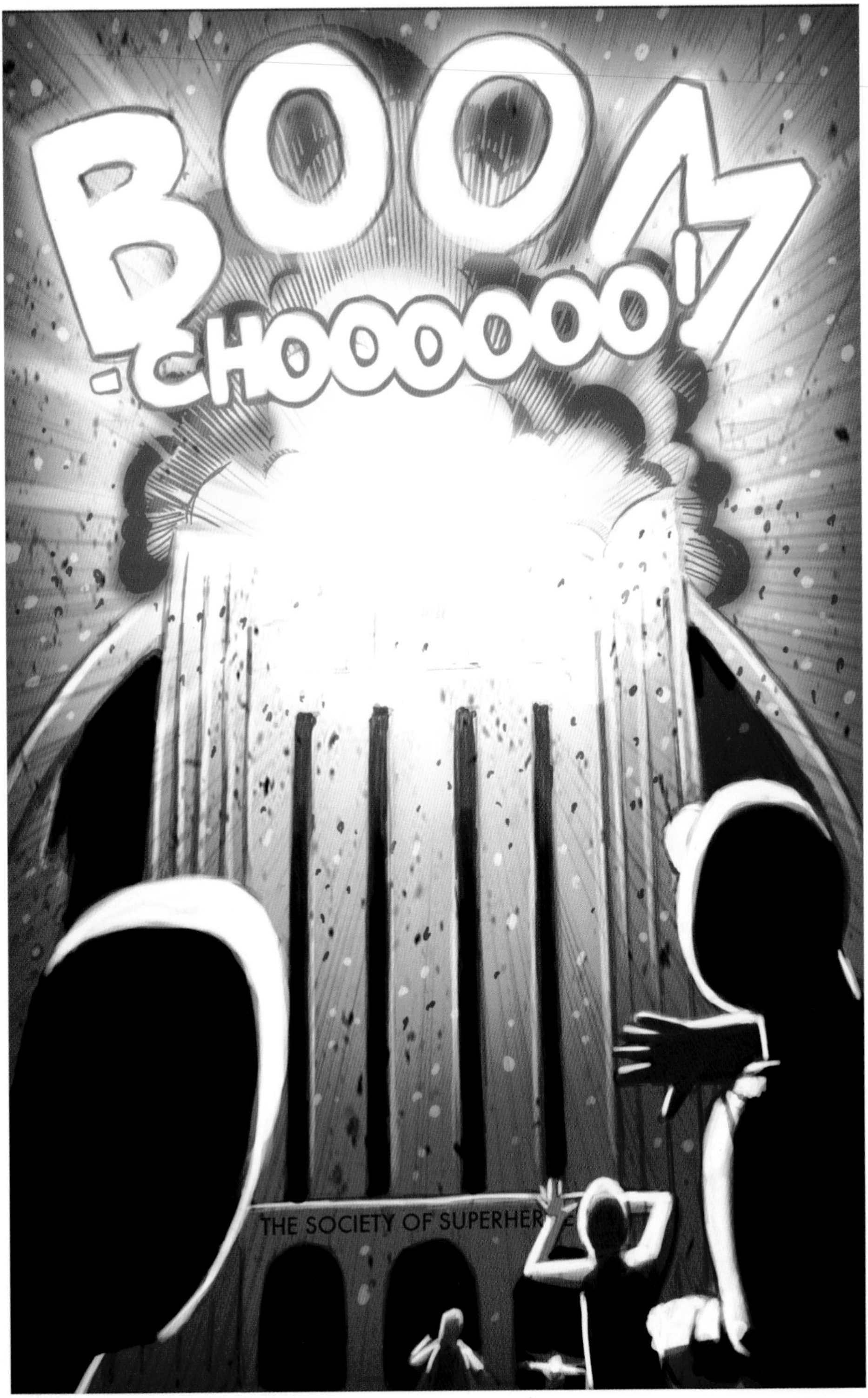
BOOM-CHOOOOOO!
THE SOCIETY OF SUPERHER

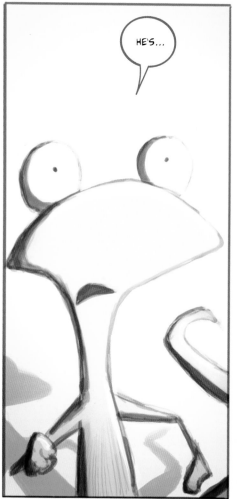

HE'S...

...GONE...

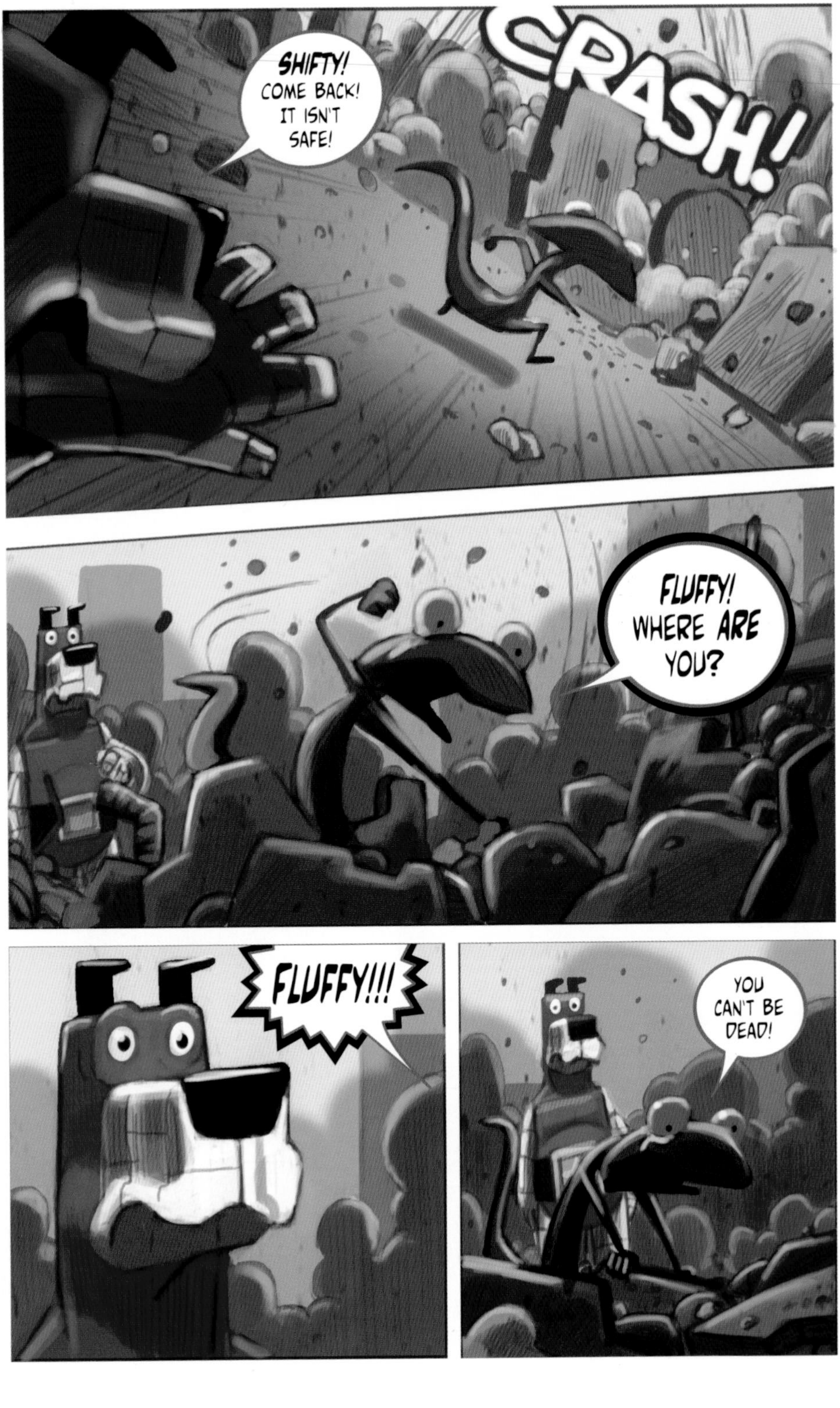
SHIFTY! COME BACK! IT ISN'T SAFE!
CRASH!
FLUFFY! WHERE ARE YOU?
FLUFFY!!!
YOU CAN'T BE DEAD!

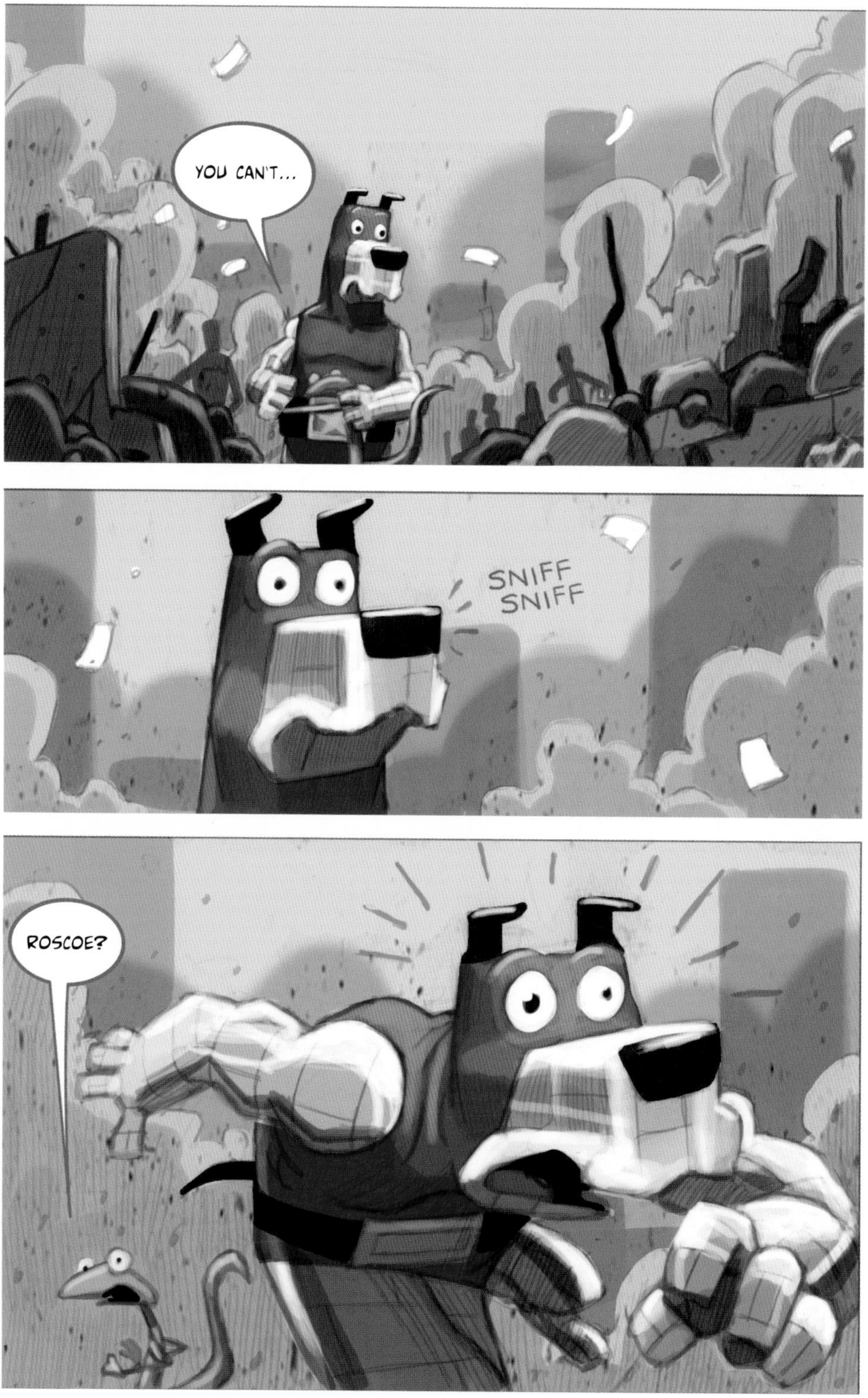
YOU CAN'T...
SNIFF
SNIFF
ROSCOE?

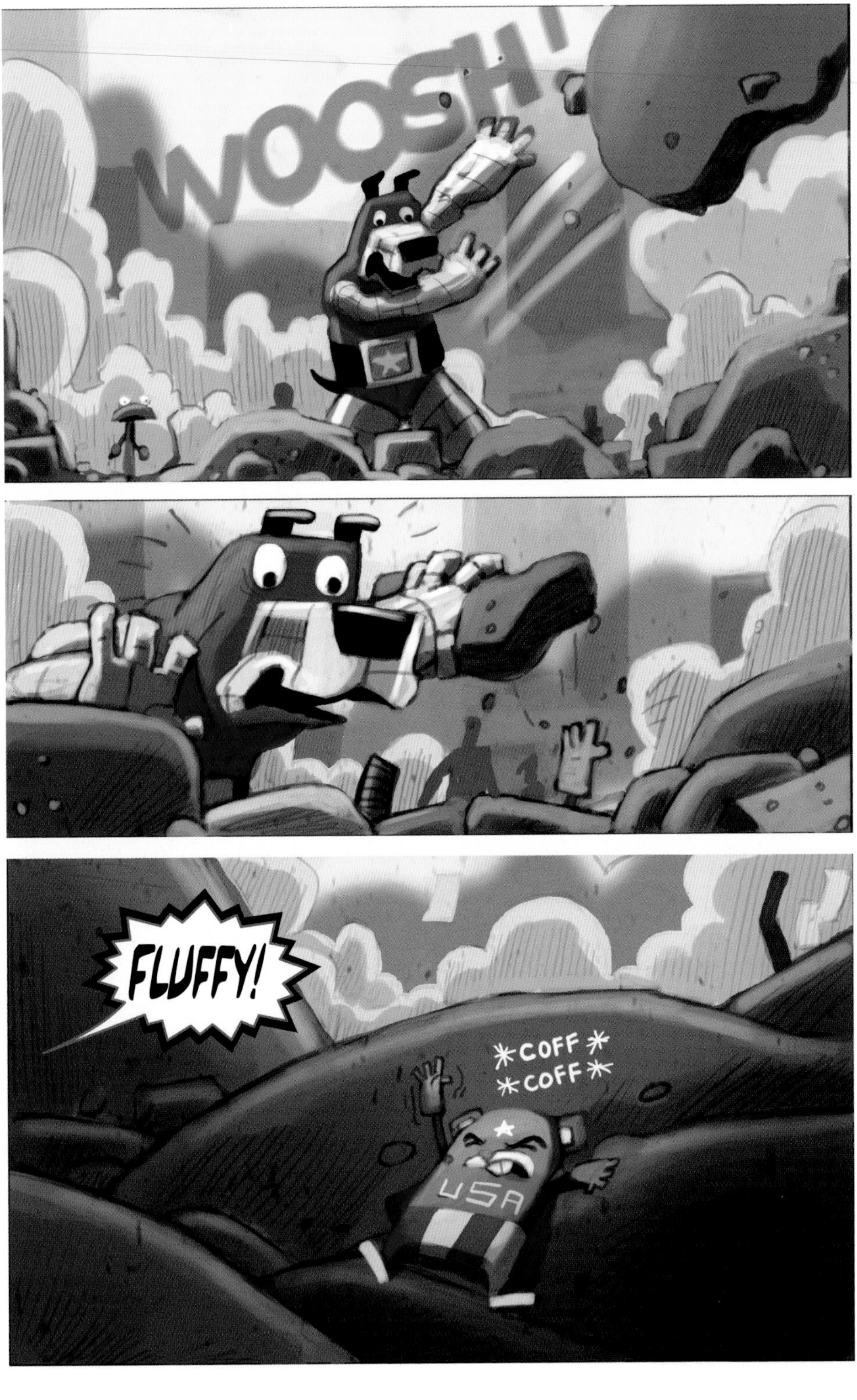
WOOSH!
FLUFFY!
COFF
COFF
USA

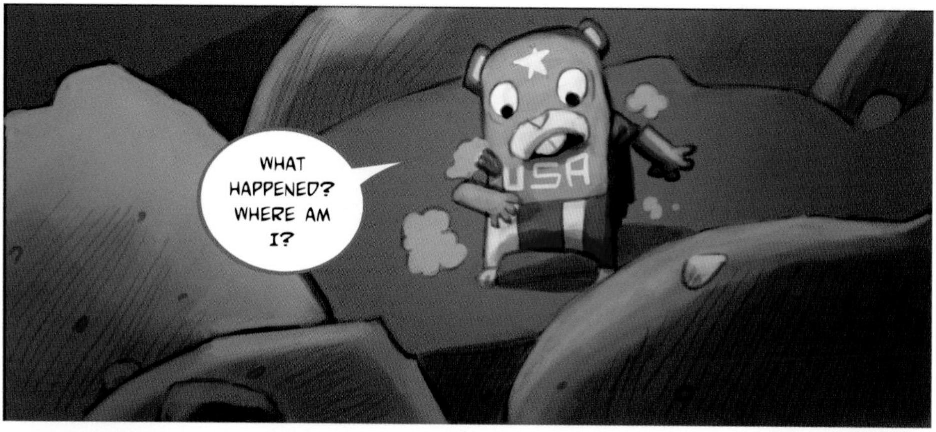
WHAT HAPPENED? WHERE AM I?

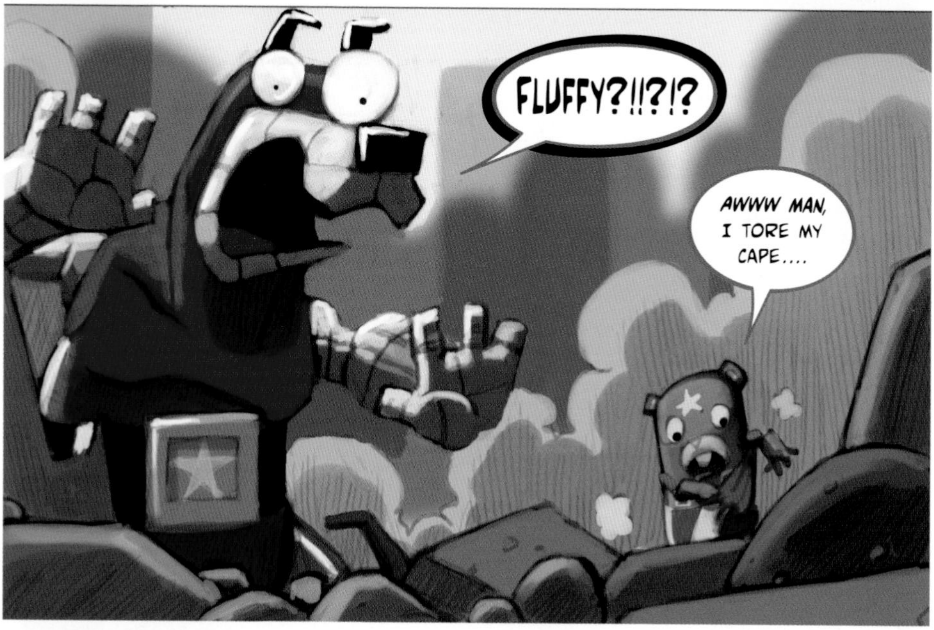
FLUFFY?!!?!?
AWWW MAN, I TORE MY CAPE....

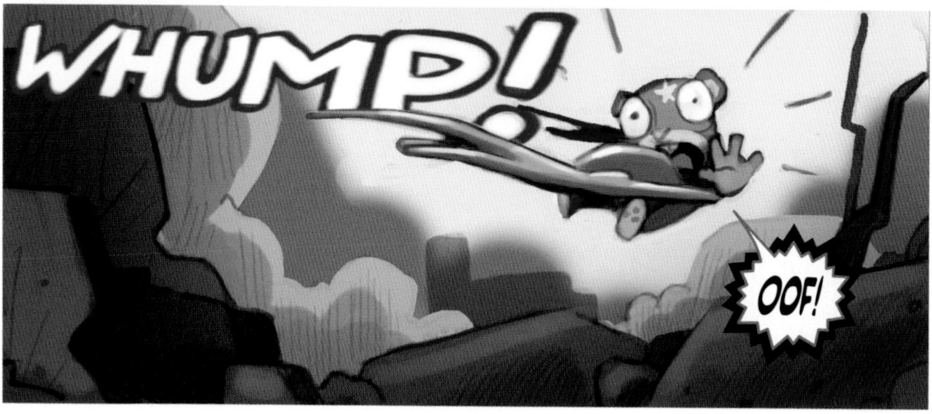
WHUMP!
OOF!

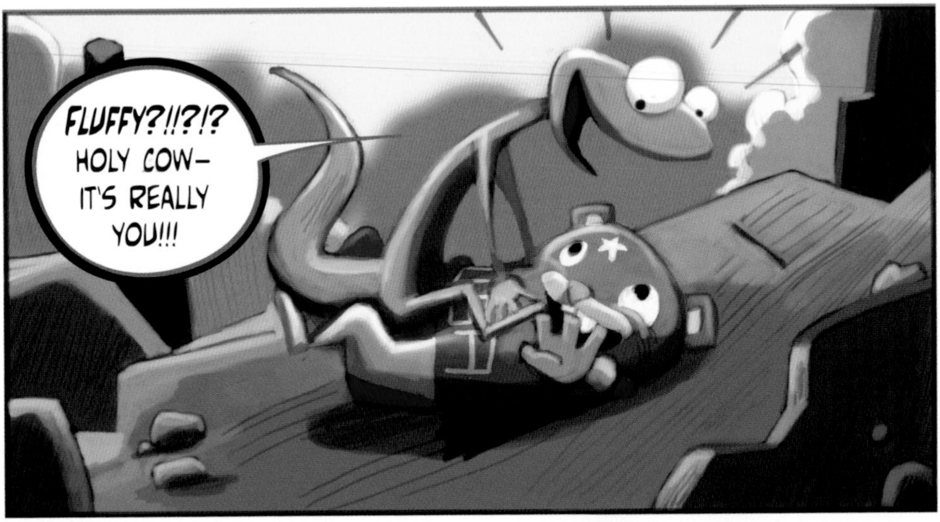
FLUFFY?!!?!? HOLY COW— IT'S REALLY YOU!!!

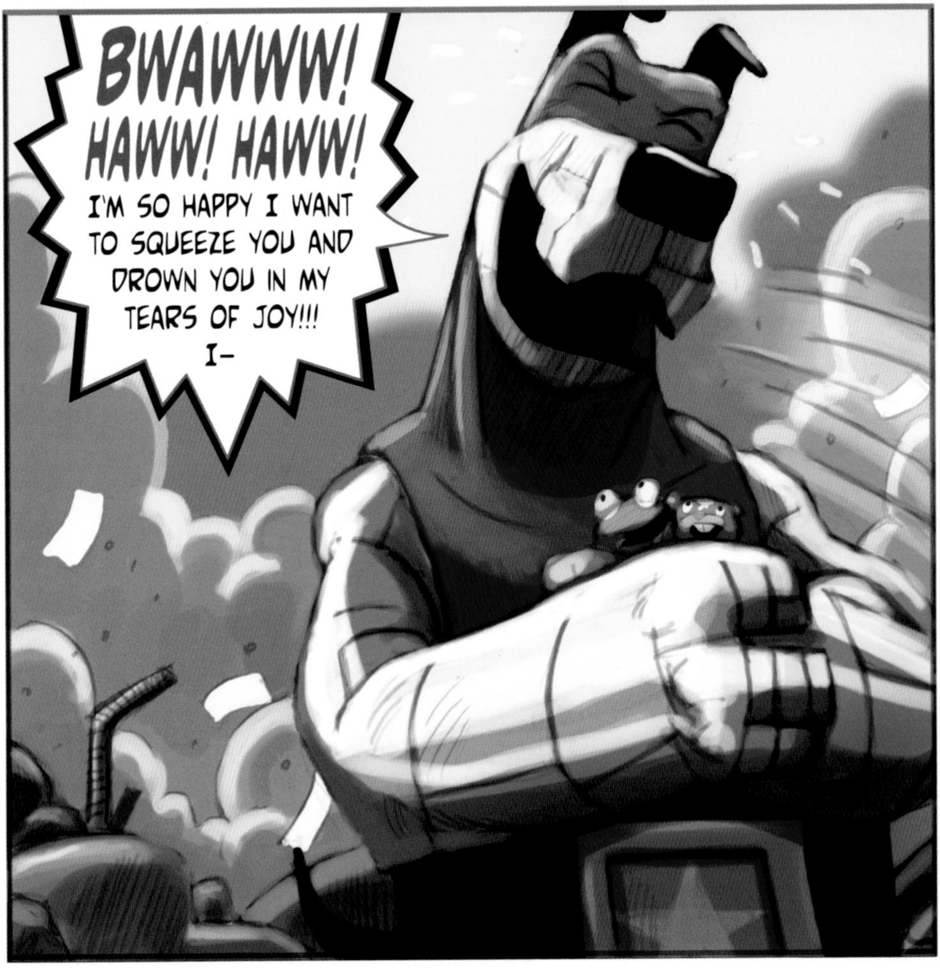
BWAWWW! HAWW! HAWW! I'M SO HAPPY I WANT TO SQUEEZE YOU AND DROWN YOU IN MY TEARS OF JOY!!! I–

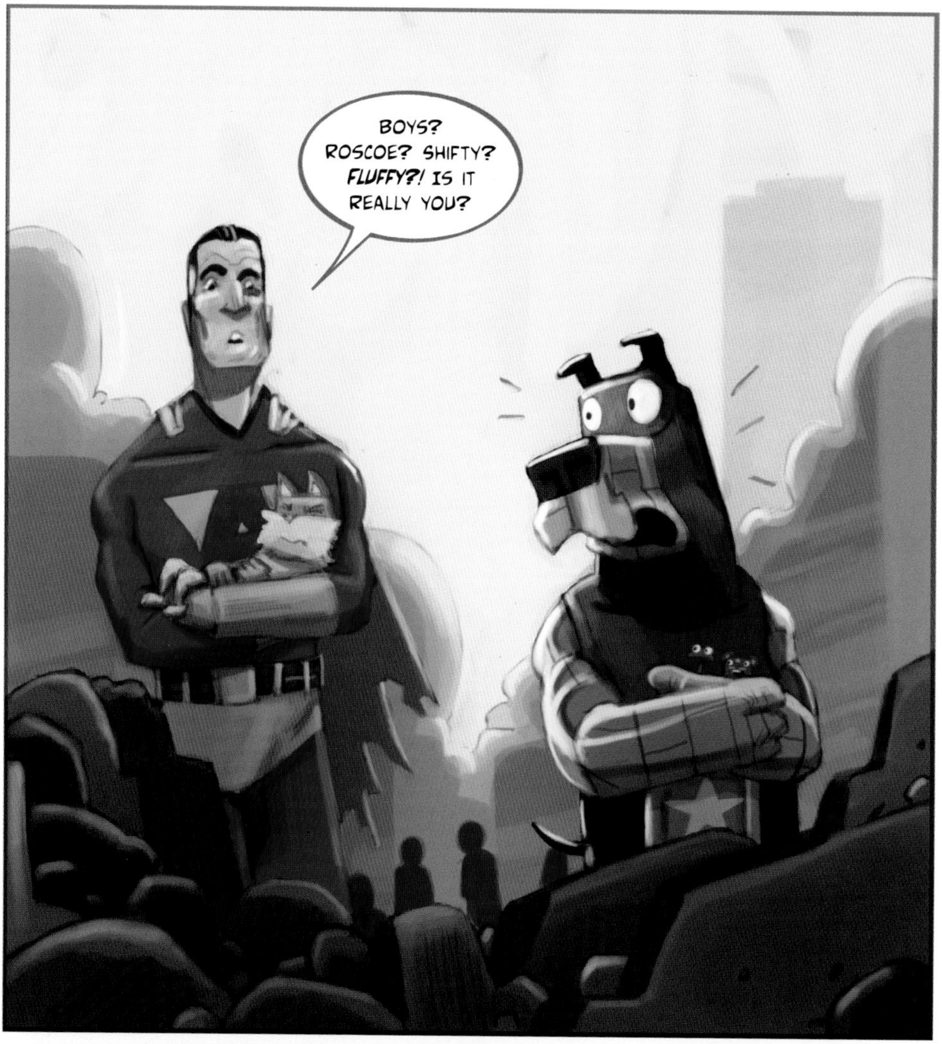
BOYS?
ROSCOE? SHIFTY?
FLUFFY?! IS IT
REALLY YOU?

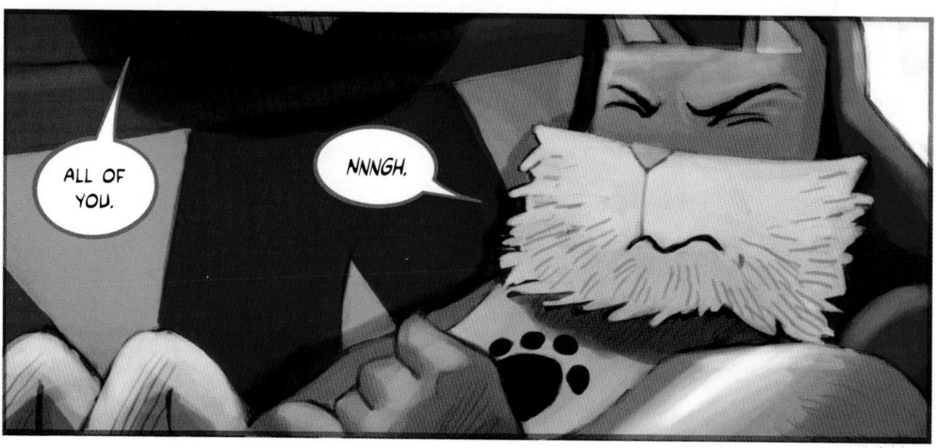
ALL OF
YOU.
NNNGH.

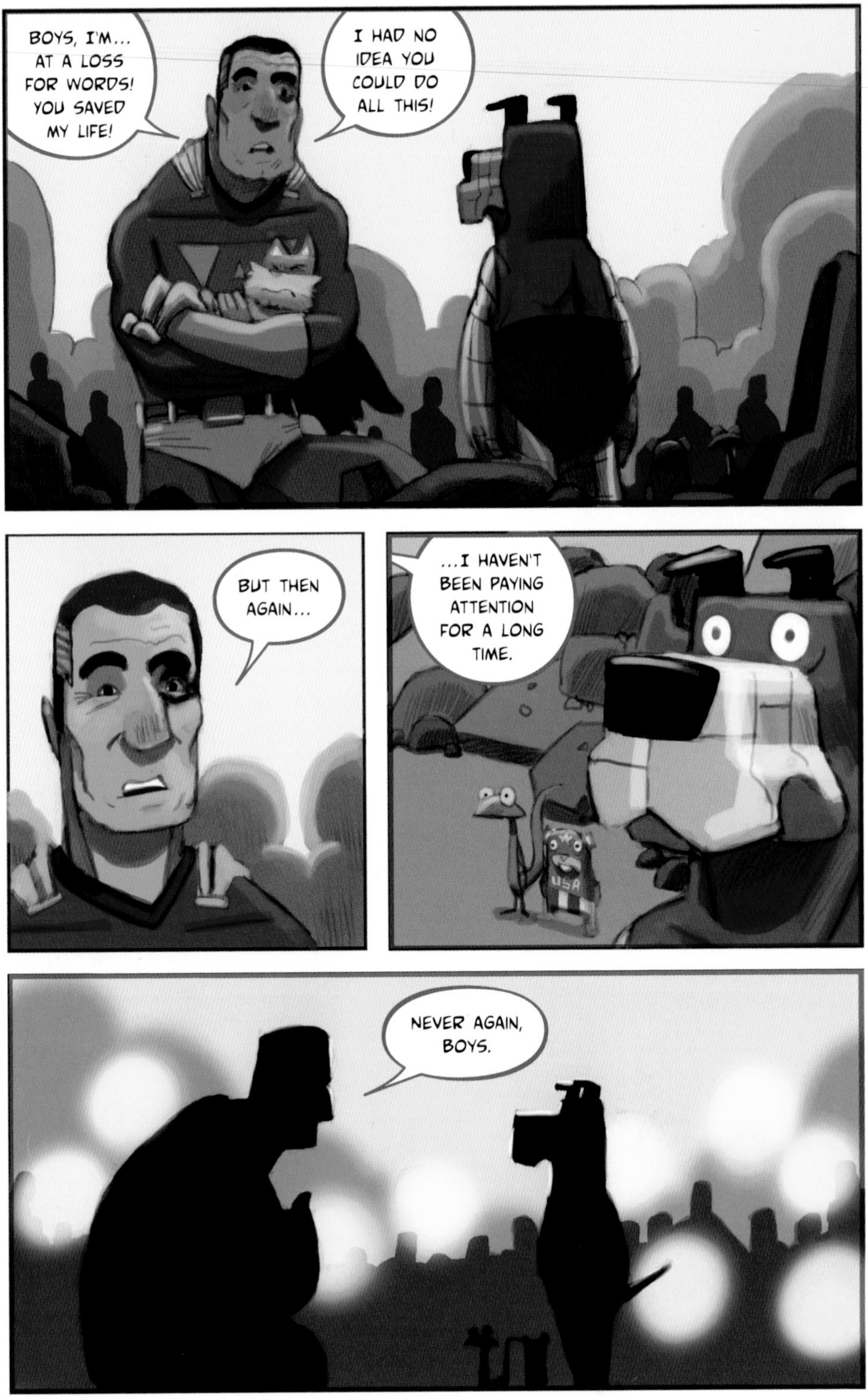
BOYS, I'M... AT A LOSS FOR WORDS! YOU SAVED MY LIFE!
I HAD NO IDEA YOU COULD DO ALL THIS!
BUT THEN AGAIN...
...I HAVEN'T BEEN PAYING ATTENTION FOR A LONG TIME.
NEVER AGAIN, BOYS.

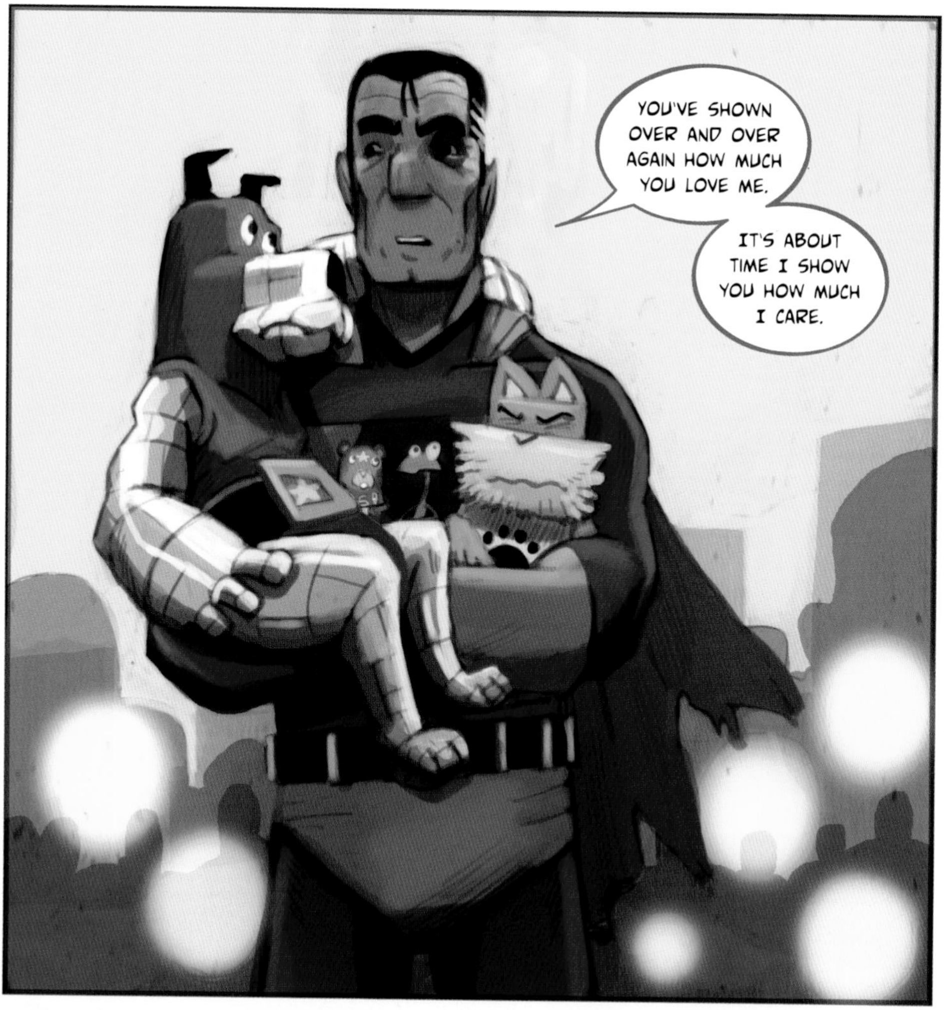
YOU'VE SHOWN OVER AND OVER AGAIN HOW MUCH YOU LOVE ME.
IT'S ABOUT TIME I SHOW YOU HOW MUCH I CARE.

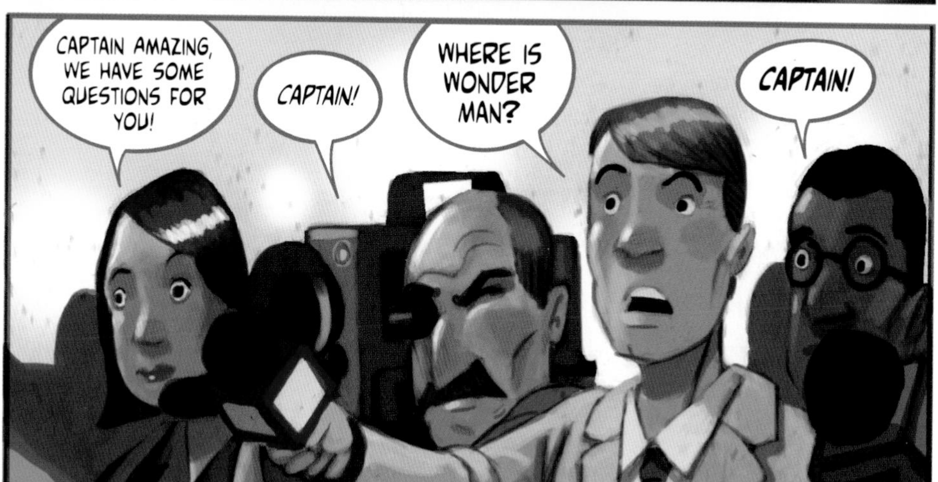
CAPTAIN AMAZING, WE HAVE SOME QUESTIONS FOR YOU!
CAPTAIN!
WHERE IS WONDER MAN?
CAPTAIN!

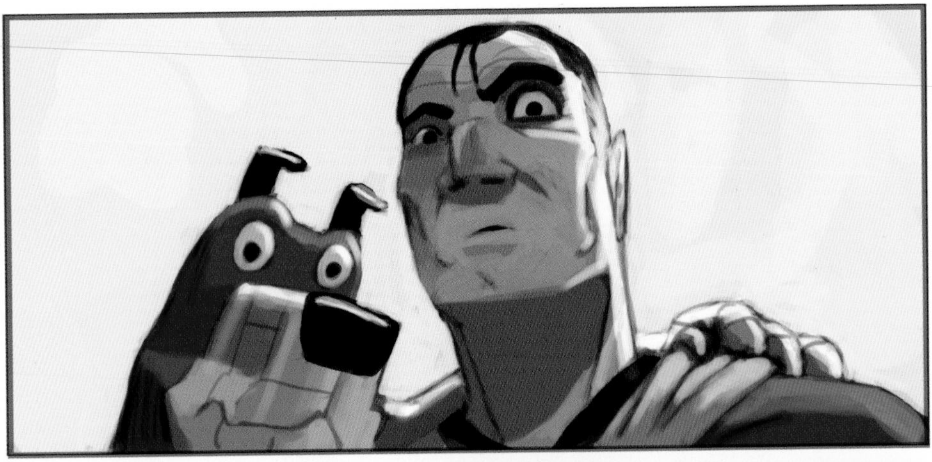

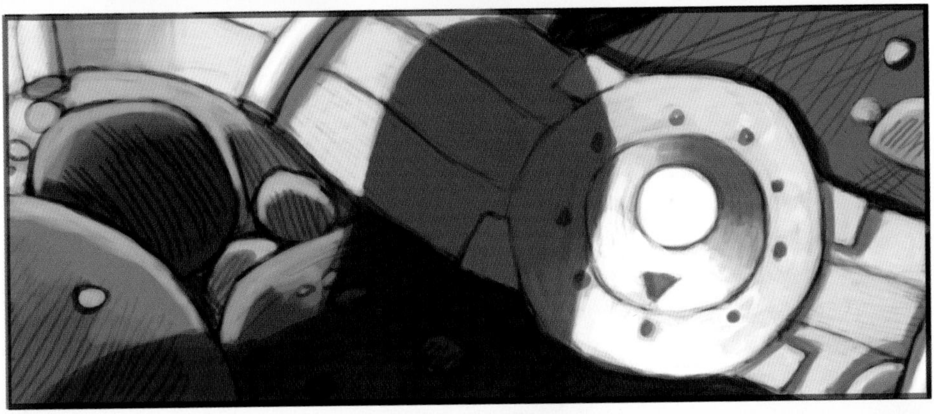

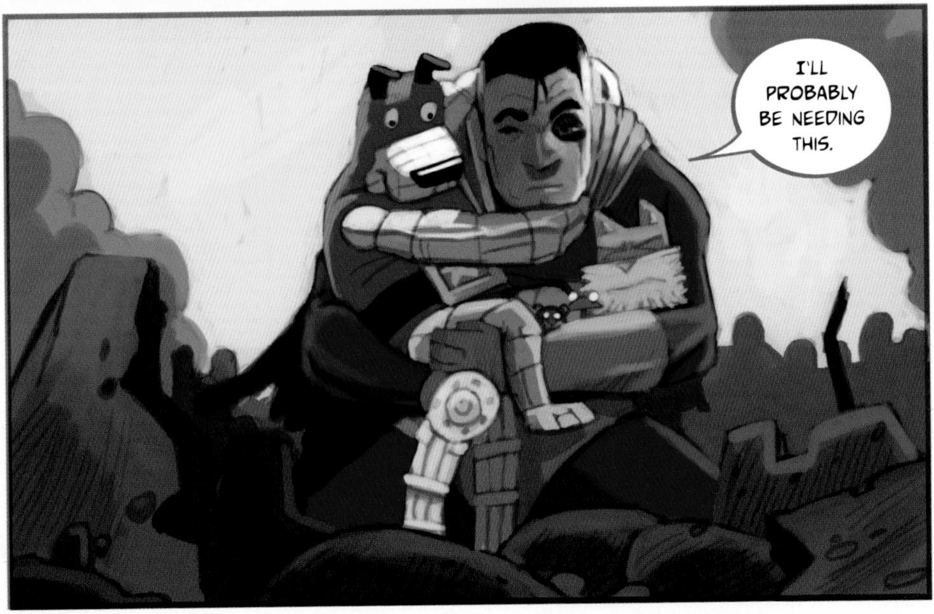
I'LL PROBABLY BE NEEDING THIS.

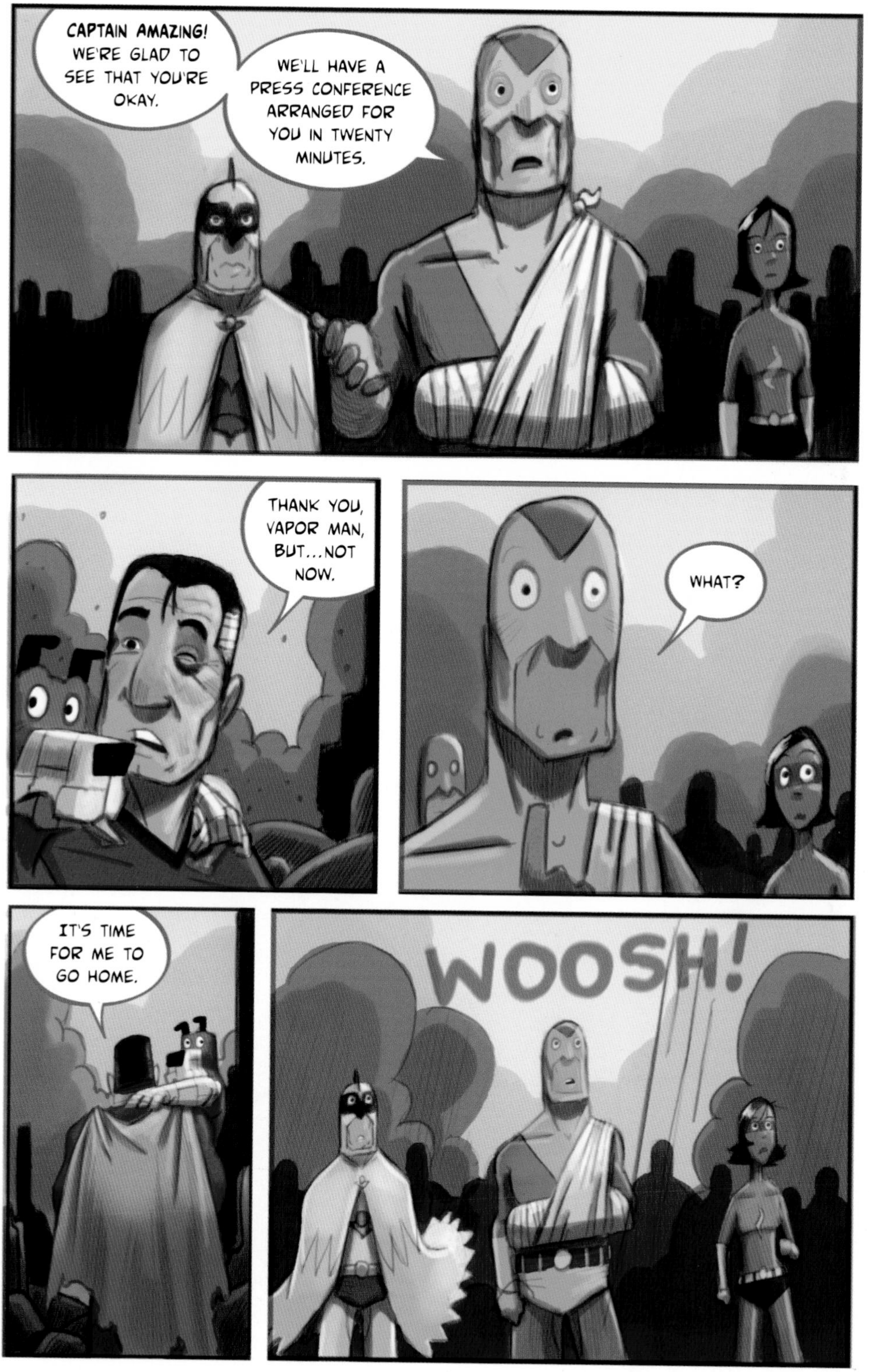
CAPTAIN AMAZING! WE'RE GLAD TO SEE THAT YOU'RE OKAY.
WE'LL HAVE A PRESS CONFERENCE ARRANGED FOR YOU IN TWENTY MINUTES.
THANK YOU, VAPOR MAN, BUT...NOT NOW.
WHAT?
IT'S TIME FOR ME TO GO HOME.
WOOSH!

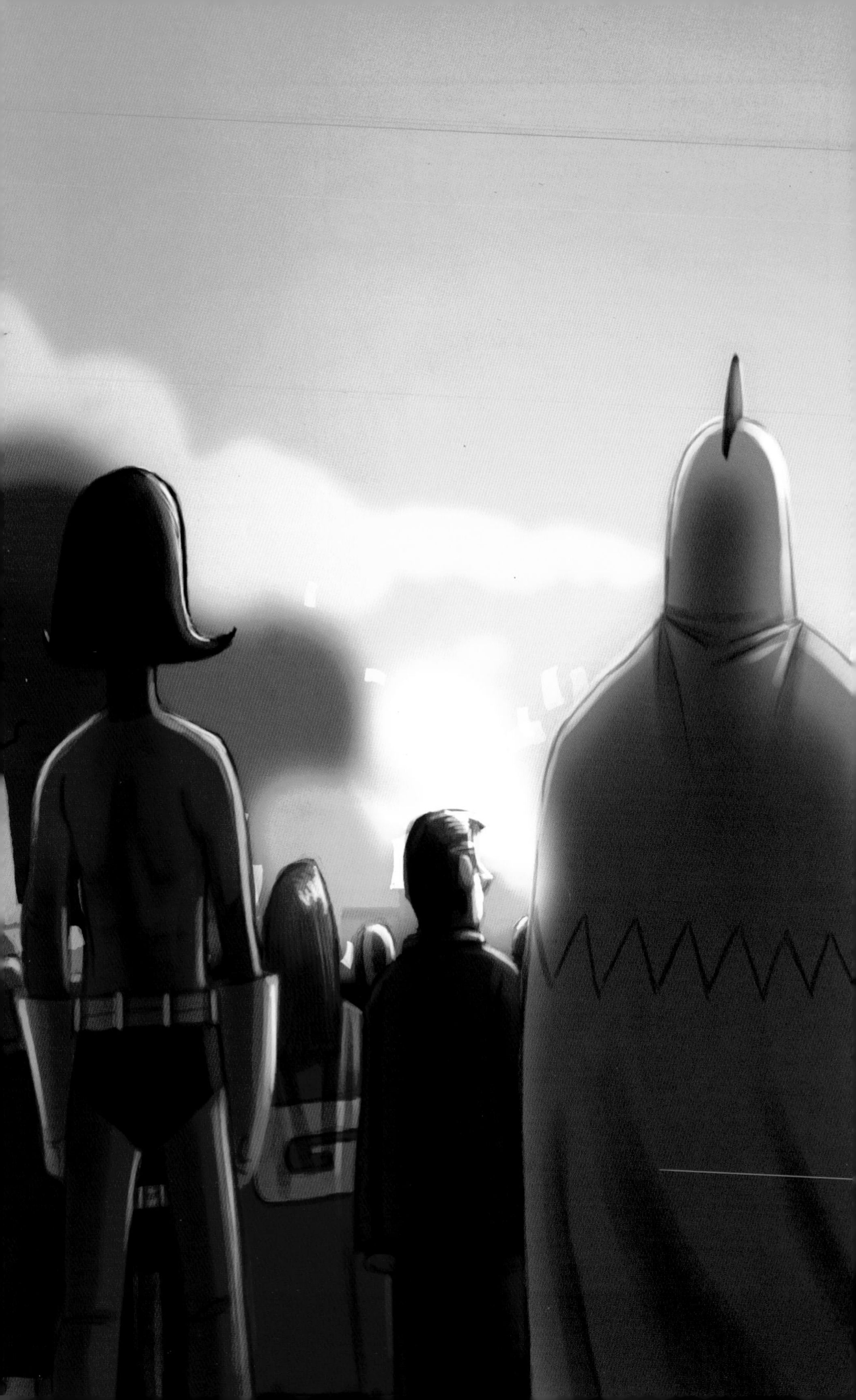

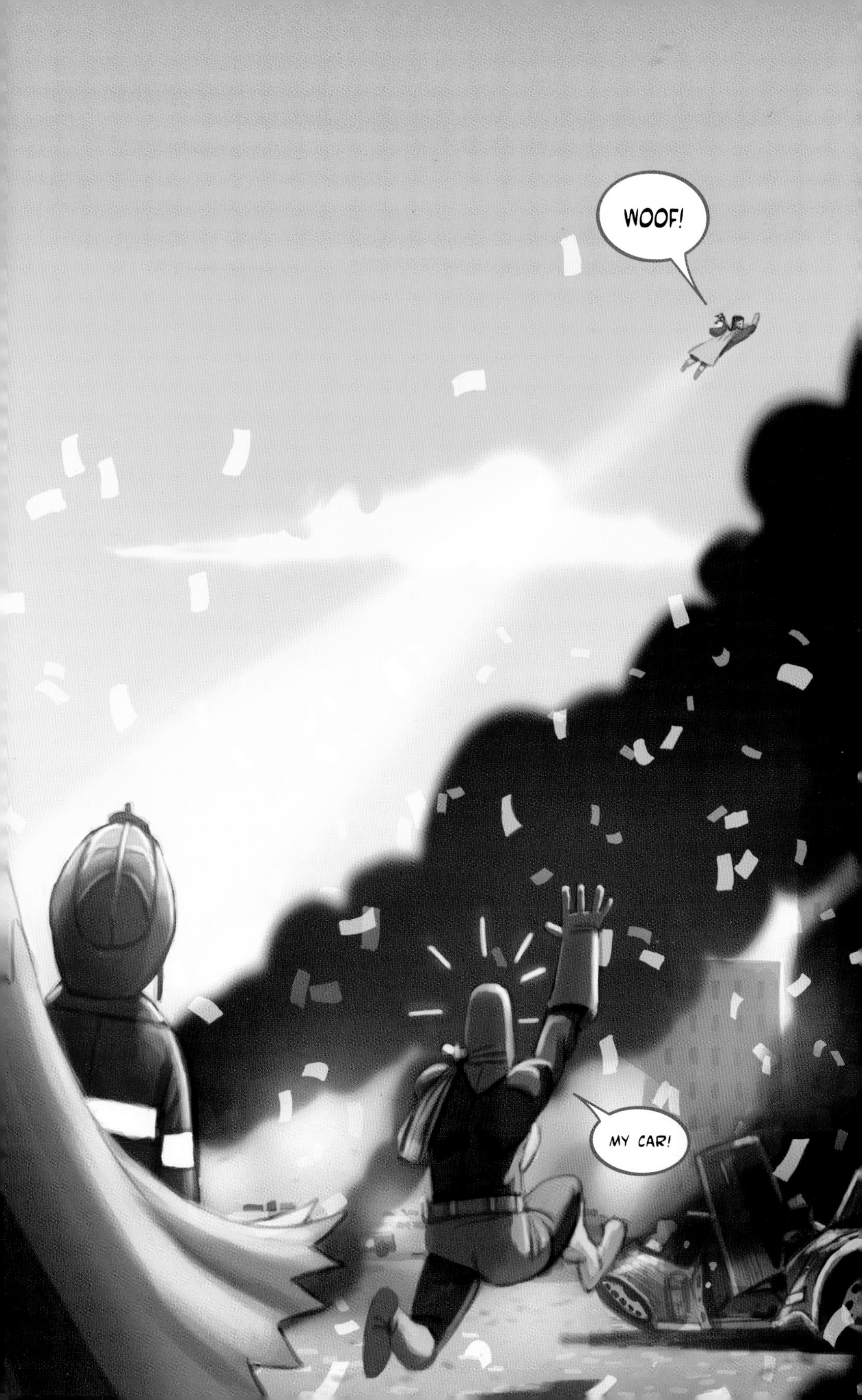
WOOF!
MY CAR!

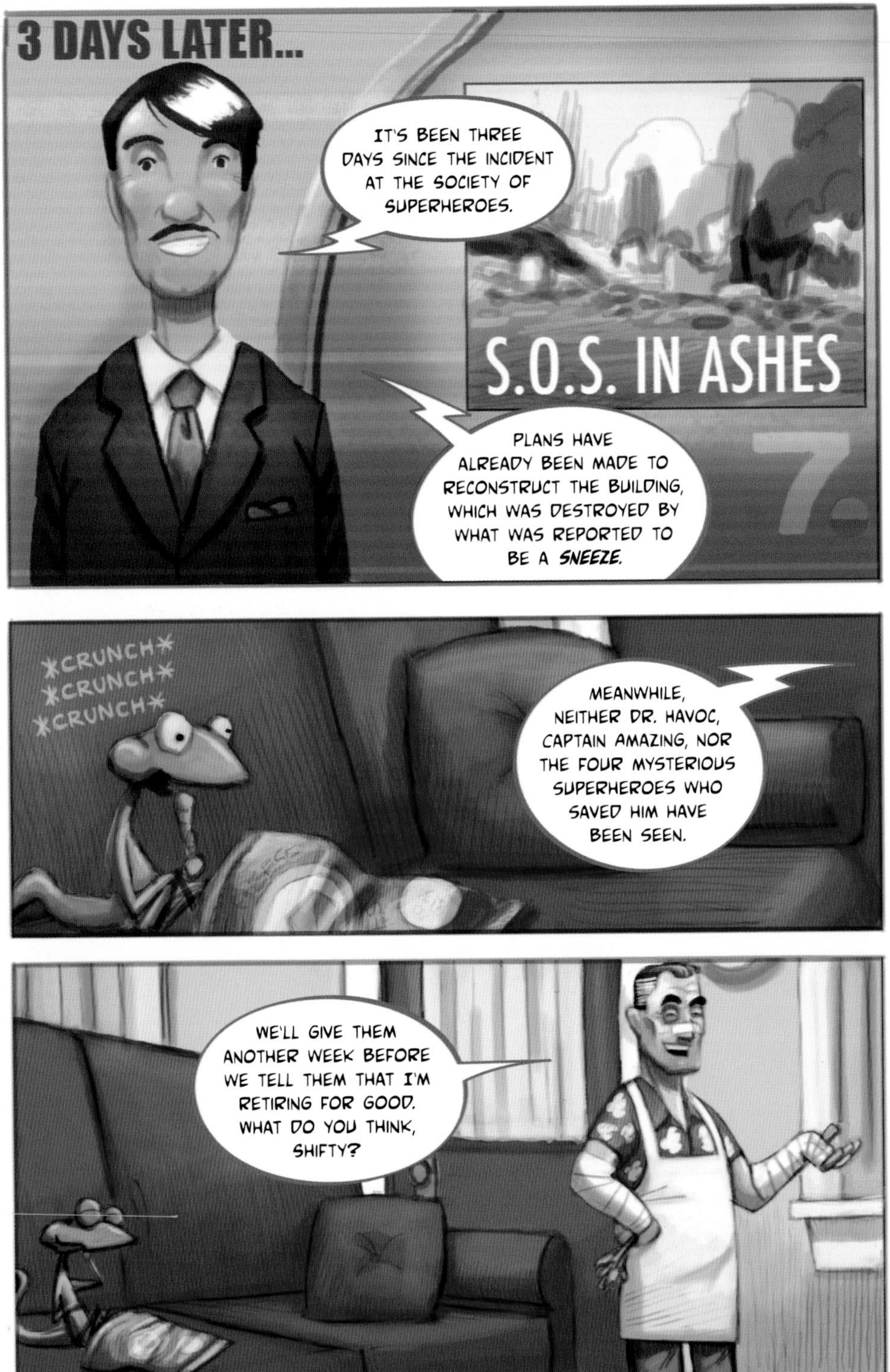
3 DAYS LATER...
IT'S BEEN THREE DAYS SINCE THE INCIDENT AT THE SOCIETY OF SUPERHEROES.
S.O.S. IN ASHES
7.
PLANS HAVE ALREADY BEEN MADE TO RECONSTRUCT THE BUILDING, WHICH WAS DESTROYED BY WHAT WAS REPORTED TO BE A *SNEEZE*.
CRUNCH
CRUNCH
CRUNCH
MEANWHILE, NEITHER DR. HAVOC, CAPTAIN AMAZING, NOR THE FOUR MYSTERIOUS SUPERHEROES WHO SAVED HIM HAVE BEEN SEEN.
WE'LL GIVE THEM ANOTHER WEEK BEFORE WE TELL THEM THAT I'M RETIRING FOR GOOD. WHAT DO YOU THINK, SHIFTY?

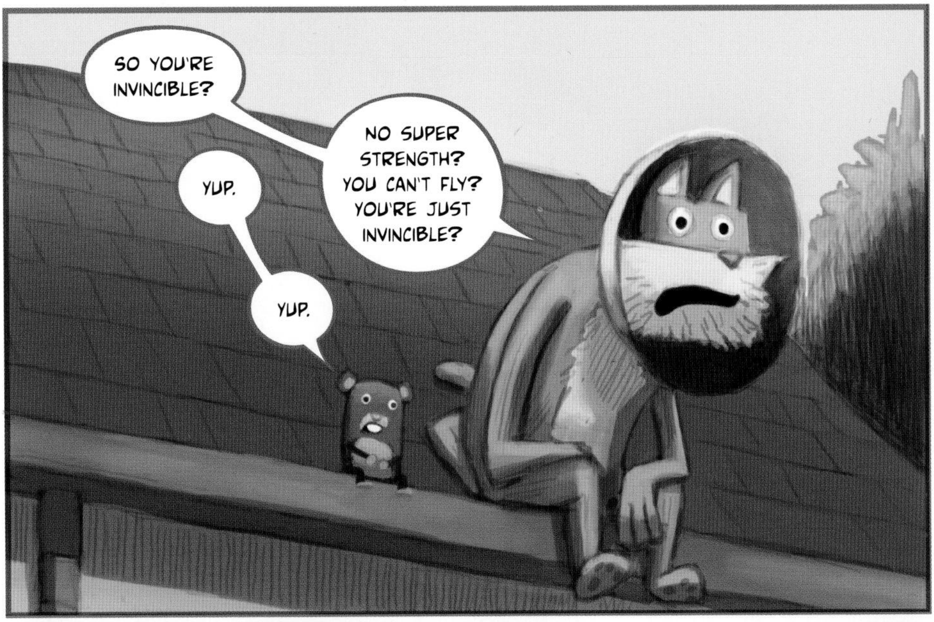
SO YOU'RE INVINCIBLE?
YUP.
NO SUPER STRENGTH? YOU CAN'T FLY? YOU'RE JUST INVINCIBLE?
YUP.

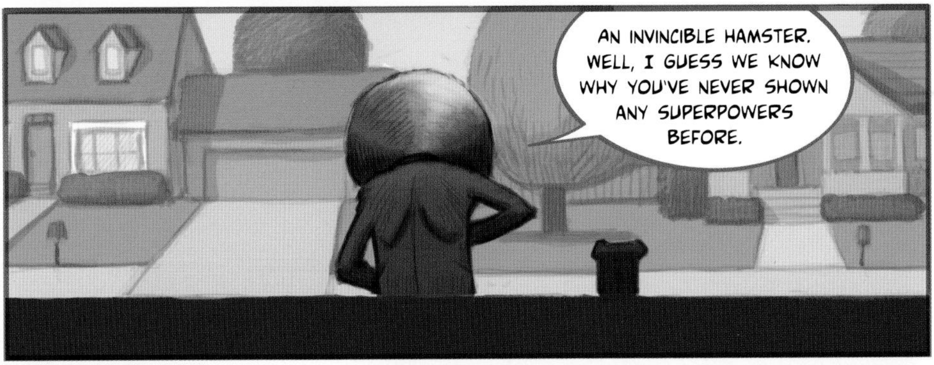
AN INVINCIBLE HAMSTER. WELL, I GUESS WE KNOW WHY YOU'VE NEVER SHOWN ANY SUPERPOWERS BEFORE.

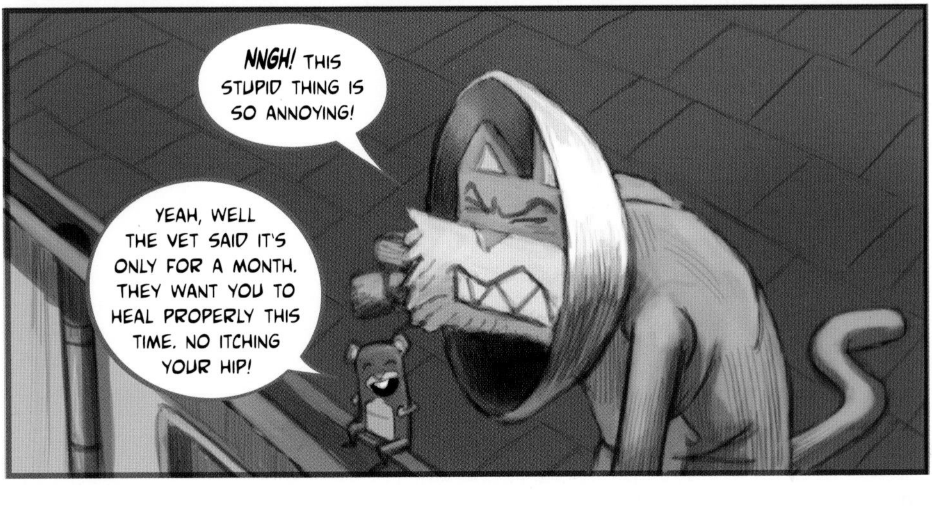
NNGH! THIS STUPID THING IS SO ANNOYING!
YEAH, WELL THE VET SAID IT'S ONLY FOR A MONTH. THEY WANT YOU TO HEAL PROPERLY THIS TIME. NO ITCHING YOUR HIP!

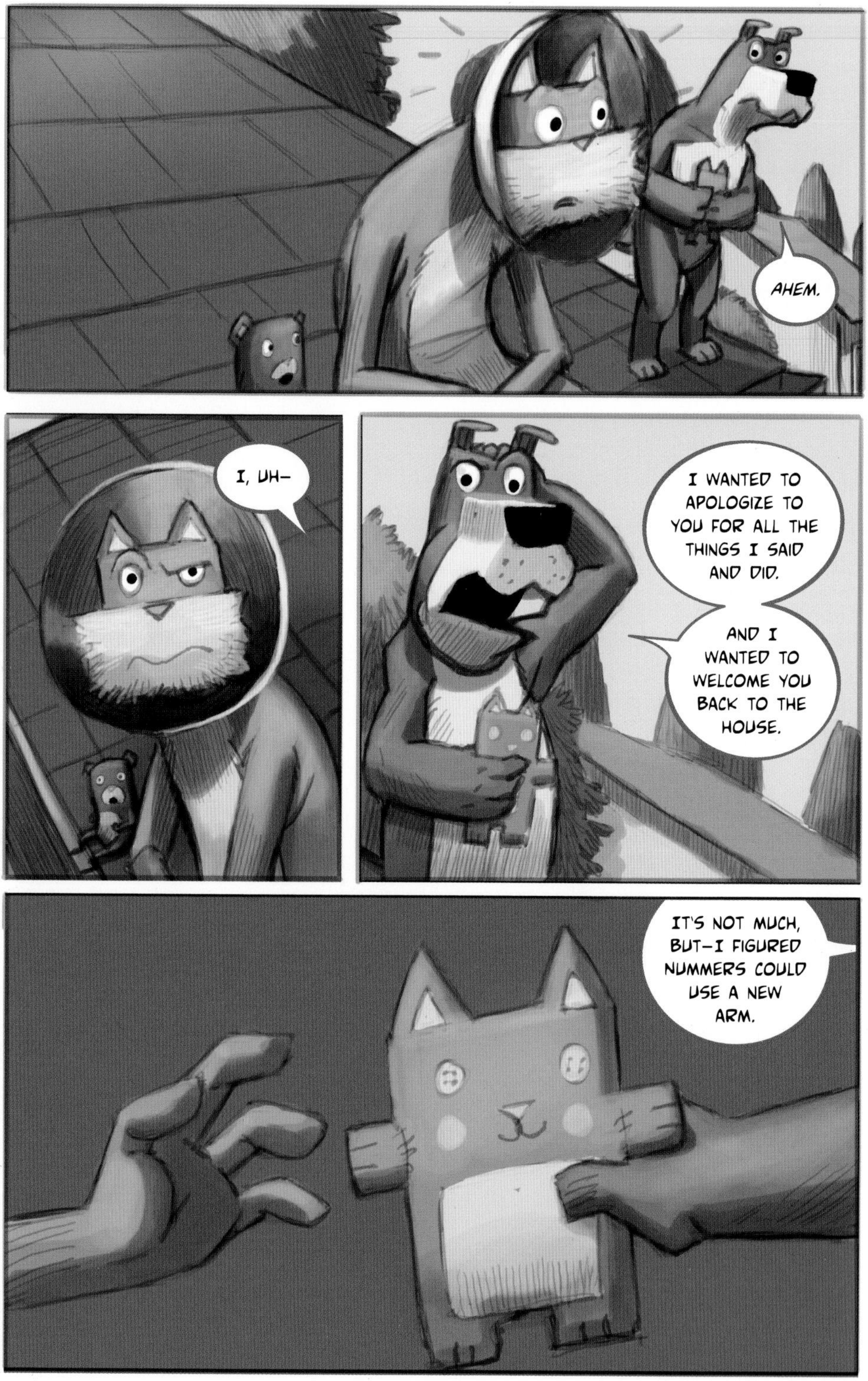
AHEM.
I, UH–
I WANTED TO APOLOGIZE TO YOU FOR ALL THE THINGS I SAID AND DID.
AND I WANTED TO WELCOME YOU BACK TO THE HOUSE.
IT'S NOT MUCH, BUT–I FIGURED NUMMERS COULD USE A NEW ARM.

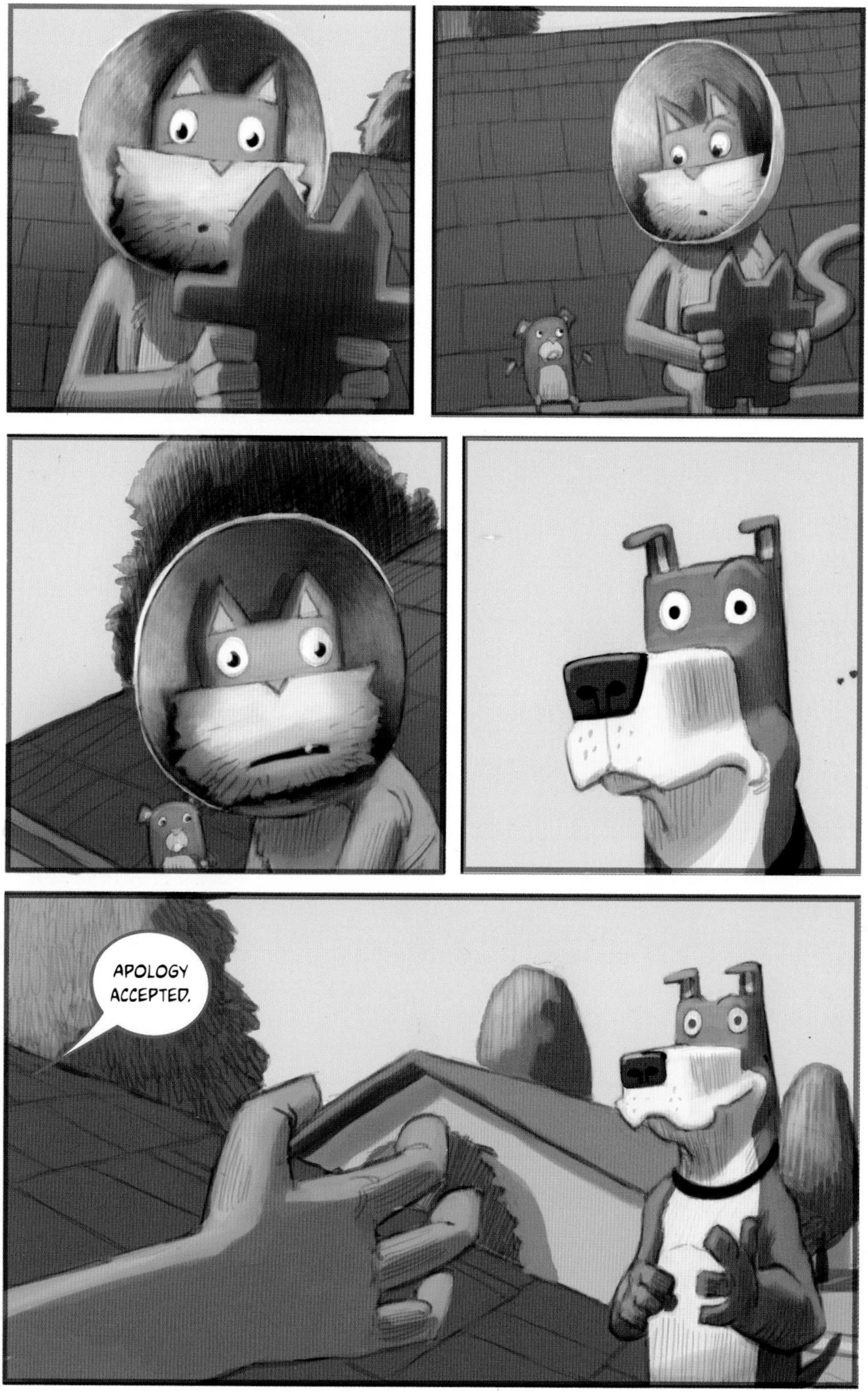
APOLOGY
ACCEPTED.

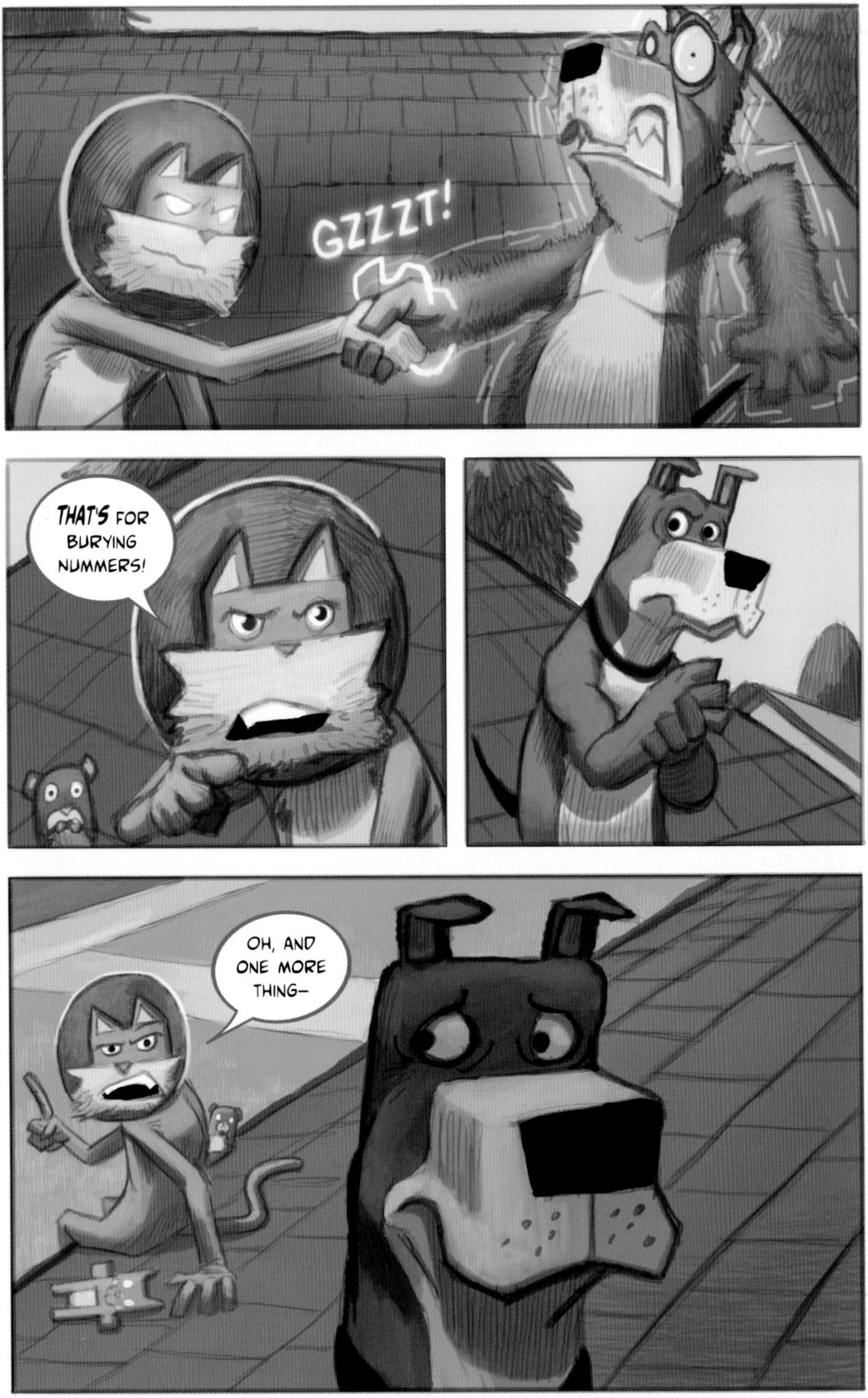
GZZZT!
THAT'S FOR BURYING NUMMERS!
OH, AND ONE MORE THING—

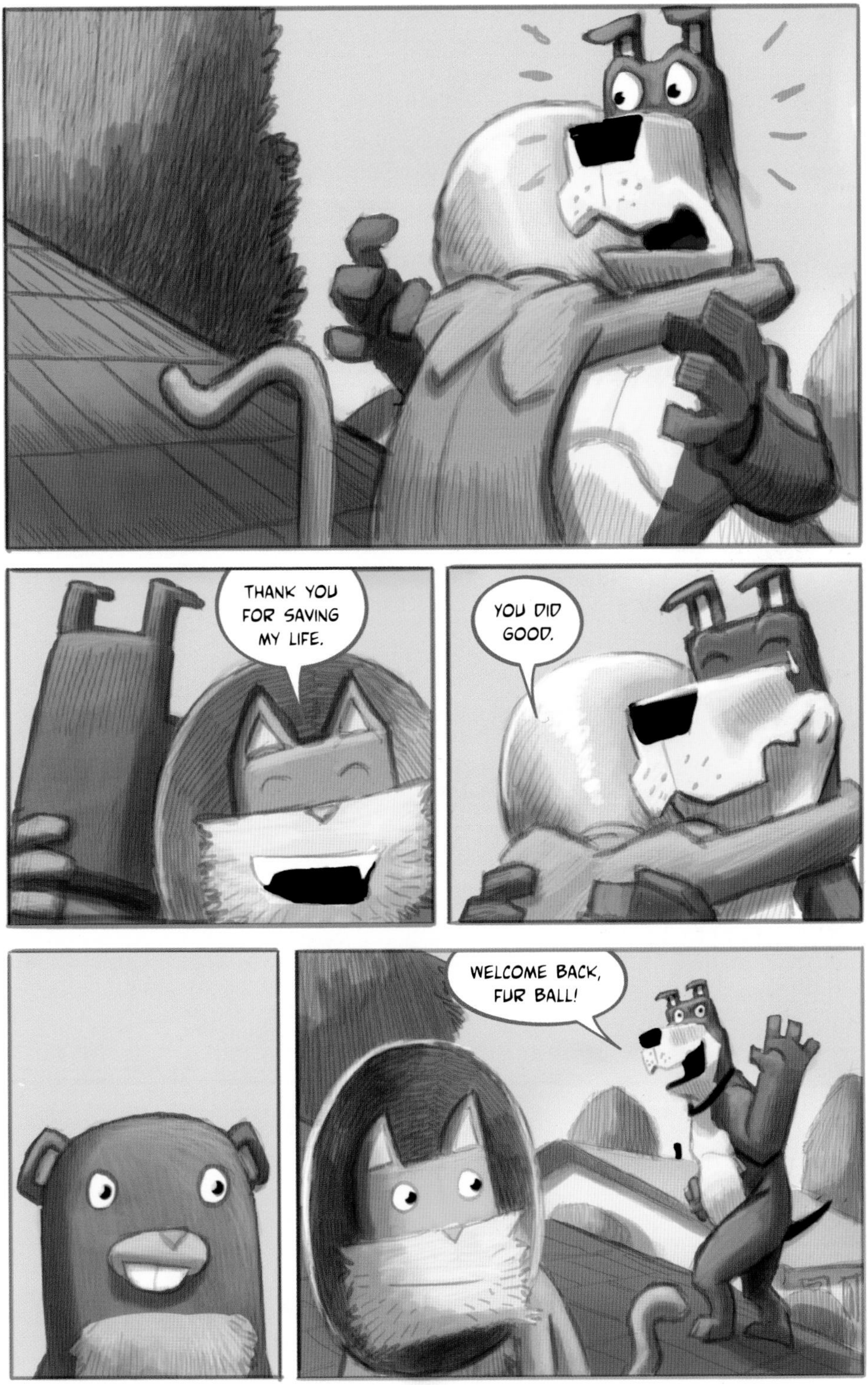
THANK YOU FOR SAVING MY LIFE.
YOU DID GOOD.
WELCOME BACK, FUR BALL!

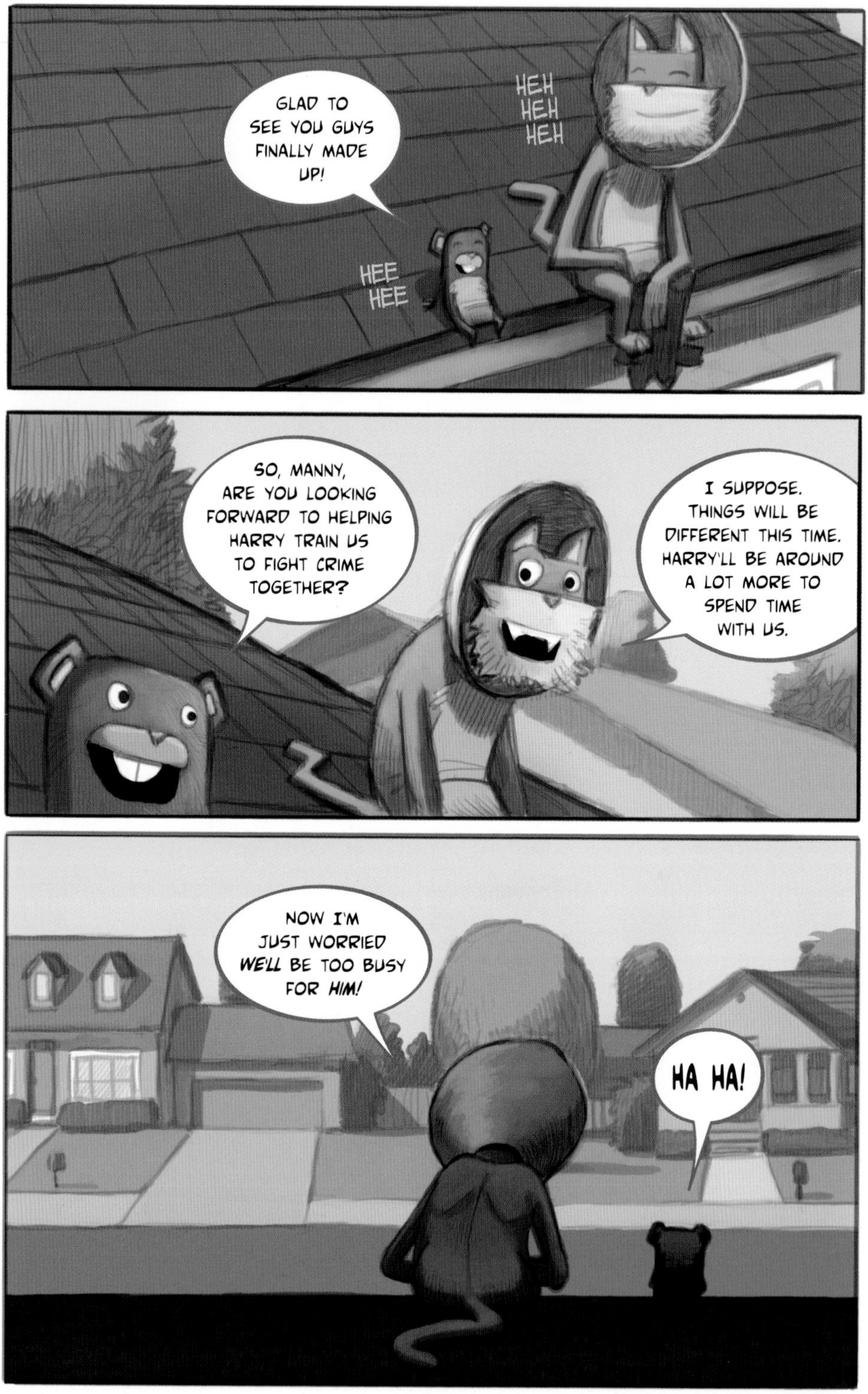
GLAD TO SEE YOU GUYS FINALLY MADE UP!
HEH HEH HEH
HEE HEE
SO, MANNY, ARE YOU LOOKING FORWARD TO HELPING HARRY TRAIN US TO FIGHT CRIME TOGETHER?
I SUPPOSE. THINGS WILL BE DIFFERENT THIS TIME. HARRY'LL BE AROUND A LOT MORE TO SPEND TIME WITH US.
NOW I'M JUST WORRIED WE'LL BE TOO BUSY FOR HIM!
HA HA!

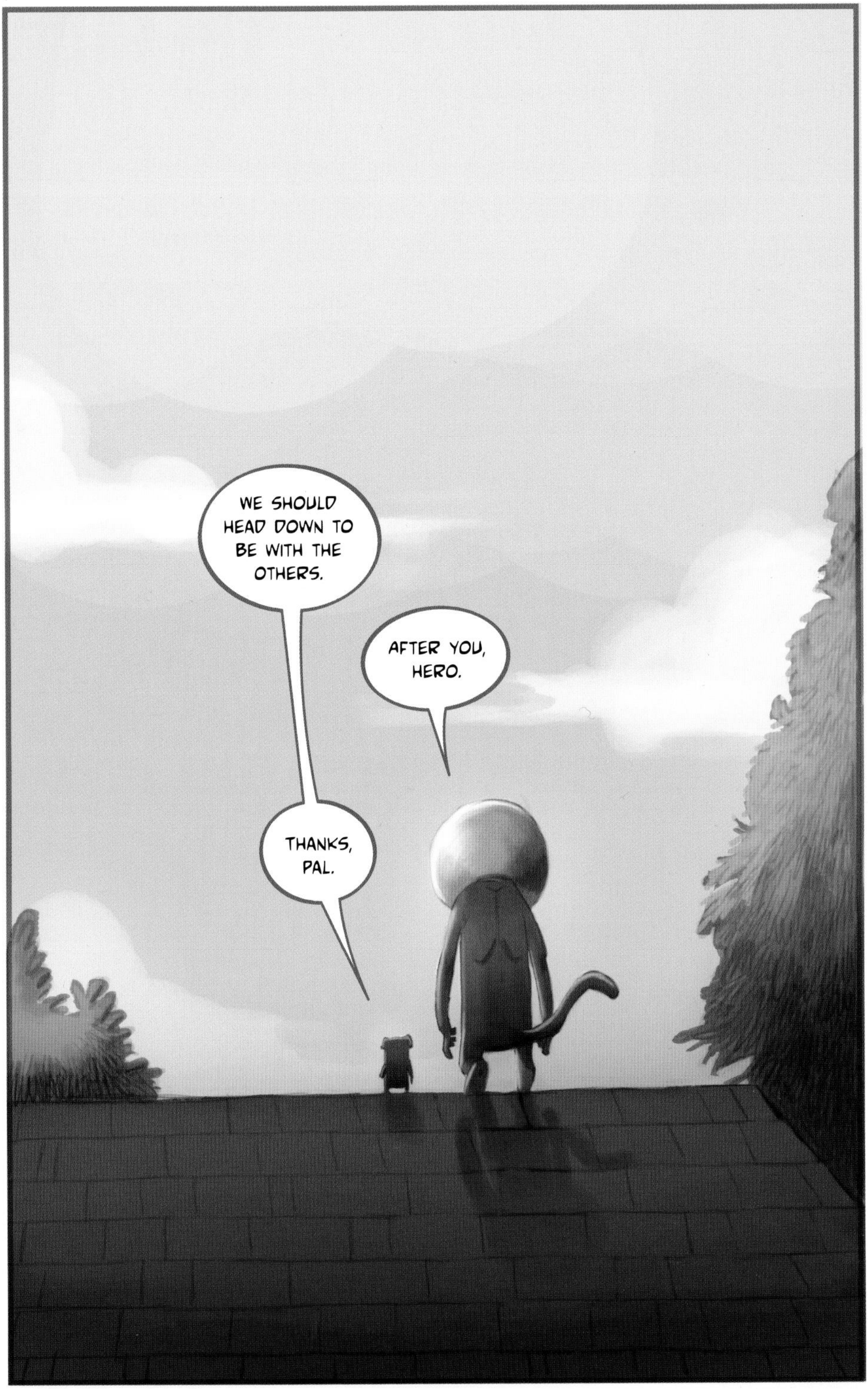
WE SHOULD HEAD DOWN TO BE WITH THE OTHERS.
AFTER YOU, HERO.
THANKS, PAL.

THE END

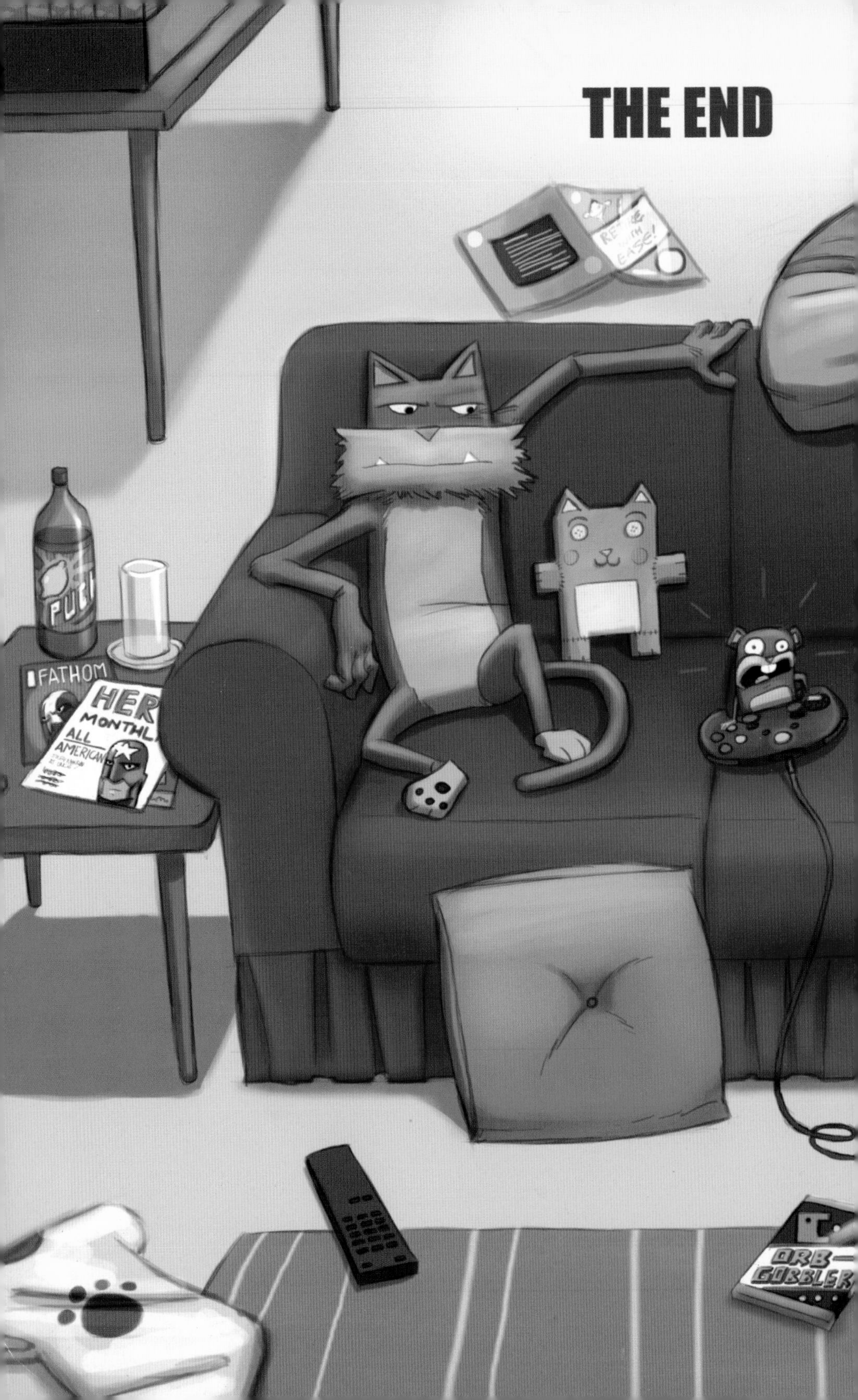
FATHOM
ALL
ORB-GOBBLER

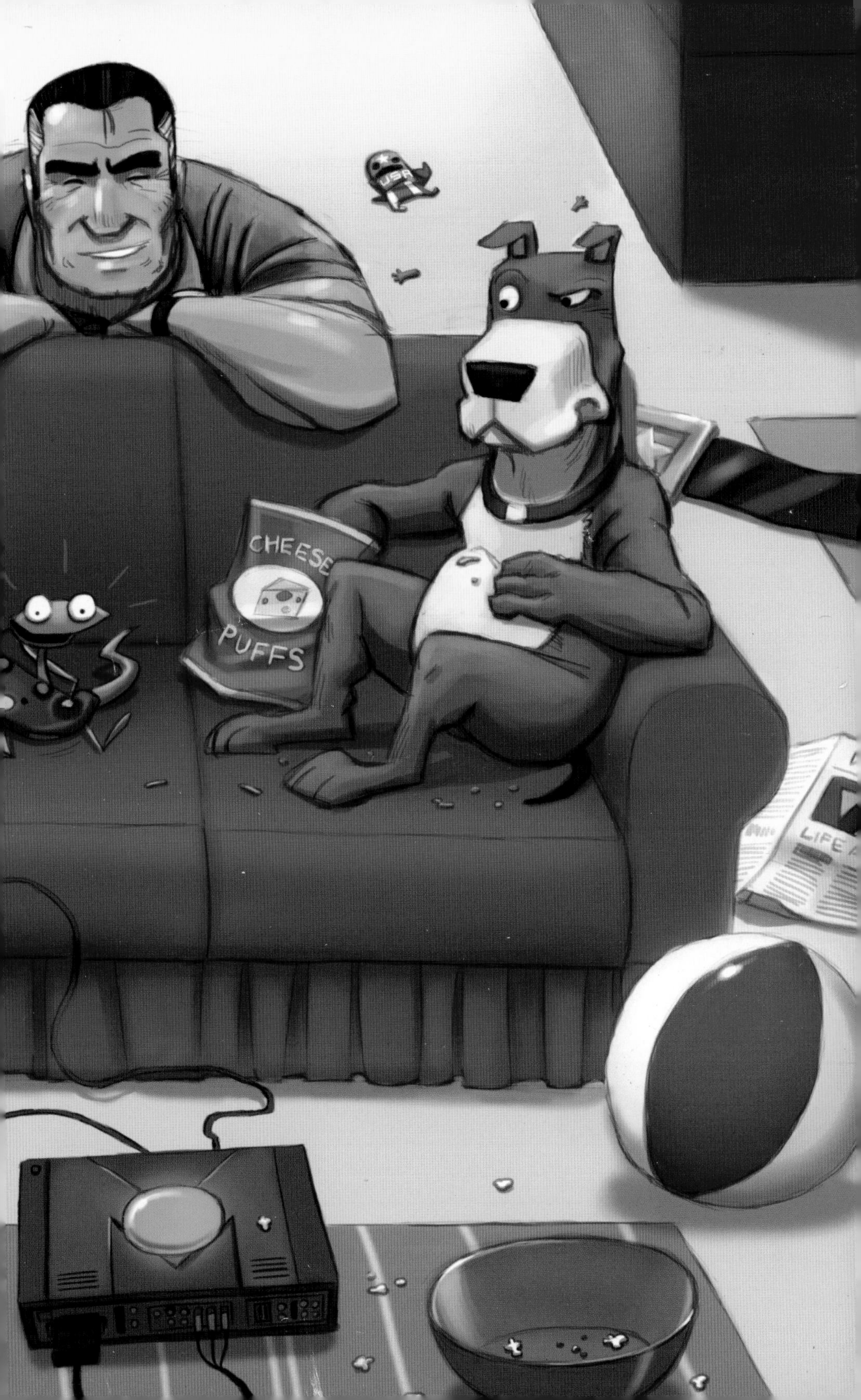
CHEESE
PUFFS
LIFE A

SOCIETY OF SUPERHEROES
SIDEKICK APPLICATION

SIDEKICK POSITION FOR: CAPTAIN AMAZING

SIDEKICK NAME: WORKAHOLIC

(REAL) NAME: DAN SANTAT

AGE: 35   ADDRESS OF APPLICANT:

SEX: MALE   HEALTH INSURANCE PROV

CURRENT HERO RESIDENCE: LOS ANGELES

SUPER ABILITY: ABILITY TO FUNCTION NORMALLY WITH LITTLE TO NO REST.

CONTACT INFO: WWW.DANTAT.COM

ARE YOU EVIL?:   Y   (N)

HAVE YOU EVER BEEN EVIL?:   Y   (N)

IF YOU ANSWERED "YES" PLEASE DESCRIBE

_____

IS ANYONE IN YOUR FAMILY EVIL?: (Y)

IF YOU ANSWERED "YES" PLEASE DESCRIB
MY CAT HAS TENDENCIES TO ATTACK MY WIFE WHILE ASLEEP.

PLEASE PROVIDE A BRIEF BIO OF YOURSELF: DAN MADE HIS PUBLISHING DEBUT IN 2004 WITH "THE GUILD OF GENIUSES." SINCE THEN HE HAS GONE ON TO ILLUSTRATE MANY OTHER GREAT TITLES SUCH AS " BOBBY VS. GIRLS (ACCIDENTALLY)" BY LISA YEE, "OTTO UNDERCOVER" BY RHEA PERLMAN, "CHICKEN DANCE" BY TAMMI SAUER, AND "OH NO! (OR HOW MY SCIENCE PROJECT DESTROYED THE WORLD)" BY MAC BARNETT. HE IS ALSO THE CREATOR OF THE DISNEY ANIMATED SERIES "THE REPLACEMENTS." THIS IS HIS SECOND BOOK.

ADDITIONAL INFORMATION: SUPER SPECIAL THANKS TO ARTHUR LEVINE, RACHEL GRIFFITHS, DAVID SAYLOR, AND PHIL FALCO FOR HELPING ME MAKE THIS BOOK SO SPECIAL (SEVEN LONG YEARS!). BIG SHOUT-OUT TO MY SIDEKICKS CAMERON PETTY, MIKE BOLDT, JOHN GIBSON, TONY ETIENNE, VINCE DORSE, AND OSKAR VAN VELDEN FOR COLORING ASSISTANCE, AND LAST BUT NOT LEAST MY WIFE, LEAH, AND MY TWO KIDS. *HUGS!*

I hereby declare that the information provided herein is accurate, valid, and a full disclosure of requested information. I am fully authorized to represent the organization listed above, to act on behalf of it, and to legally bind it in all matters related to this application.

Dan Santat

USE ONLY BLACK OR BLUE INK
PHOTO BY BRANDON KALPIN COPYRIGHT 2009